Sherwood Forest Man

Charles Beagley

First published 2016

© 2016 Charles Beagley

The moral right of the author has been asserted.

A Cataloguing-in-Publication record is available from the National Library of Australia.

ISBN: 978-0-9944161-8-6 (pbk)

978-0-9944161-9-3 (ebk–ePub)

This is not a story about
the legendary Robin Hood.
It is a story about another outlaw.

THE SHERWOOD FOREST MAN

CHAPTER 1

Once again, Jordon found himself running; running through the tall, waist-high grass of the African Savannah. Running across the close-cropped undergrowth, crunching through the charred remains of the first onslaught of the fire, by then it was too late; the wall of flames was too fierce to penetrate.

The flames were not what impeded his rescue, but more the acrid smoke surrounding the inferno. The fumes filled his throat, forcing him to gasp and splutter, until he had to mask his nose and mouth with the brightly coloured bandanna Jessie gave him. It was to mop the sweat from his face when he was out on the open plain; the very plain that had held him back.

Then there was the heat: the overpowering, relentless heat. The smarting, searing heat that dried the moisture from his skin, singing the hairs from his arms as the flames seemed to devour him; yet he could feel nothing. All the time hacking his way through the collapsing veranda, tearing at the blackened beams and shattered remains of seats and tables, frantically searching for the source of the screams.

Short of breath, eyes half closed, he finally reached the fly-screen door where he heard them and began kicking at the blazing net. He kicked and clawed at the screen. The screams grew louder, calling for him: then getting weaker and weaker.

They faded away along with the black ashes.

This was Jordon's greatest fear. This was vengeance at its worst, and his family were paying the price. Above the silence, there was a shrill buzzing, and out of nowhere, strong black arms enveloped him, pulling him back.

"No, Boss...you can't save them now...it's too late."

Halfway between oblivion and consciousness Jethro Jordan opened his eyes. It was a sudden arousal. He could still smell the burning thatch. Still feel the searing heat against his face. Still hear the crackling timbers, as he grabbed the side of his bed. Still conscious of those ghastly screams. Looking up at the ornate patterns of the mouldings on his ceiling, he listened to the infernal buzzing.

It took Jordon moments to realise the relentless, irritating sound in his head was no more than the phone, and he stretched his arm out towards the small table beside his bed and snatched up the receiver.

"Jordan," he said, sluggishly.

"Jethro...glad I got you," a voice said, as he glanced at the clock. "It's Nathan," the Chief Superintendent answered.

"Nathan...what have I done now?"

There was a laugh on the other end. "Nothing...that's not why I'm ringing," he said, laughing again. "Actually you've been pretty good lately. It's been at least a month since I had to speak to you."

Jordan sat up suddenly, "I've been on leave for two weeks."

"Oh yes...there you are then."

Jordan yawned and glanced at the clock again, "What do you want, Nathan? It's seven o'clock and I'm still on leave."

"I need to see you urgently."

Jordan grunted, "Everything's always urgent with you."

"It has to be, if I want anything done around here."

"All right, Nathan, it's too early for one of your lectures. What is it that's so important you have to talk to me now?"

"Not over the phone and not here at the station."

"You're at the station at this time?"

"Well some of us do work you know. I'll give you two hours, and you can meet me at the Old Jerusalem Inn. Quiet enough for us to have a long talk. You do know where the Old Jerusalem is."

"Vaguely," Jordan said, as he yawned again.

I thought you had already found your way around Nottingham.

"I've been busy with the house, Nathan…besides, I prefer country living."

"Ah well, you'll love this place. I understand it's the oldest inn in England, so they tell me. It's at the bottom of Castle Road Hill; just opposite the museum; you can't miss it. It's a great white edifice of a place. Don't cut through the town though, follow the A60 all the way to the canal, but don't cross it. Turn right along Canal Street until you get to the bus station car park. It's only a short walk from there…on your right, opposite the People's College."

Jordan was suspicious of the Superintendent's quiet talks. He always endeavoured to steer the conversation in the direction of Jordan joining the police force again, but that was something he vowed never to do.

He agreed to their meeting, he knew he had little option, and after returning the phone to the hook, Jordan swung his stiff legs over the bed. It was a few agonising moments before he placed his feet on the floor and directed them towards the bathroom. While he waited for the first signs of hot water, he pondered on what his old boss might have in store for him: something devious he was sure: out of the eyes and ears of his closest rivals.

Jordan ran his fingers through the running water and thought how marvellous it was to have hot water on tap at last, and glancing back through the open door to the photograph on top of the chest-of-drawers of his wife Jessie and the kids, he knew how much they would have loved this place.

He decided he wanted somewhere secluded when he first got the job with the Police Training College in Leicester. He had no experience in buying property, but when he saw the farmhouse outside the small village of Clifton-Beck, and remembered his wife Jessie showing him pictures of her dream home in the Country Life magazine, he just had to have it. Despite the term, 'Ideal for renovation,' that a legal colleague, kind enough to go with him, pointed out was a term to avoid, and usually meant years of work; Jordan paid no heed, he was hooked.

His friend was right. He had bought himself a two storey white elephant that over the next few years would need constant renovation. First, there was the slate roof, then the antiquated plumbing, and finally, a new electrical system.

It took everything he earned, there was nothing left to save, but eventually the contractors left and all was quiet; and at last, Jordon felt he could relax, until he stepped outside the house with a fresh appreciation of his surroundings.

Jordan had been so concerned with his comfort inside the house he had given little thought to the land it stood on, except to borrow a neighbour's three goats to keep the grass down. Then there was the rendering. He bought five cans of dove grey pebbledash, not because he liked dove grey, just because it was on sale, but there was never the time or inclination to use them.

One day he will, just as one day he will landscape the gardens.

Rubbing the steam off the mirror with the towel he had over his shoulder, he grunted. Shaving was one of those onerous tasks Jordan, like most men he suspects did each day without thinking. Like driving to work, the journey was always a blank.

He took particular interest this morning though, probably because he knew Nathan would come out with some remark like; 'Good God man, you look as if you've been up all night.'

At fifty-seven, Jordan had to admit he had not weathered the rigors of life as well as he should have. He poked at the white break in his right eyebrow and let out a muffled chuckle, remembering the argument he had with Ginger Bates. They were nine years old, and they were fighting over who got the cricket bat first. Ginger suddenly let go of the bat and it hit Jordon square on the brow.

He tilted his head to one side and inspected other scars he had forgotten, and concluded, even without scars he was one ordinary chap. One thing though, he mused, whether it was in his genes or just good living, he managed to hold back the ravages of the harsh African sun. With others, the dry, sunny days could put years on them in the blink of an eye, but somehow he survived all that.

Now, looking at himself in the mirror, hands clasped either side of his long square jaw, examining the barest hint of a cleft chin, he suspected those good genes had deserted him, and he was undoubtedly looking his age.

Jordan thought Nathan's window of two hours seemed a long time to get ready and drive the twenty-two miles to Nottingham. On the motorway one day, he did it in less than half an hour, although that was not taking into account the busy city traffic.

As Jordan told Nathan, that was not his preference. He had spent the last few years driving along the small winding country road from Clifton-Beck to the outskirts of Leicester, where the isolated property of the Police Training College overlooked the Leicester Canal on its southern boundary, and the rest of his valuable time was on the house. Now perhaps, it was time to visit Nottingham.

Being his first formal meeting in some time, Jordan contemplated wearing his one and only suit, or slacks and his tweed jacket, instead of his usual jeans and loose cable-knit pullover. Glancing at the window as he passed and noticing the beads of dampness clinging to the glass, it suddenly became slacks, flannel shirt and the waterproof golf jacket he had never found time to wear yet.

As autumn closed in on the country areas lying in the valley of the River Trent, early fog was usually the order of the day. Jordan noted when turning out of his drive; today was no exception. Despite his cautious start, he soon found his motorway journey to be a clear and uneventful run into the city.

Not familiar with this part of Nottingham, Jordan realised why Nathan said two-hours. He found himself in a warren of one-way streets, and parking areas allotted to days other than this day. Moreover, he had lost contact with Nathan's simple instructions, until he found himself facing the bridge that traversed the canal, and recalled he was not to cross it, but to turn right and continue along the water's edge on his left until he reached the bus station.

Ultimately, in a round about way, and still with ten minutes to spare, Jordan managed to park his cherished old Opel Berlina, and continued on to the Peoples College on foot. There, on the other side of the road, was the large white edifice Nathan referred to as the Old Jerusalem Inn.

Standing in front of the Peoples College waiting for a gap in the traffic on Castle Road, Jordan noticed the old inn looked bright and pristine against the slate grey of the old castle walls. Once on the other side, along a short gravel path, Jordan had to stop opposite the lichgate entrance between two huge hedges and take a closer look. It certainly looked old; like one of those buildings that had been added to continuously over the passage of time.

After checking his watch, Jordan stood for a moment looking at the old white rendered building, with irregular roofs and an assortment of different sized, old multi-pained windows that looked as though someone not familiar with straight lines had installed them. Nothing about the building lined up at all, but then, according to Nathan, it was a thousand years old and was lucky to be standing.

Jordan stepped through the lichgate and before he entered the inn, he glanced up at the signs on the wall. They were not difficult to miss: stretching the full width of that part of the building. When Nathan mentioned the name, Jordan was amazed. At that time in the morning, and following one of his nightmares: who cared?

Now, staring up at the enormous signs, he had to read them, and read them again. 'Ye olde Trip to Jerusalem,' was on the top sign under the guttering, and below, under a window, and what looked like a large sword, was yet

7

another sign with the explanation that it was the oldest inn in England.

Before Jordan could examine the other peculiarities of the building, he heard a short pealing chime: the introduction to the hour; and he glanced at his watch. It was nine, and as the local clock began its strokes, he entered the inn.

Immediately, Jordan's sense of smell identified the combination of fresh coffee, crispy bacon and the aroma of preserved wood, which suddenly brought to mind Nelson's Victory at Portsmouth. The Jerusalem Inn was like stepping back into another century: another time. Jordan scanned the room. It was almost empty at that time in the morning, and he soon spotted the uniformed man sitting in the far corner by the window.

The white-haired man with a ruddy complexion and a crooked nose from his rugby days saw Jordan straight away, as if he had been sitting watching the entrance for him to arrive, and raising his arm, he made a flicking gesture with his finger and thumb as if he was ordering service.

"Good morning, Jethro...have you had your breakfast yet?" he said sharply.

Jordan joined him with an anxious look, as if he wanted to get on.

"Good morning, Nathan," he said, but stopped short of answering his question. Instead, he half turned towards a large blackboard, and studied the meticulous list of chalked dishes. He had already had his bowl of bran and his tumbler of orange juice, but fell short of making himself a pot of Earl Grey.

The waitress by the counter caught Jordan's eye, with a look of anticipation on her bored face. So early in the morning he thought, and nodded. She smiled, and made her way across to their table, unfolding her order pad until she had a fresh page.

"What would you like, Sir?" she said, addressing Jordan. Nathan already had a coffee, and there was a plate in front of him, covered in singed crumbs.

"I could kill a strong cup of tea."

As she scribbled on her pad she looked up, "What type, Sir?"

"Earl Grey will do fine."

She nodded her head, made a note and turned away.

Then, as she was about to walk off Jordan changed his mind, "Oh...on second thoughts, I'll have some toast as well."

She twisted round, "With jam, Sir?"

"Have you got pineapple?"

"Sorry...we only have raspberry or blackcurrant."

"Just butter then please."

Nathan had quietly listened to the proceedings, "You better bring another coffee for me as well dear, if you don't mind," he said, finishing what he had.

When she left and Jordan turned back to Nathan, he faced a dark frown, "What's with the pineapple...jam's jam."

"A legacy from Africa I'm afraid...although it's much better here."

"I thought you were going to forget Africa?"

"I have...well almost; just a few dreams, nothing to worry about."

Nathan looked at Jordan studiously, weighing him up, trying to find the best way to start whatever it was he wanted to say, "So, Jethro," he started, and pushed his peaked cap further across the table so that he could lean forward as if he was about to divulge a secret, "How's things?"

The waitress arrived with the drinks and then left for Jordan's toast.

"Unchanged since the last time you asked me at seven."

"Yes...sorry about that. I wanted to make sure you could see me this morning. I have an important meeting with the Commissioner at two, and what we decide now will have a great bearing on what I have to say to him."

The toast arrived, and as she placed the plate on the table, Jordan thought about what Nathan had just said.

She smiled, "Don't let your toast get cold," she said.

"Thank you," Jordan replied, picking up one of the quarters.

"Well, Nathan...what's so important?"

"Ah yes," he said, sipping his coffee. "How's college?"

"You didn't ask me here to find that out."

"No...I um...wanted to know if you enjoyed your occasional excursions into field-work. It must get a bit tiresome dealing with simulations all the time."

"I enjoy the theory. It allows me to push the envelope a bit. But I must admit there's nothing like the real thing now and then."

"There you are; just what I was saying to the Commissioner."

"What's this about the Commissioner?"

"What I said," Nathan spluttered, as he took a long drink of his fresh coffee, "It's about time you had another stab at the real thing."

Jordan's eyebrow rose slightly, but he hesitated saying yes straight away; he wanted to know more first. Instead, he slowly munched another slice of toast, poured himself a cup of tea, and sat back waiting for Nathan's next disclosure. He knew how devious Nathan could be, especially when he was motivated to feathering his own nest. The mention of the Commissioner had that ring about it.

"What mess do you want me to clear up now?" Jordan said, watching that familiar expression cross Nathan's craggy face.

"Now, Jethro, there's no need to take that attitude. I've done all right by you so far. I believe in looking after my own...you know that, especially after that Kenyan fiasco. Who got you the job in the training college?"

"All right, Nathan...I'm grateful, you know that. It's just that...there's always got to be an ulterior motive with you."

Nathan glared at him, but smiled and composed himself.

"It's not like that this time, Jethro. But you're right...we do have a problem that can't be sorted out through the usual police channels."

"What can't you sort out?"

Nathan swivelled in his seat to get at the briefcase beside him, and took out a blue folder: the type that formed into a wallet, with a fine cord that wrapped around two studs sealing it. He slid it covertly across the table, "Don't look at this now...at your leisure. There's not much...but I'll fill you in all the same."

Jordan felt its weight, it was quite light for a weighty problem and he turned to Nathan for the story.

"A few weeks ago a young hiking couple came across the arm of a skeleton sticking out of the ground in Sherwood Forest. When we excavated it, we found that is was more of a dehydrated corpse than a skeleton, an old one at that, but none the less skeletal remains. We found no forensics on or near the body, no pathological clues to who he might be...yes it was male...we established that much..."

"Was there nothing else to go on?" Jordan interrupted.

"I said that. Now let me finish. To make things worse, some bright spark of a reporter has done her homework, and tied our remains in with two other unsolved skeletons that were found in Sherwood Forest over the past few years."

"Is that a possibility?"

"Good Lord no. The pathologist isn't sure of the skeleton's age, but it certainly wasn't this century. The other two skeletons are no more than five years old."

"Then tell the press," Jordon urged.

"I did...but that just made things worse. Now they think it could be one of Robin Hood's men...or maybe even the man himself, heaven forbid."

"Well...surely that can't be as bad as a serial killer."

"You'd think not."

Jordan finished his toast, washed it down with the last of his tea and sat looking at his soulful companion, "All right, Nathan...I've seen that look before. Are you going to tell me what's really worrying you?"

"The reporter who started this won't buy it."

"Lay it out for her. Invite her in for a private inspection."

"That's not good enough. It's the Commissioner. He doesn't want a serial killer stalking Nottingham, or anything to do with the Robin Hood saga brought up again. He wants a more acceptable explanation...he wants the media off his back."

Jordan thought for a moment. There was a snort of impatience.

"As I see it, Nathan, you want me to prove the identity of a corpse that could be several hundred years old, with no forensics, an unhelpful crime-scene, that's if we are talking about a crime-scene, and an investigation folder thick enough to push under my front door. What's Dent been doing all these weeks?"

"Never mind about Dent," the Superintendent barked.

"Then what about me?"

"Use your intellect; that unique analysing skill you have. This is one of those cases when you can push the envelope a bit."

"It's not any fun when people tell you it's all right."

Jordan was not happy with the hand Nathan dealt him and looked for a way out. There was none, and he owed Nathan too much.

"It's not meant to be fun, Jethro...get serious. It's about time..."

"Hold on," Jordan interrupted, "Haven't you forgotten something?"

An intent look crossed Nathan's face, "I don't think so."

"What about the minor issue of me not being on active duty...or had you forgotten that? I haven't been on an investigation for years"

Nathan smiled wryly; he was ahead of Jordan.

"Oh that...not to worry, Jethro, I had already considered reinstating you...at your old rank of course."

Jordan pondered, "I don't know, Nathan...I'm used to being a civilian."

"A civilian" Nathan let out with a snort. "You spend all day at the police college, training future police. How much more of a policeman can you be?"

"I can walk away at the end of the day...that's the difference."

"We can come to an arrangement about that."

"I see...and what about the others? They're not going to want me around them again, especially Inspector Dent. There's only room for one inspector in CID."

Nathan glanced at his watch again, he seemed anxious to be somewhere else, "I said...don't worry about him. I've come up with a solution that should address all those issues. I shall form a new special squad. Not a big one you understand, just yourself and two others: a sergeant and a constable to assist you."

Jordan shook his head at the man's amazing ingenuity.

"And I suppose you already have a name for this new squad?"

"I do. I've given it a lot of thought, and have come up with CAS."

"CAS?" Jordan exclaimed, unbelievingly.

"Yes...Criminal Anomalies Squad."

Jordan broke out in a stifled laugh, "I'll be a laughing stock. They'll be calling me the man from CAS or something equally ridiculous."

"No they won't...I'll make sure of that. It will give you the autonomy you need to call up any of the other services, and I expect the Commissioner to sign my draft this afternoon. That's why I would like to be able to tell him that you will be running the new squad."

Jordan raised his eyebrow again, and reluctantly nodded.

"Good," Nathan said, grabbing his briefcase. Then looking at his watch for what seemed the last time, he stood up and put his peaked-cap squarely on his head.

"Are we off then?" Jordan commented.

"Yes...sorry it's been a rush; wheels turning and all that."

"When do I start?"

"You already have," Nathan said, reaching out to shake Jordan's hand, "Have the weekend to tidy up your affairs. I'll see you on Monday."

He tugged at his hat, picked up his leather gloves and walked off.

Two tables away he stopped, turned on his heels and returned to Jordan.

With one hand on the table, he bent down and whispered, "By the way, Jethro. Now that you're working for me again, it's Chief Superintendent from now on," Jordan blinked, "and you're Inspector Jordan…okay?" Jordan contemplated what had just happened. "Oh and…don't forget to wear a tie when you start on Monday."

CHAPTER 2

Since Jordan's reinstatement officially starts on Monday, he decided there were two important chores he had to take care of today, since neither was assessable over the weekend.

The most important, yet at the same time, the most irritating, was his obligation to his psychiatrist, Mark Faulkner. Jordan had to ring him each time he had one of his nightmares. A call would normally suffice, but since he was also returning to the police force, in his previous role as Inspector, he was sure Mark would want to see him. Jordan's second chore was to visit the training college on his return to Leicester to clear his desk, as well as the embarrassing task of informing the Commander of yet another break.

Coincidentally, Jordan discovered that Mark Faulkner's office was only a short walk from the Jerusalem Inn, at the top of St James's Terrace. His usual approach was from the Derby, Ilkeston turn-off, and when he checked his pocket street directory, he was surprised, and a little amused, at how close they were. He had the uncanny feeling Nathan was ahead of him: since Nathan had something to do with Jordan's introduction to Mark when he returned from Kenya.

At the top of a long flight of stairs, in an unremarkable collection of offices known as the Medical Group, Jordan stood for what seemed an eternity in front of the door to Mark Faulkner's office. Staring at the gold letters signifying he was a bona fide psychiatrist, and contemplating whether his visits were more to appease his superiors than actually doing him any good; he had his doubts.

The very act of returning to his traumatic past seemed to highlight the episode, not diminish it. He could swear his nightmares were more frequent since he started recording them, than in the days when everything was fresh.

Jordan finally pressed down on the brass door handle and entered the confines of his waiting room. Mark's openly pleasant receptionist, Sandra, looked up immediately. "Ah… Mr Jordan, what a nice surprise," she said.

Jordan walked over to her small desk in the corner by the window, and stood for a moment looking at her. She had that affect on him. Beneath the soft exterior lay a hard core: a thirty-something, twice married woman of experience. Bitten once, chewed on a second time and ready for the next man who dared take her for granted again, yet still looking available.

He liked to consider his words before he spoke. "I know this might be an imposition, Sandra, but do you think there's any chance of the man seeing me today? I can go and have a walk around the city for a while if you like."

A smile crossed her face, which Jordan felt was a good sign, and she began flicking through Simon's appointment book, "You're in luck, Mr Jordan. It just so happens that his next appointment has cancelled." She checked her watch. "If you take a seat I'll let him know you're here…it shouldn't take long," she said.

Smiling at Jordan all the while, she picked up the phone as he turned to the small area on the opposite side of the room, set aside for a few easy chairs and an antique coffee table, covered with rich magazines, and as Sandra indicated, Jordan's wait was short-lived. The phone soon buzzed, and as she listened, she glanced across in his direction, nodding her head and waving him on.

When Jordan entered the room, Mark was sitting at his desk finishing his notes on the previous patient, and he looked up without breaking his concentration.

"Won't be long, Jethro...take a seat," he said, and Jordan walked across to the seat in front of the desk and sat down. He deliberately avoided the couch. He did not intend to stay any longer than he had to.

Jordan watched Mark furiously scribbling his notes: words running into words, hardly decipherable to anyone but Sandra. He was an excitable man, an athletic forty-year-old, focused on maintaining what was left of his vigour; who played squash two evenings a week and golf on Sundays.

Jordan was used to Mark's routine, just as he was used to his surroundings; not quite as bad as visiting the dentist, but there was still that unique sense of anticipation, and it was a comfortable room, the type of room you could spill all your secrets. The walls of fine books and hunting scenes appeared to merge with the antique furnishings. Just behind him, there was the couch and the easy chair Mark sat in to ask his questions. Then there was that odd forgotten wall at the end: a plain wall with a filing cabinet in the corner and a conspicuous looking door. A door Jordon suspected was for a quick retreat, away from the prying eyes of other patients that led onto the landing at the top of the stairs.

Placing his pen at the side of the blotter as he closed his notebook, Mark looked up again. "So, Jethro...you missed your last scheduled appointment, so why the sudden urge to see me now?" Then as if an afterthought, Mark eased forward with an outstretched hand.

Jordan took hold of it firmly, noticing how tanned it was against his.

"I know...I'm sorry, Mark," Jordan said, with no excuse.

Mark held onto Jordan's hand and studied his face, "You look as if you need a good sleep...the nightmares have started again, haven't they?"

"Yes...I was going to ring you; like we agreed, then Nathan rang wanting to see me this morning..."

"Ah!" Mark interrupted, looking sheepish.

"What does that mean?"

"Sorry, Jethro, it's not as devious as it sounds. It's just that the Chief Superintendent rang me the other day..."

"I knew that weasel was up to something!"

"Yes...well, I must admit, he could have handled things a little better. But then again, he means well; despite his lack of patience."

"So what did he want? Did he want to make sure I was rational again?"

"No, Jethro...nothing like that. You know I have to report to the board, and since they haven't heard from me for some time...he wanted to know if that was a good sign. He seemed quite anxious about you."

"I'm sure he did; so much for patient confidentiality. What did you tell him? Or is that a secret between you and the establishment?"

Mark gave Jordan a hurt look, "I only told him, 'No news was good news,' that you were in control of your life again."

It was a moment or two before Jordan spoke.

"You did? Well I am...you're right. I'm totally in control of my life; it's these bloody nightmares I have no control over."

Mark held back on the nightmares for the moment; he was more interested in why the Chief Superintendent was suddenly interested in Jordan, "Why are the police interested in you again? The Chief Superintendent said very little, other than to mention he used your expertise on occasions."

"He want's to reinstate me as an Inspector."

"Do you think you're ready?"

"Of course I am...that's not the problem. I'm not even sure I want to do it anymore. I've got used to being a civilian, and I like working at the college."

Mark was not satisfied with Jordan's explanation.

"It's the stress I'm concerned with. You don't want to dig up old memories, not when you've been away from crime for so long."

"It's not that type of case. This one needs more of an analytical approach. It appears the Commissioner is having some trouble with the media."

"I see," Mark let out, although he obviously had no idea what Jordan was on about. "Then we'll just have to monitor the situation; and maybe those nightmares as well. You haven't had one for a while, what brought this one on?"

"I have no idea. All I know is, it was so clear...I could hear their screams again. I don't think I ever heard them like that before."

"You've got to move on, Jethro."

"Move on! Move on! I heard them screaming! Do you know what that sounds like? I could hear each distinct voice."

"You know I don't," Mark snapped back. "And neither should you. Do you know what I mean? We've talked about this so many times."

"Yes," Jethro snapped.

"Really?"

"Yes, Mark! I know exactly what you mean. That's why I can't understand why I should be hearing them now. Do you know?"

"It's because you feel guilty...that's why," Mark replied. "You have to fight it Jethro. Every time it happens, you must say to yourself: 'This is not happening,' and you must continue repeating that until it goes away."

Jordan shook his head in despair. "I sense these images are questions that I have to answer. I see each image as a door that needs opening, and I'll find the truth."

"Jethro...that's not a door you want to open. This is 1984, Jethro, not 1952 when you lost Jessie and the kids."

"I'm an analyst, Mark. I'm trained to find answers to abstract images."

Mark could say nothing under the present circumstances. The new direction Jordan was taking could be for the good; then again, it could destroy him.

"I wish you could be sure about this new job," he said.

"It's something I have to find out."

"And I repeat...do you think you're ready?"

Jordan glanced at his watch, "I'd better be...by two o'clock it will be official."

It was the second time in as many minutes that Inspector Dent had glanced at the travel clock to the right of his Festival of Britain pen set. A preoccupation he shared with the manila folder on the desk in front of him file-named: Unknown Skeletal Remains, Sherwood Forest 1984. The original to the folder Chief Superintendent Mulholland gave Jordan earlier that morning.

These past weeks had taken a toll on him. Everyone was commenting on how haggard he looked, how grey and drawn his skin had become: accentuated by greying hair and a sullen, pockmarked complexion. His drinking was beginning to affect his decisions: although there had not been many of those lately.

Although blessed with a meteoric rise to Inspector, mainly due to his adherence to the chosen path of the division, and a passion for reading procedural manuals, Inspector Dent led an uneventful life away from the force. Returning home each day to a boring wife that gave the impression he had not been missed, while the skeletal remains in Sherwood Forest was proving to be his Nemesis.

He glanced at the clock again. It was five minutes later, and he checked his wristwatch to make sure the time was right. Two o'clock, the Chief Superintendent said on his brief memo: more of a summons than an invitation. Certainly not to meet the Commissioner and his loyal minions: 'He could just fit him in,' the memo said.

The Inspector stared at the open memo again, trying to read between the lines for that slip of the tongue. He was a detective, trained in this sort of thing, but there was nothing; the gaps were just as vacuous.

At fifty-five, Dent could do without the prospect of having to prove himself once again; but meeting with Mulholland was always that: clean cut, abundantly simple, and always a time of ultimatum. Boasting that an ultimatum kept people on their toes; made them aware of their priorities. Dent only had one priority, and it was proving too much for him.

"Where's the Boss?" a young persistent Constable called out as he rushed into the squad room with an armful of folders.

Sergeant Ward, the older detective behind the typewriter, looked up, "I wouldn't bother him right now, not if you know what's good for you."

"Well I've got some good news for him."

"I doubt it. He has to see the super at two, and he's a bit busy right now. I think he's in for the chop...we all might be in for the chop."

The young Constable slumped down on the nearest chair, "I've only just started, Sarge. It took me four years to get this job."

"No lad...Don't take me literally. I mean the case...we're going to lose the case. Do you understand what I'm saying?"

"Why, Sarge? No one will do any better than the Guv'."

"That's not the way the super sees it."

By the time two o'clock finally arrived, Inspector Dent was already entering the Chief Superintendent's outer office. A small room solely staffed by a middle-aged woman who they often described as the heart and soul of the department: and the Chief Superintendent's guardian.

Despite her tenacious reputation, they also looked upon her as an attractive commodity. Her slim, well-rounded figure was the talk of the squad room, where it remained: no man was brave enough to curry her favour for fear of the backlash.

Phyllis Montgomery looked up at the Inspector when he knocked on her open door and entered the room. He had to admit he was attracted to the woman. Despite both being married, he was attracted to the symmetry of her features, and the delicate pallor of her skin.

"Good afternoon, Phyllis, is he ready for me yet?"

She looked at him without expression, "He's in the conference room with the Commissioner at present, but he said you were to go straight into his office, and he would break off to see you for a moment," she replied, as she pushed her chair back and stood up to open the Chief Superintendent's door.

It was an austere office: polished mahogany panelling, with a large window where he could watch the comings and goings at the main gate. A deep blue Axminster carpet, with a small gold Fleur-de-lis pattern and a large desk with two chairs in front. Other than a cabinet holding the divisional trophies and the usual framed certificates on the wall behind his desk, the room was devoid of comfort. That apparently was reserved for the conference room next door.

Inspector Dent stood for a moment, noticeably conspicuous through the open door between the two rooms. The Chief Superintendent's guests were milling about, in conversation with long drinks in their hands, while others gathered around the buffet. He could see the Commissioner surrounded with his followers, but not the man himself. Then, just as the Inspector was about to turn away and take a seat, he saw him. The Chief Superintendent passed the open door, and noticing him immediately, he nodded at him before he had a word with the Commissioner and made his way through to his office.

"Ah, Richard," he said, entering the room and closing the door behind him, "Sit down man, you look uncomfortable. I won't keep you long. This damn media frenzy is causing quite a commotion; the Commissioner has got everyone on edge."

"That's all right, Sir, I know you're busy…how can I help?"

"It's this skeleton business, Richard. The Commissioner thinks we should take a different approach: something more positive."

"We're doing all we can, Sir. There's little to go on, and the new revelation that we're dealing with a much older corpse has put a completely new perspective on the investigation. We just need to adjust our sights, Sir."

"Precisely…that's what he's saying, Inspector. It doesn't seem to have anything to do with the usual day-to-day police work. He thinks we're locking up too much valuable manpower that could be used more productively elsewhere."

"What are you actually saying, Sir?"

"Wind it up, Richard. Call it a day."

The Inspector wasn't surprised.

"Then what now, Sir?"

"I want you and your squad to get on with solving some of our real crimes. To be frank, uniform are stretched to the limit, they're not coping. We've had some complaints, not about you of course," the Chief Superintendent was particular to point out, seeing the fallen look on the Inspector's face. "They're more to do with the use of our recourses. But it's all part of the same thing."

"And what's going to happen with our skeleton?"

"The Commissioner wants to continue with the investigation, if only to nullify the damage the media has done. He wants a low-profile unit to handle the unveiling of our skeleton's identity. I thought Jethro Jordan would be just the man."

"The Criminal Analyst at the college?"

"That's the man…you've met him before. He's the man we've used on a number of occasions to help us with a feel for where we're going."

"I know him, Sir…but he's a consultant."

"He was once a police Inspector, with seniority over you, I might add."

"But that was in Africa, Sir. And wasn't there some trouble?"

The Chief Superintendent suddenly looked irritated. It was easy to tell when he started repositioning things on his desk.

"That's something that need not concern you in the future, Inspector. You will have quite enough on your plate."

The Inspector knew when to give in, it was one thing he was good at, and it had saved his bacon on a number of occasions. If he was honest with himself, he was relieved. The skeleton case was not doing his reputation any good, especially with the media, who already had him pegged as a loser.

"Do you want me to brief, Inspector Jordan, Sir?"

"No. Hand all you have so far to Phyllis, she knows what to do with it," he started to walk back to his guests, "Oh and, she has all your paperwork ready."

The Inspector stood up, "Thank you, Sir."

Standing by the conference room door the Chief Superintendent turned and said; "Don't worry, Inspector; your record is still clean."

Inspector Dent was not surprised he lost the case that had captured the media's attention; he lacked the verve and charisma to gain their confidence. He only hoped Inspector Jordan was more fortunate. Somehow, he thought he might be.

Phyllis Montgomery was waiting for him. As usual, everything had been prepared, and she sat, pen in hand, for him to sign the transfer papers. She passed him his copy with an efficient smile, and he left.

CHAPTER 3

Jordan arrived at the college just after the start of the afternoon lectures, when the grounds were quiet. The grey clouds had passed and it was pleasant to see the blue sky again, and in the bright sunshine, the red brick and sandstone of the college looked alive. Jordan removed his golf jacket and took his holdall from the boot of his car. It was big enough, he thought, for the few personal belongings he had.

Not in the mood for explanations, Jordan chose this particular time to clear his personal things out of his office, but first he had to visit reception and arrange to see the Commander. It was fortunate Rosemary Springfield was on duty: a meticulous woman in her thirties, of good breeding that doubled as the Commander's secretary and general college factotum.

"Hello, Jethro," she said, finishing with a cadet and looking up. "I was expecting you earlier."

"Does everybody know what I'm doing?" Jordan questioned, putting his holdall down on the floor and leaning across the counter.

"How do you mean, Jethro?" she said, reaching down under the counter for a pile of papers, and conspicuously pushing them in front of him.

"Well...everywhere I've been today, they seem to know in advance what I want," he said, looking at the papers. "And what are these."

"Just a formality, Jethro: They are forms that need signing to do with temporarily transferring your employment and tax details to the police."

"And I suppose Chief Superintendent Mulholland organised all this the other day, like he organised everything else in my life? I'd like to know what he would have done if I had said no."

Rosemary looked disinterested in Jordan's plight, "I wouldn't know."

"Thank you," he said curtly, and grabbing the papers in one hand and snatching up the holdall in the other, he made for the stairs.

"Let me have them on your way out, Jethro," she called after him.

Jordan slipped up the stairs, passed the occasional cadet who respectfully nodded, and down the corridor to his small retreat that had offered him a secure haven over the past ten years. And dropping his holdall down by the desk, he stood for a moment taking in the familiar bookcase and large whiteboard on the far wall, still full of baffling conundrums, as if he had worked on them yesterday; instead it had been two weeks ago before he went on holiday.

He walked over to the board and studied the boxed-off groups with arrows pointing to synonymous links, and in a sudden urge not to let anyone steal his analysis; he grabbed the pad and wiped the board clean. His heart was suddenly pounding, and he leant back against the desk.

There was ten years of his life in this room. After twenty years of unsuccessfully trying to fit into different police divisions, trying to conform, trying to get over his loss, Jordan finally found a place where no one was interested in his past. A place so rich in history, he could lose himself in its traditions.

In 1910, a wealthy American entrepreneur erected it as an extensive residence on the outer fringe of Leicester. He attempted to emulate the grandeur of England's landed gentry. However, he was not to enjoy his life of luxury for more than a few years, following the onset of the First World War in 1914, and his first sight of a German airship over England. He quickly sold up, at a great loss, and returned to the relative safety of his homeland, America.

Between the first and second wars, the grand edifice became a private girls' school, and on England's entry to the Second World War, the War Office took it over to use for training spies and commandoes.

Following the war, it continued with its clandestine activities in the suspicious 'Cold War' interlude until the late seventies, when the purpose of the house had changed little: it still had uniformed occupants that trained in the art of capturing criminals, covert procedures and the use of firearms.

By now, Jordan had followed the pictures around the walls until he found himself staring out of the window behind his desk, overlooking the playing field behind the college. The white poles of the rugby goals stood out sharply against the blue sky, and he slowly realised what he might be sacrificing.

Less anxious, and a pulse-rate that was returning to normal, Jordan was still overcome with an anger he had not experienced since Kenya. He hated a life of manipulation, and in that moment he considered ringing his old boss to tell him, he had gone too far this time. He snatched up the phone and paused with his finger over the keypad: for a moment, he was actually going to do it.

Then he realised it would be a fruitless gesture; Nathan had been there for him. All the time he climbed through the ranks to Chief Superintendent, he never lost sight of his man from Africa. He stood by Jordan, defended him throughout those turbulent years, and was responsible for his life in this wonderful college. Whenever his benefactor needed him, Jordan felt duty bound to assist.

Jordan let out a sigh of inevitability as he returned the phone. He walked back around the desk, picked up his holdall and unzipping it, started to clear the draws. Not much for ten years, he thought, leaving behind college paraphernalia, and only taking that which he had brought into the old room.

Just the same, for the wide sage-green leather top of his desk: not that he ever saw it much over those years. With piles of cadet folders that could stay, he thought, his replacement could file those. Along with all the different reports, the college newsletters, monthly journals and he almost forgot; the ten year pile of police gazettes from pathology and forensics.

Then glancing at the picture of his wife Jesse and his two children, Jordan slumped back into his chair, and reached across to the silver frame and held it a moment, before a sharp knocking on the door suddenly distracted his thoughts. He looked up, and standing, framed in the doorway with her long slender fingers around the doorknob, was the last woman Jordan wanted to see.

It was Gloria Murray, the tall, busybody from communications. She had been after Jordan ever since she arrived five months ago, and for the first four he used every excuse in the book to avoid her. This last month, her persistent ways got too much for him and he found himself actually confronting her. Something he never did with a woman before.

She was too provocative for him, but to the young, inexperienced men, Gloria was a femme fatale. To other women, she was a harlot. To Jordan she was a pitiful woman he tried his best to avoid. Everything about Gloria was smooth. Her tightly drawn-back, dark hair, Hollywood make-up and minimalist ensemble was so perfect, it had to have taken her all day to maintain the illusion.

"So you're leaving us, Jethro?" she said. "I thought it was only a rumour."

"The Commissioner thought it was about time I had another lesson in real police work," Jordan said, knowing she would find out soon enough, if she didn't know already. She dealt with the college's communications after all.

"Pity," she said, "I thought we were just beginning to know each other."

Jordan carried on clearing his desk, "Yes," he said, keeping it brief. "I don't know how long I'll be away, but I'm sure you'll take care of my replacement."

"I will...I think I saw him talking to the Commander yesterday. A gorgeous young man," she said spitefully. "It should be a nice surprise to have some young blood in the place for a change."

Jordan looked up, "That should keep you busy."

"I nearly forgot what I popped in to see you for, Jethro," she continued. "I thought you might want to have a drink with me before you go."

Jordan smiled, "I don't think so, Gloria."

She flashed him one of her vicious looks, "You know what's wrong with you ... You piss people off. They'll be glad to see the back of you."

"Then you won't miss me will you, Gloria?"

Without another word, except a gasp of frustration, Gloria lurched up from the door she was leaning against, sending it crashing into the filing cabinet, and stormed off along the corridor towards her office. She almost collided with two young secretaries, who nimbly stepped to one side, and seeing Jordan, they stopped, waved at him and then carried on their way.

Jordan sat for a moment with a smile of satisfaction on his face; he had wanted to say that to the virago for some time. As he shook his head and thought about her harsh words, it began to dawn on him that she might well have been right.

Jordan was an anti-chaos fanatic, with a preference towards order. His phobia had not become compulsive yet, but he was bordering on a thin line. He was not this way before Jesse and his children were so brutally murdered, quite the opposite. On that fateful day, when he was so sure he locked the gate in the perimeter fence, a patrol made him suddenly realise the penalty of his omission.

Jordan turned his attention back to the picture of his family, picked it up, folded the stand back and slipped the frame lovingly into his holdall. He placed a few books either side to protect the frame, then he glanced around the room to see if he had forgotten anything.

The room now looked bare of his presence, like it had the first day he arrived, except for the work-in-progress he left his replacement. Then he thought about the gorgeous young man Gloria boasted about, and wondered. Either way, he wanted him to respect his room while he was away.

Jordan pulled a sheet of notepaper out of the small carrier on his desk, and started scribbling him a note. He thought for a moment. It had to be brief, succinct and to the point, but what was the point. He wanted the same room to come back to; that was the point.

He started writing: 'Whilst you're welcome to use my room, don't change it. No smoking, no spitting in the waste-bin, no eating in the room, no sleeping on the couch, despite what other lecturers do, and above all…no women. Women are out of bounds in my room, especially one called Gloria.'

Jordan paused and read the few lines he had written and laughed to himself. If he had found a note like that waiting for him when he arrived, he knew what he would have done with it. He screwed it up and tossing it into the bin, he grabbed his holdall and without turning back, he left.

The following Monday turned out to be a promising day. It had rained all weekend, with the usual foggy mornings, and Jordan contemplated the prospect of being wet on his first day, but a touch of spring had put autumn on hold. When Jordan arrived at the Prescott Lane station at seven, he found they were waiting for him. Nathan had eased his way as usual, and the respect for their new Inspector surprised him.

Everything was waiting for him: an Inspector's warrant card, his gate pass, even a place for him to park his old Berlina; Nathan had thought of everything. Although, Jordan thought with a smile on his face, it would have to be Chief Superintendent from now on, or maybe just plain Sir.

The thin folder Nathan had given Jordan at the Jerusalem Inn was hardly enough to get him started, let alone brief his new assistants. Jordan knew from experience, that he only had the profile of the case, the main files of evidence or witness statements, let alone pathology and forensic reports, were still in the pipeline.

He knew Inspector Dent's second in command, Sergeant Ward: a puerile individual that Jordan had crossed swords with before, would have muddied the waters. He would have sent the folders here there and anywhere except where he should; but he had underestimated the new Inspector's tenacious nature. He knew the game, and after dropping his holdall down by the largest of the three desks in the new CAS squad room, he set about hunting down his files.

Meanwhile, the first of Jordan's assistants was arriving at the Wellington Street front office: A bright young man in a smart grey suit, white shirt and red tie. This was the first time Sergeant Josh Crosby had presented himself for duty in civvies, and having second thoughts about the tie, he soon realised his first day was going to be a challenging one.

The chain of events that followed confused him. If it had not been for the three uniforms behind the counter, the duck-egg blue walls decorated with posters pointing out the merits of a career in the police force; home measures to combat the burglar and local organisations linked with helping those in need; Josh might have been forgiven for thinking he was in a doctor's surgery.

It was too bright and hygienic, with a plush dark blue, corded carpet, comfortable looking chairs down both sides of the room, and several coffee tables in front, covered with a liberal supply of newspapers and magazines.

"DS Crosby reporting for duty," he said to the amiable looking sergeant behind the counter.

He looked suspicious, "CID?"

"Yes, Sergeant."

The tall grey haired man raised a smile, "This is uniform, Sergeant. CID is at the back in Prescott Lane...You can't miss it."

Sergeant Crosby smiled back, and picking up the envelope with his transfer papers inside, he turned on his heels, and left. Prescott Lane, he soon found, was half a block to his right. A narrow cobbled lane just wide enough for one vehicle, and a shallow rainwater gutter running down the middle.

As he tentatively made his way along the lane looking for the rear of the police station, his eyes fell upon a familiar white sign with the letters H.M. above what looked like a copy of the police manual. It was on a huge wall that spanned the junction ahead of him, continuing each side of an equally huge wrought-iron gate.

This had to be it; he thought as he pulled into a parking space, and on arriving at the gate, he noticed a small door to one side, with a barred, glass panel in the upper half. Facing him was a keypad, and a large red button alongside.

As Sergeant Crosby pressed the button, he peered through the glass with his hands cupped each side of his head. It was a small room, with a counter down the left hand side, and another glass screen.

"Can I help you, Sir?" a voice said, from the perforated portion of the keypad.

He leant forward, "DS Crosby reporting for duty."

A few seconds passed, then there was a loud click, and the door sprang open.

Sergeant Crosby pushed the door open further, stepped into a short corridor with the counter to his left, and the door clicked shut behind him. Directly in front was another glass-panelled door looking onto a courtyard in front of a three-story brick building that resembled a warehouse, and as he turned to his left, he came face to face with a large, uniformed constable behind a glass screen.

"Papers, Sergeant," the lethargic young man asked.

Sergeant Crosby pushed his envelope through a narrow slot in the bottom of the glass, and the young man quickly slid out the papers inside. After a cursory glance, he kept back one sheet, slid the rest back into the envelope, and pushed it back, "Across the yard and through that glass door over there, Sergeant," he said. "The Desk-Sergeant will see to you."

The other glass door clicked open with a buzz, and Sergeant Crosby quickly grabbed his envelope and left the small building adjacent to the front gate. A quick glance to his left as he crossed the courtyard, and he could see the building was a guardhouse, with a small window opposite the gate. The courtyard was full of cars: some official police vehicles, but most unmarked family sedans.

Beyond the cars, between the only marked out bays with more luxury models, was the aluminium framed, glass door; and sucking in a deep breath for the third time that morning, he entered the bleak building.

To anyone already familiar with the Wellington Street front office, it would have been apparent that the extravagance stopped there, and the CID were left with a cheerless area that passed as a lobby: a small waiting area, an enclosed counter with a security door alongside and open stairs to the upper levels; he could see no lift.

As if fashioned by the confines of his environment, a grenadier-like Desk Sergeant spotted the new detective with a fixed stare, and watched him all the way across the black-and-white chequered vinyl lobby to his glass-barrier. As Sergeant Crosby leant forward to introduce himself for the third time, the uniformed Sergeant slid an open folder in front of himself.

"DS Crosby I presume," he said in a sharp clear voice.

"That's me," Crosby replied, looking surprised.

"Don't worry lad, I'm not a clairvoyant," he said, with a friendly chuckle. "I recognised you from your photograph on your new warrant card." He pushed the open folder under the glass. It appeared to be full of papers, including his stiff new warrant card clipped to the top sheet. "I need you to fill that lot in and sign each sheet," Crosby reached for his pen. "Not now lad, by the end of the day will be soon enough."

"Thanks, Sarge...I'll do that," he replied, unclipping his new warrant card.

"Sergeant Fawcet, lad," the older man barked. "I might be uniform, but I outrank you by twenty years. Remember that, and you and I will get on all right."

Crosby realised he had made his first mistake of the day, never to take a desk sergeant for granted, and quickly closed his folder. "I shall, Sergeant Fawcett. Now if you'll kindly point me in the right direction, I'll let you get on."

The Sergeant smiled and pointed towards the stairs, "Up the stairs lad...second floor. Oh...and by the way, there's a very attractive young lady waiting for you."

"Me!" Crosby questioned, pointing to himself.

"Yes. Like you, she's Inspector Jordan's new assistant."

Still thinking, Crosby turned towards the stairs, and then he stopped again.

"What about my car?" he said, just remembering.

"As I told the young lady; I'll sort you out a space by lunch time. See me then and I'll give you a code-card to get you through the gate."

That was it, the sergeant turned away as Crosby turned back to the stairs.

His first task was to find the inspector he had heard so much about, and there was the mysterious attractive young woman the sergeant sprang on him. As he left the stairs on the second landing he was warming to the idea of a female companion, but a pedantic new boss was something else.

Crosby instinctively entered the swing doors marked CID and stood for a moment scanning the busy room. He was looking for an indication that someone had noticed him, but they all seemed too busy in what they were doing, and he got the impression that this CID was going to be a lot different to Leeds.

Eventually, the sullen looking detective sitting at the first desk looked up and shot a puzzled glance in Crosby's direction. "I suppose you're another of Inspector Jordan's new recruits?" he asked, with a harsh tone in his voice.

"I'm not a recruit," Crosby snapped back, "I'm a DC of five years."

"Whatever. To Jordan you'll be a recruit."

"I'm DS Crosby."

"It's no good you introducing yourself to me. This is the real CID, your lot's down the corridor, in the broom cupboard."

There was a sudden roar of laughter from the others. The detectives were only pretending to be busy, when all the time they were listening to every word.

"And your name is?" Crosby asked, overlooking the snub.

"DS Ward," he snapped, looking back at the others, "Remember that name sonny. I outrank you, and I expect your acknowledgement each time we meet."

Crosby started to turn, "I'll ask my boss about that."

Before DS Ward could reply, Crosby pushed his way through the swing doors and turned right down the corridor.

The room at the end, temporarily marked CAS on a card pinned to the door, was not that far removed from DS Ward's broom-cupboard slur.

If it had not been for the presence of an attractive female sitting at a desk over by the window, reading the paperwork both of them had to fill in by the end of the day, he might well have looked at the sign again.

"Are you looking for Inspector Jordan," she said, looking up.

He stood for a moment eyeing the young, attractive brunette and decided things were looking up, "Yes," he replied, tongue-tied at first. "I'm Josh Crosby."

"Sergeant," she said.

"Oh...you're a sergeant as well?"

"No," she said, laughing, "You're the Sergeant. It's on your desk over there."

Crosby turned around to the unoccupied desk by the wall. She was in the desk by the window, the larger desk covered in files, was in front of the white board, and his desk, so she said, was against the wall.

Crosby dumped his things on the top, noticing a business card with his name on. It said Sergeant Josh Crosby. On the other side, it said Professor Jethro Jordan, Nottingham Police Training College, Wentworth Hill.

"Um," he let out, waving the card in the air. "And what does your card say?"

"Constable Penny Willow."

Crosby walked across and shook her hand, a small delicate hand he thought, "Is that really your name?"

"Yes it is," she snapped back. "What's wrong with it?"

He suddenly realised he had embarrassed her, "Nothing...
I'm sorry. It's a beautiful name. That's why I said that. It's so
beautiful it could have come from one of those fairy tales."

Constable Willow looked surprised, "Do you really
think so?"

CHAPTER 4

Inspector Jordan spent the last hour and a half tracing the files that CID, very cleverly sent to just about every office in the building, and not surprisingly, the last office he visited was that of the originator, Inspector Dent.

DS Ward swung round in his chair when Jordan crashed through the doors. He had a smug look on his face, but soon changed it when he saw Jordan. "I see you found the files, Inspector...sorry about that."

Jordan banged the files down on Ward's desk, accidentally spilling another pile onto the floor, "Listen to me you little turd," Jordan started. "It doesn't matter to me what you lot of useless excuses think of me, but if I catch you tampering with evidence again, or even as much as a word out of place, you'll be hearing from the Commissioner. This is his project now, and I'm not about to let someone like you get in the way of its progress. Do I make myself clear?"

Ward nodded his head, "Proper cops don't blab to the higher ups."

Jordan laughed as he picked up his folders, "That's just it old lad...I'm not a proper cop. And I'm certainly not bothered about what anyone thinks if I have a few words with my good friend the Chief Superintendent."

"We'll see what Inspector Dent has to say about that."

"Good…and while you're on, tell him to keep out of my way."

Jordan stormed out of the CID office with as much gusto as he could muster, and once outside, he sucked in a deep breath of relief. He had not reacted like that towards anyone since the time he lost control in Kenya. Although this outburst did not have the same dire consequences, it was nonetheless just as effective.

His intention was to put the fear of God into DS Ward, or anyone else prepared to disrupt his investigation, and despite their dismal failure, he was determined that his new squad was going to be a success.

Composing himself, Jordan carried on down the corridor to his new office. The door was half-open and hearing voices inside the room, he guessed his assistants had arrived. Both arms were full of folders, so he placed one armful down by the door. He wanted their first impression of him to be a masterful one, not that of a lackey doing a job he could easily have delegated.

On entering the small office Jordan walked into an overpowering smell of Jasmine; the same perfume his wife Jessie used.

Jordan crossed the small space in front of the desks, passed a surprised Sergeant Crosby, and stopped in front of the young constable. He stood staring at her. She reminded him of his wife: the same deep blue eyes. The same high cheek bones and pointed chin. The same clear skin, except the hair was different. Constable Willow was mesmerised.

"Why is your hair dark?" Jordan said, bluntly.

"I beg your pardon?" she asked.

"It's dark…it should be honey-blonde. And what perfume is that?"

"I don't wear perfume on duty…it's not allowed. Is there something wrong?"

His unusual question left each assistant wondering.

"I can smell Jasmine," Jordan continued, as if he hadn't heard what the constable had said, "Where's it coming from?"

With a look of comprehension, the Constable suddenly touched her hair, "It must be my shampoo…Yes… it was Jasmine I used."

Jordan grunted, "I'd prefer it if you used something different next time." He said, swinging round and leaving the room.

They both looked at each other with absolute amazement: Constable Willow with a sense of apprehension, and Sergeant Crosby wondering whether the tales he had heard about his new boss were true.

The Constable spoke first, "I've never had anyone complain about my shampoo before," she said, still running her hand through her hair.

Crosby opened his jacket and sniffed at his shirt, "It's a wonder he didn't have a go at my cologne…it's strong enough."

Then a voice rang out from across the room as Jordan returned with the remaining files, "You've introduced yourselves I see…that's good."

Hardly out of their state of amazement, they swung round towards the door, watched the Inspector cross to his desk, and dump another pile of folders in amongst the ones already there.

"Yes, Boss," was Crosby's automatic reply.

Constable Willow thought it was a derogatory term: a typical male attitude that isolated women in the force. She had a different kind of respect for her superiors, and chose to call Jordan, Inspector.

The Inspector seemed to have forgotten the incident of the hair and perfume, as he paced back and forth in front of his two assistants. He appeared quite a different person now. He had calmed down and was looking pensive, casting a glance now and then across the pile on his desk, until finally he perched himself on the corner, in a position he seemed familiar with, as if it was his stance when delivering a lecture.

"Right!" he started, clasping both hands together.

The two young officers sat up attentively.

"Introductions," he started. "I always believe, when I meet a new class, that our form of communication is very important. Not that I'm suggesting you're a class of course… it was a manner of speech," the sergeant and constable looked on with vague expressions on their faces. Jordan turned towards Crosby. "Of course, you, Sergeant Crosby, have already chosen to call me Boss… and that's fine."

"I prefer Inspector…Inspector," the Constable said.

Jordan smiled, still fascinated in her likeness, "Well that's settled," said Jordon. "Now…what do I call you two? I hate formality, so…forgetting rank…unless that concerns you, Sergeant?"

"No, Boss…that's okay by me."

"Good. Then I either call you by your first names or your last names…what is it to be?" Jordan asked, bending forward.

"I think surnames are a bit impersonal, Inspector," the Constable said.

"I agree," Crosby replied.

"Then Penny and Josh it is."

Jordan rubbed his hands together again.

The first of many traits were forming, Josh noted.

"Now to the task at hand," Jordan said, easing himself back on the desk further so that both legs were now off the ground. "I gather you were both briefed about our new squad, if not its function," they both nodded. "CAS (Criminal Anomalies Squad) is the Chief Superintendent's brainchild, not mine, so let's get that straight. As far as I'm concerned, our job is to identify the skeleton found in Sherwood Forest. Actually, it isn't just a skeleton. If you study the pictures in the case file, you'll see it's more of a petrified body. I'm not skilled enough to say any more, we can sort that out when we see the pathologist..."

"Do I have to go, Inspector?" Penny asked.

"You don't like bodies?"

"No, Inspector."

"Neither do I...but someone has to do it. Anyway, the only way we're going to identify this corpse is with good police work." Jordan patted the folders on his desk, "We need to break this information down into synchronous groups."

"I was trained as a strategist, Inspector," Penny interrupted,

"Good!" Jordan said, as if he didn't already know. "Then I shall put you in charge of the white board. I want you both to go through all these files and build up a profile of the crime scene. Don't look for any crime though...it happened too long ago to matter now. All I'm interested in at this moment is how that body got there."

Jordan slipped off the desk and moved towards the door.

"What are you going to do, Boss?" Josh asked.

"Well...as I said, someone's got to see the pathologist."

Josh took his jacket off and slipped it across the back of the chair, then turned to the pile of folders on Inspector Jordan's desk. Penny was already sifting through the files and stacking them in accordance with their respective links.

"You seem to be a dab hand at this sort of thing," Josh said, picking up a file.

"As I said, I was trained as a strategist, and then spent most of my recruit period in the archives. A waste of time I thought...until now."

"Look at this lot," Josh exclaimed. "We'll be here all day."

"Have you got anything better to do?"

He dropped the folder in his hand and went over to his desk, and picked up the papers Sergeant Fawcett gave him, "Christ...I said I would have this lot filled in by tonight; little chance of that now."

Penny laughed, "I'm sure we'll be finished in plenty of time...they won't take long. I had mine finished in quarter of an hour."

"Aren't you the clever little Constable?"

"I thought we weren't to use ranks."

Josh put his papers down and returned to the desk.

"Sorry...it was just an expression."

"How long have you been a Sergeant?" Penny asked.

"Five years."

"You must have been young. I don't think I've met a young sergeant before."

"One of the youngest, my super said. Then again, the West Yorkshire Constabulary is a big district. They have many constables, so they need a heap of sergeants to watch them. As soon as my statutory recruit period finished, I was asked to sit the exam..."

"Why you?" Penny interrupted.

Embarrassed, Josh laughed and said, "I'm one of those people cursed with a photographic memory."

"You're joking?"

"Give me your papers."

Penny went over to her desk and brought them back to him, but held them at arm's length at first, undecided whether this was for real, or simply a ruse to see how old she was, "What are you going to do?" She finally said, handing them over.

Josh said nothing. He took the papers, held them out in front of his face, and then one by one he scanned each sheet and passed it back to her. It took him no more than a few moments to read all the papers. She was doubtful, and expected him to recite no more than the first page, until, after a moment's pause, with his eyes closed Josh started reciting the first page.

"Penelope Willow, twenty-six, born in Penzance on January 16, 1958. Father, Henry Willow, fifty-four, retired. Mother, Jessica Willow, forty-eight, maiden name Partridge. Illnesses: Chickenpox at Six, Broken arm at Nineteen, Appendectomy at Seventeen, Miscarriage at..."

"That's enough," Penny snapped, "I believe you."

"That was only an overview of course," he said.

"Is everything in your head?"

"Oh yes," he said, nonchalantly.

"For all time?"

"If I wish to recall it...but I don't usually."

Penny went silent. Then after a while, studying the smug look on Josh's face, her eyes suddenly opened wide, and she smiled, "You cheated."

"Yes I did," he admitted, "But there was nothing they could do about it. There was nothing in the rule book about carrying the exam papers in my head."

"And that's why they chose you for this case?"

"I don't know about that. But I suppose it's the same reason why they chose a strategist and an analyst...and a stupid name like CAS."

They smiled at each other playfully as they set about sorting out the files, and jostling for supremacy, as two young people thrown together often do. That was Jordan's aim: leaving them together to come to terms with each other's distinctly opposed personalities.

Penny Willow was an innocuous young girl, hardly suited to the ordeals of a police career. Yet that was her chosen future, and she brought with her naïve eagerness, an astute understanding of the new techniques available to her.

In contrast, Josh Crosby was a nervous young man who had not yet found his confidence, and brashly hid the fact with the knowledge that he had a profoundly useful gift. His ability to draw upon it like a filing cabinet overwhelmed him at times, with a pedantic nature that fed an insatiable curiosity for detail. He had already found Penny an open book, but the Inspector's life was a background he would dearly enjoy spending time delving into.

Having kick-started the investigation, Jordan now had to familiarise himself with the central feature of the case, namely the skeletal remains found in Sherwood Forest. It was only a short drive to the Pathology Department next to the City Morgue, and he was thankful; at least, that he was a good friend of the Chief Pathologist, Chester Daniels; a regular lecturer at Jordan's college.

Unlike most of his peers, Chester was still bright and cheerful in his sober middle age; Jordan never did find out how old he really was. By all accounts, he was still athletically active, being a member of the local soccer club, where, strangely enough, he was their resident goalkeeper.

He was tall enough and broad with it, but his weather-beaten face had paid the price of countless skirmishes in the goalmouth. Not to mention the broken ankle that had left him with painful sciatica, and a slight limp he managed to hide.

Jordan punched his way through the battered swing doors, from countless wayward trolleys, and walked along the poorly lit corridor, passed an array of green doors with glass portholes, until he arrived at the buckled flaps of pathology.

It looked a desolate place, next to the service lift, and Jordan pushed his way in with his shoulder, hardly daring to touch the smudged push-plate with his hand, and stopped just short of the doors as they swung back.

He thought he had entered the boiler-house by mistake, there were pipes everywhere: hanging from the ceiling on long metal clamps. He quickly noticed the row of chromium trays on spidery metal legs, and the occasional bundle.

It was hard to see all the room; it was so dimly lit, except for a lighted area at the far end, where Jordan caught a glimpse of life: someone moving amidst the white haze of a single light. On closer inspection, as Jordan made his way passed the trays, he spotted a grey haired man bending over a table.

"Is that you, Chester?" Jordan called out.

The man looked up, with a puzzled expression on his face, and small half-oval glasses hooked onto the end of his nose.

"Yes...who's that?" he said, removing them.

"It's Jethro...Jethro Jordan from the Police College."

He turned round and put something metallic on the table in front of him. "You mean, Inspector Jordan, don't you?"

"News travels fast," Jethro said, reaching out to shake his hand, then drawing back when he saw Chester was still wearing rubber gloves.

"Oh sorry, Jethro...I've just been doing a bit of dissecting. Hold on a minute."

He walked over to a basin in the corner of the room, slid off his gloves, tossed them in a bin, and thoroughly washed his hands.

Jordan was still squinting in the dimly lit area his friend was working in, "You're going to go blind in this light."

"Sorry. This early in the morning I only switch on what I need," he replied, switching two more lights on above the table. "I suppose you've come to see our old man," he said, as another light burst into life.

Jordan shook his hand, "You heard about Dent losing the case then?"

"As you said, news travels fast. I haven't seen Inspector Dent though; it was his sidekick...DS Ward. He said you'd be down...he was right."

"Yes...I had a run-in with him earlier."

"Don't trust the man, Jethro...he's trouble."

"Thanks, but I'm already wise to him."

"Good...I just cut up the bodies; I don't get involved in gossip."

"Speaking of bodies," Jordan prompted.

"Ah yes...the skeletal remains. He's over here, there was little point in putting him in the freezer, and I didn't want to move him too much. The corpse was difficult to handle, and I'm a little concerned about its condition. It was bad enough removing him from the grave, but in this humidity, he's beginning to moult."

"Sounds like you need a dry atmosphere."

"I wish," he grunted, "I could do with a whole new lab."

Finally, in the light Jordan could see the ragged face more clearly, "There's something different about you," he said, trying to figure out what.

Chester frowned; it had been a while since he last saw his friend. Then he realised what it was and touched his chin, "Oh...it's the beard."

"You had one last time I saw you...didn't you?" Jordan commented.

"Yes, but it was much shorter then. I got sick of trimming it every day. Now I only trim it once a week," he stroked it again. "Makes me look more of a professor...don't you think?" he turned sideways for a better look.

"I hate to say it, Chester," Jordan said, "But I think it makes you look older."

"Ah well...that's life."

Just as Chester moved over towards the trolley against the wall, with a green coversheet draped over it, there was a loud thud at the end of the room. They both instinctively turned towards the noise, and saw a young man standing at the top of the aisle with a surprised look on his face.

"Ah, Jack," Chester called out, "switch the lights on at the top of the room, there's a good lad." There were several pulses of light as the tubes warmed up and the room suddenly became bathed in an eerie light. "He's my assistant...a good lad."

The Pathologist introduced Jack to Inspector Jordan, and not being familiar with recent police intrigue, he explained that Inspector Dent was no longer in charge of the case. He seemed nervous, not used to visitors, and helped to move the trolley away from the wall.

Jordan had already studied the forensic photographs of the corpse in the grave and was not expecting any surprises.

When the assistant folded back the green coversheet, the breath left him, and he struggled to maintain his balance.

The grey emaciated skin, barely covering the bones, took on a charred and blackened appearance, with small, fleshy lesions of pink skin that the flames had not consumed. It was a ghastly sight, not one he expected, and his skin went cold and clammy, as he reached out, calling for his wife, Jessie.

Chester suddenly took notice.

"Is this the right body?" Jordan said, vaguely shaking his head.

"Yes...Are you all right, Jethro?" Chester replied.

Jordan touched his forehead, and looked embarrassed. It had happened again, and in daylight this time, he thought. He closed his eyes and opened them again, and found everything was as it should be.

"I'm sorry, Chester...I was thinking of something else."

"Or someone else," Chester said, "Who's, Jessie?"

"My wife...she died some time ago," Jordan looked back at the skeletal remains on the trolley. They looked the same as the photographs, if not a little more yellow, and there seemed more skin on the bones than he remembered, and there was hair on the skull. "Did you do an autopsy?" he said to get on with his enquiry.

"Hardly," Chester said, "You need flesh and organs for that."

Jethro looked puzzled, "I don't follow."

"I can see you haven't been to many autopsies."

"This is my first."

"I see...that explains it," Chester said.

"What?"

"Your lapse of concentration earlier...it affects people in different ways. I remember one chap that..."

"Yes, Chester...that's right. Can we get on?"

"Of course... Sorry. Well, I could see the corpse was dehydrated, mummified if you like, so I had it x-rayed, and that's when I noticed the poor chap didn't have any organs. Nothing...not a sausage."

"So someone gutted the man before he buried him?" Jordan said, trying not to look at the body more than he had to. "Why is it dried out?"

"I don't know exactly. I didn't find any signs of Formaldehyde in the tissue samples to indicate embalming. But there was none, and there wouldn't have been any, since the tests proved he was very old," Chester said, looking a little dismayed. "Of course he was buried in the right place."

"How's that?" Jordan asked, becoming curious.

"The Sherwood Forest area is notorious for its dry soil, if you can call it that. It's part of a giant Triassic pebble bed. Nothing will grow there, except trees and scrub. It was strange that the other bodies had lost all their flesh in only a few years. Yet, here's our friend still quite whole, except for some abrasions on his back, as if something harsh had abraded the skin. But we didn't find anything in the grave; it was as clean as a whistle."

"You found no forensics at all?"

"Not in the grave," Chester said, picking up a small evidence bag from between the body's legs. "But I found this inside him."

Jethro took hold of the bag by its top and held it up to the light. It looked like a piece of heavily encrusted stone, "What is it?"

"It was in my report," Chester snorted as Jethro glared back at him. "It's an arrowhead. I took it to my friend at the museum and he identified it straight away. Apparently, you can find them all over Nottingham, and when he checked it against his own specimens, he dated it around eleven hundred: about the time of Richard the Lionheart. Hence my reason for saying our body was old."

"Ah!" Jordan let out with a laugh, "That accounts for the Robin Hood story in the press." Chester turned round and stared at his assistant.

"Don't look at me...I didn't say anything," he replied.

"Well I didn't...and I'm sure my friend said nothing. Besides, I deliberately told him I dug it up in my garden."

"It doesn't matter," Jordan said, passing the bag back, "Where did you find it?"

Chester picked up a large probe, beckoned to his assistant to turn the body onto its side, then pointed to the hole above the pelvis, "Just here, within the small of his back. I thought it strange at the time. It was just below the dermis, about two or three centimetres in...certainly not deep enough to have killed him."

"It seems such a small hole."

"Hardly the trouble of digging for it," Chester said, slapping the corpse with his probe with a resounding thud, as if he was striking a cardboard box.

"Have you noticed how straight he is?" Jordan commented, "As if he had been laid out in some kind of ritual. Not like the contorted corpses they usually find."

Jordan walked around the trolley feeling more comfortable, studying the way the arms crossed the chest, and his chin placed firmly on the top of his ribcage. "You said he wasn't embalmed? Yet he didn't disintegrate like the other bodies. What could they have done back then to keep him like this?"

Looking irritated, Chester reached over to the table for a copy of his report.

"Seeing that this is all in my report, Jethro, I didn't go into detail. However; we did find a substantial amount of Natron and Resin in his tissue sample."

"And what does that mean?"

"It means he was pickled. A process, I believe, was widespread at the time."

"Then this was a man of note."

"It would explain things, except why was he buried in such an out-of-the-way place, and not in one of the abbeys, if he was important?"

Jordan thought for a moment, "I don't think he was, at first. I think this was his second grave. A hurried affair by all accounts," Jordan turned to his puzzled friend. "Of course there were a lot of warring factions back then. Maybe one of his enemies dug him up and buried him there, hoping the local scavengers would dig him up and tear him to pieces."

"I'm impressed, Jethro," Chester said.

He laughed, "No need to be...that was the sum-total of my Sherwood Forest knowledge, gleaned from a tourist guidebook I bought about Nottingham. I thought I'd better find something out about the place."

"Just the same, Jethro...it has merit."

"That act would have been sacrilege," Jordan continued.

"Most definitely...That's why they preserved the body."

"Do you mind if I bring a friend of mine along?" Jordan asked.

"A friend," Chester questioned.

"Yes...he's an Archaeologist."

Chester's face suddenly lit up, "Ah...that makes sense. What's his name?"

"Simon Travellian."

An impressed smile crossed Chester's face, "I've heard of him. He was in the papers last year: something about identifying corpses in a mass grave outside Warsaw. A World War Two execution site I believe."

"Is that so?" Jordan said. It was the first he knew of his friend's exploits outside Egypt. He would have to question him about that.

"Yes...I'm sure it's the same chap. Now he'll be able to confirm how old our corpse is. Probably tell you a lot more than I can," Chester commented.

Jordan looked back again at the man from Sherwood Forest, while Chester's assistant, Jack, began to fold back the green coversheet. This time, Jordan studied the skull and sunken, closed eyelids, and he bent closer to the face as Jack stopped and held the coversheet back.

"Well Sherwood Forest man. I don't know who you are or where you came from...but I certainly intend to find out."

CHAPTER 5

Sarah Bolt, a tenacious, chocolate coated pit-bull of a woman, was the local tabloid, features reporter. Life had been difficult for her in a town built on history, and far removed from the seamy, number crunching sales of the popular press. When skeletal remains turned up in Sherwood Forest, she did her homework and discovered two other skeletons from an earlier period.

There was no proven connection, but Sarah's creative gift for scandal, managed to stir up a story of a serial burial ground. Manipulated by her own imagination, her information came from the most bizarre sources, one of which was the local Green Feather Inn. A pub coincidently patronised by the local police: in particular, the men from the CID.

By sitting within earshot of the dartboard, a handy recorder passed off as a musical Walkman and her distracting crossed legs, she was able to gather the occasional tit-bit she wanted. At lunchtime and some evenings, she sat at the end of the bar on one of the high stools, in full sight of the men playing darts, and was well within range to hear the day's problems in the CID.

All of which kept her column ticking over, until the day came when she overheard DS Ward mouthing about the unusual character that had taken over his Sherwood Forest case. There could only be one case, and she sensed a story.

Until now, she had been sitting on the edge of the case, padding out media circulars and making up the rest as she went along, until she heard DS Ward. He had taken an early lunch, something to do with finishing off a challenge from the uniform team, and overhearing Sergeant Fawcett's comments on Jordan's new assistants, he stepped in and let them know about the new squad called CAS.

She scribbled down the new name, and waited for him to come to the bar to buy another round of drinks. She had to find out about this new squad, and DS Ward looked a likely candidate.

"It's, DS Ward," Sarah said, as he dumped the tray of empty glasses on the bar and ordered a refill. She heard he fancied himself with the women, and thought this was a good opportunity to find out how attentive he was.

He turned round as he waited. Distracted by the game, he hadn't noticed her before, but seeing her sitting next to him, his eyes opened wide.

"Do you know me?" he said, surprised. He was the one who usually made the first move, not always successful, and she startled him.

"I don't, Sergeant...but I've heard of you."

"Oh," he let out, curious. "And what have you heard?"

"I've heard that you're the man behind Inspector Dent."

He looked embarrassed as he instinctively glanced across towards the others waiting for their drinks. They only had three-quarters of an hour, and they egged him on, jeering at the tall shapely redhead accosting him.

"I wouldn't say that exactly."

"Oh come now...aren't you being a little coy."

The drinks arrived, "I have to go, I'll be on duty shortly, and the lads are screaming for their drinks."

"My name's Sarah Bolt, I'll be here tonight if you're interested."

DS Ward suddenly remembered the name. Inspector Dent was cursing the female reporter who had latched onto his case, and was causing him all sorts of grief with the Chief Superintendent. It was no longer his case, and she looked too good for him to miss such an opportunity. "Okay," he said, picking up the tray, "I'll be in around seven...or thereabouts."

"Come on, Charlie," someone shouted.

"I'll see you then," she said, with a confident look on her face.

It was gone two when Jordan finally returned to the office. His friend Chester had persuaded him to take an early lunch, and what with finding out more about why Jordan accepted such a ridiculous case, and Chester's insatiable curiosity about his friend Travellian, a quick snack turned out to be a two-hour ordeal.

"I didn't expect you to be as long as this, Inspector," Penny said, when Jordan entered the room and walked over to his desk, "I thought you didn't like bodies?"

"I don't," He said, removing his jacket and draping it over his chair, "Why? Are you keeping a check on my movements?"

"No, Inspector...I just thought you'd be back earlier. That's all."

Jordan looked at his desk. The jumble of files he had left them to sort out had miraculously become neat groups, with small handwritten notes on top. Penny looked pleased with herself, and Josh was too busy scanning through pages of text to notice Jordan was looking at him.

"What are you doing, Josh?" Jordan called out.

Josh finished the page he was on and looked up. "Sorry, Boss, what was that?"

"I said...what are you doing?"

"Oh...this, I'm memorising all these files."

"What...all of them?"

"No, Inspector," Penny interrupted, "Only the ones I thought might be important. Josh told me about his unusual talent, so I thought we might use it to good purpose. Instead of wading through all this lot every time you want to check something, just ask Josh; he should be able to recall it in an instant."

Jordan shook his head. He had intended to use Josh's talent at some stage in the investigation, if only to keep reminding him of the relevant facts, but taking it this far, had not entered his thoughts.

"Well...I must say. I didn't quite expect things to be so organised. I expected the pair of you to be at it all day."

"It was Penny's doing, Boss," Josh admitted. I didn't have a clue where to start. But once I got the idea of what she was up to, I got stuck in."

Jordan sat down. His lunch was a trifle more than he usually had, and the idea of going through files for the rest of the afternoon, did not appeal to him. "So Penny...why don't you tell me all about this system you have. I presume all these neat little piles are some form of a system, even if only in your head."

"It's not so much a system, Inspector; more a logical grouping. As you can see, I've arranged them in three groups. The first group I think we can discard, because it deals entirely with the other skeletons you mentioned. Apparently, according to a few notes I found inside the folders, Inspector Dent considered they were linked with the recent discovery: part of a serial killing, or some periodic ritual."

"And you decided that theory was no longer feasible?"

Penny looked startled, "Sorry, Inspector. Unless I'm mistaken, I thought you said it wasn't possible...something about our corpse being too old."

"Quite right, Penny," he confirmed, and then glanced over towards Josh. He had heard josh was a curious young man, always full of questions. "What about you, Josh...nothing to say...no questions?"

"No, Boss. DS Ward spent three weeks going back over the witness statements on both unsolved murders, and got no further forward with the case than when he started. In fact, he wasted so much time with the daughter of the last victim; the inspector had to caution him. There's a memo in there somewhere."

"And you gleaned all that from a casual glance at the files?"

"Yes, Boss."

"See, Inspector," Penny said, "He's going to be invaluable."

Jordan thought the Chief Superintendent had obviously chosen well.

"Right," Jordan let out, snatching the files up in his hands, and dumping them at the back of his desk against the wall, "Carry on, Penny."

She moved over to the remaining two groups, "This group, Inspector, deals with all the Forensic, Pathology, Forestry and Toxicology reports. They're not very thick; it seems there wasn't much to report. Nonetheless, they needed grouping together. No doubt you will want to add to them as soon as you start coming up with new evidence."

"You think that's possible?"

"I thought that was why this new squad was formed?"

"It was, Penny. Both of you will have to get used to my methods. I find I learn a lot more by asking questions. Some may sound silly to you...even ridiculous, but they all fit in with my thinking at the time."

"I understand, Inspector," Penny said.

"I knew straight away what you..." Josh started.

"That's all right, Josh," Jordan interrupted. "I'm sure you've read quite a lot about me so far, and can recite every unmentionable trait," Josh smiled, with a knowing nod. "But you said something back then, Penny...did you say forestry?"

"Yes, Inspector," Penny said, reaching for the folder.

She passed it to Jordan. He opened the thin file, glanced at the two conspicuous sheets and the interesting folded map, and closed the folder again, "Yes...I'll have a look at that," Jordan said, pushing the folder to one side.

He looked up expectantly, and Penny continued, "This last group is all we have on the Sherwood Forest Man..."

"I like that," Jordan said, "It's better than corpse or body, and as I think I already said, skeleton doesn't quite describe him. No, from now on we shall call him The Sherwood Forest Man," Jordan stood up and wrote the new title across the top of the whiteboard, "There...that's a good start."

Penny looked up at her name and smiled, "Good, that gives us something to work to; there's little else. Witness statements from the couple who found him, a statement from the ranger who usually patrols that part of the woods, and a whole lot of other material put together by Inspector Dent, from interviews with people who thought they might know something about the gravesite," she continued.

"So he did do something in his sixteen weeks," Josh commented.

"Now, Josh," Jordan shushed, "Let's forget he exists…"

"Is this what you wanted, Inspector?" Penny interrupted.

"Very good for a morning's work," Jordan said, getting up and walking across to the window. He looked up at the darkening clouds, and then at his watch. "It's too late to do any site-work, and the light's too bad to see anything, so heads down young people, and let's see if you can wheedle anything interesting out of what we have so far. As I said, I'm mainly interested in why someone buried the Sherwood Forest Man where he was. I'll have a look at this forest file. You two can share the statements, go over them again and decide if any are worth a second follow-through."

"Boss," Josh spoke up, "I've got to fill in all these forms."

"That's okay, I'm sure Penny won't mind."

She had already picked up the pile and was back at her desk.

The remainder of the afternoon seemed to drag, and although Penny was trying to be inconspicuous, sorting through the witness statements and jotting down anything she thought the inspector might find interesting, his irritability was distracting her.

"Damn this bloody thing," Jordan exclaimed in a sudden outburst.

He was wrestling with his tie, first loosening it, then dragging it in a zigzag fashion down his chest, until finally he ripped it from his neck and tossed it in the basket. Then undoing his collar, he let out a long sigh of relief.

"Is everything all right, Inspector," Penny asked in a whisper.

Jordan smiled back at her, now in a much better mood, "Yes...I haven't worn a tie in years, except for special occasions; and there haven't been many of those lately. I can't remember the last time."

"So why now, Boss," Josh questioned, even more curious.

"When I accepted this assignment, the Chief Superintendent told me to wear a tie on Monday. Well I have; at least most of the day."

It was just before seven when Sarah Bolt entered The Green Feather. It was raining and she quickly shook her gabardine raincoat and handed it to the young girl in the cloakroom. The ladies room was the next door along and Sarah decided it was time for a makeover before she met DS Ward.

Sarah wanted to look her best, as she examined her lean face, pouting her lips as she added an extra layer for effect. She then fluffed her long, auburn hair and winked at herself. Then standing back from the mirror, she made sure her V-necked blouse was showing enough cleavage and tucked evenly into her slim, grey skirt with a slit down one side.

Satisfied that DS Ward would find her more than attractive, she tossed her lipstick stained tissue into the bin and left.

Her plan was to be there first, and she was. She wanted the opportunity to set herself up at the end of the bar where he first saw her, and she deliberately chose one of the barstools with a chromium ring just above the floor, so that she could cross her legs and hook one of her high-heels over it to steady herself.

Once comfortable, Sarah positioned her body so that she could watch the lounge door in the mirror behind the bar. She wanted to see DS Ward's face when he saw her, and on the dot of seven, he arrived. She smiled to herself, and hitching her skirt up above her knees, she waited for him to cross the room.

As soon as DS Ward spotted Sarah at the end of the bar, a feeling of anticipation struck him, overshadowed with a touch of restraint. He kept hearing Inspector Dent's scornful words, his warnings to keep clear of the woman and at all costs, deny everything.

He shook the thoughts from his head, smiled at her across the room and worked his way through the tables. That was her cue to cross her long, shapely legs. It was her intention to distract him long enough to answer her questions. She looked obvious, but then again, that was the idea.

"I didn't expect you to be here," he said, moving along the bar towards her.

"When I saw the rain, I thought twice, I must admit," she replied. "Then I remembered my promise. I don't like breaking promises."

"I'm glad you don't, Sarah," he said, sitting down beside her.

"I can't keep calling you, DS Ward."

"My friends call me Charlie," He replied, nodding to the barman. "What will it be? You look like a Bacardi and Coke girl."

"I only drink white wine when I'm working, Charlie."

He nodded again to the barmen, "So you're working are you?"

"Well I did tell you I was a reporter."

The barman laid the drinks down in front of them.

"On my tab, Geoff," he said to him, then looking back at her, he paused a moment and picked up his beer and took a quick drink. "I know who you are, and your reputation for distorting the facts."

"That's just because I usually don't have any. If you give me an accurate quote, I promise to print it word for word."

"Give you what? I'm not on the skeleton case anymore."

It was Sarah's intention to persuade DS Ward to tell her all about the new Inspector, not about him or his colleagues, but when it came down to it, he had second thoughts. The individual made no difference; asking him to renege on the police was his problem. When she flipped the switch on her small recorder, and he listened to his remarks about Inspector Jordan, and other superiors he had no recollection of, he felt a shiver run down his back.

Sarah conspicuously moved towards him so that he could see above her knees and she placed her hand on his. "You know, Charlie, both our professions are made up of give and take. You make deals with the criminals, and they give you information that will further your investigation. Everyone wins."

"And if I tell you about this new Inspector, What's in it for me?"

She brushed the back of his hand, "I can think of a lot of things mutually enjoyable...if I was given the right incentive."

CHAPTER 6

After spending most of the night examining the forestry report and other local material to do with the myths surrounding Sherwood Forest, Jordan arrived the following morning a little late.

He was beginning to fit in with his new regime, except, instead of green fields and open spaces, high walls and an iron gate now surrounded him. He leant out of his car window, swiped the keypad with his card, and as soon as the gate opened, he parked his car in the spot allotted to him by the Chief Superintendent.

He refused to acknowledge the possibility of a pair of eyes boring into his back until he turned towards the entrance, and a spotty faced young constable confronted him. He looked unhappy, but refused to move.

"Sir," he said stiffly, rolling his eyes upwards.

It was at that point that Jordan heard the sharp rap of bare knuckles on glass. Jordan rolled his eyes upwards also, and the young constable nodded, and walked on.

Jordan looked up towards the line of windows on the second floor, and saw the grim face of Chief Superintendent Mulholland staring back down at him. He looked agitated as he beckoned Jordan, and then moved back into the room.

"Have you seen today's paper, Inspector?" the Chief Superintendent said, as Jordan entered his office.

Glancing across the desk, he said, "I try not to, Sir. It's bad enough having to put up with the news on TV."

The Chief Superintendent put his reading glasses on, and held up the paper, "New 'Skeleton Case' Inspector leaves Africa under a cloud," he read, removing his glasses and looking up at Jordan, "Where do they get such information?"

Jordan shrugged his shoulders and looked complaisant. "I often wonder, Sir. It certainly looks like we've got a leak."

"Impossible," he raged, "No one knows about that period. Your records only start when you returned to England."

"They don't need to know, Sir. After all, anyone could find out I was in Africa, then all they have to do is add the words left under a cloud."

"Well leave that to me; I'll root the traitor out. In the meantime, you get on with identifying that corpse."

"The Sherwood Forest Man."

"What?"

"That's our name for him, Sir. And I should have that answer in a few days."

"The Chief Superintendent looked surprised, "Oh…good. I'll look forward to that. Can I tell the Commissioner?"

"I'd rather you didn't, Sir, it's only a guess."

The Chief Superintendent stood up and moved around the desk. "Well let me know as soon as you can. He keeps ringing me every day. God…I hate to think what he's going to say about this lot." He dropped the paper on his desk.

There was a timid knock, and Phyllis Montgomery poked her head around the door, "I've got the Commissioner on line one, Sir. Do you want to speak to him?"

The Chief Superintendent stopped short of seeing Jordan to the door and returned to his desk with a harrowed look on his face.

He snatched the phone up off the hook, "Find the truth, Inspector. This woman has to be stopped...heaven knows what she'll come up with next," he said, and then he quickly pressed the button for line one. "Commissioner..."

Jordan smiled apologetically and squeezed through the door Phyllis was holding open for him, "Does this go on all the time he said?" walking across to the door leading into the corridor.

"All the time," Phyllis said, returning to her desk.

"I'll leave you to it then," he replied, and left.

Jordan could see the whole fiasco starting all over again, and the last thing he wanted at that moment was doubtful looks and complicated questions from his two impressionable assistants. He turned on his heels and quickly left the building. It was a bright day at last, and he suspected the gravesite in Sherwood Forest would be dry and ready to inspect.

Once north of the city, Jordan pulled over into a service area and studied the map Inspector Dent left in the forestry folder. Evidently, it was the map used by the hikers' trek through the forest northeast of a small village called Merton, on the road between Boughton and Worksop. It was one of those tricky set of junctions often found in the country, where the wrong fork could take you miles out of your way.

According to the notes, Jordan was looking for an unsealed road on the left that crossed through a particularly dense part of the forest, towards the southern shoreline of a body of water called Great Lake. It was a rutted track used mainly by forestry rangers, and boat enthusiasts heading for the lower part of the lake.

It was too far along the track for what he was looking for. A short distance in from the junction with the main road was the beginning of the bridle path taken by the hikers, where a hundred metres or so in they found the skeletal remains.

Once there, Jordan drove along the track a short distance until he reached a sign indicating the start of the bridle path, where he parked the car on a wide grass verge running along a ranch-style wooden fence that was the boundary of the eastern edge of Sherwood Forest.

He decided early on that he wanted to get a feel for the surrounding land: the entry and egress of whoever buried the remains in such an exposed location. Inspector Dent's report made little mention of the crime-scene topology, let alone the flora that occupied the same burial site. Then again, assuming the burial date is correct; everything would have been different back then.

Although Jordan was a Professor in Criminal Analysis, he was more at home in the field than he ever was in a classroom. He had a propensity for the hidden truth; a gifted insight into the minutia that most detectives overlooked, and he slowly, but carefully paced out the area bordered by a perimeter of yellow and black plastic tape.

It isolated a four metre cleared space around the trench excavated along the burial site. It was void of any vegetation, leaving only a sandy, gravel substance that flowed easily through his fingers and drifted on the breeze before it finally settled. The sandy substance covered the whole area except for the gravesite, which had a covering of oak leaves from one of the last ancient trees in the forest.

When Jordan left the house that morning, he noticed the leaves beginning to swirl across the road in front of him. It was early autumn, time for the full onrush of the rustic colours that greeted him as he motored on the back-roads towards the outer ring road of Leicester and the college.

Jordan did his usual circumference of the extended trench, stopping now and then to examine a glittering object that turned out to be no more than an unremarkable piece of quartz, and the occasional splinter of wood, that could have blown in during the recent high winds. He was sceptical of any immediate success, knowing Inspector Dent's investigation turned up little more than a common arrowhead. Yet he was convinced that the clue to the Sherwood Forest Man's identity was still here.

No one in the previous investigation had seen the importance of the condition of the back of the corpse: an abraded area, that should have shown signs of settlement in the soil, where contamination is always at its greatest. This set Jordan thinking, and he pulled out the orienteering map he brought with him.

It was still early, when the morning light was low enough to cast long shadows across the open area between the higher bridle path, and the start of the dense forest. Jordan opened the map and laid it out, so that it was in the same compass position as his viewpoint. Normal maps normally show towns, hamlets and the interconnecting highways along with symbolised sites of interest. This map concentrated on the terrain. It showed tracks, such as the bridle path, watercourses, and most interestingly, the contours of the land.

Jordan stepped into the trench and squatted down as low as he could between the police stakes at both ends, as he surveyed the surrounding terrain. It was plain to see the land to his right ascended in a slow curve towards the trees, and to the left, it fell away just as slowly in another sweeping curve towards the embankment of the bridle path; leaving the unmistakable smooth gouge left by a bed of rushing water. He stroked it with his fingers. It was dry and hard.

In the bright sunlight, the incline was too subtle, and the inconspicuous hollow in the middle would have been impossible to judge. Still checking the map, Jordan could see he was squatting in a streambed that originated some distance away, north of the site. The dotted line then meandered alongside the bridle path all the way, until it diverted around a rocky outcrop, where it returned to its natural path further south.

The map gave no indication of seasonal run-off, or in fact, whether it was an ancient dry gully. With little else, this was a discovery Jordan had to confirm. If a watercourse had passed over the burial site, it would explain the lack of forensic evidence and the abraded back of the corpse. Jordan stood up and followed the ancient bed towards the outcrop of boulders. There was a link here somewhere, and he knew it, but was damned if he could see it.

Meanwhile, as Josh entered the station courtyard, he noticed Jordan's car-space was empty, and wondered, in that instant, whether he should be somewhere else. The inspector had said nothing the previous night, as Josh and Penny left him with his head buried in several folders, and Josh sat for a moment.

He shook his head, sure that this was where he should be. He was beginning to realise his new boss was a little unusual, and certainly refrained from following established police procedure. He accepted that, and decided he would no doubt find a scribbled list of duties on his desk, as he unbuckled his belt and reached over to the back seat for his briefcase. As he did so, there was a frantic rapping sound on the car window. He glanced up and saw Penny glaring at him.

Opening his door he shouted, "Where's the fire?"

"Have you seen the paper this morning?" Penny cried.

"What paper? There's more than one you know."

"I'd doubt whether you'd read the others."

Josh snorted. He deliberately avoided anything he had no need to remember. Then Penny opened her paper and thrust it into his face.

Josh read the headline, "My God…I wonder if the boss has seen this?"

Penny glanced over towards the inspector's empty parking space.

"His car's not in its spot."

"I know…that's the first thing I noticed," Josh replied.

"Do you think he's gone down to the newspaper?" She mused.

"I'd love to be there if he has."

"He wouldn't…would he?" she continued rambling.

Without answering, Josh dashed out of his car and across to the main entrance, thinking Sergeant Fawcett would know. He always knew everything that was going on around the station…sometimes before the individuals knew themselves.

When Penny caught up to Josh, he was asking the desk sergeant where his inspector was, hoping he recorded it in the book.

"The new Inspector?" the Sergeant replied, with an air of disinterest.

"Yes…have you seen him?"

"No…not this morning. Then again I only came on a few minutes ago."

"He's at the site," a dowdy looking detective said.

"Well I…" the Sergeant was about to say.

"Excuse me," Josh interrupted angrily, I asked you a question,"

"No…you asked the Sergeant a question. I just answered."

"Okay. I stand corrected. How do you know he left for the site?"

"Because he asked me for directions," the detective said, smiling as he checked his watch. "He might be just arriving about now."

"I bet you gave him the longest route," Penny shouted.

"Of course," he said, laughing.

"Come on Josh," Penny said, grabbing his arm, "We'd better get out there and see what he's up to."

"Do you want any directions?" the detective said, with a smirk on his face.

"No thanks," Josh replied, pointing to his head. "It's all up here."

With a pinched, smug expression, Penny pulled Josh to the door.

Back at the site, Jordan was no closer to capturing the suspicion that was rolling around in his head. He had hoped, following the flow of the run-off through the burial site, that the vibrations he felt as he squatted in the grave would show themselves, as they so often had done in the past, but he sensed nothing. Instead, he suddenly realised his concentration was being distracted by a loud, intermittent bleeping sound. It was coming from the line of trees over to his right, and if he was to continue, he needed to find out what it was.

As Jordan broke the tree line and headed for the sound, he caught glimpses of a shadowy figure swinging back and forth in a most erratic manner. It was not until Jordan passed the last tree on the edge of a small open area, that he realised it was a scruffy looking man swinging a metal-detector in front of him.

Jordon could see immediately that he was a man of the forest: his leathery, whiskered appearance was typical of a hermit's existence, narrowly confined to a life of fossicking. His yellow, decayed smile showed a fixed expression as he wandered through Sherwood Forest's leafy interior.

He was oblivious to Jordan's calls; hunched over his metal pole, muffled to the neck with a thick woollen scarf and wearing large orange earphones. Jordan moved round into his line of sight, and the man noticed him at the last moment.

"Oh dear," he cried, "You gave me a fright."

"Sorry," Jordan replied, moving towards him. "Could you switch that off?"

The unkempt old man looked at him suspiciously.

"You're one of those coppers, aren't you? You're here about that skeleton they found over there."

"That's right...I'm Inspector Jordan."

"It's not the same as the others you know."

"What's not the same?"

"The skeleton," he said, covering his mouth. "Oops...I shouldn't have said that. I shouldn't have said the skeleton... or the others come to that."

"What do you know about the skeletons? Jordan questioned.

"I'll get in trouble if I tell you."

"Not if you tell the truth."

The old man switched his detector off and shuffled back and forth trying to decide what he should do. The decision seemed difficult for him.

"It was me that found the other two. No, that's not right. I found one and the coppers found the other, and I got in trouble. They said old Bessie here disturbed the crime scene, when it weren't Bessie at all. She just finds the things and I dig 'em up. And I only dig a little hole."

"Old Bessie?" Jordan queried.

"Yeah...my Bessinger and Clark detector."

"Oh...I see, and what about this skeleton?"

"I found that too. But after all the other trouble I just left it."

"You just left it...you didn't report it?"

"Well...the other two came along, didn't they: The girl and the boy with rucksacks. I shouted of them, and they were the ones who called the cops. I told them I couldn't use the phone, see."

Before long Jordan soon found out the man's name was Duffy. He told Jordan how he often used the bridle path to get from the main road into the forest.

On the day in question, he failed to pinpoint it exactly; he spotted several crows fighting over something in the run-off. When Jordan questioned the area he had been pondering over since he arrived, Duffy started telling him about the floods from the upper lake that engulfed this area now and then.

Although Jordan already knew about the floods, he had no detail. The orienteering map only plotted its course, but the terrain told him this was not only a regular occurrence, it was also one of significance. Jordan allowed Duffy to continue.

"Every few years the lower lake spills over its banks and floods..."

"The lower lake?" Jordan questioned, making a note on his pad.

"Yes...you've got the Great Lake over to the west and its smaller cousin here over to the east. Anyway, it's not big enough to take heavy rains, so it runs off down this natural gully: been doing that for donkeys, long before I was born. The ground's too soft to hold it mind; it just runs until it finally soaks into the sand."

Then he returned to his story about the crows. He said he thought he found the body of a young fawn that had lost its way, and he decided to have a look. When he got there, he was in for a surprise. "There it was," he said, gesturing with his hand in the air, "all those bony fingers sticking out of the ground".

The man looked worried, just recalling the event, and Jordan consoled him with a reassuring hand on his shoulder. He also assured Duffy that he had nothing to worry about, regarding all three skeletons, and switched the conversation to the old man's preoccupation.

"I've got a licence," he let out, thinking this was another way of catching him.

"It's all right, Duffy," Jordan said, "I'm only interested in what you're looking for, and how strong your detector is."

Duffy reached down and patted the stem of his detector.

"Oh...that's all right then," he replied, with a broad grin on his face. "Bessie's the best you can get. She can find anything down to a couple of spade depths."

"Is that so," Jordan said. "And what sort of stuff do you find?"

He shoved his hand into his pocket and pulled out a handful of corroded lumps, which Jordan could see contained a few arrowheads amongst them.

"I find arrowheads the most. Then some buckles, a whole sword once, and bigger stuff like pike heads."

"No coins?" Jordan asked, with a smirk.

"Yeah...them too, but not so many. And when I do it's usually a lot."

Jordan pondered a moment with an idea that struck him.

"Did you sweep the grave site?"

Duffy looked guilty, "Yeah...I did. That was before I noticed the hand."

"And did you find anything?"

"No. It was as clean as a whistle...what I did that is."

"So you didn't sweep further down towards the boulders?"

"No...not after seeing you know what."

"How about doing it now...for me?"

Duffy suddenly looked excited, "Sure...let's go."

Duffy was not bothered about why Jordan wanted him to sweep the gully below the boulders; he simply went about his usual procedure, as if he was hunting for relics. It was slower than Jordan had expected, and he became impatient for him to reach the area beside the boulders.

He was convinced, if there was any metallic forensic material in the grave, the flood would have swept it down the gully long ago. Once it reached the rocky outcrop, instead of following the course around the boulders, it might just have become wedged amongst the stones.

No sooner had Jordan thought of that possibility, when he heard a shrill bleeping sound coming from the speaker on Duffy's detector. He rushed down the two meters or so towards the area Duffy was, and as Jordan suspected, he was at the base of the outcrop. Duffy cleared a few large stones, reached into the leather pouch hanging from a shoulder strap and pulled out a small metal implement that looked almost like a putty knife, and he started digging.

Within a few moments, his deft hand brought out a blackened lump. It would have gone unnoticed to the amateur, but to Duffy it was pure gold. He spat on it and started rubbing the crumbly mass with the ends of his fingers. Rubbing away the years of encrusted corrosion, until eventually, he produced something that looked almost recognisable. To Duffy it only brought a frown of puzzlement.

"What?" Jordan said, looking over his arm.

"It looks like an army button," Duffy said, almost disappointed.

He passed it to Jordan, who seemed just as puzzled by their find.

"Look," Duffy pointed, "you can just make out the cannon's shape."

This put a new light on things, Jordan thought, scrutinising the old button. If it had anything to do with the case, why was a soldier involved in the burial? And if that was true, the idea that the corpse was buried eight hundred years ago had no more validity than Robin Hood. Yet the body was old.

"I know who can tell you if that's an army button or not," Duffy said.

"You do?"

Duffy nodded, "My Major friend. That's who buys all my finds. He lives close by if you want to go and see him."

Before Jordan could answer, he heard Josh's voice calling from the bridle path. When he stepped out from behind the rocky outcrop, he saw Josh and Penny standing on the edge of the gully.

"Inspector," Penny called out. "We wondered where you were."

"Sorry you two," Jordan shouted back. "It was a sudden decision. The weather looked good, and I wanted to get out here before it rained again."

"It must have rained heaps since Inspector Dent went over the site, Boss," Josh said, when Jordan finally reached them. "What's there to see now?"

Jordan held out the small evidence bag he put the button in. "This Josh. It may have nothing to do with the case…but then again it could be that important clue we're looking for."

Josh was dying to ask him about the story in the newspaper, but he could see Jordan was excited. He looked all fired up for the next step in their investigation.

"Who's the man with the detector?" Penny asked.

"This is Duffy," Jordan replied, turning to the man standing at a distance. It was plain he had an aversion to groups of people. "This is, Constable Willow, Duffy and that suspicious looking fellow over there is, Sergeant Crosby."

Duffy nodded to each of them with a screwed up grimace.

"Did you want to see my Major?" he then said.

"Most certainly," Jordan said, before he turned to Josh and Penny. "Penny, you come with me…you can take notes, and Josh, I want you to go back to town and visit the council offices. See if you can dig up any information on how often this gully floods. Here's the orienteering map, I've marked the area that interests me. Oh and, try and get a periodic picture."

"Why can't I come with you, Boss?" he said, taking the map.

"Because you're the one with the photographic memory, you keep telling us. Now's the time to prove it; I want as much detail as you can find."

"Right, Boss," he said reluctantly. "Good job we came in my car."

CHAPTER 7

The mentor of Duffy's fossicking was a retired soldier called Major Sturt. He was a collector of local relics, especially anything to do with the period of Richard the Lionheart and the legendary Robin Hood. Not only was he an avid believer of the famous myth, he was the president of the local Robin Hood Society.

As Duffy mentioned, it was only a short distance away, even shorter by car, and after Jordan wangled the detector sideways into the boot, the three of them set off in the opposite direction Josh was taking back into the city.

They were heading towards Thorsby, with the forest on their left and open grazing fields on their right. Duffy looked agitated, sitting bolt upright in the front seat and rocking back and forth.

"We're here," he shouted.

Jordan slowed and checked either side. There was no side-road, just a continuous fence. "Where, Duffy?" Jordan asked.

"That big oak tree…it's one of the last hereabouts."

"But that's much further ahead."

"Oh sorry," he said. "I skip across the fence here. It cuts the corner off."

Jordan laughed, "Well we can't do that in a car, Duffy."

Penny sighed with relief. She was beginning to succumb to Duffy's odour.

Sure enough, just as they approached the old sprawling oak, Jordan spotted a narrow lane off to the right, and slowing down to avoid the ditch that carried the field's run-off, he turned and continued along a meadow with grazing cattle.

A short distance on, almost hidden by a copse of plantation pines, Jordan could see a smoking red-brick chimney, and the outline of a cottage that was all but covered in a mass of bright green ivy. As they approached, Duffy once again shouted, 'We're here,' and Jordan turned into a gravel drive and stopped.

Duffy was first out, rushing around to the back of the car and impatiently waiting for Jordan to lift the boot lid so that he could get to his detector. Penny had stepped out on the opposite side and was studying the mass of ivy that followed the contours of the cottage, with neat holes for the windows and what she could see of the front door. It was set back into the shadow: an arched contrivance of grey, aged wood around a solid planked door, with a small barred opening at face level.

There was a loud squeak as Jordan pushed open the picket gate and a broad brimmed, straw hat surfaced above the nearest waist-high hedge. Beneath the exaggerated headwear was a squat man of stocky build, if Jordan could determine that by his baggy khaki overalls, with a swollen red face, bright blue eyes and an unmistakable, white military moustache.

"Major," Duffy called out.

"Hello, Duffy, you've brought me some guests, I see."

Duffy was not one for politeness, and Jordan made the introductions.

"I'm, Inspector Jordan, and this is, Constable Willow."

"My...what an unusual name dear," he said, passing Jordan and reaching across the hedge to take hold of Penny's hand. It was hardly a handshake, more an old man's form of fondling, and Penny smiled back and said hello. Then the Major's watery eyes turned onto Jordan.

"So, Inspector," he started, "Has, Duffy done something wrong?"

"It's all right, Major," Duffy said, looking anxious, "they want to ask you about something I found," he dived into his satchel, and pulling out a small leather pouch, he handed it to the Major, then looking back at Jordan, "Do you need me any more...No...good," and before Jordan could answer, Duffy was off down the lane.

The Major laughed. "You'll have to excuse Duffy," he said, "he isn't very good socially. I scarcely get more than a few words out of him when he calls with his few pieces of antiquity, then he's off."

"What's his hurry?" Jordan asked.

"I doubt if he knows himself. He lives with his old mother over the hill just beyond those trees. He'll run most of the way back, and when he gets home, he'll wonder why he's there. She told me one day, when I called to see if they were all right, that he came home, went out to chop some firewood, and she never saw him again until it was almost dark."

"Dysfunctional is he?" Penny commented.

"No. Actually, he's very astute. I think he's one of those people with a low level of concentration, but keep him on a subject he knows about, or ask him a question about the history of Nottingham, and he'll astound you. That's our connection by the way, before you ask. I'm the president of the Robin Hood Society."

"You're not in the army any more?" Jordan questioned.

"Oh…good Lord no. That's an honorary title from my days in Korea."

"The way Duffy talked; I was expecting a World War Two veteran."

The Major shot Jordan a sharp look. "Do I look that old? I'm only fifty-two you know: probably nearer your age, by the looks of you. Were you over there? You look a career man; a Lieutenant would be my guess."

"No," Jordan replied, "I was in the Kenyan police."

The Major let out a grunt, as if he was against those who used civilian reserved occupations to get them out of service. "Anyway, I'm forgetting my manners, leaving you standing here at the front gate. Come through and we'll see if we can muster up a nice cup of tea. How does that sound young lady?" he said steering Penny around the end of the hedge and along the path to his front door.

Jordan was left to follow on behind. Not something that bothered him, it gave him the opportunity to study the Major's life-style. When he crossed the threshold onto a highly polished, parquet-floored hall, he could see the soldier in him. There was a place for everything, and everything was ordered and pristine. White stucco walls, edged with dark-oak trim, with a small shelf running around each wall. Three dark-oak doors; one open to the old kitchen with one of those huge ranges, where he could see the Major making tea with Penny, and behind Jordan, a wide staircase with an ornate newel and spiral rails.

Jordan closed the door, and noticed a tall hatstand on one side, carrying a small suede trilby and a leather jacket. On the other side was a highly polished brass shell casing full of walking sticks and umbrellas. He heard Penny laughing; at least she had managed to break the ice with the Major.

"You two seem to be having a good time," Jordan said, walking into the kitchen, and making his usual inspection.

Apart from the tiled floor and appliances, everything else was wood, even the walls and ceiling were clad in narrow planking, except for the stained-glass window looking out onto the garden.

"All ready, Inspector," the Major said, lifting a large silver tray off the range and carrying it through a door at the far end.

Penny looked at Jordan with a wry smile, carrying a round tin in one hand and a jug of milk in the other. Jordan followed.

Instead of the lounge Jordan expected, the Major led them into a conservatory. Rather than filled with exotic plants, it looked more like a workshop, come shrine to Robin Hood. In the centre of the room was a group of easy chairs and a large coffee table, where he placed the tray down and started pouring three cups of tea. Around the walls was a collection of display cases, filled with small cardboard boxes carrying delicate objects. Above them, the three walls that were not windows, where almost taken over by pictures of knights in armour, Robin Hood and old maps presumably going back to the same period.

"Help yourself," the Major said, "There's milk and sugar, and biscuits if you fancy something with your tea."

Jordan and Penny sat down and helped themselves, both looking ill at ease, especially Jordan, who had allowed the Major to distract him from the main purpose of his visit. Something he hoped to get back to with the help of Duffy.

The Major looked intently at Jordan again; with the same suspicion, he had in the garden just after Duffy left. "So, Inspector...you wanted to ask me about something Duffy found. Was it in Sherwood Forest?"

"Yes it was. I met him there near a crime scene, and once I was satisfied he had no connection, I asked him to run over the site with his detector," Jordan reached into his pocket and brought out the bag with the button in it, "He found this."

The Major put his cup down and took the plastic bag from Jordan. He turned to the window and held it up to the light, "It's an army button, Inspector."

"Yes Duffy said that."

"So how can I help?"

"He said you would be able to tell me more about it."

The Major held it up to the light again, this time stretching the clear plastic across the face. "It looks like it belongs to the Royal Artillery."

"Can you give me any more detail on that?"

The Major stood up and went across to a bench in the corner that had one of those large magnifying glasses on a stand. He studied it for a moment, "Well...without being able to take it out of the bag and clean it, I have to say it's definitely from the Artillery; you can see the carriage and gun quite plainly, even though it's badly worn. Where did you find it?"

"Down by the bridle path; by the outcrop of boulders."

"Yes...I know the spot. It's sandy soil, very abrasive."

"How old?" Jordan questioned.

"I beg your pardon?"

"The button...how old do you think it is?"

"Ah...now that does pose a problem. Between the first and second war there was a lot of transfer of equipment and stuff until they caught up and designed all new uniforms and the like," he walked over to a bookcase, ran his finger along one of the lower shelves, and grunted. "Here we are," he opened the book, which seemed to be covering badges and ribbons of the two great wars," Right…you're in luck. Here's an Artillery button that looks just like yours. It's dated 1939 – 1940."

"Does that mean this button wasn't used after 1940?"

"No…of course not…the date only refers to this button. I'd say it's a safe bet your button was from 1939 onwards; at least until the end of the war. My buttons were plastic. Then again we had to fight in dense forest, and we didn't want our buttons or badges reflecting the sun."

"I gather from what Duffy said, that he fossicks for you?"

"Yes. I clean them up, keep the best for my collection and sell on the rest. I pay Duffy a commission. It helps to keep a roof over their head."

"And you just collect Nottingham relics?"

Unnoticed during the conversation, Penny had left the nest of chairs and was examining the Major's collection, "Major," Penny stepped in.

"Yes dear," he said, turning his attention to her.

"Why do you need so many arrowheads? Surely one's enough."

"Oh no young lady," he replied, standing up and walking over to her, "They're all different, each one has its own identity," he continued, walking over to a large map on the wall. "All those different coloured pins represent where they were found. They all have their own story to tell…it's in their shape you see. The red ones belonged to the local constabulary," he laughed, "The Sheriff's men. Oh yes… despite the myth, the Sheriff was quite real. The blue were local hunters. They often missed their target you know…lost their arrows as well."

"What about all these other colours?" Penny asked.

"Some of those go back much further than the legend; what with the invading Danes, the Normans and a whole group of waring tribal factions. It's taken me years to identify this lot. They're the history of Nottingham, after all."

Jordan let out a cough; he wanted to get back to the button. The Major had side tracked him more than he would normally allow, but enough was enough. He had a desperate sense that this information was going to be difficult to pick out of the history that surrounded it.

When Penny and the Major looked round Jordan looked impatient. "Can we get back to this button? Were there any army units in this area during either of the wars? Maybe an artillery unit?"

"Not that I can recall, and I think I would have heard something; I'm involved in a number of local historical societies," the Major answered, as he slowly walked back to the table with a thoughtful expression. "Unless," Jordan looked apprehensive, "There was the LDV…that's the Local Defence Volunteers."

"I haven't heard of those," Jordan commented.

"They're called the Civil Defence now. Back in the war, they called them the Home Guard. I'm not so sure about the Great War, but certainly about the time of your button. Yes, I'd say it belongs to that period. Of course, there were plenty of soldiers coming home on leave then."

"Yes," Jordan agreed, "I thought of that, but I prefer your idea about the Home Guard. Make a note of that Penny."

"It's all right, Inspector, I'm getting everything down," she said.

Jordan was so preoccupied he missed the small notebook Penny kept bringing out of her pocket, "Are there any records left of that period?"

"Oh yes, Inspector. Everything passed over to the Civil Defence. Normally you would have to contact the head office in London, but it just so happens; we have a Home Guard enthusiast here in Nottingham."

"That's excellent," Jordan said. "I like it when everything drops into place."

"Yes, Inspector," the Major said, looking towards Penny, "His name is Lieutenant Tobias Cunningham; I'll find his address for you."

By the time the Major returned with the address, Jordan and Penny were already on their feet and poised to leave. Jordan had made it clear to Penny that their job was done here and there was more to do elsewhere. The Major handed the small card to Penny and walked them out to the front gate. On the way he picked up his large straw hat, even though the sky was looking dark and heavy, and collecting his garden hoe, he shook their hands.

"Well, Inspector, and Miss Willow, that was an enjoyable interlude. I hope you can find the time to call again; I don't get many visitors, despite my busy society work. And I hope that button leads you nearer to your outcome."

"I'd like to know more about your arrowheads, Major," Penny said.

Jordan politely smiled and nodded.

Back at the car, Jordan leant over the roof and smiled at Penny with a look as if he was notching off the clues. He glanced at his watch, "I think that good bit of detective work deserves a lunch...what about it?"

"What about Josh, Inspector?"

Jordan opened his door and slipped into the car. "I think Josh is going to be occupied for some time yet," he laughed, "despite his talent."

With the help of an attractive young archivist at the County Records Office, Josh settled down behind the Microfiche projector to search through the past fifty years of Nottingham's weather statistics. With his usual gift for sifting through pages, it was not long before the pattern of events he was looking for began to form.

They were not regular events: usually split between five and seven-year intervals, depending on the type of summer that preceded each flood. There was a sequence, and Josh soon memorised its recurrence back to 1920.

He removed the tape, and returned it to the girl at the desk. She was dealing with another customer, a young student, and he was seeking information on certain elections, the candidates and the number of voters for each year. This was the first time Josh had used the Microfiche system, and it set him thinking. If it was that easy to store information and retrieve it, perhaps her archives had information on people as well: The census, births, deaths and marriages. The myriads of forms they fill in each year, not to mention newspapers and the like.

"Thank you for that," the girl said.

"Pardon?" Josh replied, not aware she had finished with the student.

"The tape," She indicated. "Most people just leave it in the projector; they don't even have the decency to wind it back."

"That's okay," Josh said with a smile, as he walked away. Then he stopped and turned back. "By the way…would your tapes help me find something that happened in Kenya some time ago?"

"No…our system just deals with county history. You want the main library."

"Is that so? Do they store such information?"

"Oh yes…I go there often to look up my genealogy. They have all sorts of records. All the world's main newspapers, magazines…even copies of rare books."

"Sounds just what I want. How do I find this library?"

"It's the large gothic building opposite the shopping centre."

"Thank you for that," Josh said, then turned and left.

Josh soon found the library, and unlike his first naïve attempt at working the Microfiche projector, this time he felt like a professional. The library archives were much busier than county records, with young students swotting, pensioners looking back into their ancestry and a strange middle-aged woman, with a long red pencil sticking out of her frizzy hair above her ear. Her machine was directly opposite Josh's, and she kept looking up at him, and smiling each time she examined the pile of small boxes of Microfiche film by her machine.

He ignored her. It was bad enough concentrating on something he knew was wrong, than having a busybody to bother about. To make things worse, this task was proving to be much more difficult than looking for seasonal floods. He felt guilty about delving into his boss' background, but his curiosity was far stronger.

Everyone told Josh that his boss was a square peg. He had difficulty fitting in anywhere, and spent the best part of his career before joining the college, moving from one station to another. Then there was the newspaper story about leaving Africa under a cloud. That last straw hooked Josh's insatiable need for information related to Jordan's unsubstantiated secret.

There seemed to be a curtain drawn across any mention of an Inspector Jordan being involved in anything in the fifties. Josh chose that period to examine African newspaper stories because of two pieces of gossip moving around the station: first, the name Kenya, and second, the date 1952.

The biggest story at that time seemed to be the atrocities committed by a group of activists called the Mau-Mau, but nothing detailed enough to include the inspector's name, until Josh came across an article dated April 8, 1953. They captured Jomo Kenyatta, the Mau-Mau leader and jailed him for seven years. It said the Kenyan authority's envisaged recriminations, and there were many.

Further on, some months later, Josh came across another article about a Mau-Mau act of vengeance. It mentioned no one by name, just a description of the brutal murder of a senior police officer's family: burnt to death in their country home. The property had been set ablaze, and there were no survivors.

Over the following pages that seemed to span a period of several weeks, the Kenyan papers reported a rogue section in the local police, under the leadership of the man whose family was murdered. Apparently, they systematically butchered every Mau-Mau they came across. Josh continued scanning the following pages until his eyes ached, but there was no mention of any charges brought against the inspector involved. His act ghosted away, along with the Mau-Mau era.

Still not satisfied, Josh continued, page after page, until an inconspicuous heading caught his attention in the Stop Press section of the page. It read: 'British Inspector, Jethro Merrick, had his visa revoked and left Kenya today'.

CHAPTER 8

Whilst Jordan and Penny were in a good humour over the likelihood of a link between the button and The Sherwood Forest man, Josh was unusually silent. He seemed to pass off the discovery as a long shot and remained deep in thought most of the afternoon; drawing up the chart of the rainfall and floods over the past fifty years.

Jordan was going to review their position, prior to their next interview with the former lieutenant of the Home Guard. By the time Josh had charted out the flood dates on the white-board that confirmed another link with the 1940 period, Jordon noticed his lack of enthusiasm, and decided to hold off until he had an opportunity to find out what was wrong.

The white-board was finally taking shape. Penny had confirmed the details Major Sturt gave her about his friend's interest in the Home Guard, and was adding the relevant details to the line of enquiry. Josh had finished his part, and was now laboriously writing up the salient points he discovered at the county records office, in a daybook Jordan initialised to keep track of their activities.

"We've done well so far," Jordan said, looking up at the board. "A bit lopsided, but when I get my friend the archaeologist in, we should be able to put some flesh on The Sherwood Forest Man's bones."

"You're getting an archaeologist in, Inspector?" Penny questioned.

"Yes...I'll give him a call tonight."

"I thought you'd forgotten about our corpse, Boss," Josh said.

Jordan sensed a jibe, "As I think I said when we first met, I don't believe in following my nose. That's for narrow-minded people like Inspector Dent, and look where it got him. To know a person, you don't always have to tap him on the shoulder; you can find out an awful lot behind his back. Can't you, Josh?"

Josh was suddenly alert. "Oh...Yes, Boss."

He had no idea whether the turn of phrase was just another of Jordan's idiosyncrasies, or he actually suspected something. Either way, he knew eventually he would have to confront Jordon with the information he discovered.

Jordan suspected something was eating at Josh's conscience, but it was not until after they left and Jordan settled himself down to telephone his friend Simon, that he noticed the folded newspaper in the bin. Picking it up, he read the headline again, he realised they knew something was not all it should be. The fact that Josh and Penny had kept it to themselves was answer enough.

He sat with the tabloid open on his desk and kept reading the rubbish this woman had written. He knew the Chief Superintendent had, and by the sounds of it, so had the Commissioner. He also knew his friend was right: he had to stop her, but not the way he suggested; 'Make a fool of her,' he said, 'Make her swallow every lying word.' She had to be stifled with good facts, Jordan thought, but the only way to do that was to prove she had fabricated the whole thing. Jordan smiled to himself, and dropped the paper back in the bin where it belonged.

He reached for his phone, paused to recall the prefix for the London number, and dialled. He allowed it to ring a moment, as he glanced at his watch, and assured himself someone should be home by now. Just as he was about to change his mind, there was a loud click, followed by a soft female voice.

Over the background noise of a male shouting something, she said, "Hello."

"Janet?" Jordan called out.

"Is that you, Jethro?"

"Yes...is that Simon making all the noise?"

"Who else would it be? I've left him watching the chicken breasts in the pan, and he thinks they're about to burst into flames."

Jordan laughed, "Sounds like Simon all right," he said.

"Look Darling. I'd love to stop and talk, but as you can hear, I have a crisis in the making. I'll get Simon to take over... bye love."

Jordan was about to say something to her when he heard the rattle of the phone hitting something hard. He could hear a heated discussion in the background, something about sauce, before someone answered the phone again.

"Sorry, Jethro old chum. I'm being chastised for meddling with the dinner."

"So you should be," Jordan answered. When did you ever learn to cook?"

"I didn't," Simon replied, laughing, "but I'm a good adder."

"Adder?"

"Yes...you know. Add a bit of this, and add a bit of that."

"Oh I see. Yes, I remember. Goulash was your favourite... wasn't it. Only by the time you finished adding bits, you had enough to feed an army."

They laughed again.

"The good old days," Simon said, "Whatever happened to them?"

"We got married," Jordan replied, and then there was an awkward silence... "Yes," he continued, "well...I can't hold up your chicken breasts."

"No old chum...Janet will be screaming any moment now."

Jordan composed himself, "I...Err, rang because I've taken on a new case for the police. It's an unusually old corpse we found in Sherwood Forest."

"Sound's interesting."

"Yes...right up your street. It's at least eight hundred years old, so I'm told, and no one can figure out how it came to be buried where it was."

"And you want me to have a look?"

"Would you? I know it's a long way from London, but we'll pay all your expenses. I might even run to a posh meal."

"Don't worry about it, Jethro. I'm back at the museum now. I'm sure they can spare me for one day. It's only a couple of hours on the train...I might even get lucky and catch an express."

"That's great. Ring me in the morning when you're arriving."

"I'll do that, Jethro," he broke off. "Yes, dear...I'm coming. Yes, I'll say goodbye for you. You heard that I gather... must go."

"Yes, Simon, and say goodbye to Janet for me. Until tomorrow...I should be able to tell you more about our corpse then."

"Take care."

Jordan waited until he heard the click of the phone going down, and then replaced his. A lot depended on Simon's appraisal of The Sherwood Forest Man. If he could pinpoint his origin, it might give them something to work on with Nottingham's well-documented history. The city was full of those who purported to know every personage, noteworthy enough of being preserved.

Thinking he was finished for the night, Jordan suddenly remembered Mark, his psychiatrist; and wondered if he should ring him.

The incident in the pathology lab may not have been as dramatic as his usual nightmares, but it did happen in the daytime, and that in itself was worth mentioning. He checked his number in his address book, by now he should know it by heart, and dialled it, hoping he may have gone for the evening.

"Mark Faulkner," he answered.

"Mark... It's Jethro... I had another incident, only this time it was during the day...at the pathologists I might add."

"That was unfortunate," he said, "How did you explain it?"

"I didn't have to. It was dark in the room, and it was only for a minute or two. He thought I was having a turn when I saw the corpse, and I let him believe that."

"I see. So what actually happened?"

"I don't know if I told you, but we found a mummified corpse in the forest, and when I went down to see it, I thought it was Jessie. It brought back the memory of identifying her charred body."

"I've told you before, Jethro. These things will continue until you convince yourself you couldn't save them. You have to accept what happened."

"You mean accept I was responsible?"

There was a pause on the phone for a moment, "If that helps."

"I thought you were trying to get me to clear my conscience?" Jethro said.

"How can I do that, Jethro? I proved to you that you could not have prevented what happened, except by not going to Africa in the first place. You're determined to blame yourself. So...get it over with, blame yourself, and be done with it. The sooner you admit to something, the sooner the aberrations will stop."

It was Jordan's turn to go silent. "Well...I must be bad if you have to try a new tactic. Okay...I'll try it. Instead of trying to forget it, I'll tell myself it was my fault, and we'll see if it works. Who knows, it might be all I need to push me over the edge. Then instead of me having to visit you all the time, you can visit me."

"Jethro...I didn't mean it that way."

It was too late. Jordan slammed the phone down on him. It was not what he planned. Jordan knew he was the one who needed to organize himself, especially since he had so many people relying on what he made of this case. The last thing he wanted was to disappoint the very people who had stuck their necks out for him. They had made the effort, so it was the least he could do.

The following morning, it felt as if winter had decided to arrive early and cross autumn off the calendar altogether. Strong gusty winds crossed the motorway from the north-west, and the rain at times rendered the windscreen wipers useless.

When Jordan finally arrived at Prescott Lane station, he was glad to find Josh already seated at his desk busy with something. He seemed not to notice Jordan's arrival, but Jordan knew differently. The atmosphere was as chilly as the weather outside, and as Penny would be another half hour or so, Jordan thought it would be ample time for him to find out what his trouble was.

"Phew...it's freezing out there," Jordan said.

Josh looked up, "You're early, Boss," he said.

Jordan said nothing at first. He tipped his umbrella into the bin and leant it against the side of his desk. Then feeling the radiator behind his desk, he stood for a moment warming his back.

"So, Josh...Are you going to tell me what's chewing at your trousers?"

Josh looked surprised. He had not expected to face his boss with his problem so quickly: if he had to face him at all. He wanted more time to think.

"Sorry, Boss," he said, standing up and walking over to Jordan's desk, and resting one of his buttocks on the corner. "I'm afraid I've done something you won't like...in fact you might want to suspend me."

Jordan looked at the serious expression on Josh's face. He tried not to laugh, and looked equally as serious. I see…it's that bad?"

"It is, Boss…very bad. I nosed into your private life."

"Oh," Jordan let out. "And why would you want to do that?"

"Well, Boss…there's been a lot of rumour going around the station about you not being all there…and some people are even laughing behind your back. But no one will actually say why." He screwed his face up, when Jordan remained silent, "I know this sort of thing goes on when someone takes over a case…especially if it's been under unusual circumstances, but there seemed more to it. As if this had been going on a long time, and wasn't about Inspector Dent at all."

"I see…so you decided to look into it yourself. You couldn't just stay out of it. After all…it's none of your business, is it?"

"No, Boss…It's just that I get curious. I need to know things. I'm afraid that's one of my bad points…I'm sure you read about it in my profile. I hate mysteries, and it's got me in trouble a few times."

"More than a few times, Josh," Jordan reminded him. "You nearly got kicked out of the force on one occasion."

"I know, Boss…I can't help myself."

"Look, Josh, as far as I'm concerned that's one of your good points. A good detective has to have an insatiable curiosity; without that, he's just going through the motions. Your bad point is, not knowing what to do with that curiosity; and above all, not knowing when to keep your mouth shut."

"I know, Boss…but as soon as I saw that headline in the newspaper, I just had to find out the truth. I was just going to probe a little: ask people what they knew…maybe even check out a few personnel files when I got the time. But when I went to the county records office and found out how easy it was, and the archivist told me the library had a much better system, before I knew it, I was reading papers from Kenya... going back for years."

For the first time Jordan suddenly looked annoyed.

"You have been busy," he said. Expecting Josh to tell him how he switched on to the local gossip. "Well go on...you might as well tell me what you found out."

"I don't know that I found anything out, Boss. That's the trouble. All I know is the Mau-Mau murdered an Inspector Jethro Merrick's family because he captured their leader. He apparently snapped, and went on a rampage, executing all the Mau-Mau he could find...without an official trial."

"Well...as you say. You don't really know anything. All you have is a bunch of unsubstantiated facts, and that doesn't add up to evidence."

"So the police didn't cover it up? And you didn't change your name?"

"Hypothetically...when someone changes their name in those circumstances, it's not just because they wish to avoid arrest. You had to be there at the time. The country was a powder keg, and many who were involved in the capture of Jomo Kenyatta, were ultimately run-to-ground and killed."

Josh looked horrified. "Oh my God, Boss, I hope I haven't done anything to tip them off. Do you think I could have?"

"I don't know what you've done, Josh."

"I've got to undo it, Boss," Josh said, with an unusual look on his face.

"What?"

"It just struck me…if it was that easy for me to find out about this person called Merrick, someone else could do the same."

"Yes but, you're a trained detective."

"I know, Boss, but so is that newspaper reporter. All she needs is the same two clues I had…Kenya and the year 1952. And that information is common knowledge around the station."

"And by this morning's paper, we have a leak, Jordon reminded him."

"Exactly, Boss. There is one way to stop her."

Jordan looked interested, "I'm listening."

"All the information is on one spool, Boss. Without it, no one will know."

"Sorry, Josh, I can't allow you to steal it."

"I don't have to, Boss. Each spool has a label identifying the year and the topic. All I have to do is find the most unlikely subject and switch the labels. It could take them ages to realise what's happened."

Jordan's expression changed from a wry smile to one of regard. "And what unlikely subject would that be?"

"I don't know yet, Boss…Milking Yaks in Mongolia or something."

"You'd do this for me?" Jordan asked.

"It's the least I can do, Boss."

Before Jordan could give Josh the go ahead, Penny noisily broke into the room, back first, shaking her umbrella. Jordan nodded at Josh, and Josh smiled. Then Jordan turned his attention to his young red-nosed Constable.

"Here, Penny," he said. "This radiator's lovely and hot."

"Oh...are the radiators on," she said, removing her Macintosh and checking the radiator near her desk, "This one's on too...what luck," then looking over to the two men, and realising she had interrupted something, she stared at them.

"Well...have I got my make-up on wrong or something?"

"What makes you say that?" Josh said, returning to his desk.

"I have the distinct feeling you two were hatching something."

Jordan laughed, "There you are, Josh...what did I just say?"

Josh looked back puzzled, but managed a knowing smile.

"What did you just say, Inspector?" Penny questioned.

Jordan shuffled his feet trying to think of a plausible excuse that would satisfy her curiosity, and then he suddenly remembered his conversation on the same subject.

"We were talking about curiosity. I told Josh that it was the sign of a good detective. That it forced you to question everything. And here you are Penny, on a freezing cold day, when most people's brain-matter is too numb to think, let alone sense something was up, questioning skulduggery was afoot."

She smiled, not knowing whether that was a compliment, or Jordan was making fun of her. "I didn't suggest there was any skulduggery, Inspector."

"I'm sure you didn't, Penny. Forget it, I was only pointing out that it's good to sense things and question them."

Although Josh was too preoccupied in his suspicions to notice Jordan had worked on the whiteboard last night, Penny noticed straight away.

"Who's messed up my board?" she cried out.

"Sorry, Penny," Jordan replied. "That was me."

"I thought you put me in charge of the board, Inspector?"

"I did, and I know I should have waited for you to make the notations, but when I have a problem, I have a terrible habit of working it out on a board. I'm used to a much bigger one at the college, so it doesn't matter."

"Well it matters here, Inspector. Your big writing has left no room for anything else. Look how disordered it is. How am I supposed to understand?"

"Sorry again…We can have our review now if you like, instead of later."

She looked upset, "Can I take notes, Inspector, and rewrite it later on?"

"Of course you can. You don't have to stick to what I've said either. You can shorthand it if you like; as long as we can understand the gist."

"You don't have to take notes, Penny," Josh said, "I'll remember it and dictate it back to you if you like."

"No thank you, Josh," she said, curtly, "I can manage fine."

Jordan shot Josh a glance to let well alone.

"Right people… you might not understand my scribble, but I'll go through it and we can see how well we've done in such a short time. I say that because, after many weeks, Inspector Dent's squad was nowhere near this close to identifying The Sherwood Forest Man."

"We're that close are we, Boss?" Josh questioned.

"I know it may not seem that way, but we are. We now have enough leads to point us in that direction and finding that direction is our next step."

Jordan turned back to the board.

"I don't know how you expect us to follow that chaos, Inspector?" Penny said.

"What do they say, Penny? Out of chaos comes forth order."

"You just made that up, Boss," Josh said, laughing.

"Maybe so, but I'm right. I find order distracting, pushing you in directions not justified by the facts, or even the evidence."

"How can you say that, Inspector?" Penny spoke out.

"Penny...how often did you put something in a certain place just because it fitted a particular criterion, only to find it belonged somewhere else?"

Penny managed a knowing smile.

"Exactly," Jordan continued. "We have to look beyond the obvious if we want to get at the truth," they both nodded. "Now what have we learned since we started? Number one: The Sherwood Forest Man is an old man. The Pathologist estimates about eight hundred years old..."

"Why the question-mark, Boss?" Josh asked, breaking off what he was doing and casually wondering over to the Inspector's desk.

"Call it a hunch. I know that's not following the rule of evidence, but if you followed my argument on chaos, and added up all the bits and pieces relevant to his burial in a shallow grave, you would understand..."

"What if this chaos doesn't work out, Boss," he said sarcastically.

"Just to make sure, I'm picking up that archaeologist friend of mine off the train later on. So first lesson: it's all right having a hunch, but make sure it's right."

"And he will prove your hunch is right?" Penny said.

"That and other facts that I'm coming to," he turned back to the board and pointed to a diagram, "Number two: I discovered the area of the burial site was subject to periodic flooding, proving my theory that the grave was a recent one."

"That's why you wanted all that information, Boss?" Josh asked.

"Exactly…If the flooding was severe enough to abrade the skin off the back of the leathery corpse, then it would have washed away the sediment long ago. That's why I wanted all that information on the floods," Jordan looked across to the facts Josh uncovered dating back fifty years, "You've done well, Josh."

"I'm writing up more detail, just in case you want to pinpoint the actual period, Boss," Josh said. "Apparently the periods don't run consecutively, they jump about between five and seven year intervals."

"Yes…I can see. But either way, they all point to a period in the Second World War…about 1940."

"That's what Major Sturt said about that button, Inspector," Penny said.

"The one you found on the site?" Josh interrupted.

"You're not reading Penny's notes, Josh."

"Sorry, Boss."

"You can read them when we're finished," Jordan said; "In the meantime…I hope you're both beginning to see order in my chaos?" they both nodded.

"Good. For now, it's all loose pieces, just wanting one important fact to link them together. If I'm right, and that button does have a connection, then our Sherwood Forest Man was reburied by a soldier for some reason."

"That's a lot of suppositions, Inspector," Penny said.

"That's what it's all about, Penny," Jordan answered. "Now you get on and put some order into this mess on your white-board, while I go and pick-up my friend. I don't know when I'll be back. I intend taking him straight to pathology."

"What about me, Boss?" Josh asked.

"Well you said you were going back to the library to dig deeper into the 1940 flood period."

Josh's face lit up with recognition, "Oh yes, Boss...the girl said she was going to find the second Microfiche reel for me.

CHAPTER 9

As Simon's train was due in at eleven-ten, Jordan hurriedly checked his watch. He had nine minutes to spare; time enough to amuse himself with a stroll around the station foyer, look into the small vendor's kiosks, and the intriguing souvenir shop next to the machine that loudly announced your weight.

A group of small, glittering objects suspended from a rail caught his attention. As Jordan walked over to them and stood for a moment looking through the window, he could see they were clear key-ring fobs, catching the morning sunlight cascading down from the arched glass roof of the station. They were particularly interesting, because embedded in the centre of the Perspex oval, was one of those notorious arrowheads.

Jordan wandered inside and the resilient woman behind the counter looked at him eagerly, "Can I help you," she said.

"Can I see one of those key rings?" Jordan replied, walking over to her.

She opened a draw under the counter, and taking out a selection, she spread them across the backlit glass of the counter in front of him, and looked up with an inviting smile. "Which one do you like?" she said.

Not realising there was a difference, Jordan selected one and examined the smooth oval plastic, and just above the hole where the ring went through, he noticed a small coloured symbol etched into the surface. It was the Ford Motor company emblem, and checking the others, he was disappointed to find there was not an Opel one amongst them. The arrowheads were different also. Just like those the Major pointed out: some were squat and barbed, others appeared long and streamlined.

"Are they real?" Jordan asked.

"They are…I collect them myself," she said, proudly.

"How long have arrowheads been used as souvenirs?"

"As long as I can remember, and I've been selling them for twenty years."

"Always as key rings?"

"Oh no," she said, opening another draw and pulling out a cheap golden chain with an arrowhead as a pendant.

It looked imitation. She had polished it and refiled its contours, as she probably thought, to make it look more authentic, instead of something old and unrecognisable. It had the appearance of a recently fashioned piece of metal, and Jordan suddenly realised Major Sturt's passion for history.

The relics embedded in the Perspex looked authentic, "Why did you clean up the pendant arrowhead, and leave the ones in the Perspex key rings as you found them?" Jordan questioned.

"That's the council for you," she answered, "They said if they weren't sealed, they had to be cleaned back to the metal: Something to do with hygiene."

Jordan glanced at his watch, Simon's train was due, and he picked up the nearest arrowhead key ring that was similar to the Major's, "I'll take this one," he said, and dropped the money on the counter.

"Don't you want me to wrap it," she cried out as he left.

"That's all right…I've a train to catch."

She grabbed a bag advertising her shop and thrust both in his hand.

For once, the London train was on time, and as Jordan bounded up the steps of the narrow bridge that crossed the lines, he thought he spotted Simon up ahead. Although it had been sometime since Jordan last saw him, he was sure it was his friend crossing the bridge amidst the crowd of commuters from London. He had to look twice, and even then, he was not sure, until Simon was almost upon him and he called out Jordan's name.

His wide, animated eyes behind gold-rimmed glasses were what gave him away: the rest of him looked different. He looked much heavier, with little contour between his neck and jowls, and the fringe of brown hair, usually combed back across his head, was now a fringe brushed forward onto his forehead.

At first, Simon seemed to be frowning, as if he too was having difficulty. They both laughed; resigned to the fact that time had left its mark. In different ways of course: Simon was showing signs of the comfortable family life, while Jordan's single existence indicated the convenience of quick snacks and microwave dinners.

"That was good timing," Simon called out. "I expected you to be late."

"Why would you expect that?" Jordan said, turning around and walking back down the steps with him. "If you remember, I'm the pedantic one...you're the one that always had his head buried in a book or something."

"Well I've changed. I'm much more responsible now," Simon said.

"That's fine, as long as you haven't lost your touch for antiquity."

Luckily, the station was only a short car ride from the city morgue and the pathology department. Jordan was beginning to learn the quickest way from one point to another, and at the same time, avoiding all the one-way streets.

It meant using the outer main roads each time before diverting to the particular area he wanted. It was either that or walking everywhere; and like most strenuous activities, that was something he did his best to avoid. He preferred driving, but even that was becoming a nightmare that he never came across in Leicester.

Chester Daniels was waiting for them. He looked eager to meet Jordan's archaeologist friend, and had everything prepared. As Jordan introduced him to Simon, Chester shook his hand vigorously.

"I've looked forward to this moment ever since Jethro told me you were coming," Chester said, ushering a surprised Simon towards the bench in the corner.

"I'm very pleased to meet you, Professor...have we met?"

"No...but I'm familiar with your work."

Simon glanced back at Jordan, even more puzzled.

"And what work would that be?" he said.

"I mean your work on the war-graves in Warsaw."

"Ah," Simon let out. Chester's excitement suddenly became clear. "You saw the television documentary?"

"Yes...most interesting," Chester said, and before Jordan knew it, his existence had been forgotten and they were lost in deep conversation.

"Professors," Jordan called out. They looked back at him. "I brought you here, Simon for an important purpose...you do recall?"

They laughed, as Chester reached into a box on his bench, and passing out latex gloves, he pulled back the green sheet that covered The Sherwood Forest Man.

The room was suddenly silent, and Jordan studied the expression on Simon's face. There was a familiar glint in his eyes. It had been a while since Jordon last saw that, but it was unmistakably Simon's look of intense interest: the look that had kept him in archaeology all these years.

"You know...don't you?" Jordan said as his pulse raced

"Hold on a second, Jethro," he replied. "Did you take any x-rays, Professor?"

"It's Chester...please."

"Sorry, Chester...did you?"

Prepared for Simon's question, Chester picked up a large yellow envelope from the bench. Withdrawing several film-sheets, he switched on the viewing screen, and one by one, he pushed them up under the clips.

Simon walked over to the screen, took out his reading glasses, and exchanging them for the ones he was wearing, he silently studied the x-rays. While Chester and Jordan stood and watched, Simon moved back and forth examining the full skeleton, until finally he focused his attention on the skull; in particular, the films showing the front and profile nasal passages.

Chester glanced at Jordan, with a puzzled look on his face. "Have you found something of interest, Simon?" he questioned.

Simon raised his hand, gesturing for silence, and removing a small leather case from his pocket; he folded out a magnifying glass and turned to examine the mummified skull. To Jordan's horror, he bent forward and inspected the corpse's nostrils, each time referring to the x-ray, and after several grunts that sounded like he was satisfied with something, he stood up and turned to face them.

"Well gentlemen...you can forget anything to do with Robin Hood, King Richard or England come to that. What you have here is an ancient Egyptian...at least three thousand years old."

Jordan and Chester stood rigid, struck silent for the moment and stared at Simon as if he had broken a sacred law or something.

Chester composed himself first and said, "How can you be so sure?"

Simon Travellian was an expert on cultural types, in particular, his favourite passion: the ancients. He knew straight away they had an Egyptian mummy without its wrappings, but he had to make sure.

"Have you a Speculum amongst those instruments?" Simon asked Chester.

"Yes I have somewhere here," he replied, rattling through the tray of horrific implements. "Here we are...will this do?"

"Fine," Simon said, taking the long probe and inserting it into one of the mummy's nostrils, he wiggled it around until he found what he wanted. Then he unceremoniously thrust it forward until it almost disappeared inside the skull.

"There you are. His missing brain should have given you a clue. However, to make sure I checked his Ethmoid Bone and found the hole at the back of the nasal passage. And as you can see, the Speculum is all the way into the brain cavity."

"Would you mind explaining that to me?" Jordan asked.

"Look, Jethro...apart from the way the corpse is laid out, the typical cultural shape of the skull and state of the mummification, only the Egyptians removed the organs in this manner."

"But I thought Egyptian Mummies were always wrapped up."

"Usually they are. That's what threw me at first. Someone deliberately removed the wrappings. They did a good job as well...they knew what they were doing. You say you found nothing with the body?"

"Just this arrowhead," Chester said, taking out the plastic bag.

Simon waved it away, "You can forget that."

"It was in the body," Chester prompted.

"Then it was put there deliberately to throw whoever found the body off the track. No, Jethro, I agree with what you said on the phone the other night. This body was put here recently."

"How recently?" Chester questioned.

"Well...in relation to its period of death, forty...maybe sixty years, is recent."

"How about 1940?" Jordan said.

"Yes...I'd accept that."

"Have you a reason for estimating that time period?" Chester asked.

"Assuming the body was buried immediately after removing the wrappings, and taking into account the type of soil Jethro said the grave site was, I'd say that was a reasonable time. Anything longer, even this leathery tissue would start fragmenting. In fact, that was their mistake. In ordinary soil, it wouldn't have lasted long."

"I don't think it was a mistake, Simon," Jordan said, "The shallow grave, the eight hundred year old arrowhead, and the removal of the wrappings, convinces me someone wanted this body to be found, and accepted without a fuss as someone from that period, but why all the elaborate subterfuge?"

"What I'd like to know is how it got here in the first place?" Chester said.

"There's only two ways this mummy could have got into England," Simon continued: "One, legitimately via an archaeological expedition, or illegally through a private sale on the Egyptian black-market. Either way, there had to be a good reason to abandon it. It would be very easy to check on a rare specimen like this. I'd say we're looking at an illegal mummy."

"Why would you say that?" Jordan asked, just as puzzled.

"I don't know...they could just as easily have burnt it. My guess is they wanted to get rid of it quickly. In the early eighties, it became illegal to remove any artefacts from Egypt. They even went to the extent of asking the museums around the world to return theirs. They suddenly found culture."

"You said these mummies were rare, Simon," Jordan commented, "is there any possibility we could find out where he came from?"

"Most definitely…given time I could contact all the museums that have Egyptian artefacts, but they don't hurry themselves. Then there are all the private collectors. It could take some time. But if I had a lead…"

"What sort of lead?" Jordon interrupted.

"Oh…something connected with that period; maybe the museum here might help. Or maybe a private collector in the area…they always know these things."

"They don't have an Egyptian section," Chester said. "I'm afraid we might have stood a better chance if our corpse had been from the Robin Hood period."

There was a stifled laugh before everyone became serious again. Although Simon had partially identified The Sherwood Forest Man, Jordan was no nearer learning the truth than he was earlier. The fact that he knew what he was, and that he was much older than Chester originally suggested, Simon's job of identifying him was going to be much more difficult than he expected.

Jordan pondered a moment, considering his other piece of evidence, if in fact it had any connection at all. "When I said there was nothing else found with the body; that was not quite true; a few metres away we found an army button, and a local enthusiast dated it around 1940."

"Is that why you mentioned that date?" Simon asked.

"Yes. It's possible something happened around that time, involving a soldier that might just fit in with your theory."

Simon laughed, "I wouldn't say it was a theory old chum; more a desperate attempt to give some reason to this conundrum. But you're right; if you can find a link with that button and the date, then that will give me something to work with." Simon removed his reading glasses and changed them for the others, giving them a quick polish at the same time. "There's just one thing that's been bothering me, Jethro, why all the bother. I mean, whatever happened to King Tut over here, happened so long ago it hardly matters."

"Do you think he was a Pharaoh?" Chester interrupted.

"It would be easier if he was," Jethro commented.

"No...I was being smart," Simon replied. "But he was someone of note, I can say that. Only men close to the court could afford the full procedure of mummification. I doubt he was anything closer. And there's another thing, to be in this condition, up to the point of him being unwrapped, he had to have been in a sarcophagus."

"Now that's something," Jordan said. "It means we're looking for a possible stolen mummy. As for your other comment, Simon, you're right. There is no point to all this. There's no crime, no associated robbery to investigate; it's just a PR exercise to combat all the stories in the media. In short, it's the pet project of the police commissioner to outwit some bad publicity."

"Ah," he said, and Chester nodded his head in sympathy. "No need to explain any further old chum...Rather you than me...if you get my drift."

"I do unfortunately. Thank you for reminding me. I shall report to my immediate superior with the news and hope he's satisfied. Who knows, I might not need your valuable services after all."

Jordan glanced at his watch and remembered he had promised Simon a posh lunch, then looking at the eager expression on Chester's face, he realised he would have to invite him along also. Apparently they had unfinished business to discuss, and that frightened Jordan. If there was one thing he hated during his meal, it was a long, boring, drawn-out conversation.

When lunch was finally over and Chester had stopped feeding Simon's ego, Jordan drove him back to the station to catch the afternoon train back to London, and returned exhausted to the office. His plan was to settle down and put together a report on the new identity of The Sherwood Forest Man, hoping that might be an end to the investigation. Penny was waiting for him at the top of the stairs.

"Inspector," she called out.

Jordan pulled her to one side, amidst the busy traffic on the second landing.

"What's up, Penny? You look flustered."

"I saw you drive in, Inspector. The Chief Superintendent has been asking for you. He wanted to know where you were."

"Did you tell him I was taking an archaeologist over to pathology?"

"Josh did. He had quite a conversation with him."

"What...On the phone?"

"No...the Chief Superintendent came down to the office. He seemed very interested in the white-board. I filled him in, and that's when he turned to Josh and asked him where you were."

"Don't let him upset you, Penny. He's from the old school. Turning to Josh had more to do with him being a sergeant, than you being a female."

Penny smiled, "You'd better get along, Inspector. You know how he stands by his window. He's probably ringing the office right now."

When Jordan entered the Chief Superintendent's outer office, he was pacing back and forth giving dictation to Phyllis. He stopped and turned to face Jordan, "Oh there you are. It seems every time I want you, your out."

"Sorry, Sir, but I am working on this investigation."

"What about the other two?"

"They have their assignments also, Sir. It just happens that they stay behind now and then to collate the information we're collecting."

"You're getting a lot are you?"

"Surprisingly we are, Sir...all leading in unusual directions."

"Come in then and bring me up to date."

"You seem in a hurry, Sir," Jordan said, following him into his office.

"I've got another of those meetings with the Commissioner at six, that's why I've been chasing you. I know he's going to ask me how we're doing."

Jordan sat down and smiled confidently, "If it had been tomorrow, Sir I would have had it all typed up into a nice neat report."

"Well it will have to be an oral report for now. She's going to be there."

"Who's she, Sir?"

"That damned Sarah Bolt woman. The Commissioner finally granted her an interview. That's why I have to be there, and he want's some answers. He want's to know who's feeding her with all that rubbish."

"Does he expect her to tell him?"

"I doubt it...but we have to know."

"Maybe it won't be necessary."

The Chief Superintendent looked surprised, "Why?"

Jordan continued to look confident, smug even.

"Can you handle a shock, Sir? No...two shocks."

"You've got my interest."

"Well...shock number one, I've solved the mystery of The Sherwood Forest Man. He's not one of Robin Hood's men, he's an Egyptian Mummy."

The Chief Superintendent's mouth dropped open, "He's what?"

"Yes, Sir, and shock number two, he's three thousand years old."

The Chief Superintendent's face went bright red, "That's not good enough."

"It's the truth, Sir...or as near as I can get it."

The Chief Superintendent jumped up, walked over to the window, and stared out across the courtyard. "The Commissioner won't wear it. He gave express orders to squash the serial killer theory and the Robin Hood story invented by that woman, and here you are telling me about a three thousand year old mummy."

"Quite frankly, Sir, I think the whole episode is ridiculous. There should never have been an ongoing investigation, once you found out the corpse was hundreds of years old that should have been the end of it. But you've allowed this stupid woman to take control, and she's the one fuelling the fire now."

"Don't be clever, Inspector."

"Well I don't know what more I can do without incurring a lot more expense. We have the Home Guard connection to investigate. That should take up a few days, and if that actually gives us a connection with the mummy, then who knows, it might drag out for months."

"You're serious, aren't you? This corpse is actually a mummy."

"That's what I said, Sir. I just don't know how an Egyptian mummy happened to be buried in Sherwood Forest during the war."

"Where did that come from?"

"My archaeologist dated his burial around 1940. The link with the button we found and possibly the Home Guard."

The Chief Superintendent turned back from the window, with a look of resolve on his face. "Dig deeper, Inspector... you're good at that. That's why I chose you and the other two. You all have a special quality, and if anyone can solve this one, you can. The Commissioner needs something so iron-clad, no one, not even Miss clever pants, can twist and contort it to suit her needs."

CHAPTER 10

If there was anything Jordan hated most, it was a ringing phone first thing in the morning when he was running late. To make things worse, it had to be when he was only half shaved. Walking through to the bedroom, he wiped the foam off his face, and picked up the receiver.

"Jethro...don't slam the phone down on me again," the caller cried.

Jordan recognised Mark's voice immediately, even if it did sound a little higher than usual. "I won't, but I can't speak to you for long."

"I'm sorry," Mark said, choosing his words more carefully this time. "I tried to shock you...and it didn't work."

"But it did work, Mark...you did shock me."

Mark laughed, "Sorry...I didn't mean it that way. Sometimes a bit of reverse psychology shocks the patient into facing his own problems. It's supposed to be a subtle transition...but you didn't react the way I intended, and it snowballed. Sorry."

"You keep saying sorry, Mark. Believe me it doesn't really matter. I don't care whether it works or not anymore. I'm giving it all a rest for a while, and I'm going to concentrate on solving this skeleton mystery. By the way, did I tell you we found out The Sherwood Forest Man turned out to be an ancient Egyptian?"

"You can't do that, Jethro; it's a condition of your employment."

"Not exactly: it's a condition of my working at the college. And since I don't work there anymore, I don't need to report to you."

"I don't think your semantics are going to go down well with the Chief Superintendent," Mark pointed out.

Jordan laughed, "What's he going to do...sack me? That would suit me fine. It's about time I looked for a change in my life."

Mark went silent for the moment, as if he was lost for words. Then, after clearing his throat he said, "That's not the answer, Jethro."

"At the moment, Mark...it is."

"Come on, Jethro, we have to talk about this."

"You're not listening to me, Mark. Just as you didn't hear what I said about the skeleton we found being an Egyptian Mummy."

"Mummy...What mummy?"

"You see. Most people would be amazed to hear we dug up an Egyptian mummy in Sherwood Forest. But it just passed right over your head."

"My God...I'm sorry. I can see now why you need to solve this case, but I have to warn you not to lose sight of your other problem. It hasn't gone away you know, despite what you think..."

"Mark...no more talking," Jethro interrupted. "I don't want you to think I put the phone down on you again, but I really must go...all right?"

"Okay. But keep in touch."

"I'll think about it."

Jordan was the proverbial optimist. He wanted to rid himself of the hassles that plagued him, but at the same time, his insatiable need for closure, had to know who The Sherwood Forest Man really was. That would never happen until he discovered what an Egyptian mummy was doing in Nottingham.

That was Simon's job. If Jordan took too long finding that missing link, Mark's fear of a regression might become a reality.

Over the past thirty years, Jordan had become familiar with his nemesis, and wary of what brought on his nightmares. At the top of the list was always his sense of failure, or the aberrations of an idle mind. Holidays were worse, like the one preceding his reinstatement in the police. Despite his questioning the move, he was preying for an all-embracing investigation to absorb him.

By the time he arrived at the office, Jordan had convinced himself that today's interview with the former Home Guard lieutenant, would give him that link he was looking for, and he was raring to go. His reception was less than enthusiastic, despite the intense briefing he managed to pump into Josh and Penny after his meeting with the Chief Superintendent.

He expected the news of the Egyptian mummy might have filled them with more questions than he had answers. Instead, Josh had his head buried in a newspaper, and Penny was standing at the white-board, adding yesterday's changes.

"Good morning," Jordan said.

Penny looked round, "Good morning, Inspector."

Josh stood up and passed Jordan the paper, "I don't know that it's that good a morning, Boss. You'd better read this first."

Jordan's high quickly disappeared as he grabbed the paper and slumped into his seat. There was no point in removing his coat, he still had an interview to conduct, and he smoothed the paper out on his desk and looked at the bold headlines on the front page: 'Latest Sherwood Forest Blunder. Now we have an Egyptian Mummy. The suspicious Inspector now tells us the skeleton by the bridle path in Sherwood Forest is a....' He folded the paper and tossed it in the bin.

"I knew it was a mistake," he said.

"What was, Boss?" Josh asked.

"The Commissioner told that reporter about our discovery."

"He should have waited until we had all the facts, Inspector." Penny said.

"That's exactly what I said to the Chief Superintendent."

"So, Boss...what now?"

Jordan jumped up from his seat. He was not going to allow this silly women to dominate his success the way she had Inspector Dent's, "Come on...chop, chop, you two. We've got a big day ahead of us," Jordan said, with renewed enthusiasm.

Josh looked surprised, "Me as well, Boss?"

"Why not...you've finished that job at the library I assume?"

"Oh, yes, Boss. All done and dusted."

"What does that mean?" Penny whispered.

"Just something I was finishing off," Josh said furtively.

Jordan turned back at the door, "Well?"

Penny hesitated, "Shouldn't someone look after the phone, Inspector? What if the Chief Superintendent rings…like he did yesterday?"

"Somehow I doubt if he will, since he was the one who told me you two should get out more. It appears you're destined for greater things."

Josh had digested the morning's news and conscientious Penny had already tracked down the numerous activities of Lieutenant Tobias Cunningham; so neither had any restrictions that would hinder a day in the field.

It was just as well Penny checked. She found out that he left promptly for his twelve-thirty stint at the information centre, where he spent the rest of the afternoon telling tourists where to find the most interesting parts of Robin Hood country. By four-fifteen, he was back in his old uniform; teaching young Civil Defence volunteers how to save Nottingham from clandestine attacks.

By nine o'clock, they were in Jordan's car, following the ring road out of the city, to an old flint stone priory on the main road to Mansfield. It was only a short drive; someone more energetic could have walked it, as the Lieutenant often did, despite him being in his seventies.

Being a renovated church, there was plenty of space to park on the crushed granite drive, and Jordan drove around the full semicircle in front of the impressive gable end and parked facing the way he came in. Whilst the two men had no difficulty reaching the front door, Penny was struggling in her high-heels: each step digging deeper into the compacted surface.

She yanked herself forward on her tiptoes and skipped the rest of the way, just as the front door juddered open. A white-haired man immediately bombarded them with a garbled excuse for taking so long to answer the door, rambling on about being an invalid from the war. Yet when he turned to walk back into the lounge, without questioning their identity, Jordan noticed he had only the slightest of limps.

It was more of a leaning to one side: an old man's legacy of arthritis or diminishing bone density he thought. As they followed, he continued mumbling, and Jordan soon found him bent over a large refractory table, stuffing papers into a small leather briefcase at one end.

The room Jordan mistook for a lounge turned out to be one of the old sitting rooms; usually a sparsely furnished room set aside to receive guests. A huge table took up most of the central area, decorated with a narrow strip of tapestry down the centre, a silver candlestick at each end and small stacks of papers. As the Lieutenant searched through them, Jordan's curiosity noticed an old couch, two easy chairs and a small antique bureau in the corner adjacent to the French doors.

The room smelt musty, probably because the room was cold and damp. Penny coughed, and stepped back into the hall.

Jordan took out his warrant card, "Mr Cunningham, we're the police. My name is Inspector Jordan, this is Sergeant Crosby, and the young lady clutching her satchel in the hall is Constable Willow."

The old man looked passed the two men just as Major Sturt had done, "You look cold my dear. I'm sorry the place couldn't be nice and warm for you. My wife always had it warm and cosy. But since I'm out most of the day, it hardly seems worth it." He turned his attention to Jordan next and studied him. "Sorry, Inspector?" he glanced at the card with his watery eyes, "Jordan. I'm getting forgetful these days. I have to keep writing notes to myself." He lifted his hand and shook a small piece of paper, "See…Don't forget to take papers to Civil Defence lecture."

Jordan smiled, and suddenly realised the old man would have no idea what he was talking about, let alone Penny's telephone call. "You remember Major Sturt?"

"Oh the Major…of course…believe it or not, Inspector, I do recall the reason why you're here. I'm not ready for the home yet; but I do need a little prompting. Once I catch on it all floods back; especially the good old days."

"You recall Major Sturt telling you about the Army button?"

"I do. The Major and I had a long conversation about those days. I gather he told you that I was in charge of the local Home Guard unit?" Jordan nodded, Penny saw this as an opportunity to take out her notepad and Josh moved round to one of the easy chairs and sat down. The Lieutenant tapped the side of his leg with his knuckles. It sounded hollow, "Lost my leg in northern France in 1940; bloody useless after that. Mind you, it wasn't long before Jerry sent the rest of my unit packing back to Dunkirk. I got shipped home just before they arrived," he grunted, a little choked, and continued. "Anyway… all I was good for was setting up the new LDV groups around the country. And finally I took on my own here in Nottingham."

Jordan took out the plastic bag with the button in it. He showed an interest.

"I suppose it would be no use asking you if this could have been a Home Guard uniform button?"

The old man took hold of the pouch and walked over to the window. Even with his glasses, it was plain to see he had difficulty seeing the small object. "I couldn't say, Inspector. I can just see that it's an artillery button, but we had all sorts back then. I agree with the Major though, there were no artillery units here then, so it could only have come from a visiting soldier, or one of my uniforms." He handed the pouch back to Jordan. "You see...being a newly formed unit we had little or nothing to start with. No arms...no nothing, except me of course. I was still a regular so I had what they issued me with at the outbreak of war. I even had my old Webley revolver, so I was the only one who looked like a soldier...not good for moral, Inspector. Then gradually we started to get stuff: second hand uniforms, and a few old Enfield rifles." He laughed, "Even those we had trouble with."

"How so, Lieutenant," Josh asked.

"Well, Sergeant, they got the delivery mixed up. There were two types: one for the Americans that used their own ammunition and the British 303. It got so dangerous we had to label the ammunition...make sure we used the right stuff: not that we ever had the opportunity to use them. A blessing in a way I suppose."

"So it's possible?"

"Oh it's possible; Inspector...but I don't understand the significance."

The Lieutenant kept glancing over towards the coach-clock on the bureau, "I'm sorry, Inspector. I've got to be in the city by twelve, I'm working at the Information Centre in the afternoons."

"Yes I know, Lieutenant, and at four-thirty you go to your Civil Defence Group. The Major said that was a follow on from the Home Guard?"

"That's true. Although there was a few years break in between."

"So that's it then? You can't think of an event happening back in 1940. Anything will do that might give us a link with our case."

"You mean the skeleton in Sherwood Forest?"

"That's right."

"I think I would remember something like that. In those days, it would have been front-page headlines. However, I'll give it thought Inspector; you've jogged my memory now. It takes a while for the grey matter to tick over but it comes back eventually." He glanced at the clock again, "I don't suppose you could give me a lift. It looks like it might rain again this afternoon."

Jordan smiled, "No problem, Lieutenant."

As they walked out to the car, Josh brushed up against Jordan's shoulder. Penny was busy helping the old man across the loose gravel, or using him as her own support: it was hard to tell.

"Boss," he whispered.

"Yes, Josh."

"Did you here that bit about the newspapers back then?"

Jordan stopped by the car and fumbled for his keys, "Of course...that information should be in the library Microfiche files."

"Exactly, Boss. If you drop me off there on your way, I should be able to find out what happened back then before the old man goes to his Civil Defence Group."

Jordan nodded and they set off towards the city.

After dropping Josh at the library and the Lieutenant at the Information Centre, Jordan and Penny spent the next two hours going through the archive material she had collated for the same period in 1940. They were looking for a police report that might link up with an incident concerning the Home Guard, or a visiting soldier.

"Inspector," Penny called out, after a long fruitless period.

Jordan put the folder he was reading down and looked up, "Yes, Penny...have you found something?"

"I think so, Inspector; would you like to have a look?"

Jordan stood up, stretched his arms and glanced at his watch, "I wonder what's keeping Josh," he said, standing up and walking over to her desk. "I expected him back by now. He said it was a doddle using those Microfiche files."

"I wouldn't know, Inspector...he's been there a lot lately. I think he's found himself a young girl to impress. A lot go for the badge you know."

"Do they now," Jordan said, leaning across her desk. "And does that apply for women also?"

Penny blushed, and immediately turned the open folder around on her desk for Jordan to see, "There, Inspector. A small note from a Constable Ridgley, reporting a lorry crash on the Thorsby road adjacent to Sherwood Forest."

Jordan took Penny's word for it, "What's so unusual about that?"

"Well look, Inspector...it was an Army lorry."

"Umm," Jordan let out, still not convinced.

Penny pulled the folder back impatiently, "For your information, the signatory custodian of the vehicle was none other than, Lieutenant Tobias Cunningham."

Jordan grabbed back the file and studied it carefully. It was only a small report; so insignificant he was surprised Penny spotted it. There it was in Constable Ridgley's stunted writing: Lieutenant Tobias Cunningham. He checked for other sheets, but there were none. No detailed accident report, other than the vehicle skidded off the road and burst into flames. No fire report or whatever served as a forensic survey of the scene back then. It happened on September 18, 1940, and given the limited local services at the time, it was probably sufficient.

There was a loud thud as Josh rushed through the door.

"You'll never guess what I found out, Boss?"

"An Army lorry crashed in Sherwood Forest in1940."

Josh stopped dead in his tracks, "How did you know?"

"Penny found a report in amongst the old police files."

"Sorry, Josh," she said, "I'd only got half way through when the Inspector hurried us out this morning. Until then there was nothing of any interest. Then when we got back I carried on, just in case, and found this," she picked up the folder.

"I wasted my time then," he said.

"Not really, Josh," Jordan said, "There's not much here... what did you find?"

Josh took some folded copy papers out of his inside pocket and passed them over, "As you can see, the story of the accident only warranted a small piece on the back page... everything else was all about the German Blitz on London."

Jordan looked at the three different articles, surprised the incident was important enough to capture the attention of that many papers, and each one was almost identical. Then he noticed a different paragraph on the second sheet. Unlike the others, that plainly reported the fact that an Army lorry skidded off the road alongside Sherwood Forest, this reporter decided to make an observation.

He pointed out that the stretch of road was perfectly straight, the surface was bone dry on that day, and the leaves had not fallen in sufficient quantity to make the road slippery. He also questioned the suspicious nature of the fire: how in fact it started, and why it totally gutted the vehicle. He likened it to an act of arson.

Jordan said nothing. Instead, he rummaged amongst the papers on his desk until he found the paper Penny gave him with the Lieutenant's details. He reached for the phone, dialled, and asked for the Lieutenant.

"Cunningham," the voice said on the other end.

"Ah, Lieutenant, it's Inspector Jordan again."

"Inspector...what can I do for you now. I haven't remembered anything yet."

"That's all right, Lieutenant, we've had a stroke of luck. We came across an old file about an Army lorry accident near Sherwood Forest in 1940."

"It doesn't ring a bell, Inspector."

"It has your name in it. It says you were the signatory for the lorry."

"Oh dear...then it must be true, but for the life of me I can't remember."

"If we spoke to you again...say later tonight at your place? Maybe we could help you jog your memory."

The phone went silent for a moment. "No, Inspector...I think it would be much better if you came round to the council offices where I hold my Civil Defence meetings: after four-fifteen. You'll see a board in the foyer telling you what room."

"Fine, if that's more convenient for you, Lieutenant."

"It's not so much a question of being convenient Inspector; it's where I keep all my files; even the Home Guard ones. I kept all of them, right back to the very start. Each time we moved the meeting place they kept telling me to get rid of all my dusty files, but I had a feeling they might come in handy one day. I was planning to write a book about those days you see, never gave a thought that they might be helpful to the police. I mean…who would want to know about the Home Guard?"

"That sounds like an excellent idea," Jordan said. "We would certainly be interested in any files you have from that period. We might even want to borrow some for a while. See you then, Lieutenant…and thanks."

Jordan slowly returned the phone to the hook and looked up at two eager faces. He had the beginnings of a satisfied smile on his face; it was the first time he actually felt confidant that at last there was a glimmer of light ahead.

"Well, Boss?" Josh asked.

"He can't remember, despite what I said…"

"Then why the smug look, Inspector," Penny questioned.

"He has all the Home Guard files in his Civil Defence room, and believe it or not, they go back to the very beginning. How lucky is that?"

"It would have been better if he told us that in the car, Boss."

"Patience, Josh. Remember what I said about slowly does it?"

"Yes, Boss."

CHAPTER 11

Although Lieutenant Cunningham was deeply engrossed in explaining the merits of monitoring national trends to a group of ordinary civilians, he looked somewhat presumptuous, standing in his full uniform, in front of a table displaying Air Raid Warden Helmets, and other implements from the Second World War.

He noticed the police had arrived, and were standing at the back of the large room listening to his lecture, and acknowledging their presence, he promptly informed the group they could take a break for refreshments.

"Inspector Jordan, Sergeant and Constable," he said, greeting them.

"I hope we didn't interrupt anything?" Jordan said.

"Not at all, Inspector. I usually take a break for a drink and biscuits, it's just a bit earlier than usual," he replied, walking them over to a long trestle table at the end of the room. The council canteen had supplied a large chromium urn of hot water, several plates of biscuits, a bowl of tea bags, sugar cubes, coffee sachets and a jug of milk, "Can I tempt you to some refreshment?"

"Thank you," they said, and Penny and Josh prepared the drinks, while Jordan helped himself to a handful of biscuits.

"You said on the phone that you had all the Home Guard files?" Jordan said; taking the mug of tea Penny handed him.

"Yes I did, Inspector. As you can see on the table, I don't just lecture on present day Civil Defence. I find it easier to introduce the subject by telling them a bit about its origins. The first need for an official defence force and that of course means referring to the Home Guard. So the files come in handy now and then, as well as my passion to write a bit of history some time," Penny handed him a drink and he smiled at her. "All this lot keep talking about is the bomb. However, that's just a possibility these days. It's all textbook stuff," he laughed. "Don't get me wrong...I know we had Hiroshima and all that, but we didn't learn much. The German threat was different back then: the Battle of Britain, the Blitz and the imminent invasion were something we really got to grips with. It's all in my files.

"Can we have a look for that accident?" Josh said.

"Yes, why not...strange thing is, I can't remember it," he said leading the Inspector through a door into a small store-room, "but it'll be here somewhere."

Penny and Josh followed, both putting their mugs down on a small table in the centre of the room and taking out their notepads, while the Lieutenant went over to a filing cabinet next to a utility sink in the corner. Other than the table, it was the only piece of furniture in the room. The other two walls, either side of the one with the door in it, were covered with shelves; and they in turn were stacked with leaflets and assorted cardboard boxes. Josh dragged in two foldaway chairs so that they could sit and take notes as the conversation developed. Josh preferred it that way with general information, instead of overtaxing his memory.

The Lieutenant had the cabinet well organised. Standing behind his left shoulder, Jordan could see the card on the front of the top draw had a label dated at 1959 –1984, the second draw read 1948 –1958, and the bottom draw contained the whole war period, 1939 –1947. The Lieutenant groaned as he bent down and pulled the draw out.

"Here," Jordan said, "Let me do that. What file do you want first?"

"Well, Inspector, you said it was 1940, so try that one."

Jordan reached in and fingered through the dusty files until he came across the one marked, Cheetham, 1940. He pulled it out."

"What does Cheetham stand for?"

"Oh that was the house we commandeered at the time. We did a lot of that back then. It doubled as the County HQ."

Jordan passed him the file and he started to flick through it, stopping now and then to read something. He chuckled once or twice as if he was recalling a pleasant memory, and suddenly he stopped," Yes! I remember now. It's all coming back to me. I told you it would," Jordan and the others looked on tenterhooks. "Bloody nuisance it was. We were the only ones with lorries big enough." He laughed.

"Can you explain, Lieutenant?" Jordan asked.

"Oh yes…sorry. In fact, we were the only ones with any petrol. It was our National Heritage you see…we had to protect it from the bloody German bombers."

"You still haven't explained," Jordan continued.

"Sorry again, Inspector, I seem to think everyone can remember those days you see; when they can't…not enough of us left," he saw Jordan's impatient look. "All right…

In those first days of the Blitz, the government decided we should protect our National Heritage, by that I mean, all the treasures in our museums and art galleries; at least the better part of them. After discussions with everyone who could possibly have a say, they all agreed to empty the mausoleums of their treasures and ship them out into the country.

"They chose the grand estate homes as the safest depositories, and after crating the artefacts, they were sent out on trains to each county, and then ferried to each house by guarded vehicles, and who better to do that than the Home Guard. We supplied the lorries, the drivers and the manpower to load and offload the crates."

"And that newspaper report was one of those?" Penny questioned.

The Lieutenant returned to the file he was holding and read on, "Yes...Bloody nuisance, I remember now. I was furious, I tell you. I rang the HQ straight away. Told them what I thought about wasting valuable petrol on delivering artefacts."

"And what did they say?" Jordan asked.

"Bloody fools...the whole lot of them. They said we had a duty to protect the nation's valuables. I tell you, an Egyptian coffin and some Chinese pottery."

Penny and Josh were too amazed to say anything, while Jordan looked as if he was about to burst. He grabbed the file out of the Lieutenant's hand, stopping to apologise, then took several minutes reading the next few pages.

The Lieutenant was right. He had encapsulated time back then. The file was full of all his notes: his objections to HQ instructions, a preliminary survey of the most likely houses in the area, routes from the station and finally the actual roster for the driver and guards of the lorry that crashed. It was easy enough to pick out amongst several others; it was the only one with an official police stamp in the corner, denoting it was an officially recorded transfer.

Jordan glanced down the names. "Are any of these men still alive?"

The Lieutenant took the list and studied it, "Well... Graham Wilkes died five years ago, Sydney Fields went to Australia, Geoff...hold on, none of these men were involved with the crash; they only loaded the lorry at the station." He studied for a moment," Yes I remember now... Will Edgebaston was the driver and Chas Ripley sat beside him. We went through the routine the night before, and the other three were to go on ahead in a jeep to prepare for the unloading. That's right."

"So," Jordan started again, "Are either of the two in the lorry still alive."

"Chas Ripley died more than eight years ago. We always try to have a memorial for our old comrades," he paused, looking thoughtful.

"You said Will Edgebaston was the driver," Jordon said.

"Yes...now Will was still alive two years ago. He moved down to Portsmouth with his daughter, something to do with improving his health."

"Have you his number or something?" Jordan asked.

"Yes, I think so...hold on."

The Lieutenant left the storeroom and went across to the bench where he left his briefcase. One of the group, obviously anxious to get started, stopped him as Jordan turned to Josh, "Josh...take out the files to 1945, just in case there's any information carrying on from the accident."

"Right, Boss."

A little out of breath, the Lieutenant returned.

"Here we are, Inspector. I've written it down for you, and now I really must get started with my lecture again...the group's getting a bit restless."

"I understand, Lieutenant. Can I take all these files? I promise to get them back to you as soon as I can."

"Certainly...and you will let me know how you get on," he said leading them out of the storeroom. "Although I'm damned if I know what this crash has to do with your skeleton; we didn't lose anyone that night...at least I don't think we did."

"I'm not quite sure myself, Lieutenant, but I'll let you know."

They left him returning to his wartime procedures, eager to get the files back to the office, and find out exactly what did happen in September 1940.

It was unanimously decided that they should work through, at least until they had identified all the key aspects to the link with the Army button. It was obvious, Jordan's hunch that the button was of importance, was the right course to take.

It had led them to the Home Guard, the clandestine deliveries of national artefacts and the crash on the road passing Sherwood Forest. Most significantly, it led them to the clue they were looking for: the burnt out lorry had contained an Egyptian coffin.

The new questions it posed was what happened to the coffin, and why were there no burns on their Egyptian mummy? Unless, Jordan pointed out, that was the reason why they removed the wrappings.

Jordan took out the piece of paper the Lieutenant gave him, and dialled the number in Portsmouth. It always took longer when you were impatient, Jordan thought, until he heard the click on the other end and a female voice.

"Oh Hello…" Jordan said, "I'm Inspector Jordan of the Nottingham Police, is Mr Edgebaston there?"

Jordan could hear her falter on the other end. "Is there something wrong? Has someone died or something?"

"No…I'm sorry, it's nothing like that. I need to talk to Mr Edgebaston about some enquiries I'm making."

"I see…which one do you want?"

"Will Edgebaston."

"Oh…you want the father."

"Yes…If he was in Nottingham in 1940."

She dropped the phone and Jordan heard a garbled, almost hysterical woman's voice in the background. Little did he know, she was shouting because her father-in-law was deaf. Jordan did some quick arithmetic on his blotter and suddenly realised he had to be in his seventies, like the Lieutenant.

By the scraping sound, he seemed to be having difficulty in picking up the phone, then he coughed a couple of times and finally rasped, "Yes…who's that?"

"Is that Mr Edgebaston who was in the Home Guard in 1940?"

"You what? You'll have to speak up…What are you on about?"

"I'm sorry Mr Edgebaston this must be very confusing for you. But I'm looking into something that relates to the Home Guard in 1940."

The other two looked round, wondering why Jordan was shouting.

"Blimey…where did you drag that up from?"

"Lieutenant Cunningham gave me your name."

"Old Toby? By that takes me back a bit."

"You remember him then," Jordan questioned.

"Oh I remember him all right…he was a right fusspot he was. Always had to put everything down in his little book he did…I'm not surprised he still had my name. Why would you ring me? Has he died or something?"

"No he hasn't. I'm with the Nottingham police, Inspector Jordan is my name, and we're making enquiries about a Home Guard lorry that crashed near Sherwood Forest in September 1940."

"Bloody hell…What's this all about?"

"The Lieutenant told me you were the driver, and I was wondering if you can remember the accident at all."

"What was that?"

"Can you remember the accident?"

"Oh yes I remember…but I wasn't the driver."

Jordan covered the mouthpiece, "Penny…check the notes referring to the driver and his mate again," he lifted his hand, "Sorry, Mr Edgebaston, I'm just getting the notes on the accident checked again."

"You needn't bother. I'm telling you I wasn't the driver that night."

"You weren't the driver?"

"That's what I just said, isn't it?"

"How are you so sure? You said yourself; it was a long time ago…"

Penny put the open page in front of Jordan.

"Here we are…You were the driver and Chas Ripley was the co-driver; according to the Lieutenant's notes."

"That's the trouble, Inspector, he was too keen on planning, but never took the time to see if anything worked out. I know I wasn't driving that night because I swapped with a bloke called Gallagher."

Jordan paused for a moment, thinking there was that bloody spanner again. Every time he got close, there would be something to send him off at a tangent.

"Okay, Mr Edgebaston, do you think you could explain what happened?" Jordan asked, picking up a pencil and the pad at the top of his desk.

"It's not complicated, Inspector, Jack Gallagher came up to me that afternoon following the Lieutenant's briefing, and asked me if I would swap duties with him. Something about his girl coming home on leave that weekend. The pick-up was on a Saturday you see. It made no difference to me."

Jordan continued making notes, "Did that mean he was much younger?"

"Oh yes. I didn't know much about him…didn't want to."

"Why was that?"

"He was a crook, that's why they called him 'Spider', because he was good at climbing in and out of second storey windows."

"Then why wasn't he away fighting?"

"Because he was on parole. He had a choice of working in the mines or a factory, or joining the Home Guard."

"I gather you were too old?" Jordan commented.

"I was and I wasn't," he wheezed slightly and coughed again. "I had just got over a bout of consumption. I was in my thirties, they were still taking men in at that age, but not if you were ill like me. So I volunteered for the local Home Guard."

"I see. And what happened to Gallagher?"

"Now that's the odd thing. He and Ripley managed to get out of the lorry before it burst into flames, and then, within the month he was dead."

151

"Who…Ripley?"

"No, Gallagher. Ripley died years later. I didn't get to the memorial…the Lieutenant told you about our memorials I bet?"

"Yes he did, and how all the others are dead now."

"So I'm the only one left?"

"You were going to tell me about Gallagher."

"Oh yes…the whole thing was strange. I'm glad I was out of it. Anyway, a few weeks after he escaped from the crash he was practicing throwing grenades, and one went off…blew him all over the place."

"That was bad luck."

"I don't know…that's why I call it strange. We never practiced with live grenades…the Army couldn't afford any. We only used dummies. Then there was old Chas Ripley, you couldn't find a more Nottingham man than him. Born and bread there he was, and straight after Gallagher's death, he left."

"Where did he go?"

"No Idea. He just vanished…then ten years later he suddenly turned up for his mother's funeral. We were all there, and then he vanished again. But I'll tell you this; he must have stumbled on a pot of gold somewhere."

"Why do you say that?"

"Because he came from a poor family like most of us. There he was, we hardly recognised him, stepping out of his big posh car with a fancy wife, all dressed in fine clothes. And it was one of the good funerals as well, none of your pine box rubbish for him, his mother had one of those mahogany caskets."

"Maybe he won the money," Jordan suggested.

"What back then...money was short, everything was on coupons."

Jordan heard a shrill female voice in the background.

"Sounds like you're wanted," he prompted.

"You're right. You'd think she was paying for this call. I'm hogging the line she says. The bloody thing rarely rings. Is that it, Inspector?"

"Yes I think so. If I need anything else, I'll ring you again. Thanks."

"It was a nice break from the boredom of this place, Inspector. I'll have to try and get away to Nottingham again... one day, if I'm lucky."

"Thanks again, Mr Edgebaston."

Jordan put the phone down and glanced at his notes. Penny looked up from what she was doing, "What did he say, Inspector?"

"Apparently we've hit another stone wall."

"Isn't that the way, Boss," Josh said.

"It seems our Mr Edgebaston wasn't the driver that night, he swapped his roster with a man called Gallagher, a criminal by all accounts. Make a note of that Josh, and look up his record. Strangely, he escaped the crash, and a few weeks later, a grenade killed him. And here's something interesting...Chas Ripley, the man who sat beside him in the lorry, suddenly came into a lot of money. At least according to Edgebaston, he was looking a lot better off than he did before the accident; which only suggests one thing in my book..."

"He was bought off, Inspector," Penny interrupted.

"You're right, Penny. You can look into his life since 1940. Find out where he went after he left Nottingham. Check his bank accounts, and see if he had any connection with this Gallagher other than being in the Home Guard together."

"Right, Inspector…but where's that going to lead us?"

"To the answer I hope, Penny. With Gallagher dead, we don't have a clue."

"This case seems to be nothing but blind allies, Inspector," Penny commented.

"You're right, Penny. But I bet you one thing; I bet he was missing a button."

"I might have something, Inspector," Penny said.

"I was just going to call it a night," Jordan said, laughing, "What is it?"

"Well the Lieutenant was right when he said he had to make notes about everything. I've been going through these files and I've built up what happened during those few days in September. I was going to type it up."

"Just a quick summary, Penny or I'll never get to sleep tonight."

"Right, Inspector. Well…he was right about all the notes on planning the next delivery that was due that afternoon. The men's names are all here that he read out earlier, except he doesn't seem to have been aware of the two driver's changeover. Anyway, I came across a shipment manifest from a professor Ayers of the antiquities department of a museum in London, and it catalogued a number of paintings, several Chinese vases, some bronze statues and here we are… an Egyptian coffin."

"At last," Jordan exclaimed, "I can let my archaeologist friend know where the mummy came from, and he can get its history, then finally I might be able to give the Chief Superintendent an identity after all…"

154

"But what about this Gallagher chap, Boss?" Josh interrupted.

"I still want his history, Josh, just in case. And that goes for you too, Penny, get as much on Ripley as you can. I have an awful feeling there's a lot more going on here than just burying an old mummy."

CHAPTER 12

While Jordan busied himself heating up a Cornish pasty, bought on his way home before making his call to Simon Travellian, Sarah Bolt was up to her old tricks at the Green Feather as usual. Irrespective of the plan to stifle her relentless fiction, she was determined to find more fuel for her ongoing saga.

She was sitting on her usual stool at the end of the bar, when DS Ward came in, and instead of his usual glance over towards the dartboard, he checked to see if she had arrived first. Smiling to himself, he walked over to her.

"What happened to you the other night, Charlie?" she said.

He nodded to the barman for their usual, "Sorry...I've been busy, and besides, I couldn't find anything other than what you already knew about Jordan."

"Yes...I did do well, getting an interview at last from the Commissioner."

"Well that last story of yours caused a real stir. Why did you have to pad it out so much? If you're not careful you'll tip your hand."

"Because, Charlie, headlines aren't enough. My editor want's more detail; and if I can't expand the skeleton story, then I'll have to go after Jordan."

"I thought the Commissioner did just that. Now the skeleton story has become an Egyptian mummy. Surely that's good for something."

The barman served their drinks, and she quickly downed half of hers.

"One day's news…that's what it's good for," she replied. "I either need more on the mummy, or something new on Inspector Jordan."

"I'm still digging. The police files have nothing you'd be interested in, so I'm checking with the Interpol records, but so far, I've drawn a blank…the man's a complete mystery. It's as if his records have been wiped clean."

Sarah could smell a story, and pushed Charlie to dig deeper. She played on his weakness for a pair of shapely legs, despite the jeers that were echoing from the group by the dartboard. His colleagues had all arrived, and serious practice was afoot.

"I can't be too obvious," he continued.

"Did you enjoy the other night?"

"Sure…who wouldn't?"

"Then I suggest you keep digging."

Back in Clifton-Beck Jordan was drowsing in his easy chair by the fire; his day must have taxed him more than he thought. After his conversation with Simon and the exciting discovery that he knew the Ayers Foundation, Jordan settled back in his easy chair with a tall glass and a bottle of his best whisky.

Before long, Jordan was staring into the fire, the tips of the flames glowed vivid blue against the sooted fire-back, causing him to remember what Jessie had said the last time they sat together in front of theirs: It was a sign of frost. It meant the night would be bitter cold. It meant a warm bed, close encounters and falling to sleep in each other's arms.

Not this night, or any night, Jordan thought, staring into the flames as the warmth started to sting his cheeks, and as the caustic sharpness of the twelve-year-old whisky dulled his senses, he poured himself another drink.

'Fire, Fire', he heard, and the azure blue sky suddenly became bright orange and vivid yellow. Then came the screams again, the sounds of splitting wood and crackling thatch. The acrid smell of choking, eye-watering smoke snatched at his throat: drying his breath, burning and chapping his lips.

Jordan should be on fire, but he was impervious to the engulfing flames, as he hacked at the collapsing veranda, and kicked down the blazing door; tearing at the smouldering fly-screen, to get at the screams within.

The screams sounded very real, horrendously real, until they stopped and there was nothing left, except the smouldering remains of his home.

There was a loud clink of glass and Jordan suddenly jumped. He could smell neat whisky, and he was suddenly awake. He felt wet, and his head was swimming as he attempted to shake the double vision from his eyes. Then he looked down and saw the bottle of whisky had slipped from his hand and was lying across his lap. He jumped again, grasping for the bottle.

His head was still spinning. He had no idea how many drinks he had, but he could smell the whisky that was running down the inside of his trouser leg. He sat for a moment with the bottle upright in his hand, looking for his glass. A smile crossed his face and he thought; it smelt better than burning thatch.

Jordan's heart was pounding, and he thought of Mark. He told him he had his nightmares under control, but it seemed he was wrong: unless it was the whisky. He held the bottle up. It was half-empty, and he wondered how much he had spilt. It only looked a small pool soaking into the carpet.

The next day Jordan woke to discover it was Friday morning; five days into their investigation, and despite the tight tourniquet around his head, he felt satisfied. When the Chief Superintendent twisted his arm to take on this case, he had his doubts, mainly because of the mess Inspector Dent had left. He had to start all over, create his own impetus, and once in motion, drive the clues towards a successful conclusion.

Here they were, one day before the weekend, and already he could smell the green fields of the college campus. He never thought of it as a paradise, yet it took only one week away to realise how much he missed its cloistered serenity.

Jordan tried to burst through the door, into the office with a gusto that would fill his two assistants with the fire to finish this case; instead, he winced at the sound of it crashing shut behind his back.

"I'm sorry to say this, Inspector," Penny said, as she turned away from the white-board, "but you look terrible. Are you coming down with something?"

"No, Penny…it's just a hangover."

"Oh dear," Josh said, entering the conversation. "Tied one on did we, Boss?"

"I didn't tie one on as you say, Josh. It was a slow process. I started drinking by the warm fire, and instead of leaving the bottle where I should have, over on the sideboard, I had it next to my easy chair. One drink led to another."

"Sounds like you need company, Boss," Josh suggested.

"You might be right, Josh. But for the moment, the only cross I'm bearing is this case, and I'm beginning to find it a bit frustrating."

"But you've almost solved it, Inspector," Penny said.

"We have, Penny. Both of you have contributed immensely, and if I can get myself into a comfortable position behind this desk, I'm hoping our efforts this morning will push us still closer to that end."

Jordan had made up his mind that he wanted to go over the Home Guard files again. Although he trusted Penny's pedantic sense of detail, he knew from experience that prejudice could creep into any analogy without some form of control.

"So, Boss…what's on the agenda for today?" Josh asked.

It was Penny's turn to visit the County Records Office, in search of anything of interest on the fortunes of Mr Ripley, and Josh could suffer the claustrophobia of a few hours in archives; searching through the busy life of Jack Gallagher. First, Jordan thought he desperately needed a nice strong cup of tea.

Some time later Jordan glanced at his watch when he heard the door open, thinking it was one of his wandering apostles returning, but lifting his head to see, he caught a glimpse of dark blue and shiny silver buttons.

"All alone, Inspector," the Chief Superintendent called out, as he entered the room. "I expected it to be the other way around."

"If that was the case, Sir...why the call?"

"I was down the corridor seeing Inspector Dent, so I thought I'd pop in."

"Come to see if we've got any further?"

"Not really. For some reason your exploits seem to be common knowledge. I haven't found the leak yet, but he or she is doing a slap-up job."

The Chief Superintendent walked over to the white-board and stood for a moment studying it. "No further on from finding out why you have an Egyptian mummy on your hands I see. It's a damn good board; best I've seen in a while."

"That's due to Constable Willow, Sir. She's a stickler for detail."

"I can see that. And she's got to grips with the succession problem I see."

"I suppose that comes from being a strategist, Sir."

The Chief Superintendent continued inspecting Penny's notes, as if he was looking for something fresh to tell the Commissioner, and a sickening thought suddenly came over Jordan. They were wondering how the leak was able to know so much, when all the time it was here, on the wall, ready and waiting. The white-board was the indication to how far Jordan had progressed.

"The white-board," Jordan let out.

"I beg your pardon."

"It's the white-board, Sir," Jordan continued. "The leak gets the information from the white-board. Penny, sorry, Constable Willow makes sure it's brought up to date every night, so that we can make a quick start the next day."

The Chief Superintendent crossed his chest with one hand and held his chin with the other. "But all the departments use white-boards, and they leave them open all the time until they're finished."

"Yes, Sir...but they don't have anyone trying to undermine their case. I mean, Sir; no one's leaking information about Inspector Dent's new drug case. I'm sure the newspapers would give an arm or a leg for something like that. So why my piddling case?...unless it's me they're after."

"That's quite an accusation, Inspector."

"Have you a better idea, Sir?"

"Umm...I have to agree with you, it's a reasonable possibility."

"I've had no trouble with any of the other teams, Sir. In fact I've had no trouble with Inspector Dent...it's that Sergeant of his, DS Ward."

"Okay, Inspector. I'll keep an eye on him. But mind you, I won't make a move unless I have some substantial evidence."

"I wouldn't have it any other way, Sir."

Before the Chief Superintendent could say another word, they heard voices outside, and the door opened. It was Josh and Penny, they looked red faced and cold, and Penny was shaking her umbrella, until she saw who was with Jordan.

The Chief Superintendent let out his usual grunt of satisfaction, "Keep me informed, Inspector. This is the end of your first week, you've done well."

"Thank you, Sir," Josh said brazenly.

The Chief Superintendent looked over towards the other two.

"Yes...All of you...well done," he continued, nodding his head as he moved sideways passed Penny, who stood paralysed by the door.

"These inspections are getting a habit, Boss," Josh said, removing his coat.

"Are you going to stand there all day, Penny?" Jordan asked.

"Oh sorry, Inspector; I get a bit flustered when I see all those pips."

"I see," Jordan said, "You haven't been out of uniform that long."

"It feels a long time, until I see them again. Even the desk Sergeant sends shivers down my spine when I see him."

"Are you sure that's not love, Penny," Josh said.

"Oh you...he's old enough to be my father."

Jordan smiled at their bantering as they settled themselves back at their desks, until the point of what she said sank in. Then he realised that applied to him as well; he also was old enough to be her father. Yet that first day when she smelt of Jasmine like his Jessie, age had nothing to do with it.

He shook his head, and came back to the reality that it was raining again, and looked over towards the window behind Penny's desk, and saw the heavy drops blowing against the glass. "Looks like you just made it back, Penny," he said.

"It was heavy like this for a moment outside the County Records Office, so I stood for a while under the arch. Then it stopped, well...enough for me to get back to the office. I'm afraid I didn't do very well, Inspector."

"That's all right. If there's nothing to be had, that's that."

"Oh I didn't say that, Inspector. I found out when he got his money."

"Is that so?" Jordan said as she brushed a damp tress away from her face, and collecting her notebook, she walked over to his desk.

"Shall I go first, Josh?" she said, obviously respecting his rank.

"Go for it, Penny," he said, checking the files he brought back.

She turned to Jordan. He was leaning across his desk on his left elbow with his hand supporting his chin, while the other was poised with a pencil to take notes.

"As we thought," she started. "Ripley was a shadowy man. I found a record of him as an Army regular in France. It lists him as wounded like the Lieutenant, except that didn't occur until he reached Dunkirk. Apparently, his injuries happened on the beach. I couldn't find any more, Inspector until his will in 1976. Would you believe his estate was worth over eleven thousand pounds?"

"Good heavens," Jordan let out, making a note and underlining it, "Did you find out how he got that much?"

"No...but the bank was his executors. The woman at the main desk allowed me to use her phone and I rang them, but the manager was not very cooperative; to put it mildly, he said he would only speak to my superior. Although I did manage to find out that a sum of fifteen thousand was paid into Ripley's account back in 1940; he couldn't remember the date," Penny added.

"If that's so, how could he remember the amount; it wouldn't be that unusual an amount to him."

"He said, Ripley first offered him the money during one of their Home Guard meetings; he was a member also. It was all in cash: in a scruffy carrier bag. He wasn't sure at first, and he told him to bring it around to the bank. And listen to this, Inspector," Penny seemed excited. "He said, as Ripley was a friend of Gallagher, and knowing Gallagher's reputation, he had to think twice about taking his money."

Jordan laughed, "But he did."

"Yes, Inspector," she agreed.

"They're more crooked than the crooks, if you ask me," Josh said.

"Is that so, Josh?" Jordan snapped. "And what did you find out?"

Josh scooped up the files he brought out of the archives and took his place in front of Jordan's desk. Penny moved over to the white-board and picked up one of the pens, before she referred to her notes again.

"Hold-up on the board, Penny," Jordan said. "I'll explain after we learn about Gallagher. Go on, Josh…what did you find out."

"Well, Boss…the only way I can describe Gallagher is, he was a nasty piece of you-know-what. The sort that had to be a bully at school: always taking the easy way out…a proper B…if you know what I mean."

"Yes, Josh…I'm afraid I do. What about his record?"

"Ah…He has form going way back. He was born in Nottingham to a single mother who died when he was seven. No known father, and from that point on he was in and out of homes and institutions. It seems, from his petty offences like shoplifting and wilful damage, after losing his mother it was down hill all the way.

"You can see by the thickness of his file, how many crimes he was involved with. As soon as he was of age, he served his first prison sentence of eight months, and on his release, he graduated onto breaking and entering. From then on most of his sentences were no more than six or ten months. He was small-fry, a nuisance more than a major criminal, so when the war came along he was let out on parole, provided he worked in a selective industry or the Home Guard."

"So he was only a small-time crook?"

"Yes, Boss. As I said, it was all petty stuff until he went to prison."

"Umm..." Jordan mused. "The perfect stooge, easy fodder for a mastermind: someone who planned the whole thing and took the lion's share. It must have been quite a haul for Ripley to do so well, and we can assume Gallagher did better. But why was he killed?"

"Hold on, Boss!" Josh interrupted, "That's one big assumption."

Jordan became impatient with Josh's constant snipes.

"You've got to have assumptions in our game, Josh. Without them, you can't move forward. Assumptions lead to clues, and you know where they lead."

"Yes, Boss, but...we're supposed to be tying up loose ends, not finding new ones. Penny is just about to add Ripley and Gallagher to the board, now you want us to look for a mastermind. I thought this was an accident?"

Jordan looked thunderous.

"Did you pick it up, Penny?"

"What, Inspector?"

"Well what have you two been doing for Christ sake," Jordan snapped, sitting bolt upright and focusing his attention on both of them. "As soon as I read that newspaper report, criticising the validity of the accident, it set me wondering. Why did the lorry burst into flames, why was it totally gutted and why have we found the Egyptian mummy, unburnt I might add, when it was inside a coffin," their faces were still blank. "And...how did Ripley come into a large sum of money about the same time, and Gallagher was killed with a live grenade; which, by all accounts, he should not have had."

Josh noticed Jordan was now looking at him. "I must admit, Boss...putting it like that...it does sound pretty fishy."

CHAPTER 13

Even though Simon Travellian had all day to mull over Jordan's information about the shipment of artefacts, Jordan was surprised to get a call from him so soon.

Apparently, with the right approach, Simon's contact at the Ayers Foundation was most informative. So much so, Simon just had to show Jordan what he had found, and invited him down to his home for the weekend.

Despite his suggestion that Jordan should drive down to London that night and make a long weekend of it, Jordan had to decline. Rather than explain the hangover that was still gnawing at the back of his head, Jordan just said he hated driving long distances, and he would take the early train in the morning.

Jordan hated to admit it, but the inquisitive part of him wished he had left that night. He got no sleep, waiting for dawn to arrive so that he could make an early start; and when he did, he had to contend with the seasonal fog and pouring rain. Yet another part of him said it would all be worth it; he had time to dry off in the heated carriage, and before long, if Simon was true to his word, Jordan should know the identity of The Sherwood Forest Man.

Once in London, Jordan decided to take a taxi to Notting Hill instead of the underground, and before long he was looking over towards a row of swank Edwardian terraces his friends Janet and Simon called home.

A two-storey terrace, with a self-contained basement apartment they rented out to help with the mortgage; and a good-sized attic above each of the two front bedrooms upstairs. There was no front garden, only a wrought-iron railing running between each set of arched steps up to the pillared front entrance.

The arch covered the small basement alley that ran the full length of the terraces, separated only by a small wrought-iron gate for privacy, but still allowing access to the services. According to Simon, the basement rooms used to be the servant quarters in the days when the affluent lived within a carriage ride of the city.

As Jordan retrieved his overnight bag from the front compartment of the taxi, and leant across to pay the cabby, he heard his name.

It was Simon standing at the front gate, "Jethro," he called again, "You made good time then. Was it a pleasant journey?"

"Yes," Jordan said, crossing the narrow side lane the terraces were in, "I can't remember the last time I was on a train...it was quite enjoyable. I missed my breakfast, and discovered there was a buffet only two carriages away."

"Here, let me help you with that," Simon said, grabbing his bag. "I'll drop it in the hall for the moment; Janet's dying to see you."

As Jordan climbed the steps to the front door, an uneasy feeling of expectation came across him, just as it always did when he met Janet.

Simon was a good friend, but he was naïve and too trusting, Jordan thought, remembering how Simon first met Janet when she was Jordan's girlfriend at university. The three were inseparable, until Jordan decided he was sick of sociology and analysing people, and made the rash choice to join the police force. That's when he fell out with Janet, and Simon somehow fell into the routine of taking care of her.

She was like that. She overwhelmed people, especially those she loved. She drained them of their care and passion, and Jordan was too ambitious for her.

When Jordan left for Kenya and married Jessie the following year, he soon found he had forgotten Janet: or at least his love for her. She and Simon were distant memories, and he had a new life, a new wife and the signs of their first child.

Jordan was not to know at the time that within seven years, his life would collapse around him, and he would be looking to his friends again for support. It was not his intention to seek their solace: they thrust it upon him, and as he turned in on himself, they pulled him back, and rekindled old friendships.

That was one reason why Jordan moved to Leicester, and found all manner of excuses for not visiting them as often as he should. Without Jessie, he suspected Janet still had awkward feelings for him. Feelings, in latter years, that slowly evolved into a tendency to mother him.

"Jethro," she called out from the open door, "You naughty boy," she continued, opening her arms to greet him. "It's been too long between visits."

Jordan embraced her, and immediately felt the softness of a woman in his arms again, as she pressed her body up against him, squeezing him tightly, not wanting to let him go. And he not wanting to be let go.

Straight away Jordan noticed there was something different about Janet, and as he smiled at her and answered her pressing questions, he pondered on what it might be. Then picturing the last time he saw her, he suddenly realised what it had to be; she had matured, and in the process, had put on weight.

Since her days at university, she had always been a slight girl, painfully thin at times, as if she was slimming. She was a picture of prettiness: always smelling of Rosemary, with fair, silky long hair, and a fresh complexion envied by every girl on campus. Now she looked plump, even buxom by today's standards, and her complexion was vital and rosy, with the first ominous signs of age creeping into her eyes and around her mouth.

She now had the figure Jordan preferred, except in Janet's case, he suspected it was a sign of middle age. As she broke free from him, and turned to walk back into the kitchen, Jordan felt she had never looked more beautiful.

As he held her fingers at arms length before she broke free, he had to stop himself from looking into those deep blue eyes, the same ones he fell for all those years ago. He had to accept a lot had happened since those days at university.

As usual, Simon was naïve to the chemistry that reignited in front of him, "Come on you two," He called out, anxious to get Jethro's bag inside, and the door closed. "You can get to know each other again later."

"And guess what Jethro," Janet said, as she entered the kitchen. "I've got your favourite drink, and that fruit cake you liked so much."

Jordan smiled and attempted to look enthralled, but suddenly, all he could think of was a weekend of his favourite things, and that old urge to grab the woman he once loved, "Sounds just wonderful," he said.

Jordan had no idea why Janet thought he liked brandy and fruitcake while lunch was cooking. He had never had them in the past, or recalled ever telling her they were his favourites, and decided she was mixing him up with another beau.

All Jordan wanted to do was get on with Simon's news, but for some reason, every time he broached the subject, Simon moved on to something else. Jordan suspected Janet was responsible, saying, 'I hope you two aren't talking shop,' each time she caught them talking about anything other than the good old days. By the time lunch was ready, Jordan had given up trying to get Simon started and was resolved to let things take their course.

She poked her head around the door, "Lunch is ready," she said.

There were laughs all around, and the charade began.

It was easy to see a lot of planning had gone into the meal of roast beef, Yorkshire pudding and large plump, jacketed potatoes. Although it was one of Jordan's favourites, he was always surprised to notice, being a Yorkshire man, automatically meant he ate Yorkshire food.

Nonetheless, Janet's intention to make Jordan feel better fell flat on its face. The meal went over with more nervous laughter than any sensible conversation, and it soon became evident that certain subjects were taboo, which left little else to talk about, except Jordan asking questions and Janet answering them.

Despite her well-planned meal, Janet's effort to keep him happy had misfired, and he was furious. "That was a fantastic meal Janet," he said, wiping his mouth with a napkin. "And yes...all but a few nightmares now and then, I've almost forgotten about Jessie and the kids, the police are still putting up with me and I'm still going to see my Psychiatrist."

With surprised looks on their faces, Jordan stood up and left the room.

Janet followed Jordan and caught up to him in the lounge, just as he was about to sit down in one of the easy chairs. Her happy face suddenly looked sad, and her brow took on the frown of a question, "How are you really, Jethro?" she said.

"Don't go down that path, Janet...I'm coping all right."

"You don't look as though you are."

"Well I am. It gets harder when I'm with people who know, but I manage to overcome that," he looked into her eyes again, they were glazed over, and she looked as if she was about to cry. "I know you're trying hard to avoid things that might encroach on my sadness, but I'm used to that, so just be yourself."

"That's why you've neglected us all these years."

"Maybe...or maybe it's because I've been trying to build a new life for myself. Not very successfully, I admit, but I'm getting there."

"And there have been no women in that new life of yours?"

"I'm afraid not. I don't seem to attract women any more."

"You mean you don't go out looking for them."

"Whatever. I'm happy enough with my work."

"You can't do that all the time," Janet said, sitting on the arm of his chair.

"That's why I switched to teaching, before I was dragged into this police case."

Janet laughed, "I bet you're cursing me."

Jordan looked at her with a puzzled expression. "What a strange thing to say."

"Well you didn't come to see me. You want to know what Simon found out about the Ayers Foundation."

"That was my purpose...I admit."

"All right, Jethro, I'll make a deal with you."

"Sounds interesting," he mused.

"If I leave you with Simon all afternoon, I want your undivided attention for the rest of the weekend."

"Won't Simon have something to say about that?"

"Oh, Jethro," she said, slapping his arm and standing up, "Is it a deal?"

"Sure...I promise you my absolute attention."

As Jordan busied himself with a paper he found on the coffee table next to his chair, he heard the front door slam shut, and turning round to his right, he noticed Janet walking down the steps. Simon entered the room, went over to the window and watched her walk along the lane in front of the terraces.

"She's gone," he said. "I thought it was going to be tomorrow before I got a chance to speak to you about the mummy...then she changed her mind."

"Changed her mind?"

"Yes. She gave me explicit instructions not to talk shop until you had a chance to settle in. I mean old chap...you're only here for the weekend, how long do you need to settle in for Christ sake."

"Did you tell her that?"

"No...not in as many words."

"Sounds like you're hen pecked, Simon. You should have told her I didn't come to see her, I came to hear what information you have."

"Good God no, Jethro. If I told her that, I wouldn't get her out of the bedroom all weekend. She likes to think there's still something between you."

Jordan's mouth dropped open, "And you don't mind that?"

"I know it's not reciprocal old chum. You can't kid me that you've forgotten about Jessie and the children. It's written all over your face."

"Yes...I know. And I just told Janet that."

"Ah...so that's why she's gone out."

"Yes...and I have to warn you. She made me promise to give her my full attention if we get our business out of the way this afternoon."

"Okay. I can live with that. I'll get my notes."

Jordan decided to play it by ear. He did not intend to cause a rift between his two friends, and if things looked like getting out of hand, he could always get an early train back home. He suspected life in the metropolis was different from less sophisticated places like Leicester, but to what extent he felt he was about to find out.

Simon returned with his notebook and a handful of papers.

"What's that lot?" Jordan asked.

"This friend of mine, Greg Chapman, told me what he knew, and was good enough to let me have some copies of Ayers last expedition."

"So my Sherwood Forest Man is theirs...is he?"

"Ah...that I can't say; but it's a good bet he is."

Simon dropped the papers onto the coffee table between the chairs and went over to the sideboard. "What's your poison?" he said, dropping down a large central flap and exposing his drinks cabinet.

"Have you got some white wine?" Jordan said.

"Should have some here somewhere; Janet likes a tipple before bed."

Simon rattled amongst the bottles and brought out a Riesling. It was already open as he guessed, and he grabbed a bottle of whisky for himself.

Dropping the bottles down on the end of the table, he held out the other hand holding the glasses. "You don't mind a whisky glass do you?" he said.

"Anything will do. I've drunk out of china mugs before now."

Simon thumped into the other chair and put the glasses between them, and pouring a wine in one and a whisky in the other, he relaxed back in the chair with his arms stretched out, "What does this remind you of?" he said, with a smile on his face.

Jordan thought for a moment. It had to be significant; otherwise, Simon would not have mentioned it. Then he remembered: the university common room, when the teachers were engaged in other activities.

"The university common room," Jordan said.

"Right...I thought you'd forgotten for the moment. It took them ages to find out who was breaking into their cupboard and nipping their booze/"

"Yes...and old Baggers couldn't do anything about it. The church board wouldn't allow any drink on the campus. I remember threatening him with a letter to the Governor... that quietened him down a bit," Jordan boasted.

"I'll say," Simon chuckled, "Then he went and found a new hiding place."

"I know. I bragged I would find it...but I never did."

Simon took another gulp, finished his drink and poured another. He looked sad for the moment, "Those were the days old chum," he said.

"I'd go steady on the drink," Jordan said, sipping his wine. "We haven't started yet. I'd hate to think what Janet would say if she found you drunk when she got back. Probably blame me...'A bad influence as usual,' she'd say."

"I doubt it. It won't be the first time that happened."

Jordan suspected Simon's melancholy mood might get in the way of telling him all about the Ayers mummy and he slapped the arm of his chair, "Well...this won't get the tale told."

"Pardon?" Simon let out from his momentary lapse. "Oh...yes, sorry, Jethro." He took another drink, smaller this time, and reached for his notes. First, he pushed the pile of copies in Jordan's direction. "I don't need these. I copied them for you: background information, something for you to read on the train."

"Good...I'll do that."

"Now, Greg...that's my contact at the Ayers Foundation, he's one of those laboratory technicians. He does all the remedial work, looks after the antiquities... you know." Jordan nodded. "Anyway, when I told him about your find, he just about had a breakdown. He told his boss, Mr Lyle, and he in turn got onto his insurance company. There was mad panic for a while."

"Why contact the insurance company?" Jordan asked.

"I questioned that at first, until I was told they paid Professor Ayers a large sum of money in compensation for his loss; which meant they now owned anything that was found. Not that there was much chance of that, since it was all burnt."

"Until I came up with their mummy," Jordan joked.

"Exactly...Greg said when he got back to me, that it would devastate the Foundation if they had to pay that money back. That's why they let me in."

Jordan laughed, "I can understand why. They want you to prove my mummy doesn't come from their collection."

"I know," Simon agreed, taking another drink. "But I don't really know how I can do either; there's no real way of proving you found their mummy, without the wrappings, and the cartouche that's usually painted onto the outer lining."

"What's that?" Jordan asked.

"It's an oval with hieroglyphics inside denoting the mummy's name, rank and years of his life, or in the case of a Pharaoh, his dynasty."

"So that's why the wrappings were removed? I thought it was because they might have been burnt in the fire."

"Probably that too. They would have got rid of anything that might tie him in with the shipment," Simon said, shaking his head. "Anyway, I'm digressing. I don't know what the outcome of the introduction of the insurance company will be, maybe they'll contact your office, I don't know, but I did find out who the mummy was. Or might be...damn, I'll just have to assume the mummy is the same one sent to Nottingham in September 1940."

"The official manifest is included in with those copies. It covers some valuable paintings, statues and a collection of Ming pottery, and the coffin. Now that was something special. In fact it was Professor Ayers' one-and-only successful expedition."

"Is he still alive," Jordan asked. "I have a feeling I read that he died."

"He did...some time ago. Ayers went back to Egypt in 1954 to clear up the last of the Vizier's tomb..."

"Vizier?" Jordan interrupted.

"Yes...our mummy, Jethro, but I'll come back to him shortly..."

"I'll have to start taking notes," Jordan said.

"If you wish, but it's all in the copies...Anyway, Ayers and Naseby, and before you interrupt me again, Naseby was his partner from the beginning until Ayers died in 1955. He was in a mysterious car crash in Cairo."

"Mysterious?"

"Yes. The police suspected he was murdered, but were unable to ascertain whether it was a case of murder for gain, or he was just one of the statistics of the day: Robbers, religious fanatics...that sort of thing."

"That's very interesting," Jordan said, with a glint in his eye.

"It's all in those papers, Jethro, so get to it later...on the train."

Jordan laughed, "All right, Simon...I'll let you get on."

He glanced at the clock on the mantelpiece, "I'd better...her majesty will be back soon. Anyway, Ayers and Naseby went out to Egypt in 1924, but instead of looking for a Pharaoh in the Valley of the Kings, like Carnarvon and Carter, Ayers, who was the leader of the expedition, chose to search over towards Thebes, in amongst the tombs of the Notables. His reason for this was, he was not looking for valuables like the others, he wanted to learn about the people and their kingdom; and the only way to do that was to study the men who actually ruled the kingdom."

Jordan smiled, and nodded his head, "The Vizier's."

"Exactly... And the high priests, although in most cases they were the same." Simon looked back to his notes, flicked over a few pages and stopped, "Now...the coffin that was brought back from Egypt: the same one that was shipped to Nottingham, was that of a Vizier called Hykotep, and he was the high priest and advisor to the Pharaoh Horemheb.

He was responsible for the Pharaoh's treasury, his spiritual path through life, his major building projects and most interesting of all, the building of the Pharaoh's final resting place."

"He was a powerful man then," Jordan commented.

"One of the highest, until he was usurped by Ramses. That was before he became the Pharaoh himself. However, Hykotep still managed to amass a fortune."

"Was that part of the Ayers expedition?"

"No...despite finding out Hykotep had no heirs, they never found his fortune. Ayers was forced to leave Egypt when the Italian's crossed the border in 1939, and when he finally returned in 1948 to continue his dig, but the upheaval at the time forced him to return to England. As I said earlier, he didn't finally return to Egypt until late 1954, and within the year he was dead."

"What happened to Naseby?"

"Oh he continued. Although Ayers had managed to bring most of Hykotep's antiquities back with him in 1939, there was still a lot of fieldwork needed, and I gather Naseby was still hoping to come across the treasure. Apparently he wouldn't give up, and after his partner's death, he took on another partner, the father of the Mr Lyle I spoke of, and they started an export company in Cairo. Since the Egyptian restrictions, you could only do work in the registered site, and only with the Egyptian officials permission: hence the rationale in forming an Egyptian company."

"What happened to them?"

"Lyle had a funny end...almost the same as Ayers in fact. He died in a car crash somewhere around Andorra I believe. Naseby, I understand, is still alive. Barely that is, he'll be in his eighties now. Oddly enough, he was born in Nottingham, and I do believe he returned there when he retired. Bought a mansion I think."

"That's interesting," Jordan mused, "I'll look into that. By all accounts he looks as if he has a lot to answer for."

"I hope you're not thinking of going after him, Jethro. He's a very powerful man. Exporting antiquities from Egypt must have paid off, unless he found that treasure after all… and forgot to tell anyone."

CHAPTER 14

Darkness seemed to fall suddenly in the city, probably because its congestion masked the waning sunset. Back home in Clifton-Beck, Jordan could sit at his window for an hour or more and watch the sky gradually change from an autumn blue-grey to all the shades of orange through to indigo.

Here in Notting Hill it was like switching a light on and off. One minute they were mulling over the copies of Simon's information, and the next he was leaning over the end of his chair struggling to switch on the standard lamp. They had had a few drinks by then and the resounding slam of the front door sounded distant, but the message was clear: Janet was back, and they had better be finished.

Simon jumped, gathered up the bottles and glasses, and stored them back in the cabinet; then jumped back in his chair just as the lounge door opened.

"By it's warm in here with the door closed," she said, looking cold, "I hope you washed up the glasses Simon. It smells like a brewery."

"I'll see to them later dear," He said, looking round.

"Now my love, if you don't mind, while I get my surprise ready."

Simon's eyes rolled to the top of his head and he let out a weak sigh, as Janet took off her coat and jumped into his chair by the fire. She was carrying a plastic bag and she leant forward and brought out a brown paper bag.

She spread it open with her fingers and waved the bag in front of Jordan's face, tempting him to look inside, "Remember these," she said.

Jordan obliged her with a smile, surprised by what was in the bag. It was full of chestnuts, the type the street venders used to roast on open hot coals. She giggled excitedly, and raking the fire until she found some hot embers, she threw on a few nuts. Then she reached over to the lower shelf of the bookcase in the alcove next to the fire and brought out a board game. Like the nuts, she held it up for Jordan to see, and rifle his memory for a period he could hardly remember.

"When was the last time you played Monopoly, Jethro?" she said.

He shook his head, "I have no idea."

"Then it must have been when we were at university."

Jordan had to call upon all his reserves of patience and good will to indulge Janet's need to revisit the past. He thought the promise he made was to be nice to her over the weekend, and to accept her mothering, her passionate embraces and the hours of reminiscent conversations.

Despite Jordan's eagerness to get back home and sift through the new information Simon had supplied him with, he realised he was about to become eighteen again, and enjoy what he had with Janet and Simon.

They would spend there winter evenings together in the boy's room roasting chestnuts and playing Monopoly. It was an ongoing game: an intellectual game that seemed to go on forever and regardless of Janet being there for Jordan, Simon was always part of the activity. Janet had recreated everything, as if she wanted to return to that time, even down to the hot toddies in front of the fire.

When Simon returned with a poker and stabbed it into the flames, she poured out the same rum they had at university. When the poker was hot, Simon dunked it into each pewter mug until the contents sizzled, and it gave off a heady aroma.

As the evening progressed, Jordan easily fell in with Janet's charade, and he had the uncanny feeling she had played out the sequence of events many times before. It was not a difficult transition. The past years of repressed feelings, the guilt that he might forget Jessie and the children too soon and the terrifying thought that he may have grown used to a monastic existence, had left him cheerless.

Used to lying in on Sunday, Janet's early call came as a shock, and once again, she had everything planned. Her excursion started straight after a full, old-fashioned breakfast: the very same Mrs Haggerty of his lodgings used to serve up to her horde of young intellectuals. Simon must have told Janet about the bacon, sausage and eggs, with plates of fried bread, and mugs of steaming tea to follow.

As soon as they washed the dishes, they wrapped up for a day out in Notting Hill. Visiting the busy street market first, where they challenged the validity of the local antiques, bartered with vendors, screwed their faces up at the offer of jellied eels and sampled small china bowls of cockles in vinegar.

After an outdoor meal of fish and chips in a Bavarian style beer-garden, Janet headed for the park. It was a rude awakening for Jordan, bringing back so many memories, as he watched the children playing on the swings, until they passed the bowling greens, and Jordan's eyes really opened wide.

There in front of them was the most magnificent lake. It had everything: a small wooden pier and lines of moored rowing boats, just like the ones the three of them went on when they were at university. He recalled a warm summers day and fighting over whose turn it was to row. Jordan glanced at the other two. Janet had already secured a boat, while Simon just stood looking as if he was eighteen again.

There was a scramble for the oars. It was laughable; here they were, three fifty-year-olds acting as if they were young again. Jordan decided he had no desire to challenge Simon's eagerness to row, instead he settled back in the twin seat at the stern relaxing with Janet at the tiller, listening to the water lapping the sides. It was a gentle accompaniment to the squeaking oars, swivelling in the rowlocks, and Simon looked at ease, as if this was part of a regular regime.

The ducks scattered out of his path and somewhere in the park, Jordan could hear children laughing, a carousel playing and in the distance, the melodic strains of a brass band. A small island in the centre, crowded with foraging water birds, acted as a barrier to the different activities of the park, and as their small craft circuited its perimeter, they ventured into each quadrant of different sounds.

It was a short idyllic interlude. As the sun dropped behind the distant trees, a chill breeze fell across the lake and suddenly rippled the surface, sending the ducks scurrying for the shelter of the island. Janet shivered, and sadly uttered it was time they made for home. Simon nodded, and rowed for the pier.

By the time they reached the small row of terraced houses, the three adventurers had returned to normal. Little passed between them as Simon put a match to the fire, and Janet busied herself in the kitchen. Jordan had already packed his bag earlier that morning, including Simon's papers, and brought it downstairs and placed it in the hall by the door. Janet saw him, stopped a moment with a tray of tea dishes, looked resolved to his leaving and carried on into the lounge.

"What time do you want to leave?" she said, on her way back to the kitchen.

"There's a train about six, it'll get me into Leicester around eight," Jordan said, "I think that's late enough. I have a busy day ahead of me."

"Busy sorting out my new information...I warrant," Simon said, standing back from the fire. It was blazing now and he started adding the small knobs of coke from the scuttle in the hearth. "Five minutes should do it, Janet," he shouted.

She returned with a plate of thick slices of bread, placed it on the centre of the coffee table alongside the tea things, and left the large teapot down by the fire.

"My last concession to our past, Jethro," she said, reaching for the long fork Simon passed to her. "Do you remember toasting bread in your rooms?"

"I do," Jordan replied with a smile. "I remember everything we've done today Janet, thank you...it was a pleasant surprise."

"We've tried to keep the tradition alive, Jethro," Simon said, kneeling down by the fire and opening up a hot area in the middle. "It can be difficult in these modern times, but we try, and there are still a few old places about."

"Well it took me back…I can tell you. I haven't visited any of those experiences since our time at the university," Jordan mused.

"It's a pity you left so soon, Jethro," Janet said, placing a thick slice on the fork and handing it to him. "You might have had a different life."

Jordan stared into the flames and started toasting, "I don't regret doing what I did; only going to Kenya."

"You wouldn't have met Jessie then," Simon said.

"No…and she would still be alive."

"You don't mean that, Jethro?" Janet said, buttering the slice he finished, and passing him another. "You wouldn't have had those years, or the children."

"No…you're right," he said, turning back to the fire.

It finally came into the conversation. They had avoided the subject all day and everyone felt better for it. Jordan caught his train, after a few tears and vigorous handshakes, and as far as Jordan was concerned, that was the end of it. Although Janet's recreation of the past was an enjoyable interlude, it was not something Jordan would like to do too often.

He settled down to Simon's copies and immersed himself in the life and times of a powerful three thousand year old Egyptian Vizier.

The following morning, the last thing Jordan wanted to do was face the Chief Superintendent and listen to how well he did on the golf links that weekend. An ordeal he had to endure as soon as possible, if he wanted to find out if he was to proceed with the case.

Despite Simon's new slant on the evidence, he had finally identified The Sherwood Forest Man, and that was the Commissioner's aim. Would it be enough for the press, in particular, Sarah Bolt, or was she now interested in him. If he was clever enough, Jordan might substitute his own skin for one of the wealthiest skins in Nottingham. It was against his nature to embroil people in scandal, but he had the feeling Benjamin Naseby was overdue.

Jordan looked up at the Chief Superintendent's window as he stepped out of his car, instinctively feeling his eyes upon him. He pointed to himself and then stabbed his finger towards the grim face at the window, the Chief Superintendent nodded and walked back into his room.

"Good morning," Jordan called out as he came through his office door.

Josh and Penny were already at their desks and they looked up, surprised to see their boss so cheerful.

"Someone must have had a good weekend, Boss," Josh commented.

"Yes, Inspector," Penny joined in, "Tell us all about it."

"I'm afraid you'll have to be patient for a while yet. His majesty caught me arriving, and wants to see me post-haste," they frowned. "However, I have brought you a lot of reading matter," Jordan said, delving into his bag and retrieving the bundle of Simon's copies, "Have a read through, it's all about our mummy. I'm afraid we can't call him The Sherwood Forest Man any more. He's an Egyptian Vizier called Hykotep, and he served Pharaoh Horemheb, three thousand years ago."

"My goodness," Penny let out, and walked over to his desk.

"I suppose you want me to remember this lot, Boss?" Josh said.

"I don't know yet, Josh. This meeting may see us all out of a job."

The door to Phyllis's office was open, and she was sitting at her desk looking as if she had been waiting for Jordan to arrive.

"I hope you've got some good news, Inspector," she said, getting up and walking over to the Chief Superintendent's door, "He's been waiting for you."

Jordan gave the surprised woman a hug, "Phyllis...I think I might just make his day," he said, as she opened the door.

She looked at him suspiciously, and poked her head through the gap, saying, "Inspector Jordan's here, Sir...are you ready for him?"

"At last," Jordan heard, as he entered the room.

"Good morning, Sir," he said, and moved over to the desk.

"What?...Oh yes, good morning, Inspector," he replied looking up from a folder he had open in front of him, "I hope this isn't a wasted visit like last time."

"But, Sir...each time I call I manage to push the case that much further."

"I want a conclusion, Inspector...not an interim report."

"I have a conclusion for you, Sir. I think you can safely tell the Commissioner that the case of The Sherwood Forest Man has been solved."

"It has?...good!" he said, looking at Jordan's bland expression. "Well...are you going to tell me, I'm not clairvoyant you know."

"Yes...sorry, Sir. I spent the weekend with my archaeologist friend, who I had looking into the likely sources of the Egyptian mummy, and he discovered the shipment to the estate near Sherwood Forest, where the lorry crashed. It belonged to the Ayers Foundation, which in turn led to the identity of the mummy in the coffin," Jordan noticed the blank look. "You did tell the Commissioner."

"Of course I did. That's why he said it wasn't enough without an identity that could be tied down to an owner."

"I don't remember him saying that, Sir."

The Chief Superintendent looked impatient, "No well… you're not the only one who can keep things to himself."

"I can't understand why, Sir."

"Never mind that…just get on with it."

"Yes…right, Sir. Well, you will be pleased to know he was a very important man back then. He was a Vizier to an Egyptian Pharaoh."

"Did you find out why he was buried?"

"No, Sir…but I have a good idea."

"So…why didn't you look into it?"

Jordan shook his head, "Sir, I was under the impression my task was to find out who he was. It would be a whole new investigation to track down the evidence of all that led up to his burial, and somehow I don't think you'd like the complication."

"What complication? Isn't it complicated enough?"

"Sir…I think you should tell the Commissioner and leave it at that. I'll go back to the college, and you can get back to life as usual."

The Chief Superintendent stood up, walked around his desk and confronted Jordan, "Do you think life will ever be the same again? I know that look, Inspector. You've dug something up, haven't you?"

"More like I've disturbed a hornet's nest, Sir."

The Chief Superintendent frowned, did an about turn and slowly circled his desk, "If I catch your drift, Inspector, you're giving me two choices: a quick chat with the Commissioner and that's the end of it, or this hornets nest you speak of."

"That's correct, Sir."

"You know bloody well I can't agree to the first without knowing the second, so you had better sit down and explain."

"Are you going to sit down, Sir?...I think you're going to want to."

"Oh very well."

Jordan composed himself. He spent part of his journey home last night rehearsing this very situation. He decided to keep it clear and concise. It was only a suspicion after all; and he had no idea whether his old mentor had any connection with Benjamin Naseby or not.

"Sir...Right from the beginning of this case, there have been far more questions than answers. At the root of each situation, regardless of the person involved, one name kept cropping up. He was involved with the original discovery of the mummy in Egypt, the transportation back to England, the shipment here during the war and I suspect, three murders in the process."

The Chief Superintendent almost choked, "You what?... Who?"

"His name is Benjamin Naseby, Sir."

The redness drained out of the Chief Superintendent's face, and he suddenly looked as if he was about to keel over. "Oh no, Inspector, it must be a coincidence. He just happens to be one of Nottingham's biggest benefactors. He supports most of the institutions, and countless local companies. Despite him being a recluse, he's a powerful man...he owns the Courier."

A stunned look crossed Jordan's face, "The Courier?"

"Yes. I gather he doesn't manage it any more, but he's still the major shareholder. And in a small place like this, that counts for a lot."

"How many coincidences do you want, Sir. Sarah Bolt works for the Courier."

"My God…that explains everything."

The Chief Superintendent stood up again and paced the floor.

"Can you see it now, Sir? As soon as Naseby heard we found his mummy, you can bet he told Sarah to muddy the waters. He wouldn't have to explain a thing to her, she's a natural pariah; he just had to say he was settling an old score. There was never a real story there in the first place, and with the help of the Commissioner, they closed that chapter in his life forever. There certainly isn't anyone else left to tell the tale, except his partner's son. And since he stands in line to inherit the lot, he's not going to say anything."

"The Commissioner…What am I going to tell the Commissioner," the Chief Superintendent exclaimed, "I'll wait for your report…that's what I'll do. We can't make assumptions like that without proof."

"That's just it, Sir, I don't have any."

"Then find some for God's sake. But whatever you do… tread carefully. As I said, Inspector, he has powerful friends. And that includes the Commissioner."

"I suppose you won't be contacting the college yet?" Jordan asked.

"Never mind the college…you just find me that proof."

CHAPTER 15

When Jordan returned to his office, he noticed Penny had moved her chair alongside Josh's desk and they were busy studying Simon's papers.

"You can start memorising that lot after all, Josh," he said, going over to his desk. "I think we're going to be here for a while yet."

"I thought we just had to identify The Sherwood Forest Man, Inspector," Penny spoke up. "And by the looks of this, that's just what you've done."

"It's a whole new ballgame now, Penny," Jordan said, walking over to the white-board and picking up the eraser.

Penny had already removed the pictures, but had not started copying the notes as Jordon asked, before deleting everything. As Jordan started cleaning the board with long sweeping strokes, she jumped up and called out, "I haven't copied those latest notes yet, Inspector."

Josh looked up from the papers, "That's all right, I can remember."

"Forget it, Josh," Jordan said, finishing off, "Everything's in the files if we need it. We're starting a whole new board," he picked up a red marker, "and instead of The Sherwood Forest Man, we have another man called, Benjamin Naseby," he wrote the name in large capital letters at the top of the board.

"I thought we weren't going to use the board again, Inspector," Penny said.

"That was because I found out the leak was using our board for his information," Jordan laughed, "This time I want him to find out. I want it to get back to that vixen Sarah Bolt. I want her to know we're investigating Benjamin Naseby,"

"Who's Benjamin Naseby, Inspector?" Penny asked.

"He's only Nottingham's richest man," Josh interrupted, "Sorry, Boss."

"That's all right. You're correct. You've obviously noted in the papers that Naseby has played a circumstantial part in every aspect of our investigation. I suspect, for some reason, he killed his partner professor Ayers to get control of the expedition into the Vizier's tomb. He killed, or had killed, the Home Guard soldier Jack Gallagher; and further down the track, killed his second partner, Willy Lyle."

"That's a lot of circumstantial guesses to prove, Boss," Josh said.

"And we haven't got any time to lose," Jordan said, turning back to the board and segregating it into three parts with two broad, downward strokes. He then chose a black pen and headed each section with a name: Professor Ayers, Jack Gallagher and Willy Lyle, "There," he said, "That should look interesting."

"What am I going to put under each name Inspector?" Penny asked.

"It doesn't really matter, Penny. It's bait. I want this to get back to Sarah Bolt, and in turn to Benjamin Naseby. Then we can sit back and wait for his reaction."

"And while we're sitting back, Boss, what do we do?" Josh said.

"Well there's not much we can do about Professor Ayers, except send a fax off to the Cairo police for a copy of their files. Who knows, we might get lucky. Spot something the Egyptians missed. As for Gallagher, it's too late to find out who substituted the grenade…but, I shall add the information to the board, as well as the others, just to let them know, we know," Jordan paused, studying Willy Lyle's name. "Willy Lyle might be different. The files on his accident, or murder in 1969 might still be open, that's only fifteen years ago. We could look into that."

"That still means we're going to be waiting for other people to do something, Boss, they might be too busy…or not bothered after all this time."

"True," Jordan replied, as he noted the main points of each incident on the board, "Penny…Lieutenant Cunningham took a fancy to you. Why don't you go round to his house and see if you can squeeze any more out of him about Gallagher."

"What am I looking for, Inspector?"

"How he got hold of a live grenade would be a good start. Then you can use that strategist's mind of yours to find out who gave it to him."

"All right," she said, returning to her desk and gathering her things.

"I'd ring him first. You know how busy he is."

As Penny checked the files for Cunningham's number, and the itinerary of his crowded day, Jordan turned to Josh and thought for a moment.

"Josh, I remember you telling me you could look at old newspaper reports on that Microfiche contraption at the library?"

"That's right, Boss."

"Well...how much of these papers have sunk in?"

"A fair bit, Boss...why?"

"Do you think you could remember enough about Willy Lyle's accident in that place...what did they call it?"

"Andorra, Boss."

"That's right. You could see if there are any newspaper reports."

"Actually, Boss...it was just outside Andorra. Apparently Lyle and Naseby set up their business in Andorra because it's a tax-free state; close to Spain and France; the accident was some distance away."

"Why those places?" Jordan said.

"I don't know, Boss...that's just what the papers said..."

"He's in, Inspector," Penny interrupted.

Jordan turned to catch her at the door, "Okay, Penny, do your best," then he turned back to Josh, who was checking the papers again.

"Anyway, Boss," he continued, "Andorra sits on top of the Pyrenees and there's only three ways out of the place: north to Toulouse, south to Barcelona and east along the mountain passes to Perpignan on the Mediterranean. And as it happened the accident occurred in one of those passes."

"Can you remember which one?"

"That's what I was checking on, Boss."

Josh continued flicking through the pages of information.

"Here it is, Boss...Pas de la Casa."

"Good. That should be enough to go on. Let's see how good you are on that machine, and at the same time I can have a look at that girl Penny was talking about."

"Oh she was in the County Records Office, Boss."

Meanwhile, Penny managed to find her way back out of the city to Lieutenant Cunningham's old converted Priory. As she turned around in the drive she noticed the curtains moving in the large front window, and by the time she stopped and grabbed her briefcase off the back seat, a beaming old face looking through her windscreen confronted her.

"Good morning young lady," the Lieutenant said, as she stepped out of the car.

"Good morning, Mr Cunningham. I hope this isn't too much of an inconvenience. We're tying up a few loose ends."

"Does that mean you've solved the case then?"

"Almost. The Sherwood Forest Man has turned out to be an old Egyptian mummy...very important by all accounts."

"The Sherwood Forest Man?"

"Yes...sorry, that's the case name we gave him."

The Lieutenant took Penny's arm and led her towards the house, and once inside, he directed her into the kitchen, "You don't mind interviewing me in here do you dear, only it's a bit cold this morning, and the old grate that I use to heat the water keeps the place nice and warm. I've just made some tea, would you like a cup? And there are some biscuits on the table...or I have fruit cake if you'd rather?"

Penny remembered the Inspector's comment on how this man talked, 'Non-stop' was his actual phrase and she sat down at the long refractory table in the centre of the room, "I'd love a cup of tea thank you, and biscuits will be fine."

He looked cheerful, pleased to have company, and pottered with the cups on the dresser top next to the grate. As soon as he finished he brought a tray over to the table, and after setting out the dishes, he went over to the grate where the teapot was warming on one of the hot plates.

"There you are...shall I be mother?"

"Please do," Penny said, as she opened her coat and unzipped her briefcase.

As soon as the Lieutenant had poured the tea, he sat down opposite her, waited for her to sugar hers, and select a chocolate biscuit.

"My wife liked chocolate biscuits. They were her only concession to a little bit of luxury. The Army pension isn't that big you know; that's why I supplement it with my jobs in the city. They're not too taxing, and they help pay the rates and the like," He laughed. "Silly really...Here I am being paid by the state, and I have to pay it back to them in rates and rent; quite ridiculous."

"I thought this was your own house Lieutenant," Penny questioned.

"Oh no...it's a trust house. I just look after it, and I pay a miniscule rent. It's like one of those estate houses that belong to the Dukeries."

"Dukeries?" Penny said.

He laughed again, "I don't think you have time for me to explain our Feudal system to you dear, it's quite complicated."

Penny suddenly realised she had been distracted from the purpose of her visit, "Then I had better get on then, Lieutenant," she said, taking out her notebook.

"Do you know I actually like being interviewed? It makes me feel important. That's the other reason why I go out to my little jobs. I get all sorts of people asking me questions. And if I can give them an answer, they look so pleased, and I feel as if I've done something good...I feel important again."

"Well I'm glad, Lieutenant," Penny replied. "Now...down to my questions."

"Fire away dear lady."

"Right. Can you remember the grenade practice, Lieutenant?"

"I certainly can. Only because it was a regular part of the Home Guard regime. I can't remember a specific occasion though."

"Oh dear. I was hoping you might remember the day Jack Gallagher died."

"I remember that day, but I'm afraid it was because he was our only death. I didn't witness the accident myself...I was in London that day, visiting our national HQ."

Penny looked particularly disappointed. "The Inspector thought you might have been able to throw some light on the live grenade, since he found out that the Home Guard only used dummies."

"That's true...I recall questioning it myself with the depot that supplied the ordnance. Most remiss of them I said."

"Yes...we have that report in the papers you loaned us."

"And you will have noted that the Sergeant of Arms at the depot said it was possible that a live grenade could have got mixed up with the dummies on the delivery lorry. Sometimes they dispatched both types together."

"Would it be possible for someone to bring a live grenade into the camp?"

The Lieutenant studied her question for a moment, sipping his tea, "I suppose anything would be possible back then. We had a security check of sorts, but their hearts weren't in it, they weren't professionals you see. A few of the old ones looked upon their function in the Home Guard as a duty...

mind you they were proud of it. But the others...they were just a bunch of malingerers."

"So there was no one to check the grenades?"

"Oh I didn't say that. When we were doing anything that was dangerous, either Sergeant Fletcher or myself conducted the manoeuvre. I'm surprised really. All live ordnance was marked...unless..."

"What, Lieutenant?"

"I just had a terrible thought. Someone could easily have scratched the mark off. It was only a small spot...everyone knew what to look for."

"Does that mean your guards were lax?"

"I'm afraid so. As I said, they were not professionals, they were not looking for enemies within, and they did not expect a German invasion. Being a professional myself, I built in certain safeguards. In the case of handling armaments and the issue of ammunition, I made sure each man signed a munitions book. That way I could keep track of the movement of materials."

"Was that in case of theft, Lieutenant?"

"Oh yes. You have to understand, there were many subversives about at the time, and the chance of any of our material getting into their hands was a major worry. In fact...thinking about it now, I wouldn't be surprised if the switching of the grenade might well have been an action to disrupt the unit."

"But you knew all your men?"

"That's true...but remember I was in London on the day."

"But the Sergeant would have known a stranger."

"Yes...I suppose you're right. However, at the time, there was an exchange of personal from other units, and my intension was merely to register their attendance. Also there were certain government allowances, as in the case of Jack Gallagher; on assignment from prison."

"So…as long as they had a uniform, they got passed the guard."

"I have to admit that was a possibility."

Penny studied what she had just noted down and finished the biscuit she was trying to eat, "What about this register you kept?"

"I still keep them. Would you like to see the one for that period?

"Yes please," Penny said, picking up her cup.

The Lieutenant went over to a bookcase, bent down unsteadily to the lower shelf, and after running his finger along the dusty spines, he pulled out the one marked 1940. It was not unlike a school exercise book with the old watermarked cover, and back at the table, he opened it and flicked through the pages. Stopping at one particular page, he read a few lines to familiarise himself with that day, to make sure it was what he was looking for, and slid it across the table to Penny.

"Here we are…the munition roster list for the day Gallagher died."

Penny looked down the list of seven names. The first she recognised was Gallagher's, and then Edgebaston, but the others meant nothing to her. Then she refocused on the last name. It rang a bell, she had seen it somewhere recently, but for that moment, it eluded her.

"What's this asterisk for?" she said, pointing to the name in question.

The Lieutenant leant across the table and turned his head, "Oh that…it's my legend for a visitor from another unit."

"Visitor?"

"Yes," he said, sitting back in his chair. I forgot to include those. As I was trying to explain earlier, our units were not that professional, in fact, usually the local bank managers and butchers managed them...the local bigwigs so to speak. So the government arranged training and lectures with the units like mine that did have a regular overseeing them." he let out a laugh. "My training methods got plenty of interest, I can tell you, and this Corporal Lyle was one of them."

As soon as she heard the name, unlike reading it, she remembered Benjamin Naseby's partner, Willy Lyle, and the detail of his death in a car crash outside Andorra; the very accident the Inspector and Josh were investigating at that moment.

She felt a sudden feeling of elation. As the Inspector had suspected, all these deaths had too close a connection to be a simple coincidence, and now the link with Gallagher's death, and the certain prospect that Lyle had switched the grenades.

Penny was anxious to get back. She glanced at her watch and the Lieutenant did the same. It was later than she thought, almost time the Lieutenant left for his first job in the city.

"Any chance of a lift dear?" he said.

"Yes, I'll wait till you get ready. No rush."

As Penny waited for the Lieutenant, she wandered out into the hall and into the sitting room. She walked over to the window and looked at the garden she admired so much the last time she was here. It was a large sash window, and from its lofty position, she could see beyond the top of the hedge that formed the boundary at the front of the property. As she ran her gaze over the roofs of the parked cars on the main road, she suddenly became curious.

On her way through the city from Prescott Lane, she had noticed a green car following her. It turned when she turned, sped up to catch the lights and stayed with her all the way out of the city. Suspicious, Penny pulled into the next car-parking bay and watched the small green car turn off to the right.

As it turned she managed to get the last numbers on its plate, and she scribbled them down on the corner of the newspaper on the passenger seat. She waited for a few moments, and when she thought the road was clear, she continued on to the Lieutenant's old priory.

Here it was again, unless she was becoming paranoid.

"Mr Cunningham," she called.

"Yes dear, I'm ready," he said, entering the room.

"No...it's all right. I wasn't chasing you. I just wanted to know if you knew who owned that green car parked outside your house. Is it a regular?"

"Where dear," he asked, changing his glasses.

"There," she pointed, "just behind the Land Rover."

"Yes...I see it. The Land Rover belongs to the man next door, but I haven't seen the green car here before."

"I see," Penny said, walking away from the window. "Just wait here for a moment while I check it out."

"What's wrong dear," the Lieutenant said, but Penny was gone.

Penny had to know if the green car was the one that followed her out of the city. She had no intention of another cat and mouse drive back to the station.

Unfortunately, the gravel drive was no help to her covert approach to the entrance on the main road. She became aware of a movement behind the hedge, heard a car door slam and saw the car backing up to leave its parking place.

It was the same car, Penny was sure of that; as she got a good look along the side of the Land Rover before she edged along its front. She took out her warrant card, and holding it up in front of her, she intended to present herself to him as he pulled around the Land Rover. She readied herself to shout stop.

As Penny cautiously moved forward, she had not considered the Land Rover's height, and neither did the driver of the green car. He swung out into the oncoming traffic, stopped a second, and then dashed out into the next gap.

By now, Penny was poised on the corner of the Land Rover's right wing, ready to step out and brandish her card.

His eyes were on the traffic, and he was in a hurry to get away before she saw his number, or worse still: got a look at his face.

She stepped forward, thinking the green car was still paused to move, but found to her horror he was on top of her.

The Lieutenant saw everything.

When Penny rushed out of the house with, what sounded like an exciting arrest, he followed her and stopped at the top of his drive. Everything happened so quickly. One minute she was crouching behind the front of the Land Rover, and in the next instant, he stood horrified, watching her flying through the air.

The green car came out from behind the Land Rover just as Penny stepped forward with her card in her hand. Its left side caught her right hip, spun her around and tossed her across the drive like a rag doll, where she collided with a large tree, and slumped in a heap at its base.

The Lieutenant dashed back into the hall, dialled 999 for an ambulance, and by the time he reached her crumpled body, the green car had left the scene. Crying, the Lieutenant reached over to the small piece of plastic lying on the ground, it was her warrant card, and he gently slid it back inside her coat pocket.

CHAPTER 16

Feeling like a spare wheel, Jordan went to look for a drinks machine, whilst Josh scanned through the papers popular in Andorra and southern France at the time. Their biggest problem, should they be successful, was reading the reports that most likely would be in Spanish or French. Jordan had a smattering of French from his time in Africa, and Josh said he was good with Spanish. As it turned out, the Spanish was in an unusual Andorran dialect.

When Jordan returned, he found Josh had fulfilled his boast. He tracked down various reports from Spanish and French sources, and was in the process of copying each paper before he moved on to the next.

"How do you know if they're what we want?" Jordan said, over his shoulder.

"Does it matter, Boss? They're all full of the names we're after, and they talk of a crash on the Pas de la Casa."

Jordan started reading the French copies, and immediately spotted the names of Willy Lyle and Benjamin Naseby. They appeared lengthy reports, not only covering the accident itself, but also going into their offshore activities. Despite his rusty colonial French, Jordan soon realised they were suspicious of the English company that was using Andorra as a tax haven.

In one paragraph, the reporter dealt more with their shady exports of valuable antiques, than the accident itself.

"In spite of my shaky French, Josh, this stuff is pretty damning," Jordan said. "We seem to have picked on a pet grievance, according to the French."

"Not unusual for the French, Boss," Josh replied, still copying the Andorran papers account of the accident.

"It seems to centre around their export of Egyptian artefacts...French archaeologists apparently got their noses put out of joint," Jordan commented.

"This looks good as well, Boss...what I can make of it," Josh said, squinting at the screen, and jotting the words he could not understand, down in his notebook.

"I thought you could speak Spanish fluently?"

"I don't think I said fluently, Boss. This stuff's all in some kind of dialect."

"Copy what you can. What we don't know we can get translated."

"Inspector Jordan?" a female voice called out.

They looked back towards the counter. A young woman was calling Jordan's name as she walked down the row of Microfiche machines.

"Inspector..."

"Here," Jordan called out.

She smiled at him and quickened her step, "There's a call for you up stairs, Inspector...it sounded urgent."

"What now," Jordan said to Josh, "You carry on here while I see who this is."

"Right, Boss."

Jordan finished his drink, tossed the cup in the nearest bin and followed the young woman up the stairs. She half turned as he caught up to her.

"You're the first policeman I've seen in the library."

"Is that so," Jordan replied. "Do I sense a question in there somewhere?"

"Oh no, Inspector…I was just pointing out that the library was a strange place to dig up clues; if that was the purpose of your visit."

"I agree. But now we've found your Microfiche room, I think you might see us a lot more often in the future."

She stopped at the top of the stairs, turned to face Jordan, and gave him one of those promising smiles. "I look forward to that, Inspector," she said, as she pointed over to the counter on his right. "The phone is on the end of the counter, Inspector. If you press nine, it will connect you to the outside caller."

When Jordan got through, he learned it was Sergeant Fawcett on the other end. He sounded excited, hardly making any sense.

"Hold on, Sergeant," Jordan said, "what's that about Constable Willow?"

"Sorry, Inspector…I really liked the girl."

"What do you mean, you really liked the girl? What's happened?"

"She was knocked down by a car on the Thorsby main road, Inspector."

"My God…where is she?"

The Sergeant's use of the past tense horrified him.

"They took her to the General, Inspector. I gather she's on the operating table as we speak. I've notified the Chief Superintendent."

"So she's alive then?"

"She is…just."

"Did it happen at Lieutenant Cunningham's house?"

"At the bottom of his drive, Inspector; the old man's in a right state."

"Is he at the hospital?"

"No…He wouldn't leave the house. The medics took care of him there."

"Good…I want to question him."

"What about Constable Willow, Inspector?"

"I'll send Sergeant Crosby."

"Where will you be if I need you, Inspector?"

"I need to see the crime scene. We have to get as much as we can on the car."

"I already have an accident team there now, Inspector."

"And I'm sure they're doing a good job, Sergeant, but I have to see for myself and find out what happened from the Lieutenant before he forgets. I can't do anything at the hospital if Constable Willow's in surgery, and if she does come round, Sergeant Cosby can question her."

"I don't think you'll get much out of her today, Inspector."

"Probably not."

"Good luck then…all the old man kept muttering was it was a green car, according to the Constable. No number plate or driver description."

"We'll get him. Thanks, Sergeant…must go."

As Jordan put the phone back, he had to stand for a moment and stop himself from shaking. He had no idea why, but he was suddenly feeling the same pain he did when they told him his wife Jessie and the children were dead.

Barely composed, Jordan sucked in a deep breath and made his way back to where Josh was deeply engrossed in the story of another accident, or in both cases, fowl play. Apparently, the story had occupied the papers for several days.

"Boss…look at this," he said, when Jordan approached, and he saw his reflection in the screen, "Guess whose car Lyle was driving when he crashed?"

Jordan could not answer. Josh looked back from the screen. He could see something was wrong straight away. The man he thought of as hard and self-occupied, looked on the verge of crying. His eyes had glazed over, and he was finding it difficult to compose himself.

"Boss…What's wrong? Who was on the phone?"

Jordan swallowed deeply. He knew time was of the essence, and he took in another deep breath, "Collect up the papers quickly, we're going."

"You didn't answer me, Boss?"

"It's Penny."

"What about Penny?" Josh was worried now.

"She's been knocked down by a hit and run."

"Knocked down?"

"Do you have to keep repeating everything I say?"

"Sorry, Boss…but you're not making much sense."

Jordan grimaced, "She was knocked down by a green car outside Lieutenant Cunningham's house…is that clear enough for you?"

Josh looked down at the pile of paper and scooped it into his hands, "Yes, Boss…let's go…which hospital?"

Jordan took hold of Josh's shoulders, "Sorry, Josh. She's in the General."

Back at the car Jordan felt composed enough to tell Josh what he planned, "I'm going to drop you off at the hospital, while I go and see if I can make any sense of what the Lieutenant saw before he forgets."

"What about Penny, Boss?"

"It won't do her any good if we're both sitting waiting for her to come out of Surgery. I need to get onto the crime scene before it goes cold."

"Don't you want to be there when she comes round, Boss?"

"I'll get there...okay?"

As luck would have it, the General Hospital was on the outskirts of the city, only a short distance from the Lieutenant's house. They had cleared the area in front of the old priory and the Accident Division was still busy investigating the scene.

Jordan parked further along the main road and walked back, slowly looking at the marks already sprayed on the road, where the green car hit Penny.

"Bad business, Inspector," Sergeant Morgan spoke out on seeing Jordan.

Jordan stopped in front of the drive, "Terrible business, Sergeant. Have you anything more on the car yet? Did you get any witnesses other than the Lieutenant?"

"The Lieutenant?"

"Yes...Mr Cunningham was a Lieutenant in the Second World War. He still likes to be referred to in that way."

"Oh...sorry, Inspector, I didn't know. And it's a negative to your question."

"Do you mind if I have a look around."

"No, Inspector, we've just about finished here."

Jordan nodded with a smile and passed the Sergeant as he entered the gravel drive. The first thing he noticed was Penny's car, "Are you taking Constable Willow's car back to the compound?" he called back to the Sergeant.

"If that's what you want us to do, Inspector."

"Just let me go through it, see if she left anything behind."

"I'll get one of the Constables to see to it, Inspector, if you can find the key."

Just as Jordan reached Penny's car, the Lieutenant opened his front door and stood at the top of the steps looking shaky, "What a catastrophe, Inspector."

"Go inside, Lieutenant," Jordan said, opening the car door, "I'll be in to see you in a moment. Go on...don't stand there shaking."

The old man turned around slowly and went back inside, leaving the front door ajar. Jordan knelt on the driver's seat and slowly cast his eyes around the interior. He had no idea what he was looking for, but thought she might have left something that she would rather he brought to her in hospital.

There was nothing. No clothing, handbag or briefcase she usually carried. Then Jordan tried to imagine what she was doing at the bottom of the drive without her car. She must have walked down to the front for some reason, in which case, she was not in the process of leaving. Maybe looking at the garden while the Lieutenant was getting ready, assuming she was giving him a lift as he did on the first occasion; it was about the same time.

In that case, Penny must have left her bag inside the house, and the key would still be inside; it was not in the ignition. As Jordan eased himself up off the seat, he noticed the small pen she used to make notes. It was lying in the folds of a newspaper, and when he picked it up to return it to her bag, Jordan caught sight of the large scrawl on the white area at the top of the page.

He turned the paper around and saw it was three numbers: eight, nine and seven, and he suddenly realised they might well be the numbers of the car.

"Constable," he called out as he got out of the car.

"Yes, Inspector. Can I take it now?"

"Not just yet. I have to find her bag for the key, I think it's inside. But I found this on her front seat," he passed the young man the paper." You'll see there's three numbers scrawled on the margin. They look as if she wrote them while she was driving, probably couldn't get the letters. Give it to Sergeant Morgan, it might be important...you never know."

"I'll do that straight away, Sir, while you get the key."

When Jordan stepped into the house and headed towards the sound of clinking dishes in the kitchen, he had no idea the Lieutenant was so upset. He said he was making a cup of tea, the panacea of all ills, but as far as Jordan could see, he was just going through the motions.

"Oh, Inspector...how terrible," He uttered, as soon as he saw Jordan in the doorway, "She was just about to take me into the city when it happened. It's terrible... Absolutely terrible...Is she all right?"

Jordan walked across to him and touched his shoulder, "We have no news at the moment. Apparently she's still in the operating theatre."

"I'm not surprised," he said, sitting down. "I've seen a lot in my time, Inspector, but I never saw anyone fly through the air like that. She..."

"Lieutenant," Jordan interrupted. "Please...don't fill your mind with such things. I want you calm and collected. I want your professional, military eye for detail, and that acute sense of recall you keep telling me about."

He jerked his head back and took on the manner of a military man again, "I understand, Inspector...but it's all a blur really."

"No it isn't. You just think it is. So let's go over what took place a piece at a time...you'll be surprised what you can remember."

"Well...she said she would give me a lift...just like you did, Inspector. She was putting her notebook away in her briefcase. It's still there where she left it."

Jordan looked down at the small plastic pouch. He unzipped it, took out the notebook and zipped it up again, "Damn!" he exclaimed, seeing her bag alongside, "I forgot about her key."

Jordan opened her bag, and rummaged through the usual rubbish filling the bottom of her bag, but no key. Then he had the awful feeling she might have been carrying it in her coat pocket, until he noticed the small zipped pocket in the lining, and opened it. There, inside, were two sets of keys: a large bunch that obviously looked like house keys and another hanging from the arrowhead key-fob he gave her. He laughed, then rushed out to the waiting Constable.

"Sorry, Constable," he said, "I had a job finding them."

"That's all right, Inspector. By the way, I gave the Sergeant that newspaper with the numbers on, he's passed them on to Registrations."

"Good...Now take Constable Willow's car back to Prescott Lane."

"Is there anything you want me to say to Sergeant Fawcett, Inspector?"

"No. I have the feeling he'll know more than I do. Just give him the Constable's keys, and tell him I'll see him later."

As the Constable turned out of the drive, Jordan turned back into the house to finish his interview with the Lieutenant. By now, he had composed himself sufficiently to continue with the job he started, and Jordan sat down at the table again.

While the Lieutenant busied himself with the tea things, Jordan picked up Penny's notepad and slipped it into his inside pocket before he forgot, and at the same time, he pulled her bag and briefcase close to his arm. He had a lot to remember before he left for the hospital, not the least of all what she might need. However, that would have to wait.

The Lieutenant placed a cup of tea in front of Jordan, "Thanks," he said, "I could do with that," and sipped the hot sweet beverage slowly.

The Lieutenant sat down opposite, "How can I help, Inspector?"

Jordan opened his notebook, "Well the first thing I want to know is, where you were when the car hit Constable Willow?"

"As I started to say, Inspector, the young lady was waiting for me. She was looking out of the window, and she saw something."

"What was that?"

"I don't know really, except...she asked me if I knew who owned the green car outside. When I said I didn't, she told me to wait while she went out to check...I presume she meant the driver. I was curious, so I followed her as far as the front door, where I watched her walk down the drive."

"What happened then?" Jordan said, making notes.

The Lieutenant sipped his tea and studied the question with a far away look in his eye. "She looked as if she was creeping up on someone."

"Creeping...are you sure?"

"Yes, Inspector. You know how it is when you want to walk quietly, and you're treading on something noisy. You sort of crunch-up your shoulders and let your arms hang out from your body...as if you're saying, 'Be quiet.' But the gravel drive was against her," he shook his head and put his cup down. "Then the next thing I noticed, she was right up against the Land Rover."

"What Land Rover?" Jordan snapped.

"There was one of those big Land Rovers on the corner of my drive. It belongs to the man next door, and the police asked him to move it further along."

"I see...right, what then?"

"I couldn't see much, as you can see, there's a hedge in the way. One minute she was standing by the front wing of the Land Rover, and the next, she was flying through the air... terrible it was. And she hit that big tree on the opposite side of the drive, and crumpled down into a heap on the ground."

"I gather you went to see what you could do?"

"I did, Inspector. I know about first aid, but I could see straight away, her injuries were beyond my experience. I therefore made her comfortable before the ambulance arrived, checked to see if she had any bleeding wounds and her airways were clear. She was unconscious of course."

"Well, Lieutenant, I'm sure that helped."

"I hope so, Inspector."

"Did you see the car?"

"Yes. I could only see the roof from the window, when she pointed it out, but when he hit her and drove off into the traffic, I could see it was one of those small cars. It was green...apple green."

"Nothing else?"

"I don't think so, Inspector...It all happened so quickly."

"That's good...you've done well, Lieutenant," Jordan said, closing his notebook, "You never got your lift, do you want one now?"

"Oh no, Inspector, I couldn't go to work now. My mind's too full of the accident. Thank you all the same."

Jordan finished his tea, and placed his business card on the table, "I think that's a wise decision. Anyway…if you need anything, or recall any other details, give me a ring," Jordan said, poking his finger at the card. Then he picked up Penny's bag and briefcase, and made his way back to the front door.

The Lieutenant followed Jordan as far as the threshold, just as he had done with Penny, and watched Jordan all the way along the drive, where he hesitated for a moment; looking back at the old man. He looked lost as he lifted his hand in a timid wave, before he turned to go back inside, and Jordan continued around the hedge and back up Thorsby main road to his car.

CHAPTER 17

By the time Jordan arrived at the hospital it was dark, and as he made his way along the lighted corridors towards casualty, he wondered what he could possibly say to Penny that would put her at ease. He had to find out how bad she was first, so his first priority was to find the doctor on duty.

The Matron took exception to Jordan's point that police injured on duty should take precedent over other cases, especially when her superiors needed access. The doctor was with a patient and the deeply intimidating look the Matron was giving him said it all, and to make things worse, Josh was nowhere in sight.

Eventually Jordan found Penny's room. At least she was in a private room, not amongst those in the main ward, and a young, tired looking uniformed Constable was sitting by Penny's bed.

"Oh, Inspector," she said, looking up, "you've arrived at last."

"Does that mean anything in particular, Constable?"

"No…I mean, only that Sergeant Crosby has been pacing about wondering where you were, and telephoning the station every ten minutes."

"Is that where he is now?"

"No, Inspector...he went out for something to eat."

"I can't understand his problem. He knew I was at the crime scene."

"Apparently the phone there isn't working."

"I see." Jordan said, glancing over to the lighted bed and the small frail looking person lying there so still. All he could hear was the machine clicking, keeping pace with her heart and all the other parts of her it was monitoring, "Any news? I'm still waiting to hear from the doctor."

"We know nothing, Inspector. I think that's why Sergeant Crosby was so agitated. He asked the nurse several times, but she just kept saying she could only tell a relative, or her superior. No one's looked in on her yet."

"Well it can't be that bad then."

The door suddenly opened, and a young bushy haired man with black rimmed glasses poked his head inside the room, "Inspector Jordan?" he said.

"Here...are you the doctor?"

"Yes. I was here when they brought her in."

Jordan stood up and went over to the door and followed the doctor outside into the corridor, "So, doctor...how is she?"

"She's a very lucky girl," he said.

"I gather you can tell me the extent of her injuries, I'm her superior."

"Yes I can. We have to be careful you know; we get allsorts trying to find out about patients...I'm sure you're used to that, especially the media."

"Oh I know the media, have they been in yet?"

"Yes. A brash young woman I understand. She wouldn't take no for an answer until your Sergeant Crosby jumped in and escorted her from the building. She was screaming all sorts of abuse at him. But he got rid of her."

"Yes," Jordan laughed, "I'm sure he did."

"I wish I could handle women like that," the tired looking doctor said.

By now, they had reached the doctors office, and they went inside where it was more comfortable, and especially private. Jordan had a need to sit down. For some reason he suddenly felt quite dizzy.

"Are you all right, Inspector?" the doctor said, looking at him the way doctors do. "You don't look at all well."

"Too much happening all at once on top of an empty stomach. I have one almighty headache, but it will pass," he said, looking up. "You were saying."

"Ah yes. Where do I start? No major injuries, that's a good thing," he said, studying the folder he picked up off his desk, "a lot of small fractures, nothing serious, and a few cuts and abrasions. She did get a good whack on the head though: a tree by all accounts. It gave her a nasty gash on the side of the head, which we had to stitch. I don't think she'll be very happy with that, but we can look at it later. Then there's her left shoulder, her worst injury. She broke her scapular in three places, and we had to put a plate in it, that's why she was in surgery so long. I'm afraid you won't see much of her this side of six weeks."

"What about the other fractures? You said she had a few."

The doctor looked back at her papers again, "Ah yes... they all seem to be adjacent to the left, top side of her body; probably where she came in contact with the tree. Other than the bad breaks in the shoulder blade, she had small fractures in her wrist and forearm on the same side, one on her pelvis and two more in her upper thigh. All those are superficial;

they should easily knit themselves without any help from us, but she will need complete rest."

"Here in hospital?"

"Not necessarily. In fact we would prefer it if she rested at home. We need the beds you see. After a couple of days she shouldn't need any monitoring."

"What about her head?"

The doctor glanced up at an x-ray on a lighted screen.

"Ah yes. I am concerned about her concussion. We've done a brain scan, but if she doesn't come round within the next few hours, I think we might need to take her back for a more thorough examination."

"So she's unconscious at the moment?" Jordon asked.

"She has been since we brought her in."

"Is that normal with these accidents?"

"As I said, Inspector, it's normal if she comes round soon."

"Right," Jordan said, standing up, "I'll go and watch over her then."

"I'd get something to eat if I was you, Inspector, and possibly a good night's sleep wouldn't go amiss. We'll ring you if you're needed."

"You're probably right, doctor, but I'm here now, so I'll wait for a while. Then I'll think about what you said."

"As you please, Inspector," he said, leading Jordan out of his office. "Oh by the way, have you any idea who her relatives are, or someone to contact."

"I'll leave the details with Matron."

"Much obliged."

When Jordan returned to Penny's room, he realised she never spoke of her family. He knew Josh was an orphan, but Penny never said much about her home life.

"Constable, contact Sergeant Fraser and ask him to look up her nearest relative. He needs to contact them about the accident."

"Is it that bad, Inspector," she said.

"Good Lord no, Constable. She's fine. Subject to a few broken bones, she should make an early recovery...it's standard procedure...all her private details will be on her enlistment papers."

"I'll do that now, Inspector."

"Oh...and when you're finished, I'd call it a day if I were you."

"I'm still on duty, Inspector."

"I see...then see if you can rustle up some tea and sandwiches."

Jordan was now alone with Penny in the semidarkness, with only the light from the small lamp above her bed and the red and green lights of the equipment against the wall. He sat down exhausted in the chair at the side of her bed, and stared at the frail looking figure with wires coming from patches on her head and body. The usually feisty young girl, almost half his age, looked small and vulnerable.

With her right arm strapped up in a harness, and the other lying limp on the bed, Jordan reached out and took her hand in his. It was warm, alive, and he sat there hoping his strength might transfer to her, and she would soon waken from the black fog that enveloped her.

Holding Penny's hand was like slipping back into a world he dared not imagine he would ever know again. He felt the rapport between them the first time they met. On reflection, he realised it was the smell of jasmine that reminded him of his wife Jessie.

In the dark, he could imagine all manner of things: their evenings together holding hands on the veranda, watching the sun go down behind the African Savannah and Jessie's gentle touch; in a way had melded them together. He had to pinch himself when he woke in the morning and saw Jessie lying beside him asleep; unaware he was admiring her: just as he was with Penny now.

She fostered that feeling in him, despite his mature, professional mind telling him he was possibly transferring his latent frustrations. Maybe that was part of his guilt, and all he really wanted was to exorcise those feelings.

Penny suddenly realised she was awake. She had difficulty feeling her body. There was no immediate awareness of the accident, the mass of wires attached to her, or the cumbersome contraption holding her arm in a horizontal position; she could feel nothing. She thought she was dreaming, until she saw the ghostly figure sitting next to her, saying things she could not understand.

Confused, Penny lay still. If this was a dream, she wanted to know what the strange man was saying, and why he was holding her hand. She had a sensation that she did not expect, but she realised his hand was in hers. A spiritual hand, she thought, and uncannily her fear gradually turned to an overwhelming calm.

"You don't know this, Penny," Jordan suddenly found himself saying, "nobody does, but once I sat by a bed just like this, holding my wife's hand. She was dead you see, but I didn't believe that. I told her anyway. I told her how much I loved her. I told her the children were waiting for her. I told her I would be joining them soon, but first I had a job to do, that would put everything right."

In the corridor outside Penny's room, Josh hesitated when he heard Jordan's voice. What he could see in the darkened room looked bizarre, and he shuffled his feet as he entered. The sound refocussed Jordan, and he stopped talking, not realising he was actually saying anything, and he let go of Penny's hand.

"Is that you, Boss?" Josh said, as if he hadn't seen him.

"Yes, Josh…it's me," Jordan replied, clearing his throat, "The doctor says Penny will be all right after some rest. Apart from some cuts and abrasions and a few minor fractures, her only real problem is a broken scapular."

"Scapular, Boss?"

"Yes…you know… her shoulder blade."

"Don't tell me, a man with a photographic memory, doesn't know what a scapular is," Penny suddenly let out."

Jordan jumped to his feet and lent over the bed, and Josh joined him on the other side. "You're awake!" Jordan said, "Look, Josh…she's awake." Jordan was unusually elated, until he realised she might have heard him talking to her," How long have you been awake?" he questioned.

"Just now…I think," she answered, "when you were talking to Josh."

"Never mind," he said, forgetting all about his soul-searching, "you're with us now…that's all that matters. Isn't it, Josh?"

Josh was still thinking about the scene he interrupted, "Err…yes, Boss."

Whether Jordan realised it or not, he had inadvertently allowed these two people into his innermost thoughts: the secret place where only he could deal with his nemesis. Even Mark Faulkner had not entered that place. One he would cherish the thought of invading; but Jordan never gave him the opportunity.

Maybe that was his mistake. Even though Jordan would not admit to his young assistants knowing, he felt better for it

"Right, Josh," Jordan said. "This young lady needs her rest; she's been through a terrible ordeal.

"That's just it, Inspector," Penny said, trying to move, "I can't remember a thing. It's a complete blank."

"You don't have to," Jordan assured her, "it will all come back in time."

"Don't you remember anything?" Josh said.

"Nothing...do you think it's because of my head injury?" she said again, feeling the bandages on her head with her good hand, "and what's wrong with my other arm...is it where the car hit me?"

"You see!" Jordan said, "You do remember."

They laughed, Penny let out a whimper as she began to realise how bad she really was, and her two male companions looked relieved. Then the fluorescent lights came on, and a surprised nurse stood in the doorway looking at Jordan and Josh sitting on the edge of Penny's bed.

"What's going on?" she said, loud enough to wake the dead. "You two shouldn't be sitting on the bed like that, you'll upset the balance."

She was referring to the contraption holding Penny's arm in a rigid position, and in the semidarkness, neither had noticed the counterbalance strung across the ceiling on wires, and poised above the end of her bed. It was low enough for Jordan to have caught it when he leant across to check on her. He was lucky.

"I'm sorry, nurse, I'm to blame," Jordon said. "I didn't want to put the lights on in case I disturbed Constable

Willow here, so I just moved around in the small light from her bed lamp. I wasn't aware she was hooked up to a counterbalance."

"Very well, Inspector...it is Inspector Jordan, I assume?"

"It is."

"Good...that's why I came down. There's a Chief Superintendent Mulholland out in the corridor, enquiring after you."

Jordan walked over to the open door and looked out into the corridor. The Chief Superintendent was talking to the duty Constable and looking round; he nodded to her and walked towards Jordan.

"How is she," he said, shaking his head from side to side. "It's an outrage, when a police officer can't go about her business without being knocked down."

"She's doing fine, Sir," Jordan said, taking the Chief Superintendent's elbow and leading him to one side. "She doesn't remember anything about the accident yet, but I'm sure she will...at least the doctor doesn't think she's damaged her head."

"So you don't know what took place, Inspector?"

"I didn't say that, Sir. I've been piecing things together from what the witness said, and the beginnings of some notes she was making. Apparently, she suspected a green car was following her all the way from the station, right up to the point when she stopped to check on him. She wrote that he suddenly turned off. Then after her interview with Lieutenant Cunningham of the Home Guard, she noticed the car parked in front of his house."

"Cheeky bugger,"

"Exactly, Sir...anyway, the Lieutenant's story was that she went outside to check on the car, and as she approached, he suddenly took off up the main road towards Thorsby, knocking her down in the process."

"And he didn't stop?"

"No, Sir."

"So all you have is this Lieutenant's eye-witness account and her note about the car following her from the city?"

"Not quite, Sir...She managed to scribble the car's three numbers down on a newspaper...Eight, nine, seven, and Sergeant Morgan is having them checked out by Registrations right now. We should hear something soon I hope."

"It's a bit thin, Inspector."

"I don't know, Sir. How many small green cars do you think have those three numbers? And I might add, also have damage to its left side."

The Chief Superintendent's left eyebrow rose slightly, and he nodded his head, "Well I want everyone onto this. No one knocks a police officer of mine down and gets away with it. Now let's see how she's doing."

Jordan escorted him into Penny's room. Josh jumped up from his seat, Penny looked amazed and the Chief Superintendent beamed with confidence.

"Fine show, Constable Willow," he said, walking over to her bedside.

"It didn't seem that way at the time, Sir."

"Damn plucky....that's all I can say. You males ought to look to your laurels with women like this on the force. How are you feeling dear?"

Penny managed a smile, "I don't really know at the moment, Sir. They've got me so pumped full of sedatives, I can't feel a thing."

"Sorry to hear that. The doctor tells me you'll be out of here in no time, and then you can rest at home. Take all the time you want, Constable; I want you back in the office, fit and ready to face the world again."

"Thank you, Sir," she said, "I don't know what I'm doing yet."

"It's early days yet, Sir," Jordan said, "but we'll sort something out."

"Good work, Constable," the Chief Superintendent said. "Don't you worry about a thing until you're better. CAS will carry on looking for the culprit," he let out a false laugh. "And finish off that mummy case...what do you say, Inspector."

"Almost tied up, Sir. And everything's pointing towards Naseby."

He suddenly looked embarrassed. "Yes...well don't forget what I said."

With that to remind them, the Chief Superintendent nodded at Penny and left the room. Out of courtesy, Jordan followed him.

"Sir...I meant what I said. We've all but linked Naseby to three killings, and now I wouldn't be surprised if I found out he had a hand in Constable Willow's unfortunate hit-and-run.

"And I meant what I said, Inspector. Be very sure of your facts."

CHAPTER 18

When Jordan walked into the office the following morning, he was surprised to find Josh filling in the new sections on the white-board. Unlike Penny, he was filling in the blanks from memory, only stopping for a moment to turn and nod.

"Morning, Boss," he said, and continued writing.

"What's this...taking over Penny's duties already?"

"I remembered what you said, Boss, about the leak using our board to get his information. So I thought I'd give him some more."

Jordan stood behind him reading the Gallagher section first, smiling to himself over Josh's last entry. He had managed to work in the connection between Ayres, Naseby and Gallagher, highlighting the change with the rostered driver.

"I'd like to see Naseby's face when that gets back to him," Jordan said.

Josh Laughed, "What about this, Boss," he said pointing to the entry on Ayers' section dealing with his suspicious accident, "Do you think that says it?"

"Oh yes, Josh. You'd have to be a fool not to get the point of that...and what about Lyle's death? Have you had time to memorise all those papers yet?"

"The French I had to take your word for, Boss, but the Spanish, dialect or not, I managed to get a good idea of what happened that day."

Jordan sat down at his desk, "I'm all ears."

Josh walked away from the board and sat on the corner of Penny's desk, "Well, Boss...as I see it, Naseby and Lyle had their business registered in Andorra, that's well before the whole thing was changed back into the Ayers Foundation, and all the papers seemed to agree that it was a tax haven enterprise. Apparently the main office was still in Cairo, and the Andorran office acted as an import link with Egypt."

He stood up and started walking between the desks. At the other end of the room, he turned and started again, "According to the reports, Naseby and Lyle used to make a regular trip to Marseille, evidently they had a gallery there, and the only route they took was across the Pyrenees, through the Pas de la Casa to Perpignan and along the coast road. Now here's the thing, Boss, an Andorran reporter familiar with the Pyrenees, said it could not have been an accident; at least not the way Naseby described it. He was there on the pass chicane with the police, and he said the circumstances were all wrong."

"How come?"

"Well, Boss...Imagine a chicane, you know...one of those..."

"I know what a chicane is, josh, I've driven round enough over the years. I even drove over the Pyrenees on my way to Spain once...in the snow."

"I bet that was scary?" Jordan nodded impatiently. "Right, Boss, sorry... Anyway, this particular part of the Pas de la Casa has a sharp S-bend top and bottom, with a straight bit in the middle. At the top, there's a wide

232

semicircle used as a sightseeing area for cars to pull into. Now Naseby said the point of this journey was so that Lyle could show him a chalet he wanted to buy; apparently he was keen on skiing and he thought the rented chalets were to expensive."

"Is this going somewhere?"

"It is, Boss…just a little background. I've got it all up here," he said, pointing to his head, as he shrugged his shoulders.

"Having a photographic memory, Josh is all very well if you can control it; you know, fast back and forward, or flick through to the vital piece of information."

"I know, Boss…it's difficult at times, but I'm getting there. Naseby said they stopped and walked over to the edge and looked down at the slopes. Then as Lyle pointed out the chalet to him, they noticed the car slowly rolling forward. Lyle dashed over to the car, opened the door to secure the handbrake. He said he had to lean into the car to reach it…"

"How ridiculous."

"Exactly, Boss… and the police must have thought the very same, because Naseby made the statement that the car was moving very slowly at that moment. It wasn't until Lyle jumped in that it picked up speed, then it just seemed to get faster until it was racing down the hill and off the bend at the bottom."

"You said this reporter refuted that?"

"Yes, Boss. The account I gave you was Naseby's statement to the police. The reporter said, where it was parked in the semicircle it would have been impossible for the car to run down the road between the chicanes. Depending on its position, it could only have run across the road into the rock face or forward into the bollards on the edge of the sightseeing area. For the car to have run down the road, it first had to leave the semicircle."

"I see," Jordan said, thinking. "Did they say anything about an autopsy?"

"Yes, Boss, the same reporter pointed out that the pathologist said Lyle had an unusual injury to the back of his head, when almost all other injuries were on the front of his body. Also…that injury in itself would have been fatal. Unfortunately, the police were unable to ascertain whether that was the first injury. Apparently there were other's that could also have caused his death."

"And Naseby got away with it."

"How's our invalid then?" a loud voice interrupted them.

They turned and saw Sergeant Fawcett coming through the door.

"She's doing well, Sergeant," Jordan answered.

"She was Lucky, I'm told. The Chief Superintendent is going around the building telling everyone how brave she was, how we need more like her. She's becoming quite a heroine."

"I can imagine," Jordan said. "Did you come up with anything on the car?"

"Yes I did. They've traced it to an address in London."

"You have?" Josh uttered.

The Sergeant passed the paper he was holding over to Jordan.

"Why am I not surprised?" Jordon said. "This Victor Strand, Sergeant, have we contacted the Met yet? We need someone down there."

"All in process, Inspector. I informed them of the situation, and they're fully aware that an officer was involved. But at present the premises appear empty, and according to a neighbour, the green car hasn't been there for a week or so."

"Well I hope someone's watching out for him."

"The car's details are with every patrol unit between here and London Inspector; we can't do any more than that."

"I know, Sergeant...it's the waiting that gets you."

"Sergeant Morgan's on the lookout locally. If you ask me, the car's still here somewhere. I mean...why would a private investigator from London be following one of our detectives?"

"Precisely, Sergeant," Jordan agreed.

"Well...I don't know about you two, but I've got a station to run," the Sergeant said, turning on his heels and walking back to the door. He stopped and paused. "Let me know if there's any change with Constable Willow."

"I will, Sergeant," Jordan said, turning back to the board. He glanced at Josh, "There's something else you can add to the board. Let them know we have all the driver's details. Give his name, address and the fact that he's a private detective."

"Right, Boss," Josh said, picking up the paper.

Jordan was still engrossed in the board. "Have we got any further on Ayers' death in Cairo? That would be something."

"Interpol haven't got back to us yet, Boss, I'll make a note to chase them up."

"What else have you got in that head of yours? Did you come across anything on the business set-up?"

"Yes I did, Boss," Josh said, with a broad smile on his face. "It was a bit convoluted, but I managed to construct a bit of a family tree...of sorts."

"Let me jot this down, Josh...I've a feeling I might need to refer to it."

Josh settled himself the way he usually did when he was about to refer to something in his memory, then he puckered his mouth with a firm expression, and nodded his head. That was his way of saying he had it.

"Right, Boss...ready?" Jordan nodded, pen poised, "The first indication of any alliance between Ayers and Naseby, was in 1924. Naseby left university and joined Ayers expedition to Egypt. That partnership ended with Ayers death in 1955."

"That was the car crash in Cairo?"

"Yes, Boss."

"That was a long partnership in Egypt?"

"Well it wasn't really. If my memory serves me right, the expedition had to leave Egypt in 1939 when Mussolini crossed the border. And what with all the unrest in Egypt after the war, Ayers didn't return until 1954."

"He only had another year then," Jordan commented, finishing his notes. "And you have no idea what happened to either of them in between?"

"No, Boss. The Ayers' papers are a bit vague on that period. That's when Lyle came in I think. Lyle and Naseby were at university together, but lost contact when Naseby joined up with Ayers; I don't know why. Anyway, when Ayers died in 1955, Lyle suddenly turns up as Naseby's new partner in Cairo," he laughed, "and that lasted until 1969, when Lyle himself was killed in a car crash."

"Yet another coincidence."

"Yes, Boss. Now here's the strange bit. The company, Lyle and Naseby, continued until Naseby retired in 1981. However, it was Lyle's son this time. He was only twelve when his father died, but Naseby put his father's share in trust for him until he was twenty-one."

"What was the share-holding then?"

"Naseby had eighty percent, Lyle junior twenty percent."

"So he didn't try and cheat him then?"

"Apparently not...And when Lyle junior was of age, Naseby resurrected the Ayers Foundation, with Lyle the sole director."

"Even stranger," Jordan uttered, "Unless his guilty conscience was pricking him, and he wanted to atone for Lyle's death. I bet the son doesn't know."

"We don't really either, Boss."

"No...you're right. But I'd stake my future on it."

It was the following day when Jordan got a call from Penny's mother in Penzance. She had been talking to the doctor about visiting her daughter, and the young man Jordan spoke to informed her Penny was ready to go home.

"Hold on, Mrs Willow," Jordan said, assuredly. "I haven't heard anything myself yet, but Penny only lives in a one bedroom flat, hardly comfortable enough to rest up after an accident."

"Then what shall I do? I'm quite prepared to stay over and look after her."

"What about, Mr Willow?"

"Oh he's all right. Give him a good book and the television and he's right for weeks. We've talked it over already, and he said I have to look after Penny until she's fit for work. And the doctor said that would take about six weeks."

"Too long to be stuck in a bed-sit," Jordan said, pausing for a moment to think. "Leave it with me, Mrs Willow; I'll come up with something."

"Oh good, Inspector, it's most generous of you. Shall I come down by train this afternoon...or is that too early?"

"You do that, Mrs Willow, and I'll have you picked up at the station and driven directly to the hospital to see your daughter. By then I should have sorted something out. If not...you and Penny could always stay at a hotel for the night."

"Good. I'll ring you when I know what time I'm arriving."

Josh was not going to be in directly, something about checking up on what happened to Professor Ayers in Cairo. He was getting impatient, waiting for Interpol to get back to him, so he thought he might just have the same success he had with his other searches in the Microfiche archives.

It was just as well. When Jordan put the phone down after speaking to Penny's mother, it rang again. This time it was Phyllis Montgomery.

"Inspector? It's Phyllis."

"Good morning, Phyllis, what can I do for you?"

"Good morning, Inspector. This case you're working on, would it have anything to do with a man called Christopher Lyle?"

Jordan was surprised, "It would...Why?"

"Well the Commissioner rang this morning, saying he's arranged a meeting with a Christopher Lyle and a Mr Bradbury..."

"I don't know any Bradbury, Phyllis...is he a lawyer?" Jordan interrupted.

"No, Inspector...he's a representative of the Ayers Foundation's insurance company, and the Commissioner want's you to be there as well."

"I see," Jordan said, "Sounds very mysterious. Did the Commissioner arrange it? What did the Chief Superintendent say?"

"He doesn't want to know about it. Frankly, I think he's hoping this is the end of the whole affair. It's been a nightmare. But if you want my opinion…"

"Please do, Phyllis," Jordan jumped in.

"Well…Marjory, that's the Commissioner's secretary, told me her boss's good friend, Mr Naseby, had something to do with it."

"Ah…now it all makes sense."

"It does?" she let out. "Then I can tell him you'll be there at lunchtime?"

"Where, Phyllis?"

"Sorry…the Grand of course…Twelve-thirty sharp"

Jordan arrived at the Grand ten minutes early to check himself out in the toilet and make sure he was presentable. He could still hear the Chief Superintendent's plea for him to look the part when he arrived on his first day, and that meant wearing a tie; and now he was thankful Penny fished it out of the bin and placed it in his top draw.

As he straightened the damn thing around his neck, there was another reason for being early: Jordan hoped to scrutinize his opponent from a vantage point before meeting him, he laid great store in first impressions, and asked the Concierge where he seated the Commissioner and his party.

His eyes sparkled. It was plain to see the Commissioner was a valued patron, and as usual, he was taking drinks with his guests in the lounge.

"Lunch will be at twelve-forty-five, Sir," he said.

"Thank you," Jordan replied, as he moved away.

Jordan found a perfect location to spy on the party. There was a fretted screen drawn across the pillared opening between the lounge and the dining room, to separate the areas and retain the warmth from the blazing open fire in the lounge. The Commissioner and his guests were sitting in a nest of leather easy chairs arranged around the fire with a large coffee table between them.

Jordan had no trouble recognising the heavy set, boisterous figure of the Commissioner; he was the one talking, and had a large drink in his hand, while the other two had left their's on the table.

The fair man on his left looked like Lyle, Jordan suspected. He was the younger of the two, and had that flair of an entrepreneur about him, whereas the other man looked sharp. He had black, well-trimmed hair, a blue pinstriped hand-made suit, and of all things a matching hanky to his tie, in his breast pocket. Although the young man also wore a suit, it was softer, probably worsted, and it was light grey.

He was sitting at ease. Unlike his companion, he sat uncomfortably leaning forward in his seat, with a black briefcase in front of him.

Jordan glanced at his watch. It was twelve-thirty, and he moved around the screen at the end nearest the foyer, and approached the nest of chairs from the arched opening. The Commissioner, who placed his drink on the table and turned in his seat with one arm outstretched, immediately recognised him.

"Ah, Inspector...on time I see."

"Always, Sir...couldn't be late for one of your lunches."

"I hope you're hungry...I'm famished," he uttered, with a snort as he shook Jordan's hand. "This is Christopher Lyle and the serious looking gentleman is his insurance agent Mr Bradbury...I'm sorry, I didn't catch your first name?"

"Malcolm, Sir."

Jordan shook Lyle's hand first. It was a strong grip, as they tested each other, then he walked around the chairs and shook Mr Bradbury's. He was not surprised to find him a weak comparison, unless he had nothing to prove.

As if by signal, a waiter was at the Commissioner's side before Jordan sat down opposite the other two, "What will it be, Jethro," he said, becoming personal.

"I'll just have a white wine thank you."

Then the Commissioner snatched up his drink and took a large gulp, nodding to the waiter for another before he left. "So Gentleman," he started, "Now we're all here, what was it you wanted to talk about?"

They looked at each other, and as if by prearrangement, Lyle spoke first, "I have three major concerns about the Inspector's investigation. One, as I'm sure you are aware, the insurance company owns the mummy you found in Sherwood Forest, and as it is of no real purpose to them, the Ayers Foundation has agreed to reimburse the insurance on that particular item. Two, I am concerned about the adverse publicity the Foundation is receiving over certain allegations. And three, it has come to Mr Naseby's attention that these allegations are of a criminal nature."

The Commissioner could see the rage building up on Jordan's face and replied first. "I'm sure Inspector Jordan would like to answer your questions in more detail after lunch, isn't that so, Inspector?"

"Undoubtedly, Sir," Jordan said, "Although, it strikes me Mr Lyle..."

"Christopher, please."

Jordan smiled and nodded, "Christopher...it strikes me that you are a little confused. In the first place, there have been no official comments regarding who the subject is in

Sherwood Forest...only fabricated newspaper reports. In addition, there have been no allegations made about you, the Ayers Foundation or Mr Naseby, criminal or otherwise. Therefore, I can only assume your Mr Naseby has a crystal ball, or he has a very good pipeline to my investigation."

As soon as the Commissioner's fresh drink arrived, he took another drink and laughed. "There you are gentleman... we're a bit premature."

"I don't think so, Sir. I only said these details were unknown. That doesn't mean they won't be shortly," Jordan said.

"Are you in the process of making charges, Inspector?" Lyle said.

"I need to question you first, Christopher. I assumed that was the purpose of this meeting. You wished to clear yourself of any suspicion."

"Lunch is ready, Commissioner," a precise voice said from the side.

The Commissioner turned to the young waiter, "Ah yes... good, how about something to eat to calm the waters?" he said, followed by another forced laugh.

This was Jordan's first experience of the dreaded Commissioner, and straight away, he knew his time in the department was numbered. He cared little about losing his job, as long as he could clear-up this mess first. First impressions told him Christopher Lyle had nothing to do with Naseby's crooked past.

That was not to say he was a complete fool, on the contrary, he seemed to have a bright head on his shoulders. Whether or not he knew the history behind the Ayers Foundation, and allowed it to continue, was another kettle of fish that Jordan was determined to find out.

Until now, he only had one major suspect, and that was Naseby. All the rest were petty scroungers, out for what they could get from the scraps that fell from the table; and that included the private detective that knocked Penny down.

CHAPTER 19

Despite the Commissioner's efforts, the lunch turned out to be a cool affair. The Commissioner had decided, against the Chief Superintendent's advice, that they should explore the ground before Jordan laid any specific charges against Nottingham's most noted personality. Although Naseby was not able to attend himself, Christopher Lyle was now in charge, and perfectly capable of protecting the good name of the Ayers Foundation.

Back in the nest of chairs with another round of drinks, Jordan was keen to bring this farce to a head. He could see the power emitted from Lyle's insistence that nothing suspicious surrounded the mummy found in Sherwood Forest, was placing the Commissioner in an awkward position, and decided to bring out one obvious fact that would make them think seriously about their next move.

"Mr Lyle...how did you arrive at the conclusions you aired before lunch?"

"I'm not sure, really. The media reports I guess."

"Reports that stem from Mr Naseby's newspaper, I might add."

"Why bring him into this...he's over eighty for God's sake. And he's far too ill to be bothered in what's going on in the world."

"So that means you had to manufacture the news items."

"I did not...I resent that, Inspector."

"Well, Mr Lyle, there's been no official comments, yet you seem very well informed. Since the reporter responsible works for Mr Naseby, I can only assume he instructed her to meddle with the facts, and when I think of that, I ask myself why. And here you both are."

"All right...it was, Benjamin. He called a meeting to discuss the ramifications of the mummy being part of the 1940 shipment."

"And Mr Bradbury here is naturally interested?" the Commissioner said.

Jordan looked over towards the smart man who had said very little before, or during lunch. He came across as a listener. One of those people who posed no threat on the face of it, until they produced a damning report that would make anyone wish they had kept their mouths shut.

"Ah...Mr Bradbury," Jordon said. "You haven't said much up till now. Perhaps you might like to say a word. I'd like to know why you're here."

"I'm simply looking after my company's interests, Inspector."

"You could have done that without this meeting. But I suspect you're looking to get more out of this...am I right?"

Mr Bradbury smiled. Christopher Lyle looked anxious and the Commissioner sat clutching his drink. Jordan nodded his head for an answer.

"All right, Inspector," Lyle answered instead. "When Mr Bradbury's insurance company heard about the possibility that the mummy in Sherwood Forest could be part of the 1940 shipment, they asked the question: how could this be so, if the rest of the shipment was destroyed in the fire?"

"Exactly," Jordan replied, "a question you might regret. Naseby understood the ramification... that's why he held the meeting, got his reporter to distract the police from the truth and made sure he had an informant to keep him apprised."

"Have you got any proof of that, Inspector?" Lyle asked.

"I know exactly what happened, I just don't know why... unless it was greed."

Lyle laughed, "That's ridiculous, Inspector. I was only twelve at the time, and my father didn't join Benjamin in Cairo until Ayers died in 1955."

"Your father knew Naseby back in their university days. As far as I'm concerned, he was in touch with Naseby all the time. He didn't have the capability that Naseby had to go to Egypt to make his wealth, but he helped in other ways."

"I don't believe you, Inspector," Lyle said.

"You only have to look at Mr Bradbury's face to know I'm right. I'm sure his company has a fine network of investigators capable of working it out. Am I right, Mr Bradbury?" Bradbury said nothing, but the smile on his face said everything. "Of course I am. He knows the proceeds of the valuables, allegedly lost in the fire, were ample to fund Naseby's grand plan, the last thing I haven't figured out yet... the last piece of the jigsaw."

"That's enough," the Commissioner said. "This was an unofficial meeting Christopher to allow you to explain the Inspector's unusual claims. I have to admit, you've said more to reinforce them, than dispute them. I think you had better seek the advice of a lawyer, and inform Benjamin while you're at it."

As the two men left the Grand's lounge, the Commissioner beckoned Jordan to stay where he was. "You were sailing against the wind there for a while, Inspector. I'm sure you realised Christopher is a friend of mine, just as Benjamin Naseby is. God man...we go back years. He supported my election for Commissioner."

"You didn't think he supported you out of friendship, did you, Sir? He must have half of Nottingham tied up with spies and the like, ensuring his empire survives against all the odds. However, right will out, Sir. Who would think a small Army button could bring down someone so powerful."

"Army button?"

"Yes, Sir...you should read your reports."

"You haven't got him yet, Inspector. You said yourself, you still have to find out the why...and you told Christopher that."

"Deliberately, Sir. Two can play at the game of muddying waters."

Jordan glanced at his watch again.

"What's with the watch, Inspector? You've been checking it out ever since lunch. You obviously didn't learn how to treat your superiors."

"I'm sorry, Sir. I meant no offence by it. It's just that I promised Constable Willow's mother I would find somewhere for them to stay..."

"How is Constable Willow?" the Commissioner interrupted.

"Very lucky I'm told, Sir. She's due out of hospital right now, but she has to be cared for during the next six weeks. That's why her mother is here."

"And you promised to take care of it, because her daughter only lives in a small, one bedroom flat, and as yet you haven't done that?"

"How did you know, Sir?"

"Even the Commissioner has his spies, Inspector. I know everything that goes on in my ward. You should remember that in future."

"I don't suppose I shall have to now, Sir."

"I shall be talking to you later about that, Inspector. In the meantime, I want you to carry out your promise to Mrs Willow. Go and collect them at the hospital, and take them to the Sherwood Lodge. You'll find I have arranged everything. A double room, complete service and full pay until Constable Willow is back on her feet. Then...and only then, will we have a talk about the future of CAS."

"I thought that was just a stopgap measure until I sorted out this mess."

"It was, Inspector...until I realised how valuable it was."

Josh was waiting for Jordan when he returned to the office, anxious to tell him Penny's mother had arrived, and was at the hospital waiting to be collected.

"You must be mad, Boss," he said.

"I already know that, Josh, but did you have anything particular in mind?"

"She told me you were taking them somewhere to stay."

"Yes I know. I don't know why I said that, but I did. So let's finish up here and I'll go and pick them up. What did you find out about Ayers' death?"

"Not much, Boss. That Naseby is one cool character. He must have paid someone to kill Ayers, because he was in Thebes at the time. And that's over three hundred miles away."

"You don't think he would have done it himself. I'm sure he got Lyle to kill Gallagher..." Jordan suddenly paused. "Unmistakably, that's why he killed Lyle himself. The pattern fits. If you notice, he keeps sweeping the ground clean; leaving no one to hold anything over him. I wouldn't be surprised if he killed the Ayers assassin when he got back to Cairo."

"It's still all circumstantial, Boss."

"I know, Josh. But I've got one thing in my favour."

"What's that, Boss?"

"Pride...It's one of the sins you know. Naseby didn't have any children of his own, that's why he adopted Lyle's son, and went back to the Ayers name."

"I don't follow, Boss."

"Well. He's dying, so Lyle said, and even as far back as his retirement, he started setting the ground so that his empire was free of any encumbrances. His own company was tainted, but the old Ayers Foundation, despite his part in it, was untouched by any corruption or aspirations of greed..."

"How do you know that, Boss?" Josh interrupted.

"Ayers wasn't after the wealth that came from tomb-hunting, like Howard Carter and his lot, he was only interested in the history."

"But if Naseby's money went into the Foundation..."

"I know, Josh...but as far as he was concerned, he had already laundered it, and since his retirement, and all his philanthropic activities, that period of his life would have been forgotten. Until the mummy turned up."

Josh laughed, "I can't understand why he didn't let it burn with the lorry."

"That's what's been sticking in my craw all this time, Josh. There has to be a reason, and I think it's the answer to everything."

"What are you going to do with Penny and her mother, Boss?"

"Until my lunch with the Commissioner, I was so desperate, I even considered letting them stay at my place… it's big enough."

"Yes, Boss…but two Willow women under the same roof."

"I know, Josh, I wasn't looking forward to it. Then the Commissioner saved my bacon. He told me he had arranged for Penny and her mother to stay at the Sherwood Lodge for the duration of her recuperation."

"The Sherwood Lodge, Boss."

"There you go again…repeating everything I say."

"I know, Boss, but the Sherwood Lodge. Even I would gladly step in front of a car to stay at the Sherwood Lodge."

"It's that good, is it?"

"I'll tell you something, Boss, when Penny comes back after staying there, we won't be able to talk to her without an invitation. All the top people stay there: the rock stars, film stars, even Commissioners," he laughed. "I bet Naseby owns it, and six weeks, Boss. Is that how long Penny's going to be off?"

Jordan laughed, as he walked towards the door, "I'm afraid so."

Jordan left Josh worrying about how he was going to cope while Penny was recuperating in the Sherwood Lodge, instead of wondering whether she would have a job to come back to. The case was almost complete, and then there would be nothing except casting his net again, while Jordan returned to his life at the college.

As Jordan Steered his old Opel Berlina around the semicircular drive of the mock-medieval twin gabled front of Sherwood Lodge, he remembered Josh's description of the hotel's clientele, and hesitated in parking amongst the elegant Rolls', Jaguars and other luxury cars he could barely name.

Before the Opel's wheels had hardly stopped, a horde of bright blue waistcoats, gently negotiated Penny into a wheelchair, loaded the bags onto a chromium trolley and ignored Jordon as if he were no more than a cabby. But a familiar voice saved Jordan's embarrassment. The voice of a person he thought was still in his office.

"Jethro...am I glad to see you," the Chief Superintendent shouted.

Jordan stepped out of the car and leaned over the roof. His old mentor was walking across from the entrance, with his usual anxious look.

"I thought you had tucked yourself away for the season, Sir."

"Don't be funny, Jethro, I'm still your superior."

"That's why I said, Sir...Sir."

"The Commissioner has everybody on edge. He said you were on your way an hour ago. Where have you been?"

"I do still have an investigation to work on, Sir, and if you had forgotten, another young assistant of mine called Sergeant Crosby needs my direction."

"Yes, Yes...of course. Come along now quickly."

"What about my car, Sir?" Jordan let out.

"What about your car?"

"Well...they won't get it towed away or anything silly like that. I mean, it does look a little out of place amongst all these other cars. What about yours?"

The Chief Superintendent grimaced, "I came with the Commissioner. His is the midnight blue Jaguar over there."

"My, my...gives you something to aspire to, doesn't it, Sir."

Jordan soon learnt the reason for the Chief Superintendent's anxious expression; so did Penny and her mother: after the past weeks adverse publicity, the Commissioner had decided to make the most of his new heroine. Constable Willow was the bravest young woman since Mary Wilson, whoever she was. Only instead of injuring herself rescuing passengers from an express train derailment, he promoted Penny as the woman who put her body in front of a criminal's car.

There was no mention that the incident may well have been an accident; the mere fact that the driver continued without stopping was the crime. It didn't matter that he might not have seen the slip of a girl in those last moments before he pulled out into the traffic. She was a heroine, and the police needed that.

"I bet you didn't expect this," Jordan whispered into Penny's ear.

She turned around quickly, innocently brushing her mouth across his face.

"Oh, Inspector...I'm sorry, you caught me by surprise."

"I think we were all caught by surprise," he said.

"I meant...oh no, it doesn't matter. I thought you were taking me somewhere quiet to rest. I hope he doesn't expect me to say something."

"He won't," Jordan said, moving away and heading for the Commissioner.

"You surprised us all, Sir," he said, alongside the bulky figure.

"I thought you lost your way, Inspector."

"Just tying up loose ends, Sir. Life has to go on, show or no show."

"You think this is too much, don't you?"

"Not risking your disapproval, Sir…Yes."

The Commissioner smiled as he shook another hand, "You're skating on thin ice again, Inspector. I'd try to join in if I were you."

"I don't care, Sir. Sack me please; I'd really like to go back to the college. But before you do that, Sir…give a thought to your brave girl. She's just got out of hospital, and she wasn't prepared for all this."

The Commissioner looked across towards Penny and her weary mother.

"Of course…I'm sorry, I didn't think. So many young people today would give their eye-teeth for this type of popularity."

"Not when they're nursing a fractured scapular, and multiple contusions."

"Yes you're right; maybe when she's fit again…A commendation ceremony."

"Let's find out what really took place first, Sir. We don't want any more adverse publicity, do we? I'm sure the driver of the green car is at fault, but as for being a criminal…I'd wait on that angle until it's proved, Sir."

The Commissioner was as good as his word. Although, even his request to allow Penny to rest, was overshadowed with tasteless platitudes. Nonetheless, the bright blue entourage wheeled Penny away into the lift and her mother smiled back at Jordan from across the room.

She had no need to say anything to him at that moment, her message was obvious by her grateful expression, and Jordan nodded back before he turned away from the festivities and went looking for his car. Jordan wanted to slip away from the clutches of the two men who could ruin his life, but before he had reached the edge of the arc of stone flags in front of the entrance, a tailored voice called his name.

He tried to ignore the call.

"Inspector Jordan," it came again, louder.

Jordan stopped and half turned to see a tall figure dressed in a black suit. It was the Concierge, and he was standing by the double doors with one hand limp by his side, and the other poised across his midriff as if he was about to click his fingers.

"Was there something?" Jordan said.

"A call for you, Inspector...it sounds urgent."

Jordan followed the precise man back into the foyer, where guests were milling around the counter, and directed him into a small office.

"Here?" Jordan asked.

"I thought you might want some privacy, Inspector,"

Jordan smiled, "Thank you...that's most considerate."

"Just press number one when you're ready."

Jordan waited for the Concierge to leave and picking up the phone, he pressed the first button, "Hello...who's that?"

"It's Josh, Boss," he said excitedly.

"Checking up on me at the posh establishment are we?"

"No, Boss...You'll never guess where I am at this moment."

"Surprise me."

"I'm at the residence of Benjamin Naseby."

Jordan hesitated to answer at first. Either Josh had made a huge blunder without telling him first, or the good luck

Jordan was praying for, had finally come their way. He composed himself, "Can you repeat that, Josh?"

"It's true, Boss, I'm actually ringing from Naseby's mansion. Well...the kitchen to be exact...just outside in the hall."

"And what are you doing there?"

"We've got the driver of the green car."

Jordan had to put his hand over the mouthpiece to stop Josh hearing his excited outburst; someone had to remain detached and in control. "I think you had better explain, Josh, from the beginning, and what you're doing in Naseby's kitchen. And please...make it simple."

"Sergeant Morgan got a call from a man called Bixby. He works as a gardener for Naseby, and he saw the police notice on the television about the missing green car. Apparently he noticed the car behind his gardening sheds or something, anyway, it didn't click at first until he had a word with the butler."

"You're getting complicated, Josh, don't forget we all don't have photographic memories. What does the butler have to do with the car...is it his?"

"No, Boss, but the butler introduced Mr Bixby to the owner of the car. His name is Victor Strand, and he's staying in the chauffeur's residence."

"And that's where you are now?"

"I went with Sergeant Morgan, Boss. He's arrested him, and he's sitting in the kitchen waiting for you."

"Has he been cautioned?"

"Yes, Boss, but I asked Sergeant Morgan if I could ring you. I knew you'd like to question him...and why not at Naseby's...who knows."

"Has Naseby said anything?"

"No, Boss...not a peep. The only person I'm dealing with is the butler, and he won't let any of us outside the kitchen area without a warrant."

"Okay...I'm on my way."

Although Jordan had to check his map for the location of Naseby's mansion, once he turned off the Long Eaton road, all he had to do was follow the police cars.

There was one on the corner of the main junction, another two parked on the grass verge just short of the main gates and several others scattered all along the gravel drive up to the main house. Then a constable diverted him passed the front section along a narrow lane to a collection of outbuildings, and another group of police cars.

Sergeant Morgan was leaning into one car talking to the driver, and Jordan pulled up alongside. "Sergeant," he called out, "Where's the catastrophe?"

The Sergeant turned round, "I beg your pardon, Sir."

"The catastrophe...why all the cars?"

"Oh sorry about that, Sir. The call went out on the radio and everyone responded. We've got the man who knocked Constable Willow down, Sir."

"I know that, Sergeant, that's why I'm here. If you'll take my advice, I'd get this lot out of here and back on the road. All Naseby has to do is complain to the Commissioner and you're mincemeat."

The Sergeant had not realised the association. When it dawned on him that Naseby was the Commissioner's friend, he grabbed the radio off the driver and told everyone to leave the area, "What about Strand, Sir?"

"You stay back with one car, and when I finish, you can have him."

Sergeant Morgan's face lit up again, and he escorted Jordan to the rear entrance of the house. The butler was hovering around and wanted to know the name of the other man. Jordan showed him his warrant card.

"I don't think this is proper procedure, Inspector. You should have a warrant before invading Mr Naseby's property."

"Your name, Sir?" Jordan said, noticing Josh coming out of the kitchen and acknowledging him with a nod.

"Cartwright, Inspector."

"Well, Mr Cartwright. The man in the kitchen is a wanted felon, and is about to be arrested. And since I understand he is staying in Mr Naseby's residence, I shall be arresting Mr Naseby also for aiding and abetting."

"You can't do that! Mr Naseby is an invalid."

"I don't care what Mr Naseby is. He has given shelter to a felon, and I would be surprised if said felon is not working for Mr Naseby, which makes his situation much worse. And as for you, Mr Cartwright, you will be detained for further questioning also."

"You can't do that."

"But I can, Mr Cartwright. I understand the gardener approached you several days ago about Mr Strand's car, which meant you had to know it was wanted by the police, and that also makes you guilty of aiding and abetting."

"I'm the only one who can look after Mr Naseby. He's dying."

Jordan studied the butler for a moment. "Very well, Mr Cartwright, I will allow you to go and see your employer and explain the situation. That doesn't mean I'm about to let you off. All it means is, that I'm prepared to discuss the matter with Mr Naseby prior to his own imminent arrest."

"Oh very well," the butler said and left.

Jordan turned to Josh, "Right…where's Mr Strand?"

Josh led Jordan down the hall and through a panelled door that opened out into a large tiled room. Straight away Jordan could see it was a large kitchen. It was the sort of kitchen usually found in restaurants, with two walls of cupboards above benches; an enormous range occupied a third wall and in the middle of the room was a long workbench.

Sitting at this large bench was an equally large man, who looked hot and very nervous. He also looked like a private detective: one of the sleazy types that earned their money spying on unfortunate husbands and wayward wives. He was trying to sport a small groomed moustache, but it was almost lost in the heavy jowls that hung either side of his red face, enveloping the shirt collar that was cutting into his neck.

In front of him was a plate of beef and vegetables, with the knife and fork still arranged neatly by the side of his plate, as if he was just about to start his lunch, or for some reason he had lost his appetite.

"Not hungry, Mr Strand?" Jordan asked.

"What's all this about?" he grunted.

"You know very well what it's about, Mr Strand. You've already been cautioned, with details of your crime."

"What crime? And who are you?"

Jordan took out his warrant card and showed him, "I'm Inspector Jordan. I'm the superior officer of the young female Constable you knocked down outside Lieutenant Cunningham's house the other day. Remember?"

"It was an accident. She stepped straight out in front of me."

"That may be so, Mr Strand. But you ran down an officer of the law who was displaying her warrant card, and you left the scene without rendering her assistance."

"I didn't know. Not until I saw the television that night."

"Then why didn't you come forward then?"

"I...I got scared."

"You mean you already have form in London, and there's another thing, Mr Naseby was paying you to spy on the police...isn't that so?"

"I'm not going to say any more without my lawyer."

Jordan turned round, biting his lip. "Take him away, Sergeant. We'll see how loyal he is to Mr Naseby when he's spent some time behind bars."

Just as a constable handcuffed him, he swung round looking as though the police could not touch him: not with a friend like Naseby.

"Oh and let me give you something to think about, Mr Strand," Jordan added. "We have several murders that need tying up."

When they led Strand out of the back door, he shouted. "You can't pin any murders on me, I was only asked to keep an eye on you lot."

"Yes..." Jordan said, looking at Josh, "He'll be easy meat now, Josh."

With his head stooped in sullen defiance, Strand looked as though he was about to answer Jordan's questions. Jordan nodded his head at the officer holding him and he brought him back to the bench. Strand slumped back into his chair.

"You know, Strand," Jordan said, sitting down at the table. "You may think this is only a trivial incident, worth no more than a fine or at worst a month or so in prison, but you've forgotten one thing..." Strand looked up when he heard that. "You already have a string of petty offences against your name, and if I remember your file correctly, the last judge you came up against, remarked that he would lock you up and throw away the key if you came in front of him again."

Strand turned back to looking at his lunch and laughed. "Just about everyone here has a record, and that includes that greasy bastard of a gardener. You want to check his record... you'll find he has more skills than just planting flowers."

Jordan nodded his head towards Josh, and Josh reciprocated, knowing what his boss wanted. It wouldn't go down well in court if his main witness had a criminal record, especially one that would question his credibility.

"My point, Mr Strand is...you could make life much easier for yourself if it was brought to the court's attention that you cooperated with our inquiry."

"I want that in writing," Strand mumbled.

Jordan banged his hand down on the bench, making Strand jump and the peas on his plate to cascade across the table, "This is not up for negotiation, Strand!" Jordan shouted, as he glanced up at the officer behind his seat, "Take him away."

"All right...all right," Strand cried out, "I was hired to keep a check on who you were visiting. That's all...I swear."

"Who hired you?"

"Mr Naseby of course. He wouldn't allow anyone else to see me. One on one he always said, the safest contract a man could have."

"He used your record against you, didn't he?"

"Oh yes...like everyone else. He has cabinets full of dossiers on people. I ought to know...I found out most of the information in them, and I suppose he had someone else doing it before me...they go back years."

"You've seen them?"

"Yes. He has a great big steel vault in his room...they're his bargaining chip."

"Why get drawn in, your offences are only minor."

"They're only what the police know about...and I'm not enlightening you either, you'll have to get a warrant for his files."

"All right, Strand," Jordan said. "That's helped your case, but you're still in custody. I'll have a word with my superiors. See what they think about your mitigating circumstances, but I think you will have to do a lot more before they forgive you for knocking down a police officer."

"Such as?"

"Well...testifying against Naseby would be a good start."

"I don't think it'll go that far, Inspector. Their names are upstairs with the rest," he laughed again; "There's even a file with your name on it."

Jordan thought there would be and gritted his teeth. "Take him away...and pick up the gardener as well while you're on."

They bundled Strand outside towards the waiting van, Jordan closed his notebook and stood up. He glanced across at the large window in front of him, the recovery vehicle had arrived to collect Strand's green car and take it back to forensics, and he watched Josh giving the men their instructions before he headed back towards the kitchen.

"All done, Boss," he said on entering.

"Is it?" Jordan replied turning away from the window, "I wonder...somehow I have the awful feeling it's just the beginning," he shifted his eyes up towards the ceiling.

"Somewhere up there, Naseby has the means to blow the lid off this town, and what's the betting he'll use all those files to stop our investigation dead in its tracks."

"Files, Boss?"

"Yes, Josh!" Jordan replied. With his hands on his hips, Jordan swung round and faced the window again. "My God… will this never end?" He turned back, his face tight with pain. "Strand said Naseby has a vault full of files with dossiers on people. All the most important people in Nottingham and anywhere else he might need protection. He said Naseby even has a file on me. Maybe even you and Penny, and anyone else with something to hide."

"I haven't got anything to hide, Boss."

"Are you sure…no unpaid parking tickets, unrequited loves you abandoned?"

"No, Boss…at least, I don't think so," his mouth dropped open. "You don't think he knows about Kenya, Boss?"

"Oh I'm sure he does…every sordid detail."

"It's a wonder he hasn't tried blackmail, Boss."

"That's not what it's all about, thank goodness."

"Then what is it about?"

"It's about security, Josh. As I said before, Naseby has one driving conviction. He want's to leave this Earth as clean as he came into it, and he's collected all this information to guarantee that."

"Inspector Jordan," the butler said, walking into the kitchen. "Mr Naseby will see you now, Sir. He can't spare you much time, his rest period is imminent."

Jordan turned around surprised, "Is that so…good."

"I must warn you first, Sir; this is not to be a formal interview. Mr Naseby only wants to meet with you to discuss a few ground rules."

"I'm sure he does."

"He means what he says, Inspector. If you want any conclusion to this matter, I suggest you do as he says...he's used to getting his own way. I will time your visit, so brevity is of the essence. You will be alone, there will be no notes taken until he says so and he has a button to call me should he becomes distressed."

"Does he realise the situation he's in?"

"Oh yes, Inspector, more than you can imagine. But I must add, he is a dying man, and as such, has no fear of any future prosecutions."

"Then why bother with this charade?"

"Because, Inspector; Mr Naseby, like yourself, needs a certain form of closure to this investigation. Your discussion is to decide on whose terms."

"On whose terms?" Jordan lashed out.

"I'm sure you can understand that, Inspector."

With that remark, the butler turned and led Jordan out of the kitchen. Josh followed until Jordan stopped him at the bottom of the stairs.

"No, Josh...you heard the man, this is just Naseby and myself. You head back to the Sherwood Lodge and see how Penny's getting on. I'll join you there before long, and we can all have a nice chat about where we stand before I present the Chief Superintendent with Naseby's ultimatum."

"Ultimatum, Boss?"

"Yes, Josh. That's what all this is about."

CHAPTER 20

Jordan was surprised when the butler ushered him into the bleak room at the end of a long corridor, after the sumptuous luxury of the rest of the house. It was no more than a hospital room. No bigger than was necessary to hold a nest of easy chairs around a small glass coffee table on one side; a multi-functional hospital bed with all its instruments and equipment to monitor a dying man on the other, and in the far corner, a floor to ceiling steel door with a large spoked wheel to lock it shut.

In his initial scan, Jordan had time to notice a red light beside the wheel before his attention returned to the bed. He had overlooked the chrome wheelchair by the window. The drawn blinds left that side of the room in semi-shade, and when a ghostly shape moved forward, Jordon was surprised.

"I've been waiting for you, Inspector," a soft, rasping voice spoke.

"You have?"

"Oh yes. I knew you'd come eventually. But I'm afraid you're too late."

"Am I?"

"Yes, Inspector...I'm dying, you see. I have Multiple Sclerosis, with only a month or two left. You should have come earlier."

"I'm sorry, Mr Naseby," Jordan said quietly, with an air of calmness, "Maybe you can tell me what all this is about, then we'll both know."

Naseby nodded to the butler, who obediently wheeled him out into the centre of the room near the nest of chairs, with a mass of tubes and cables following him.

"Will that be all, Sir?" the butler said, placing a jug of water and glass on the table, "Shall I draw the blinds?"

"No...thank you. Leave us...and don't fuss."

As the butler left them alone, Jordan noticed Benjamin Naseby looked like a caricature of the ruthless mogul. In fact, the picture of the old man in a wheelchair out of an American detective novel came to mind; except this was not America, and Naseby did not have a beautiful wayward daughter.

He was alone in his great mansion with no one to inherit his fortune, and with only months to live: all his scheming and planning had been for nothing. Yet he was still manipulating, controlling the destinies of those around him: if not by the simple power of his fortune, by the ultimate threat of their own pasts.

"Sit down, Inspector, I hate looking up at people."

Jordan slipped into one of the easy chairs, "You didn't answer my question."

The old man smiled. "Pour me a glass of water, this oxygen makes me dry after a while. A bit heady as well. Normally my body feels like a dead weight, but after a while it disappears and I'm floating on air."

He was referring to the tubes coming from behind his back, over his ears and connected to a small plastic device plugged into his nostrils. His eyes looked bright, yet discoloured and watery. He looked as if he was on something more than oxygen, and Jordan wondered whether he would get any sense out of him.

He passed Naseby the glass of water, forgetting he was probably unable to use his hands, and noticing a kinked straw beside the water jug, Jordan dropped it into the glass and held it up to Naseby's lips. He started to shake, every part of his body was shivering with the effort it took for him to open his mouth.

He took a long draw on the plastic tube and nodded when he was finished.

"That's better," he said, "See what I have been reduced to. I can still speak, but not for long," he chuckled, coughed to clear his throat, and sucked in a deep breath. "I feel like the disappearing man."

Jordan was getting impatient, "My question."

"Ah yes. You want to know what started all this. Well... as you can see I am no longer a threat to anyone, yet I am still capable of dealing a devastating blow. Through others I admit...and what's behind that steel door," he chuckled again. "Yes, Inspector, I saw you looking at my vault, and I'm aware that you know what's behind it, and what damage its contents could do to so many people's lives."

"What has that got to do with the charges I can bring against you?"

"Oh no, Inspector...I don't think so."

"You sound confident."

"I am...I'll be dead before the prosecutor can even draw up the papers."

"Maybe so, but I can do a lot of damage to your empire... dead or alive."

"Yes you can, Inspector. And you have answered your own question."

"I fail to see how."

"We both have the power to destroy lives. But if you think for a moment, we won't really be achieving justice at all... will we?"

Jordan had to agree with the spiteful old man. All he wanted was a place in history. His name recorded amongst the notables of Nottingham and he would set everyone free. On the other hand, Jordan also had to admit, his crimes were long gone, and with the only person left to seek revenge, the very one Naseby wanted to continue his empire.

Christopher Lyle was the last person to believe Naseby killed his father, and Jordan immediately knew: here was his bargaining chip.

The old man sat motionless. His tremors had subsided, except a slight flicker at the corner of his mouth, and the look of anticipation on his face.

"So, Inspector...do we agree?"

"Do you mean the fact that it's a stalemate?"

"Hardly a stalemate, there are options."

"Such as?"

"You close the case and give me a written guarantee that it will not be opened again, and I destroy the files."

"That sounds too simple."

"Why...I think it's a perfect solution."

"What's to stop me from opening the case after you're dead and the files have been destroyed? More likely, you destroy a false set of files, or better still, what if there are no files at all. I know Victor Strand told me he helped prepare them, but he works for you, so who am I to believe."

"I understand your distrust, Inspector, but this is a time when we have to trust each other. But…if you insist on having some indication that they are real, you will find something to wet your appetite behind the cushion of your chair."

Jordan leant forward and pulled back the cushion, and sitting against the backing was a thick blue folder with a flap held down by a Velcro tab. He slipped his finger underneath and opened the folder. Inside was a collection of documents, paper clippings and photographs. They all referred to a period in Kenya that Jordan was trying to forget: A period in his life he would rather not have occurred.

On top was a photograph of his wife Jessie and the children; and underneath that was another of Jomo Kenyatta. They brought tears to his eyes, and he looked up at the evil old man.

"What made you so evil?"

Naseby's expression changed, within the limited range of his atrophied muscles. It was an unusual expression, caught between shock and apprehension, but the truth was in the eyes; no one had dared to call him evil before.

"Inspector…your hatred of me won't solve anything."

Before Jordan could answer, the door opened and Cartwright entered the room, "Sorry, Sir…it's time for your therapy. Hans is waiting outside."

"There you are, Inspector. Your time has run out. I shall give you the opportunity to discuss this matter with your superiors, but I'm sure my good friends will come to the right decision. Meanwhile keep the file if you want…it's only a copy, and let Cartwright know when you wish to negotiate."

"I have one condition before any negotiations, despite my superior's decision. I want to know what happened."

"Don't worry, Inspector. I intend telling you everything, if I know the case will not proceed. That is my condition."

A huge muscular man in white trousers and singlet, walked into the room with an armful of towels, and prepared the bed for Naseby's treatment. Jordan closed the file; he had no need to see its contents, and left it on the chair. Then following the butler out of the room, he made his way along the corridor and down the stairs.

Standing at the bottom was a young uniformed officer, and Jordan looked at his enquiring face, "Was there something, Constable?

"Sergeant Morgan asked me to wait and see if you required any help with Mr Naseby," Jordan looked blank for the moment. "He said you might want someone to help you escort him to the station...Sir."

"Oh no, Constable," Jordan said with a smile. "That won't be necessary," he walked with him to the door and stood at the top of the steps. "I see everyone's gone...you might as well get back to the station."

When Jordan arrived at the Sherwood Lodge, it was late afternoon. Dark clouds were racing across the sky from the north, bringing with them the first drops of icy cold rain. As Jordan stepped out of his car a small boy in a bright-blue uniform rushed across the flagged patio with a large umbrella that was almost lifting him off his feet, and Jordan made a grab for the handle he was hanging onto for grim death.

"Here young man, let me help you with that," Jordan cried out.

"It's all right, Sir," he chirped, "I'm supposed to escort you inside. I can't allow you to get wet; the Concierge would have my guts."

"Then let's both hold the umbrella."

Inside Jordan thanked the boy, nodded towards a suspicious Concierge, and made his way up the grand stairs to Penny's room on the first floor. A blast of hot air greeted him when Penny's mother opened the door. She looked pleased to see Jordan, and Penny looked round and shouted across the room.

"Oh, Inspector...Josh said you were going to be here ages ago."

Josh walked out of another room, "Hi, Boss...you're late."

"My interview with Naseby took a little longer than I thought."

"Sit down here, Inspector," Penny said, "The fires wonderful."

"I will...and how's our heroine today?"

"Inspector," she exclaimed, "I'm not a heroine. I'm just a silly girl who thought she could stop a car. I didn't think. I thought he could see me coming round that Land Rover. Obviously he couldn't."

"It's all old history now, Penny," Jordan said, "We have the man and he's pleaded guilty to leaving the scene, although he says he didn't see you."

"Why was he following me?"

"Yes, Inspector," Penny's mother chipped in, "I would like to know that."

"He was working for Naseby."

"You got him to admit that, Boss?" Josh asked.

"Yes...eventually, when I threw in a couple of murders."

Penny laughed, "If only he knew."

"Yes," Jordan agreed, laughing himself. "If only. Anyway, apparently it's all for nothing. Naseby has enough information on the people who count in Nottingham to cause the biggest stink since Robin Hood."

"Does he really intend releasing those files, Boss?" Josh asked.

"Oh yes...he's very serious; unless I can make a deal for him."

"Would you do that, Inspector?" Penny asked.

"I wouldn't, Penny, but I'm duty bound to inform the Chief Superintendent, and he and the Commissioner might well bow to Naseby's demands."

"What about the case?" Josh asked.

"Either way the case is dead, but I intend to find out what happened."

"It sounds a lot about nothing to me," Penny's mother let out.

"Maybe you're right, Mrs Willow," Jordan said, looking at his watch. "But I must get back and report to the Chief Superintendent."

"Do you have to, Inspector?" Penny said, "I was hoping you would stay for dinner. They serve it up in the room you know. Anything we want."

"I would dearly love that, Penny, but duty calls. Josh can stay, there's no point in you going back to the station tonight."

"Thanks, Boss...I just fancy a nice juicy steak."

"Stop, Josh," Jordan said, picking up the phone, "I might just make it back before dinner if I hurry," he dialled the Chief Superintendent's private number, the one he gave him that first day in the Old Jerusalem, "Sir?... it's Inspector Jordan...Yes, I've just finished, and I need to speak to you urgently tonight...soon as possible. I think you might want to see the Commissioner when you hear what I have to say."

Penny suddenly reached across the back of the couch with her good hand and caught Jordan's arm, "You will try to get back, Inspector...please."

"I wish I didn't have to leave, but I have to. As soon as I know, I shall ring and tell you I'm on my way. If not you carry on and have your meal," a disappointed look crossed Penny's face, "I can always stay for dinner tomorrow."

"Of course you can," she said.

"Josh...Walk me to the top of the stairs," Jordan said.

As they left the room Josh turned to Jordan with a suspicious glance, "What's up, Boss? You did tell Penny everything?"

"Not quite, Josh," he replied stopping at the top of the stairs. "Naseby really means business, and I don't know how I'm going to stop him. I can't even guarantee he's not bluffing. He showed me my file, and it was terrible. I don't know how he got hold of it all, but he has everything. More than the Kenyan police did."

"Then you've got to make a deal, Boss."

"I don't think that will be up to me, Josh. He seems to have a file on just about everyone that matters...maybe even the Chief Superintendent and Commissioner. I don't know what they're going to say."

"I bet they'll tell you to make a deal, Boss."

"Maybe so...but that's not my worry. I need to guarantee he won't pull a fast one just out of spite. And I have to get at those files before he dies."

"You'll just have to use his adopted son somehow."

"What did you say?"

273

"His adopted son, Boss...you know, Christopher Lyle."

"That's right...he doesn't know Naseby killed his father. If he did, he would destroy the Ayers Foundation, and ruin Naseby's name."

"Doesn't Naseby realise that, Boss."

"I don't know, Josh. We talked about Lyle, but we talked about so many things...I can't remember if his knowing came into the conversation."

"I think you would remember, Boss."

"I'll find out though...next visit. And you're coming with me."

"I thought he only wanted a one on one, Boss?"

"Well he's going to have to live with it...isn't he?"

Chief Superintendent Mulholland was impatiently waiting for Jordan when he finally arrived back at the station. He watched him dash across the car park outside his window in the pouring rain, and returned to his desk to hear what he had to say.

When Phyllis ushered Jordan in without the usual ceremony, and quickly closed the door behind her, they just stared at each other across the room.

The Chief Superintendent stood up, went into a small ensuite and returning with a towel, tossed it across to Jordan, "Here, dry yourself before you make a mess on my carpet," then he sat down, reached into his draw, brought out a bottle of whisky and two glasses and poured a stiff drink in both. "Get this down you before you catch cold," he continued, pushing the glass across the desk.

Jordan sat down and picked up the glass. "Thanks, Sir, I needed that. It's hell out there on the roads. Do you know I nearly got sideswiped twice?"

"Never mind about the traffic, tell me about Naseby."

"I don't know where to start, Sir."

"Well you had better start soon, Inspector; I have a meeting with the Commissioner this evening...so make your statement a brief one."

"Brief, Sir? Is a catastrophe brief enough?"

The Chief Superintendent took a large gulp of his whisky and glared at Jordan, "And what does that mean? You're not exaggerating again?"

"I wish I was, Sir. The truth of the matter is quite simple, Naseby has a dirt-file on just about everyone who holds an important position in Nottingham, and he threatens to make the dossiers public if we continue with the case against him."

Chief Superintendent Mulholland's face went grey, and he drained his glass. He offered Jordan another as he filled his again, but Jordan refused, knowing he still had a lot of driving to do that night, "My God," he uttered, "My God."

"My very words, Sir."

"He's got to be stopped, Inspector."

"I think that's your job, Sir...and the Commissioner's."

"Can't you do anything? Raid his place, take the files and destroy them."

"You didn't see the vault there in, Sir."

"Then what? We can't just let him disclose all the cities dignitaries close guarded secrets without doing something. It...it would be like another Wall Street crash...we'd have bodies everywhere."

"I understand, Sir...he has a file on me," the Chief Superintendent gave him a questionable look, "The Kenyan affair, Sir."

He responded, "Good Lord...not you as well?"

"Yes, Sir, and I think he has one on you and the Commissioner...he hinted as much. He said you two would be the first to suffer."

The Chief Superintendent blustered and had another drink, "This is terrible, Inspector...it's going to ruin the force."

"Well I don't like saying this, Sir, but you could always agree to his terms."

"I've got to discuss this with the Commissioner. Did you give him any promises? Any of your usual suggestions?"

"No, Sir. It wasn't that type of meeting."

"Then what type of meeting was it?"

"It was very short, Sir. I threatened Naseby with several charges, before I knew about the files of course, and he came back with his ultimatum. When he announced he would run the files in the local papers. I did make one point though, Sir, should you agree with his terms, that I would need certain conditions."

"What sort of conditions?"

"Firstly I would like to ascertain for myself the validity of the files, check that they are in fact what he says. I then insisted on being the one to destroy the files."

"Good...although I think you might get some resistance from the Commissioner about checking on other peoples so-called secrets."

"I wouldn't actually read them word for word, Sir; just verify that a random selection is what Naseby claims...no more."

"I suppose someone has to do it. What's your opinion about ditching the investigation? You and your team have put a lot into it. And then there's Constable Willow, she took a pretty bad knock."

"Oh I don't think Naseby would mind if we charged the driver, Sir, and as far as the case is concerned...it amounts to nothing really. Although we're sure Naseby was responsible for the robbery in 1940, the murders that ensued and anything else on the way that we don't know about yet, it's all pretty well circumstantial. Then there's the point that we could never get him in front of a jury...he only has a few months to live. So all I could do was threaten his good name, and in turn, that of the Ayers Foundation; which more importantly, would bring his adopted son Christopher Lyle under suspicion."

"What about this Lyle? Do you think he's mixed up in all this somehow?"

"I don't think so, Sir. When I questioned him, he seemed to have swallowed Naseby's line over the years, and let's not forget...Naseby has looked after him, and looks like leaving everything to him when he dies."

"The threat was a good move by you, Inspector."

"I thought so, Sir. At least it gives you a reprieve. As he said, now we have something on each other, and that has to stand for something."

The Chief Superintendent suddenly looked decisive. He finished his drink with one gulp; put the bottle and glasses back in his draw and stood up, "Right! I'm going to see the Commissioner...where will you be?"

"I thought I'd drop in on Penny, Sir."

"Good Idea. I'll ring you there."

The Chief Superintendent never did ring. Jordan spent a pleasant evening with Josh, Penny and her mother, without a thought for the potentially disastrous outcome he would have to face if the Commissioner did not agree.

For some reason, Jordan was relaxed; whether that was due to the two whiskies he had earlier, the rich meal and fine wine, or the companionship of friends: it was of little concern to him. What did concern him was, the possibility that Naseby's venom might rub off on them, and they would become known as the ones who foolishly opened Pandora's Box.

The following morning the Chief Superintendent was standing at his window when Phyllis walked into the room with that morning's mail, "Inspector Jordan's here, Sir," She said, beckoning him with her other hand behind the door.

"Show him in, Phyllis."

Jordan entered the room with a suspicion that it was the end of the road, but sensed the journey still had some way to go before it reached that.

"Sit down, Jethro," the Chief Superintendent said coolly. He looked a burdened man. Uneasy in what he was about to ask of his good friend.

"I'm always suspicious when you call me Jethro."

"So you should be."

"What does that mean?"

"It means I have a dirty job for you," he ushered Jordan to sit. "This wasn't my idea by the way. He want's you to get Naseby to open the vault, it doesn't matter how, use the suggestion you made of wanting to check the files if you like, but as soon as you have it open, you must secure it. There will be a team of experts outside waiting for your call," he looked at the disbelief on Jordan's face. "Is that clear?"

"That's mad...what about the security?"

"The Commissioner does not want the files destroyed. He sees this as an opportunity to discover who to trust in Nottingham."

"You mean take over from Naseby."

"As you wish...I want nothing to do with it, and I advise you to do the same."

"Then what?"

"We will raid Naseby's house. If what you say about the important people in this city, we shall have no difficulty obtaining a warrant."

"Very well, Sir."

"You what...I thought you would object."

"I want to finish this, Sir...under my own terms."

CHAPTER 21

When Jordan returned to his own office, Josh was standing in front of the white-board looking studious, with one arm across his chest and the other supporting his chin. He was engrossed in something, and he was not aware that Jordan had entered the room and was standing behind him.

"Found something interesting, Josh?" Jordan said.

Josh jumped back, "Oh, Boss, you shouldn't creep up on people."

"Well normally, you're not so absorbed. What's got your attention?"

"I was thinking about what we talked about last night, Boss...you know... the bit about whether Christopher Lyle was implicated in all this."

"And I said, I didn't think he was. He comes across to me as being a naïve idealist, and an idealist certainly wouldn't get himself involved in fraud or any other type of felonious activities."

"I know, Boss...but I just thought you'd have to be pretty naïve to miss some of Naseby's shrewd tactics over the years. I mean...he must have heard something."

Jordan paused for a moment. There was something in what Josh said, and he had to admit, judging character was not one of his best attributes. "You might be right, Josh, but it's all immaterial now. The Chief Superintendent has decided that I have to go ahead with Naseby's ultimatum."

Jordan was not about to let Josh know the truth of what was about to take place. If anything went wrong, he wanted him and Penny out of the way.

"You're going to make a deal with him, Boss?"

"That's right, Josh."

"So what about Strand? We can't hold him too long without charging him."

"He'll be charged today. As far as I'm concerned, he's not part of Naseby's deal. He'll have to go down for the lesser charge of hit and run."

"Good, Boss. I don't think it would have gone down well in the station if you let him go...when are you going to question him?"

"I'm not...you are. I'm going to contact Naseby's butler and arrange our next meeting. In fact I'll ring him right now, see if Naseby's ready for me."

"I thought I was going with you, Boss?"

"Somehow I don't think Naseby is going to let me near the files yet, and that's when I want that photographic memory of yours."

"You said you weren't going to read them."

"That's right, Josh, and if I went through them, within the first half dozen I wouldn't know what I was reading. If they were genuine dossiers they'd be totally different from each other, and only someone with an eye for detail like you, could tell me if they followed a pattern and were copies or were obviously different."

"I could do that, Boss...just say when. Now I'd better get down to Strand; see what I can get out of him."

Just as Josh was about to leave the room, Jordan remembered something, "Oh Josh," he stopped and turned. "Strand told me he knew about the files because he was one of the main contributors, so there's a good chance he spent time in the vault. He may even be familiar with its operation. Give him the impression it would help his case if we knew more about the vault."

"Right, Boss...I'll make that my first priority. What about the vault's combination while I'm at it?"

Jordan laughed, "Now that would be something."

By the time Jordan reached Naseby's house, he was in no fit state for an interview, let alone the clandestine mission the Chief Superintendent expected him to carry out. His initial intention was to fill in as many blanks as he could before even attempting to turn the tables on Naseby. How he did that he was not sure.

There was only one principle objective, and that was to get the vault opened, but that posed a problem. Naseby was in no condition to open it himself, so that was left to Cartwright or whoever was in the room with him at the time; yet Jordan had difficulty accepting Naseby would allow a stranger to open the vault. That would be Jordan's first priority.

As soon as Cartwright ushered Jordan into the room at the end of the corridor, Naseby's personality seemed to take charge of the proceedings. It was as if his loss of motor function had diverted what power he had left to his brain, and he set the agenda immediately Jordan entered the room.

"Well, Inspector...what's the verdict?"

Jordan took his seat while Cartwright laid out the water jug and glass.

"I have authority to discuss terms with you," Jordan found himself replying, as Cartwright returned with a drinks tray, on which was a bottle of white wine, suspiciously the same type he ordered at the Sherwood Lodge, and a glass. "I didn't ask for a drink Cartwright," Jordon said.

"Have one, Inspector," Naseby said, as Cartwright wheeled him over to the nest of chairs, "We have a lot to talk about. My time is still limited, so if you want to here about what led up to the mummy in Sherwood Forest, you had better sit back and listen: the first instalment today, second tomorrow and files the next."

"I was hoping I could verify the files today."

"I'm afraid not, Inspector," he replied, nodding towards Cartwright, who gave Naseby a drink before leaving the room.

In a way, Jordan was relieved, just as he was when he persuaded the Chief Superintendent to abandon his idea of a special force waiting for his signal. If he wanted Jordan to settle this matter, it had to be under his terms. Naseby was no fool, and one slip-up could easily turn into a catastrophe.

"Very well, Naseby," Jordan said, picking up his drink. "I'll allow you the privilege of starting first. Fill in all the blanks and you can have your deal."

Naseby flashed an arrogant glare. He hated being patronised.

He started with his unusual chuckle, it was probably the nearest he could come to a real laugh, and it was without feeling. Jordan had no idea whether or not he was being cynical, amused by what he was about to say or simply clearing his throat. Either way, a deep breath followed as he settled himself to start.

"I don't know if I can even remember what happened back then…it was so long ago. And there wasn't a master plan or anything like that, one thing just led onto another, and whatever entered my head at the time."

"Detail isn't important," Jordan interrupted, "it's the chain of events that interest me…how an Egyptian mummy turned up in Sherwood Forest?"

Naseby nodded his head towards his drink and Jordan obliged while Naseby stared at him all the time. It was hard to tell what was going on behind those grey, watery eyes, but Jordan was certain of one thing; Naseby was back there at the beginning. Then he shook the straw free of his mouth and he spoke again, sharp and clear this time, as if he had remembered.

"You have to realise, Inspector, back then I had no idea what I wanted to be, other than follow my Idols."

"Now that's something I didn't expect you to have."

"Oh yes. There were a few at that time, but Howard Carter stood out above the rest…I suppose, because he found all that treasure," he chuckled. "Let's face it, Inspector; the young are always chasing rainbows, especially when there's a pot of gold at the end."

Jordan felt Naseby needed prompting.

"Was that when you decided to be an archaeologist?"

"I don't know. When I enrolled at university it seemed the easiest to get into at the time, and the workload was far less than most courses, but that came much later. What you have to realise, Inspector, is there are two types of archaeologist: on the one hand you have the Ayers of the world, who think of nothing more than the history, and the story behind the lives of a particular period," he chuckled again, "And…

on the other, you have people like me. Like Carnarvon and Carter, who seek the glory...and of course the rewards that go with it."

"And of course, you did very well."

"I did...I don't deny it."

"Then what?" Jordan asked, trying to keep him moving.

"Sorry, Inspector...it's so easy to fall back into that time. It was about 1924, I think; I had finished my course and was looking for a new outlet, when I heard about Professor Ayers' expedition to Egypt. I had no idea what he was looking for. I didn't care much... I just wanted to get out there. It wasn't until we continued on to Thebes, instead of the Valley of the Kings where Carter was, that I realised I was on one of those historical digs. Treasure was not one of Ayers interests.

"His dig was in the barren hills above Thebes, in an area none as the Tombs of the Notables: high ranking officials that served the Pharaohs and Ayers' burning passion was what these men might have left behind as an epitaph to their lives."

"And Vizier Hykotep was one of those men."

"Very good, Inspector. I can see you have done your homework."

"I have a very good friend who's an archaeologist."

"That would explain it then. However, we didn't find his tomb straight away. In fact, we didn't find his tomb until five years later, after several years excavating priests and the like that we had never heard of. It wasn't until we came across a builder of quality tombs, whose grand epitaph was a list of his customers; and it was a fine list, I had to agree. The names were awesome.

"Nevertheless, excavating his tomb and deciphering all the evidence pointing to the officials of the Pharaohs, took time, and then Ayers wanted to go through them one by one.

The robbers had sacked some, but others were still intact, and that's when it got interesting. We discovered these men had as much wealth as some of the Pharaohs did...they had been powerful men. As I had majored in hieroglyphs, Ayers left that monumental task to me. He was happy digging amongst the tombs, day after day, and he had little interest in the artefacts."

"But you had."

"Oh yes. As I said, we found the position of Vizier Hykotep's tomb along with several others on a steep hillside. Ayers as usual, was determined to excavate the tombs in their chronological order, and it was at least another year or more before he finally arrived at the Vizier's tomb. When we eventually broke through into the main room after all those years, all we found was just another tomb the robbers had pillaged long ago. It was a shambles, and all the robbers had left behind was a collection of damaged furniture and a few ceremonial funereal jars.

"While Ayers went about restoring the main room, he left me with all the jars...hundreds of them, all filled with pieces of papyrus. At first I couldn't make much sense out of them, until almost a year later, I finally discovered there was a distinct grouping in the scrolls. As I began to link them together, it became evident that the first fifty or so jars I examined fell into three categories: One, the Vizier's activities over the years, which excited Ayers no end; two, information on the layout of his tomb; and finally, a detailed breakdown of its contents.

"I immediately alerted Ayers to the possibility that the Vizier's tomb was much larger than he first thought, and the information I gathered enabled him to break through one of the decorated walls, and find a whole labyrinth of rooms on the other side. This extensive exercise gave me time to study the contents description, and I soon found out the pieces of papyrus were an indication of a vast fortune, maybe even as extensive as they found in the tomb of Tutankhamun."

"What did Ayers say to that?" Jordan questioned.

"I didn't tell him. He was so excited to find a tomb that had not been disturbed for three thousand years; I decided to keep the information to myself for a while. Besides, I hadn't deciphered all the papyrus yet, but I did ascertain one thing early on: Vizier Hykotep was clever enough to realise his tomb would be raided."

"What back then? I thought that was a much later pattern."

"Oh no, Inspector... the robbers ransacked the tombs almost immediately, that's why they employed specialist builders to design elaborate tombs. The trouble was they overlooked the fact that the builders most probably plundered the tombs themselves, or sold the plans for a handsome sum. Either way, Hykotep found a way to guarantee his wealth would be waiting for him on the other side."

"And how did he do that?"

Naseby gestured for another drink, satisfied his thirst and continued.

"I found what I considered to be the most important piece of papyrus yet. The trouble was, it was written in parables, but I managed to decipher enough to realise the answer was on his coffin, which Ayers hadn't found yet."

"I thought you said he had broken into the tomb?" Jordan asked.

"He had. But Hykotep had designed his tomb to be a labyrinth of false rooms with blocked off passageways; each one taking days to dismantle."

"His delaying tactic?"

"Yes...but there was a much cleverer plan. I discovered amongst his puzzling parables a clue to kill the builder and the men chosen to work on the burial chamber. 'Once interred, he would provide their last meal,' it said, but I was confused, how could he provide a last meal if he was dead?"

Although Jordan wanted to know everything, Naseby's account was beginning to tire him, "So what happened then?"

"Don't be impatient, Inspector; this is one of those stories that are full of clues. Have you not realised that by now?"

"I can't say I have."

"Well I had discovered a vast treasure, and all I needed was the clue to unlock its whereabouts; which meant Ayers had to find the sarcophagus holding the coffin, with the clue for me to continue. That was my first step on the shaky road of destiny. I decided I didn't want Ayers to know of the Vizier's wealth; meaning I had a problem on my hands when I finally worked it all out."

"When in fact did that actually occur?"

"Ah...that's when fate decided to step in and change my life, Inspector: in the guise of shiny black jackboots."

"I don't follow."

"Mussolini man...he invaded Egypt and put an end to our dig. We couldn't return until after the war."

"Hold on," Jordan interrupted, "My archaeologist friend told me Ayers managed to bring the Vizier's sarcophagus back to England in 1939."

"Not quite. The sarcophagus was an enormous thing made of black basalt; Ayers brought the coffin back. He broke into the burial chamber just before the Italians moved into Egypt, and he crated it up, along with what artefacts he had and returned home. He wasn't going to let the Nazis get hold of his work. They were very interested in that sort of thing you know. At least Hitler was."

"And you followed."

"Yes. I spent the war years working on the rest of the papyrus."

"Where did the robbery come into it?"

"You fathomed that out as well, Inspector?"

"I told you I had most of the cards."

At that point, when Naseby's tale was finally beginning to interest Jordan, the door opened and Cartwright quietly interrupted, "I'm sorry, Sir, but there is a Sergeant Crosby on the phone for the, Inspector...he says it's urgent."

"Oh very well. Don't be long, Inspector, or I shall forget where I was."

Jordan leant over him when he stood up, "I doubt that Naseby," he said, then followed Cartwright out into the hall where there was a telephone on a small table.

"Is that you, Boss?" a voice said when he picked the phone up.

"Yes, Josh...what is it?"

"Thank goodness you haven't gone into the vault yet."

"How do you know I haven't?"

Josh sounded excited and sucked in a deep breath, "Because if you had, you might not be talking to me now."

"You're not making much sense, Josh."

"I'm sorry, Boss. I've just finished my interview with Strand, and he told me the oddest story about Naseby nearly suffocating him in the vault. And following that, he almost incinerated the files."

Jordan paused for a moment and checked that he was not overheard.

"Josh...just settle down and recall what he actually said."

"Right, Boss...It seems the vault is fitted with an anti-burglar system, only this one doesn't just warn you of an intruder, it sucks all the air out of the vault and suffocates him. Strand found this out when Naseby caught him looking at the files, instead of dropping what he had into a filing basket like he usually did..."

"Wait a minute, what's this about a filing basket?"

"Apparently, Strand dropped what he had in a basket for Cartwright to check and then he filed it in the vault. He's the only one who goes into the vault."

"Okay, I'm with you now...Carry on."

"Right...well Cartwright was helping Naseby when Strand came in and as the vault door was open; he walked inside, and got curious. The next thing he knows the vault door slammed shut and he hears a pump sucking the air out. A few minutes later, when Strand was gasping for air, the door opened again and Naseby told him the next time he did that he would be dead."

"So what about the incineration."

"Oh yes...Strand was so furious, when he stepped out he pushed the button to close the door, but instead of the vault door swinging shut, two doors slid out of the architrave, like lift doors, and LED numbers on a small panel started counting up from zero. And Naseby screamed for Cartwright."

Jordan glanced at his watch, "What happened then?"

"Cartwright pushed Strand out of the way and punched a button again. The numbers stopped, and the doors slid back again. Only this time he said he felt a gush of hot air hit his face. He said it was really hot."

"Did he tell you what button?"

"No, Boss...I was lucky to get that much."

"All right, Josh thanks for the warning. I haven't time to get my head around what you just said, Naseby's into an interesting part of his story, but I want you to go back to Strand and go through the sequence again. I want to know what he did to turn that vault into an incinerator."

"Okay, Boss. Do you want me to ring you back?"

"No...I don't think I'll be long now. And Naseby made it quite clear that I wouldn't get to see the files until our next meeting, or the one following that."

"Right, Boss...I'll get back to Strand."

Jordan was about to replace the receiver when he wondered if Cartwright had been listening in, and still with the phone to his ear, he pressed the hook. All he heard was the continuous purr of an outside line, and satisfied his call had been a private one, he replaced the phone.

"Sorry about that, Naseby," Jordan said, re-entering the room.

Cartwright was in the process of freshening Naseby's hands and face with a damp cloth from the en suite, and returning it, he shot Jordan an unusual glance.

"I hope you're not going to keep Mr Naseby too long, Inspector."

"I think that's up to Mr Naseby, he's the one doing all the talking."

"Don't fuss Cartwright," Naseby said, "I'll ring when I'm finished."

"Very well, Sir," he replied, and left.

"Now, Inspector...where was I?"

"You were going to tell me about the robbery."

"Ah yes. As I said, we had to return from Egypt, that was 1939, and as you can imagine, England was in turmoil at the time. Everyone was preparing for the war with Germany.

I was forced to register with the army like most able-bodied-men at the time, but as it turned out I was too old at thirty seven, so I was offered the option of serving in a reserved occupation."

"What did that mean? I've heard about it."

"It meant you had to serve in a capacity that helped the war effort for the duration of the war. Something like mining, factory work, in the hospitals or something else in one of the ministries...you know the sort of thing."

"What did they catch you for?"

"I was lucky actually. When I started telling this old Sergeant from the past war, that I didn't really have any skills, I didn't fancy being an Air Raid Warden or enlisting in the Home Guard, he started running his finger down the long list he had in front of him, and he suddenly stopped with a broad smile on his face.

"Apparently the government had become very concerned when they heard Hitler was ransacking Poland and France of their national heritage: you know, all the treasures they had locked away in their museums. Consequently they decided to form a department, strictly confined to coordinating plans to safeguard our treasures."

"But what about the robbery?"

"I'm coming to that, Inspector...you want to know what led up to it I assume?" Jordan condescendingly nodded, "Nevertheless, I saw this as an opportunity to get my hands on the Vizier's coffin. It was just a thought mind you, I knew I had to have the opportunity to study it, and I didn't want to alert Ayers by making contact with him again. I don't know whether I mentioned it earlier, but we had a falling out. I didn't want him to take the coffin out of Egypt so early."

"The Robbery, Naseby," Jordan said impatiently.

"Yes. Well, some months later, during the first week of the Blitz, I noticed on my list of museums and galleries ready to transport their artefacts, that the Ayers Gallery, that was its name at the time, had set aside a shipment for dispatch to a designated estate. Since I was the one who selected the destination and organised the shipment, I brought forward my plans.

"I must point out that after my return from Egypt; I made contact with my old university friend Willy Lyle again. If my plan to steal the Vizier's coffin was to be successful, I needed someone with me who had certain contacts: people on the fringe of society that were capable of pulling off this delicate manoeuvre. I didn't have any capital you see, and although my prime objective was the coffin, there was enough money in the other artefacts to pay these people and set Willy and myself up for life. Or at least fund the coming expedition to find the Vizier's treasure."

Suddenly a shrill alarm interrupted Naseby, and Cartwright entered the room again with the big man in white, Han's muscles rippled as he carried his pile of soft towels to Naseby's bed, and Jordan knew his time was up.

"Damn," Jordan cursed.

"Sorry, Inspector," Naseby said, as Hans wheeled him back to the bed. "I promise tomorrow's meeting will start with the Robbery."

CHAPTER 22

Despite Jordan's preoccupation with Naseby's intriguing disclosures, he was becoming aware of a disturbing change in his emotions. Instead of the expected euphoria of discovering his suppositions were proving right, he was beginning to experience an overwhelming sense of apprehension.

It was not a feeling Jordan had become aware of immediately. A pervasive process had crept up on him and suddenly escalated after Penny's accident. It had crossed his mind that he was getting through the day without a flashback, along with the realisation that his nightmares had stopped.

Jordan was plagued with the thought that something serious was about to happen or worse still, nothing at all. He had put up with his nightmares for thirty years, and to be without them was something he dared not imagine.

When Jordan backed into his parking spot, he pushed himself back into his seat as far as he could and waited a moment. For some reason he found himself holding his breath, and let it out in a sudden rush, that caused him to gasp. He really wanted to look up at the Chief Superintendent's windows without him seeing. He sighed with relief, there was no stern, frowning face for him to hide from, and he quickly left the car and dashed across to the entrance.

Signing in at the desk Jordan's stomach let out a loud rumble, and he suddenly realised he had missed his lunch.

Sergeant Fawcett also realised the fact as he smiled and walked over to the counter, "Are you thinking of going down to the canteen, Sir?"

Jordan felt his stomach, "Yes...I suppose I should. Although I don't really fancy canteen food at the moment, perhaps I'll treat myself to a sandwich."

"I'd hold off on that if I were you, Sir," the Sergeant advised. "The Chief Superintendent's looking for you."

"I didn't see him at the window."

"Probably because he has the Commissioner with him."

"Oh great...that's the last person I want to bump into. What are they doing?"

"I'd say they were having lunch about now in the conference room."

"How do you know?"

"I just sent the caterers up to his office."

Jordan suddenly looked more cheerful, "Oh well...I can wait till he's finished then. Pass me the phone and I'll ring Phyllis."

To Jordan's dismay, when she advised the Chief Superintendent that he had arrived, they called him up straight away. Apparently, they were just talking about Jordan and his interview with Naseby, and wanted to know how he got on.

Jordan looked glum as he replaced the phone on the hook, unlike the Sergeant's cheerful expression, "Can't get out of it, Sir?"

"So it seems, Sergeant."

"Cheer up, Sir...if you let them know you missed your lunch, they might offer you some. Or better still; let your tummy do the talking for you."

Jordan laughed sarcastically and moved on up the stairs. "Oh, Sergeant...let Constable Crosby know where I am, you know how he worries."

By the middle of the afternoon, Jordan finally entered his office, and all he wanted to do was drop into his seat and sleep. Josh looked surprised, walked over to Jordan's desk and planted himself on the corner.

Jordan opened his lids and stared at him. "What do you want?"

"Are you all right, Boss?"

"No. I've had a torturous time with Naseby, and as soon as I got back the Chief Superintendent invited me up to have lunch with him and the Commissioner."

"Sounds nice. Was it a good meal?"

"I don't know...I didn't get much of a chance to eat it."

"Asking a lot of questions, were they?"

"It was endless. I know what that bugger of a Commissioner wants. He's only interested in getting his hands on Naseby's files. But he won't get them, not if I have anything to do with it," he sat up. "By the way...did you get any more information about the vault out of Strand?"

"It depends on what you call information, Boss. It was like drawing teeth, and because I only got it out of him bit by bit, I can't guarantee its validity."

"Run it by me."

"Right...As far as I can work out, to get into the vault, you first have to dial in the correct combination: a green light comes on next to the opening. Then you have to turn the wheel to disengage the dogs, I think that's what they call them. Those big metal bars that go into the architrave. Then you press the green light and the door opens," he glanced back at his notes, "Yes…that's right."

"That's all very well, Josh, but how did he nearly suffocate Strand, and what about the incinerator?"

"I'm coming to that, Boss. I have to tell you the sequence, because it all depends on the light. That's the one that goes green when the door opens."

"Okay, Josh…in your own time."

He clasped his hands about his face and thought for a moment, running through the sequence in his mind. "Okay… Now the light goes red when the door is open. That's right, but if you press it again, the inner doors shut and that's when the vault evacuates the air, but it doesn't lock. You have to turn the wheel to do that. The door shutting is a security device to catch burglars, or in this case kill them. I suppose Naseby doesn't want them to tell anyone what's in the vault."

"But someone has to be in the room to shut the door."

"Oh no, Boss. That was going to be my next point. In that mode the door stays open for five minutes, then it closes on its own. Apparently, there's an overriding switch above the architrave when Naseby or his butler are inside. But Strand told me they never go inside together."

"He doesn't trust his own system by the sounds of it. In any case, Naseby can't use his hands. He has to be fed and cleaned like a baby."

"That's not quite true, Boss; not according to Strand. Seemingly, he has used his hands on occasions. It's just that it takes so much out of him, he doesn't."

"Okay, there's no light on when the door is shut and locked. When it's unlocked it goes green, and when the door opens it goes red."

"Right, Boss."

"So what happens to make the vault incinerate."

"Ah…that's when it gets tricky, Boss. Strand wasn't sure about that bit. All he remembers is hitting the button, which should have closed the door. He thinks he hit both, because he says he saw both lights flash before the red light came on again. It was certainly red when the lift-like doors slid out from the architrave. And that's when a small glass panel above the lights lit up with numbers and started counting up, before Naseby nearly lost it, and Cartwright took over."

Jordan found himself running through the sequence as Josh had. It sounded complicated, but when he thought about it, it was quite simple really. The trouble was Josh kept persistently asking Jordan questions about his lunch, but time after time Jordan skimmed over the surface, preferring not to divulge the true nature of the Commissioner's interest in the files.

He joked about the sumptuous turkey and sliced pork the caterers delivered in heated tureens, compared to the shepherds pie or bangers and mash that the canteen served up. How trifle with real cream was far more palatable than suet pudding. Josh laughed, and their conversation drifted back to Jordan's dilemma with Naseby's vault.

"Are you really going to incinerate the files, Boss?"

"If I can. The trouble is; I'm not sure I really understand how the damn thing works. Don't forget…It will have to be a spur-of-the-moment thing."

Josh considered a rehearsal might be in order, and when he finally summoned the courage to suggest it, he was surprised to find Jordan thought it was a good idea. Josh had no way of knowing Jordan was a great believer in enactments.

Jordan cleared his blotter, went over to Penny's desk and unscrewed the caps off a red and green bottle of ink that she used to highlight her records. Placing them on the blotter, he motioned to Josh.

"What, Boss?"

"The door, Josh...we need a door."

Josh looked around and decided to use a portable radiator that was not in use yet, and wheeled it across the floor to Jordan's desk.

"How about that, Boss?"

"Perfect," Jordan said, holding one end while he swivelled the other.

This was not what Josh had in mind, but it sufficed.

"Right, Josh," Jordan started. "You handle the door and I'll try and remember the light sequence. Josh readied himself. "Okay," Jordan continued. "Let's assume the combination has been dialled in, you've turned the wheel to unlock the dogs, and the green light comes on. I press the green light," he gestures to Josh to pull back the radiator, "as the door opens, the red light goes on."

"Perfect, Boss," Josh calls out.

"Right. Now the door is open and the red light is on. If I wanted to close it I would press the red light, but if I wanted to incinerate the files, I would press both simultaneously," Jordan thumps his clenched fist down on top of both ink caps.

"Whoosh, they're gone, Boss."

"I don't know. It sounds too simple. The same mistake that happened to Strand could happen anytime. There has to be a safety device."

"I don't think so, Boss. That's how Strand made the mistake."

Jordan shrugged his shoulders, picked up the caps and screwed them back onto Penny's inkbottles, while Josh wheeled the radiator back across the room.

"It's all immaterial really, Josh. They're never going to let me get near the vault. What with Cartwright watching me like a hawk and that gladiator of a masseuse called Hans ready to crush my neck, I'll be lucky to examine anything. Still, a deal's a deal. I have to verify the files before I accept Naseby's terms."

"Everything will go according to plan, Boss, you'll see."

"I wish I had your confidence."

Visiting penny and her mother at the Sherwood Lodge was becoming a routine, not to mention a grand evening meal at the expense of the department. The suspicious Concierge was no longer glancing down at his log of visitors to see if Jordan and Josh were on his list. He casually looked up, and on seeing them, courteously smiled.

In the room, Penny glanced up and her face suddenly glowed. "At last," she said, turning around on the couch, "I've been waiting for someone to call all day."

"I would have thought, living like a lady would have been sufficient," Jordan said, glancing over towards her mother sitting on the opposite couch, and giving her a warm smile. "You should be making the best of things. The department aren't going to pay for this luxury for ever you know."

"I know," Penny said, with a sigh, "But do you know something, Inspector; you can have all your luxury as far as I'm concerned."

"You're joking, Penny," Josh said, walking around to the drinks cabinet, "Can I, Boss? I'm gagging for a drink."

Jordan looked at his watch, "I suppose so. You're still on duty for the next five minutes, but who's counting."

"That's all this is to you, Josh," Penny said, "A place where you can drink and eat yourself silly at the department's expense."

"Of course...and to see the best girl in CAS."

Penny laughed, "Silly...I'm the only girl in CAS."

"Well there you are," Josh said, opening a bottle of lager."

"Do they go on like this all the time, Inspector?" Penny's mother asked.

"All the time," he said. "Now you can see what I have to put up with."

It was too early to order a meal yet, so the three of them sat around the fire talking about the state of the case, while Penny's mother went for her usual stroll around the hotel.

Penny laughed, "She doesn't think I know, but she goes off to the games room and plays poker with the old men."

"Poker?" Jordan questioned, while Josh almost choked on his beer. "Your mother plays poker? At her age."

"Oh yes. She's quite a good player actually. She learnt in one of those old peoples community centres. They played whist at first, then bridge, and when they finally got sick of that they learnt to play poker."

"Well I never," Jordan said. "Does she play for money?"

"Oh yes...and she wins."

Then, on the dot of eight, Penny's mother returned for her meal. No one said anything, preferring to let her think she was having some fun on the side.

"So, Inspector," Penny continued, "You're in the last stages of the case?"

"Just tying up loose ends now, Penny," he bluffed.

She changed her position, this time, resting the contraption she was still supporting, on the arm of the couch. "I'm going to miss everything," she said, by the time this thing comes off, you'll have Naseby behind bars."

"I don't think so, Penny...you mustn't have heard me. Naseby has only a month or so to live. By the time I draw up all the charges he'll be dead."

"Then what has all this been for?"

"We didn't know when we started...did we? Besides, we had to clean up the riddle of the Egyptian mummy in Sherwood Forest."

"Oh yes...our Sherwood Forest Man."

"Exactly. It hasn't been for nothing. Anyway, both of you had some good training through it. You've got your first case under your belt, and wherever you go from now on, it will stand you in good stead."

"What do you mean? Wherever we go," Penny said.

"Well I don't expect to be an Inspector after this. I was only engaged to sort this lot out after all. And when it's done, I'll return to the college."

Penny looked glum, and Josh was beginning to, when Penny's mother looked at her watch and spoke up.

"Are we having our meal now?"

It was unusually late when Jordan arrived back at his cold house in Clifton Beck; much too late to start the fire he had taken great pains to arrange before he left that morning, and he made straight for his small stock of drinks in the lounge.

He had hung on at the Sherwood Lodge until Penny's mother asked if he and Josh had any homes to go to, and they left, much to Penny's disappointment. She had trouble sleeping also, except her difficulty had nothing to do with nightmares.

Jordan sat by the unlit fire drinking his whisky wondering what was wrong with him. He had wished for a nightmare free night for years, and now that he appears to have that wish, he can't sleep. His problem was the anticipation. The wondering whether he has finally left his wife and children's deaths behind. The thought of being able to start a new life again after thirty years, was frightening.

The drink he had absorbed up to this point he thought may be enough to send him staggering off to sleep, but it was not enough, he was still wide awake, and the memory of that day back in Kenya was as strong as ever.

He poured another, this time bringing the bottle back with him to the couch, and he decided to take advantage of the clarity he was experiencing. In the past, his mind had kept that point in time cloaked with a veil of unclear flashes of what might have happened. According to Mark, it was his subconscious mind's way of keeping the truth from him, and softening the guilt.

Now, for some inexplicable reason, he could look upon the event as just that: an unfortunate incident that came about by the misfortunes of the time.

When Jethro Merrick stepped out onto the veranda that morning, a warm breeze coming across the burnt grass of the African savannah brushed his face. He remembers wondering why he agreed to come to this God forsaken place: the flies, wild animals, disease, unfriendly natives and the relentless heat.

Jessie had walked him to the flyscreen, kissed him goodbye and immediately stepped back inside, lest the flies invaded the house. He smiled at her and their fingers touched on the stiff mesh, and he said goodbye again; he wouldn't be late.

In reality, Merrick had no idea when he would be back, the Mau-Mau where being particularly difficult since their leader was captured, still harassing the local farmers and any traffic that was stupid enough to travel alone on the dirt roads. The fact that there was no cover, made little difference to the Mau-Mau: they could hide in grass no higher than their ankles, but where Merrick lived, it was up to his waist.

Merrick thought the first three false calls were the pranks of the tribal boys, getting their own back for being banned from the local tavern, but it was not until he asked his driver to stop, so he could check the map, that he suddenly realised they were being slowly drawn farther away from his normal route.

Merrick called the station on the radio, but there was no reply, and when he changed the frequency to contact the other patrols, he found to his surprise that they too were all doing the same thing: chasing shadows.

By the time Merrick got back to the station, everyone was dead. He could see his comrade's revolvers were still in their holsters, yet they had all been hacked to death. His black driver was certain it was the Mau-Mau; no more than three or four, yet they slaughtered half a dozen men and women that knew nothing more than typing reports. Merrick said that was why they wanted the patrols out on the road, until the patrol north of his house returned.

It was Sergeant Grant. He was red faced and angry, but more than that, he was fearful of facing his good friend Jethro Merrick. He had to tell his friend that his place had burnt to the ground, his livestock run off, his tribal workers murdered and worst of all, his wife and children were lost in the blaze. By the time Merrick got back to his homestead there was nothing left, except eleven black bags.

That was when Merrick, and those on patrol that survived the massacre, banded together to hunt down those responsible. Their pursuit of the Mau-Mau took on a sinister momentum; they slaughtered far more than three or four.

Jordan poured himself another drink, and for the first time, he felt he knew what really happened back in Kenya. His memories came flooding back: not only the good times, but also the bad ones that followed his wife and children's death. The time when he and his friends reverted to animals, no better than the savages they hunted, until they too became criminals, locked away from public scrutiny.

Then his friend, Nathan Mulholland, a Superintendent in the English police, flew over to fight on his behalf, and with the help of the British Government, the African authorities released them into British custody.

There was no getting away with what he had done, but there was no public trial either, they feared their actions would jeopardise the rebuilding of Kenya. Merrick, his chosen name then, received a suspended sentence, an unspecified duration of psychotherapy and a reduction in rank.

He needed a new start in England, and that was when Merrick decided to change his name to his mother's maiden name. She was pleased; he now had a biblical name that stood for: Excellence...Friend of God.

CHAPTER 23

It was the second day of Naseby's confessions. Jordan arrived at the station early, made his appointment with Cartwright for ten o'clock, and settled down with Josh and the files they had put together on the Sherwood Forest Man, for a two-hour brief on the robbery and murders that subsequently led to Naseby's downfall.

Despite knowing Naseby would not live long enough for a trial, Jordan wanted to end this case efficiently, as if the court had indicted Naseby.

After sorting through the files on Penny's desk Jordan placed his hand on the first pile and looked across at Josh. "I might be away a little longer than last time Josh, because I want to see if I can get Naseby to open the vault today instead of tomorrow. If I can, you know what the outcome will be, and I shall ring you."

"Why did we go through all the files then, Boss?"

"I know we're not going to be able to charge Naseby, but when it's closed, I want to be able to present a complete case. I would have preferred you to be along on Naseby's journey, so that you could type it up from memory, but I think it's better this way. When it comes down to it…it was only to do with Naseby and myself."

"If that's the way you want it, Boss."

"It is Josh, but in the meantime, I want you to go through each stage of the case and prepare a statement as if he was being charged...all right?"

"I understand, Boss. You'll provide the conclusion in each case when you get back. I still need more detail on the truck robbery, and Gallagher's subsequent murder. I already know about the Vizier's mummy, and how it got to England, and the bit about Naseby being put in charge of the countries valuable assets."

"Don't forget what happened before 1940. That's important. We need to prove what happened then was part of Naseby's grand plan, and that everything that followed was a continuance of that plan. The Vizier's treasure, although he hasn't told me about it yet, Ayers' death, circumstantial or otherwise, and there's Willy Lyle's death also, but that doesn't fit in until much later. You need to establish his presence in all this, back when Naseby murdered Ayers," Jordan prompted.

"It's become complicated, Boss. Who would have thought finding an old pile of bones would have turned out to be a sixty-year-old saga. Still...who would have thought you could have made this much of it, certainly not Inspector Dent."

"Why bring his name into it?"

"I bumped into him in the canteen yesterday. He came and sat down beside me and asked how you were getting on."

"Oh...and what did you say?"

"I told him you had solved the case and was in the process of charging someone," he laughed, "I didn't mention Naseby, Boss."

"But he did."

"Yes...how did you know?"

"Well as I said earlier, I had suspected DS Ward of being our leak for some time, and as he was Dent's confidant, it stands to reason that he would keep him informed of our progress. How did he react to the arrest?"

"He laughed, Boss."

"He laughed?…Did he say why?"

"He said we would never get Naseby to court."

Jordan laughed this time, "And he was right," Jordan said, glancing at his watch. "Anyway, Josh…I must get off to Naseby's. Sorry you're stuck in the office, but it's better than being stuck in the car outside."

"That's all right, Boss. I think I'll enjoy going through the case again. Up until now, we've just been adding new chapters without any revision, and we rather lost track of the events. Now I can sit down and build it up from the beginning, see how it developed over the years."

"That's good, Josh, I'm glad you see it that way," Jordan answered as he opened the door to leave. "By the way… don't forget to put in all the dates; they'll sort of give the tale substance…if you know what I mean."

Josh nodded and walked across to the files on Penny's desk.

For some reason, when Jordan entered the familiar room that had become Naseby's prison for the past ten years, Naseby looked more agile than he had done.

"What's wrong with your boss?" Jordan asked Cartwright, as he went through the regular routine of laying out Naseby's water and Jordan's white wine.

"I don't quite know what you mean, Inspector."

"Well look at him. His eyes are bright, his complexion is rosy and he looks as if he could rise right up to the ceiling, if it wasn't for all the wires and tubes holding him down. Has he been drinking?"

"You know he isn't allowed alcohol, Inspector. No... the doctor came this morning and decided to give him an injection to lift his spirits. He thought his condition was deteriorating too quickly. And when Mr Naseby told him of your visit, and that he needed his whits about him...you can see the difference."

"He's as high as a kite," Jordan said.

"I heard that, Inspector," Naseby said softly, "a little cocaine now and then helps me focus my thoughts."

"I would have thought it would do the opposite, Naseby," Jordan said. "I want you focused today. I want the whole story cleared up. I'm not going to let this saga drag on any longer than it has to...and I want to verify the files today as well."

"My, Inspector...what a lot of 'I want's'," Naseby said, as Cartwright wheeled him round to the nest of chairs. "We'll see...I mean about the vault. The story is nearly finished anyway...the end is very near."

"They'll be no 'We'll see,' Naseby. If we don't settle this today, to my satisfaction, I shall lodge the papers with the prosecutor tomorrow morning. Then once they're in his hands, they're as good as public. I'd hand the lot to your reporter Sarah Bolt if I didn't know she probably knew more than me already."

"I'll give you this, Inspector; you've done a thorough job. Pity you weren't working for me...you could have done well. Nonetheless, I may be a little high at the moment to help me get through this ordeal, but I'm also very tired, and I too want to see the end of all this," he beckoned for a drink and Cartwright put the straw to his mouth, and after he quenched his thirst he continued. "I'm happy to do as you say, provided you can promise me that none of this will taint the Ayers Foundation."

"I have no wish to interfere in the Foundation's good work Naseby. If I see no signs of them connected to your conspiracy, then they have nothing to fear. The case will be closed as promised."

He meandered for a moment, and then looked up sharply with a glint in his eye, "Do you know how much I'm worth, Inspector?"

"I'm not really interested."

"The Commissioner is."

"Is that so?"

"Yes...he was very interested when I told him I had set aside a sizeable sum for the police benevolent society."

Jordan was surprised, "I bet he was. But if you think that will make me reconsider my position...you're sadly mistaken."

"Oh dear, inspector, you're too perfect. Life must be a terrible bore. Still...I just thought you would like to know, not everyone thinks my money is tainted."

Jordan sipped his wine slowly. "Are you finished...can we get on with the interview now?" He said, taking out his notebook.

Naseby settled into his story-telling mode, and pursing his lips as he stared over towards the opposite wall, he started, "Yes, Inspector, we were in the first week of the Blitz. A bomb hit St. Paul's, not too severely thank goodness, and the docks were in a bit of a state, so they pressed me to find a home for the nation's treasures.

"The Crown Jewels, the National Gallery and the British Museum were already taken care of, it was the smaller, and greater part of the national collections that needed help. As soon as I came across Ayers' establishment, and read the artefacts he was sending out of the city, I realised this was my chance. Since I was born and bred in Nottingham, and the major estate there was on the list of acceptable residences, I chose to send Ayers' shipment there. As I said earlier, I had already planned how I was going to achieve my goal, which not only needed the cooperation of the local Home Guard, but the mysterious environment of Sherwood Forest.

"That's where my good friend Willy Lyle came in. He organised to infiltrate one of his men onto the driving roster, as well as a back-up lorry to carry away the artefacts. At first we thought of hijacking the shipment, but that would have given the police too much of an opportunity to do their forensics, question the driver and chase the trail of the stolen valuables through the usual fences.

"No...the robbery had to be done in such a way that the driver could say he had amnesia, and the lorry with all its contents was burnt beyond recognition. There had to be a crash on the road through Sherwood Forest. The lorry would have to roll over and burst into flames. They arranged to leave a petrol can in the wreck; it was against the rules, but who was going to question the oversight after everything was lost. Petrol was difficult to get hold of at the time, and it was a common enough practise to carry a spare can, just in case."

Naseby gestured for another drink, he seemed in a hurry, and was soon recalling the incident again. "Lyle provided a couple of men to pick up the shipment at the station, whilst we drove another lorry to the crash sight. I had spent all week loading the lorry with old materials that could easily be construed as the burnt remains of Ayer's collection, and I was quite prepared to sacrifice a broken pot or two to salt the ashes...it made it look more believable."

"I suspected all that, Naseby," Jordan reminded. "And that you used the collection to finance your search for the treasure, but what happened to Gallagher?"

"He got too big for his boots. The robbery went off so well, he thought he could blackmail me to give him a bigger share. I left Lyle to take care of him."

"And what about Ripley?"

"He was an unambitious little man. He was highly delighted with his share and gave us no trouble at all...except when Lyle had to get rid of Gallagher."

"He wanted more money as well?" Jordan suggested.

"No...he was just frightened out of his whits. Lyle told him to leave Nottingham, and not to come back, if he wanted to live. We didn't set out to kill anyone, Inspector. Gallagher brought that on himself."

"Okay...Now you have the money to search for the Vizier's treasure, and you went back to Egypt with Ayers."

"Hold on, Inspector, you make it sound as if it all happened overnight. It was nearly fourteen years before we got back. There was a war on remember, and it wasn't until 1948 before Egypt was reasonably stable again, but still a dangerous place to be moving around in. Then there was the terrible upheaval when Israel came into existence. Egypt was at war again, along with its neighbours Jordan, Syria and Lebanon, there was no way they were going to allow excavators back into their country. Then there was the Suez Canal crisis in 1950, so it wasn't until 1954 when Ayers got permission to return.

"It was just as well really," he started chuckling again, "After all that I didn't break the code until 1952. I knew it was on the Vizier's coffin somewhere, but my hieroglyphics weren't as good as I thought. I kept copying small sections and taking them round to scholars, hoping I could then piece together what they had deciphered. They all said the same. They could see it was only a fragment, and they needed the whole thing to get the true picture.

"Nevertheless, I did it eventually, or at least I discovered where the last clue would be. The funny thing was; it was under the stone sarcophagus all the time."

"The clue was?"

"No...well yes, to discover the clue I had to move the sarcophagus, and in doing so, I discovered the subterranean vault," Jordan looked vague. "Have another drink, Inspector and I shall explain."

Jordan poured himself a drink and glanced at his watch. He was concerned that he might not have time to get at the vault before Hans came in for his daily physiotherapy session with Naseby, "I thought you said you were almost finished?"

"I am, Inspector, have patience. When Ayers and I left the site in 1939, we stoned the entrance up, more to protect the tomb from the elements than any would-be thieves, and during those war years we thought no one would be interested."

"And was it still walled up?"

"Yes it was. The permit we had still entitled us to work the area, but it was made quite plain to us that there would be no more plundering of Egypt's heritage." Naseby wheezed, "They hadn't cared a damn, and now they were interested. Anyway, over the next six or so months we completed the tidying up of the Vizier's tomb, I had to be extremely careful, if I wanted to find my clue without Ayers knowing, while he finished off deciphering the pictograms in the Mastaba Chapel: that's the place where the entombed persons relatives could leave offerings."

"I'm not really interested," Jordan said, watching his time slip away.

"Sorry, Inspector…I was having no luck finding the clue I wanted. I had misread the scroll somehow, there were no identifying hieroglyphics at the base of the sarcophagus, and when I was just about to give up, and sitting with my back against the stone having a drink of water, I spilt the canteen. I jumped up, brushing it off myself as you do, and I didn't think that it was so hot it would dry so soon. Then I noticed the pool of water draining away through the crack in the stones. I knelt down, took out my spatular and started removing the old mortar from between the flags. As I did so, instead of it building up either side, it fell straight through."

"The vault you were looking for was underneath the sarcophagus?"

"Exactly…There was nothing I could do while Ayers was about, so I made arrangements for him to have an unfortunate accident."

"You had him killed?"

"If you like, and I'm sure you know the rest. I called my friend Willy Lyle to come over and help me, and to get around the new regulations, we opened a company with an Egyptian partner, registered to export local artefacts. It was becoming quite an industry by then: taking genuine artefacts and dressing them up to look like cheap imitations. The locals had become experts at the trade."

"And you slowly plundered the Vizier's tomb?"

"That's right, Inspector."

Jordan finished o ff hi s no tes, an d he lped Na seby wi th another drink before his last two questions "What happened to Lyle?"

"Ah...My good friend Willy Lyle; he was never interested in money like me. His only use for money was to spend it, have as much enjoyment as he could; he was a strong believer in the saying; 'You can't take it with you,' and as he got poorer, I got richer. You see, my pleasure was not in what I could get out of the money, but what I could do with it, and as he spent his share, I invested mine."

"And he thought you were getting a bigger share."

"Right again, Inspector. So...eventually he had to go, otherwise he would have spent everything. I decided enough was enough when he asked me to go and see his latest extravagance: a chalet on the slopes of the Pyrenees..."

"Sorry to spoil your recollections Naseby," Jordan interrupted, "but once again I managed to find out all about what happened to Lyle on the Pas de la Casa. It was in all the local papers at the time. I just wanted you to admit that it wasn't an accident."

"Well, Inspector, it seems that I already did. I wasn't proud of it, but he would have ruined my plans for the Ayers Foundation. I told him, I expected Christopher to take it over one day. Lyle couldn't care less. He was one of the worst hedonists I ever met. Funny thing is, he was never like that when we started."

Jordan had almost reached the end of his interview, "And one final question Naseby, Why did you bury the Vizier, when you could have burnt him?"

He chuckled again, "They always say it's the smallest things that bring you down. I didn't have time to get the mummy out of the coffin, nor did I want to. So often did the

Pharaohs have amulets and other objects implanted amongst the wrappings, I thought it would be wise to check him out with the coffin."

"And did he?"

"There were a few pieces, but nothing that would guide me to the place where he hid his fortune for the afterlife. By the time I had finished with him he was no more than a husk of dried flesh and bones, and I wasn't about to wrap him up again, or get rid of him in a matter-of-fact way. He was a Vizier after all, and he deserved better. So...knowing that Sherwood Forest was a mass of Triassic pebble beds, I decided he would be well suited to the dry environment. And in case he was found, I placed an arrowhead in his body to delude the parochial constabulary that he might be from the time of Robin Hood."

"And of course you engaged the help of Sarah Bolt."

"Yes I did. She didn't know the truth. I just played with the ideas she was promoting at the time. She was all for stirring up the old skeleton murders; which I didn't have anything to do with by the way."

"I never thought you did."

"Good...But I underestimated you, Inspector. I never thought you would bring in an archaeologist. Why didn't you leave it with the pathologist?"

"I couldn't do that. But that wasn't the small thing that caught you."

"It wasn't?"

"No...I found an army button at the burial site. There was no way that could have belonged to your corpse, nor even one of Robin Hood's men."

"Gallagher!" He called out. "Lyle was against the idea of him burying the Vizier, I should have listened to him, but I didn't. I knew best, and I was more concerned with deciphering the coffin."

Jordan stood up, "I think it's time to check the vault, Naseby."

He looked reticent at first, but almost immediately, he smiled and pressed the button on the cord hanging across his shoulder.

Cartwright walked in, "Did you want something, Sir?"

"Yes, Cartwright," Naseby said, turning towards him, "Open the vault for the, Inspector." Cartwright looked surprised, "Go on...it's all right."

Cartwright went across to the large wheel on the front of the steel door and dialled in the combination. Then he turned the wheel anti-clockwise until Jordan heard a series of sharp clicks as the dogs slid back. As Cartwright moved across to his side of the door Jordan noticed the green light had come on, Cartwright pressed it, and the door opened back with a loud whoosh of air.

It was obvious, closing the vault evacuated the air, as the green light went off and the red one shone brightly. So far so good, Jordan thought; the sequence of lights was as Josh had explained to him. Now was the difficult moment.

Cartwright stepped back and ushered Jordan into the vault first, just as Jordan glanced over towards Naseby. He was silent, and his face had taken on an apprehensive look, almost expectant.

"Inspector," Cartwright said.

Jordan stepped to one side and took hold of Cartwright's arm, "No, Cartwright, you first. Step in and move to the back of the vault."

Cartwright shot a glance at Naseby then reluctantly stepped inside, and as he did so, he lifted his arm and flipped the switch above the architrave. It was a quick movement. If Jordan had not been aware of the safety override, and was expecting it, he might well have missed it altogether.

Before Jordan followed, he turned to face Naseby. "Aren't you worried I might find all your secret papers, or maybe even a stash of undeclared banknotes? And what about all the jewels you must have found amongst the Vizier's treasure?"

Naseby attempted a laugh, "There are no jewels left, Inspector, and as for any money, I leave all that at the bank, along with my papers. There are only files."

He was telling the truth. Jordan had intended to make only a cursory check of the cabinets that lined both sides of the vault, but no sooner had he started randomly opening one, he found himself curiously forced to open another.

Before long, he was checking every drawer. There was so much material on just about everyone that was anyone; he wished he did not intend to destroy the contents. There was a whole cabinet on the major players in the police: the judiciary, the council, even the fire brigade. Then there was the commercial section, tradesmen, manufacturers and shopkeepers, Naseby seemed to have something on all of them, but nothing of his own: no business documents or anything private. It was just a vault to contain the dossiers of sinners. He turned and looked out towards Naseby.

"I can see how you have so many people eating out of your hand, Naseby. This lot would frighten the life out of anyone."

"I consider it a good bargaining chip, Inspector."
"What's to stop someone else using these when you're gone?"

"You clear my name in writing and they will be destroyed."

"And what's to stop me calling my men in right now and taking the lot?"

"You must take me for a fool, Inspector," he replied curtly. "The moment anyone tries to break into my vault, it will be their last."

"I know about the air being sucked out."

Naseby laughed, and Cartwright followed.

"Their fate would be far worse than suffocating," Naseby declared.

Jordon knew what that fate would be.

Satisfied, Jordan turned round in the confined space and stepped out of the vault, before he gestured for Cartwright to follow. He had no idea whether the switch above the door would do anything to hinder his plans, and he left it, so did Cartwright. As soon as Cartwright left the vault, Jordan placed his hand on the two buttons.

"Is this the button I press," he said, depressing them both under his hand.

At first, neither Naseby nor Cartwright realised what button Jordan had pressed, they just looked surprised. As soon as the architrave doors slid shut instead of the vault door and the red numbers started counting off, Naseby screamed out to Cartwright, and he jumped towards Jordan.

"Step aside, Inspector," Cartwright shouted, reaching for Jordan's arm.

Despite his genteel demeanour, Cartwright was a powerful man. His huge arms enveloped Jordan immediately, wrapping around his chest like a boa constrictor, as if he had no sense of combat other than crushing his victims to death.

Even though Cartwright was a tall man, and his grip was far stronger than Jordan anticipated, Jordan had not forgotten his police training in Kenya.

Somehow he managed to writhe around so that he was facing the ferocious grimace of a desperate man; his gaze split between watching Jordan and the increasing red numbers; as if there was still time.

The veins in his temple looked as though they were about to burst, as Jordan wrestled one hand free, and cupping Cartwright's chin, he pushed his head back, as Naseby could be heard screaming vitriolic commands in the background.

Cartwright was still too strong. Jordan could feel his own strength waning against the relentless surge of power he was wrestling. As he strived to hold his own, he recalled the black tribesmen of Kenya; they too were tall and powerful, without fear or motive, other than to kill.

He remembered the way they killed Jessie and his children, and the rage he knew then suddenly took hold of him again. Cartwright's face suddenly became the face of a Mau-Mau tribesman, with a gaping, snarling mouth of snowy-white teeth, and Jordan felt young again.

He took hold of Cartwright's free hand, and gripping his thumb, Jordan bent it backwards, and at the same time, he pushed the whole arm forward until Cartwright's thumb reached his shoulder. Then Jordan heard that familiar crack, and Cartwright's ear-splitting scream.

Cartwright went limp, and Jordan was able to break free, and stagger back, just as Naseby attempted to scream and curse, but instead, only a feeble sound came out, as he coughed and spluttered.

The drug-induced agility had left Naseby as Cartwright reeled in agony, clutching at his broken thumb until he finally collapsed in a writhing heap on the floor, and Jordan was relieved to be alive. He had forgotten what he had set in motion when he pressed the two buttons, until a loud shrill alarm echoed around the room, as the vault reached its temperature; and he knew the files were gone.

With his nostrils full of the acrid smell of charred paper, Jordan glanced back at the numbers on the screen until they had counted back to zero. Cartwright had stopped screaming by now and was rolling back and forth on the floor, while Naseby had become silent; his head slumped on his chest.

Jordan walked back to the nest of chairs, reached down for his glass of wine and emptied it. Then he turned to Naseby. There was no reaction when he lifted Naseby's head; his eyes were staring blindly, with large gaping black holes for pupils. He felt for a pulse, there was none, and he guessed his nemesis was dead.

"That's not the end of it you know," Cartwright mumbled.

Jordan looked across at him, "It is for you. You're under arrest for impeding a police officer in the performance of his duty, and anything else I can think of."

Leaning against the corner of the bed, supporting his broken thumb, Cartwright sneered, as Jordan opened the door and went for the phone on the stand, "You've got Lyle to face now," he shouted after him.

Jordan picked up the phone and dialled the emergency number. "And what will he do?" he called back.

Through the open door, Jordan could see Cartwright attempting to lift himself up onto the bed. He must have been in excruciating pain, but he managed it and grabbing hold of a towel with his good hand, and holding one end in his teeth, he wound the rest around his broken thumb. Then he glared back at Jordan.

"He has the same powerful friends."

CHAPTER 24

As Jordan waited for the services to arrive, he stripped a pillowcase from its bolster on Naseby's bed and turned it into a sling for Cartwright's arm. Then Jordan walked over to the large window overlooking the gravel drive and looked across the meadow towards the main road.

Before long, he heard the wailing of a siren, and shortly after, saw the red and white flashes amongst the distant hedges. The ambulance arrived first and the medics soon confirmed that Naseby was dead, before they turned to the sorrowful figure of Cartwright and started attending to his hand.

Surprisingly, the second to arrive was the Pathologist, Chester Daniels. Jordan met him at the front door and walked him back to Naseby's room.

"How are you, Chester, the body is this way," he said.

"Hello, Jethro," Chester replied, shaking Jordan's hand. "I wondered what you were getting up to," he continued, stepping to one side for Jordan to lead the way, as he looked around the massive house, "So this is where it's taken you to?"

"Yes it has. You were quick…you've beaten everyone but the ambulance."

"Funny you should say that, I was only five minutes away when my assistant called," he said, poking his head into the room. "All right chaps?" he questioned, seeing the medics working on Cartwright. They nodded back.

"Naseby's over here, Chester," Jordan said.

Chester stood and looked at Naseby's limp body for a moment, he'd seen enough dead people for it not to mean anything, but this was the first time he attended someone so powerful. "What's that smell, Jethro?"

Jordan sniffed the air. Although the alarm had drawn his attention to the smell, the excitement of the moment had masked it. It was strong now, and acrid; the same smell he recalled when lighting the fire. It was the smell of burnt paper with the touch of firelighters, only in this case, it was probably the paint off the cabinets.

"Oh that! That's the smell of burning dossiers."

Chester shook his head; he had no time for riddles, and bent down to check Naseby's body. He then glanced around the room. "By the look of this room, Jethro, I gather Naseby here was an invalid."

"Yes...Multiple Sclerosis I understand. Oh and, he had an injection of cocaine just before I arrived. His doctor said it would energise him for his interview I believe. The butler over there knows all about it," Jordan nodded his head in Cartwright's direction.

Chester looked at the pathetic man. Cartwright was standing now, ready to go with the medics to the hospital, "What happened to him, or is that something else I shouldn't ask about?"

"I had to subdue him, Chester."

"Oh...I see," Chester remarked with a sense of understanding.

"What about, Naseby," Jordan asked.

"I would have to say, looking at his condition and the state of this place, not to mention his Multiple Sclerosis that he died of shock."

"He died of shock?"

"Yes…although the cocaine would not have helped."

"It never does, Jethro,"

"Is that it?" Jordan said, hoping for something medical.

"That's it, Jethro, until I perform an autopsy," he closed his bag and stood up. "Cases like this…I imagine he only had a short while to live, can go just like that. His whole body was ready to give up, and what with the extra stimulant, and whatever went on here earlier, it was all too much for him. I won't know what actually killed him until I get him on the table."

Jordan walked him back to his car. It was getting crowded now, despite the enormous semicircular drive in front of the house. The ambulance was just leaving as the fire brigade arrived, and following them was the mortuary wagon for Naseby, and two police cars. There, at the far end of the chain, was the familiar red car driven by Josh, who had to pull off onto the nearby meadow.

"Okay, Chester," Jordan said, leaning into his window, "I needn't tell you I would appreciate a quick turnaround on this."

Chester laughed, "Oh I'm sure you would. There's going to be a lot of people knocking on your door, if I'm not mistaken."

"You're right there…Take care."

Just as the pathologist managed to work his way around the other vehicles, a loud car horn hooted Jordan as he turned back to the house. It was Josh. He pulled into the space left by the pathologist and jumped out of his car.

"Boss," he shouted, "What's happened?"

Jordan waited for him to catch up, "It's finished, Josh. All the files have been destroyed and Naseby's dead."

"Dead!" Josh shouted, stopping, "How...how did he die?"

"He just did. That was the pathologist. He's doing an autopsy straight away, so we should hear something before the end of the day."

"The Commissioner isn't going to like that."

"Who cares...I know a lot of people who will."

"Did you get a chance to go through the files like you said?" Josh questioned, as he followed Jordan back into the house and up the stairs.

"I did. It took longer than I expected actually. I got so interested at all the important names that I almost blew it. Then I made sure I was last to leave the vault and followed your instructions to the letter."

"And they worked?"

"Can you smell that?" Jordan said, as they entered the room.

Josh held his nose as they walked over to where two fire fighters were trying to prise open the doors to the vault.

"This is it then?" one said, on seeing Jordan.

"Yes...it's a vault containing papers in cabinets, and they caught fire. Probably faulty wiring or something," Jordan replied, "I wonder if the mechanism still works?" he continued, turning to Josh, "Did Strand say how you opened it again?"

"No...he just said you press the red button to close the outer door."

Jordan laughed, "I suppose it doesn't really matter now," and he pressed both buttons again. Suddenly the sliding doors jerked open and a cloud of smoke poured out, catching everyone by surprise.

"Back gentlemen!" one of the fire fighters shouted, "it might be toxic."

While Jordan and Josh moved across to the nest of chairs, the fire fighters donned their breathing apparatus and entered the vault.

"I think we had better sit down, Josh," Jordan said. Glancing down at the table, he noticed the bottle of wine was still half-full. "Just the thing," he said. "I don't know about you, but those fumes have left a nasty taste in my mouth."

Jordan noticed the expression on Josh's face, and passed him the bottle, as they dropped into the chairs to wait.

When the fire fighters finally cleared the vault for Jordan to enter, he was surprised in the mess he had made. Imagining his fire at home, seeing the few papers he used to light his fire with, curl up into a black sandwich and then suddenly explode into flames. Everything was black, and the draws were hanging out haphazardly as the fire fighters checked for smouldering embers. Apparently there were none; just slabs of charred files.

Whilst Josh stood outside the opening, still holding his nose and looking a little apprehensive, Jordan randomly poked through the draws with a pen to see if anything had survived the inferno, but nothing had. Each black slab he touched shattered into ash and dropped to the bottom of the draw.

"Well that's the end of that," Jordan said, walking back to Josh. "By the way, why did you come out to the house? I thought I told you to stay away?"

"I hadn't planned to, Boss. I understand why you didn't want us involved, but when I heard the commotion downstairs, and Sergeant Fawcett told me what was up, I just had to follow the others. I kept thinking of what Strand said about the butler almost killing him in the vault."

"All right…you're forgiven. But only if you write this lot up and put it with all the other reports I asked you to complete."

"I have, Boss. I have them all in neat piles waiting for you to check and sign them off. Even the arrest warrants… although, I don't expect you'll need them now." He paused for thought. "God, Boss, there's going to be a stink over this."

As so often has been the case during this investigation, Josh was uncannily right; and Jordan soon found himself seated in front of the Chief Superintendent's desk, whilst his unhappy mentor paced back and forth in front of the window. It was a silent moment, while both seriously considered their positions.

Jordan's thoughts had focused on an easy finish to the day: finalising the reports Josh prepared for him earlier, and tidying up loose ends, while considering the actions he believed diligent for the events that took place. He imagined he would be congratulated for a fine job, offered a drink and maybe even an invitation to diner later, but as the Chief Superintendent swung round, and Jordan caught sight of his looming silhouette, he realised it would not be today.

"What were you thinking of, Inspector?" he snorted.

"College…Sir?" Jordan remarked.

"Don't be flippant, Inspector," the Chief Superintendent snarled, banging his fist down on the desk as he passed, before he finally sat down.

"I don't see what all the fuss is about, Sir."

"Oh you don't. After destroying valuable evidence and killing the main suspect...you say you don't see what all the fuss is about."

"It was an accident, Sir. Part of Naseby's safeguards. As for Naseby's death...that could have happened anytime. It was probably the cocaine he had injected into him before I arrived that did it; the pathologist said as much. He said a man in Naseby's condition shouldn't have been taking cocaine."

"I don't believe you, Inspector. You never did anything by accident."

"It makes little odds now, Sir."

The Chief Superintendent glared at Jordan, stood up again and started pacing the floor again, "Have you got this in writing?"

"I'm expecting the pathology report later today, Sir."

"The Commissioner's furious you know."

"I'm not surprised...he wanted the files for himself."

"I don't..." he stopped, bent down over Jordan's shoulder and continued in a whisper. "I don't want to hear you talking about the Commissioner like that."

"It's true, Sir...I saw the files. There's one on just about every member of the Judiciary: no one has escaped. The Council, Public Service...even you, Sir. Did you know he had a file on you?"

The Chief Superintendent looked culpable. "It was brought to my attention."

"And did it influence the way you conducted yourself, Sir?"

"That's a matter between me and my maker."

"I wonder if that's the way the Commissioner thinks, I doubt it. According to his file he shouldn't be running the police, he's been riding shotgun for Naseby for years. You might tell him that when he undoubtedly asks you to consider my present circumstances. Because if you don't, Sir...I shall."

The Chief Superintendent's complexion turned grey. "I hope that's not what I think it is, Inspector? The Commissioner is a man to be feared."

"Not any more, Sir. There are many people in Nottingham who would consider me a hero, and pushed the wrong way I might just tell them. Like you, Sir, they all must know about the files. I don't need to show them anything, just a mention that I made sure the files were what Naseby said they were before I burnt them."

"So you admit it?"

"I don't admit anything, Sir. The Fire Brigade will confirm the vault combusted while the doors were closed. Oh and, I don't think you'll get any argument from the Chief over that point either; there was a file on him in there as well."

The Chief Superintendent sat down at his desk again, this time he looked as if he would be there for a while, at least until he opened his afternoon mail. It was still sitting where Phyllis left it on the far corner of the desk. It looked conspicuous, as if, knowing the Chief Superintendent's mood: she had crept in, left the envelopes there, and crept out again.

He looked up under his bushy eyebrows. "I suppose all this is written up?"

"Waiting for my signature, Sir."

"Then I suggest you spend what's left of the day, making sure every statement is perfect; including the episode this morning. That includes the Pathology report, Fire Brigade report and any other report that might confirm your story.

When I go to see the Commissioner, I don't want to have to sit there explaining something you missed."

"Does that include a report on all the names on the files, Sir, including your own and the Commissioner's? I can still remember his details. It was a pity I didn't allow Sergeant Crosby to inspect them with me. He has a photographic memory you know...you did know that, Sir?"

"Oh for Christ sake...Get on with it."

Jordan did just that. He spent what was left of the day with Josh going through his collection of statements and reports, and when they finished, Josh turned to Jordan and looked at him with questioning eyes.

"What?" Jordan asked, signing his last paper.

"What do we do now, Boss?"

"Do you mean now...now, or now... the future?"

He laughed, "I mean it's seven o'clock, Boss. Are we going to see Penny?"

"Ah...you want another slap-up free meal."

"Is there anything wrong with that, Boss?"

"No...of course not. It's just that I thought I might have a private word with Penny. You know...alert her to the possibility that she might not have a job to come back to. Or at least the same job."

"I could always go and watch Mrs Willow beating the men at poker."

"You could that. You might even learn something."

"That's an interesting thought, Boss."

By the time they arrived, Mrs Willow had already left for her assignation, and Josh made a U-turn and left the room immediately.

"What was that all about?" Penny asked, as Jordan walked round to the drinks cabinet, poured a stiff drink and refilled Penny's lemon juice. "He didn't even ask how I was," she continued, studying Jordon's vacant expression.

"Don't worry, Penny, he thinks of you all the time. But tonight I asked him to go and watch your mother until we have dinner."

"Why? She's perfectly capable of looking after herself."

"I know. It's just that I wanted a private word with you."

Penny's eyes lit up and she turned her body to face Jordan, who had sat next to her. He was sipping his wine, and she tried to see if there was any hint of a clue in his expression. As usual, there was none. Jordan was still as elusive as ever.

"So...what was so private you needed to talk to me on our own?"

"Oh yes...well, as I intimated yesterday, Josh and I were on the verge of finalising the case, and if you remember I told you how pointless it was because Naseby was dying," she nodded her head impatiently. "Well I concluded it today, and in the process I killed Naseby," her eyes opened wide, "or at least my actions caused him to go into shock...which killed him."

"Oh, Inspector...what's going to happen now?"

"Well obviously I'm going to be under a lot of scrutiny for a while, but don't let that concern you. I made sure you and Josh were well out of it...naturally I shall take full responsibility...Which brings me to my point..."

"At last," she interrupted. "I thought you would never get there."

"Yes, well...there's always been the likelihood of CAS being disbanded, we discussed it enough times. And that means, when you get out of that thing," he pointed to her brace. "You might be looking for another job."

"Oh dear, Inspector," she cried, taking hold of his hand. "I hoped we might be working together for quite a while."

Jordan pulled back, "It's always been on the cards, Penny. You know that I have to return to the college," he laughed. "That's if they'll have me."

Penny's face suddenly looked horrified. "They won't put you in prison...will they? I don't think I could stand it if they locked you up."

Jordan looked at Penny disbelievingly. He had no idea she felt that way about him. He still didn't. He thought he was seeing more into her words than there really was, and became frightened to respond.

"Penny I don't want to hurt you, but..."

She interrupted him again, "No, Jethro...I can call you, Jethro?" he nodded with a sour smile. "I sensed something the first time we met, remember? You sensed it too. It was as if we were drawn together."

Penny was frightening Jordan now. "No Penny...I smelt my wife's perfume...that's all. I confused you with her."

"You're doing it again, Jethro. You're hiding behind your wife's death. I know you loved her and the children, but it's time to move on...you need someone else."

"I'm a lot older than you, Penny. Can you imagine what that means? I must be the same age as your father."

"My father's ten years older than you."

Jordan let out a deep sigh, "Oh God...how did this happen? No...when did it happen, you can't be in love with an old man twice your age."

"I said I felt something straight away, but I really knew that night when you visited me in hospital."

"When I visited you in hospital? What about that night?"

"Remember? When I was coming round."

"I remember well...Josh and I were very worried about you."

"No, Jethro, it was just you, sitting in the dark by my bed."

"You remember that. I thought you were unconscious?"

"That's what made it so exciting. I came round...and...I don't know why, but when I heard you talking to me like that...I couldn't tell you I was awake. I just listened. It was sheer poetry."

"You were confused, Penny. You were still under the influence of the sedation, and you must have had quite a jolt to your head."

"Please don't spoil it, Jethro," she cried.

Jordan suddenly felt a mixture of rage and passion welling up inside him. He remained silent; his eyes darting back and forth as he frantically searched his thoughts for a sane reply. "It wasn't you, Penny."

"Pardon?"

"I was talking to my wife...I'm sorry," Jordan finally said, standing up and walking around the couch to get another drink. He did not return, but stood by the cabinet. It was safer, less friendly. "I suppose you do deserve an explanation, but I had no idea you were awake, and the emotion of the moment got to me I guess. In a way it was an act of clearing my conscience."

"Clearing your conscience?" she snapped.

"Yes...I was saying something I wanted to say for a long time, and never found the right moment. Seeing you there in the half-light over your bed made me a little delusional. I let myself imagine Jessie was still alive, and I had an opportunity to make my peace with her." tears started to flow down

Penny's face. "I said all the things I wanted to say to her, but never had the chance to. I wanted to let her know I would be joining her soon: as soon as I had dealt with the murderers who set our house on fire and killed everyone in it."

"And did you?"

"Oh yes. I butchered them all, and as many others that I came across. That was until I was caught and sent back home, after a very convenient enquiry."

Penny looked apprehensive now. The steam had gone out of her, and she wiped her face and considered what he had said. "Is that all true?"

"Oh yes. That's why they put me on suspension indefinitely, and I ended up teaching at the college. They wanted to keep an eye on me. I regularly go to see a psychiatrist you know."

"You do?"

"Yes…although I put off going to him for a while since my nightmares stopped. The Chief Superintendent was furious."

"Nightmares? Oh, you're having me on, Jethro. You're trying to frighten me off aren't you? Trying to make me think you're some sort of maniac."

Jordan moved behind Penny, and bending over her, he kissed her on the cheek, "Everything I said was true. And yes…I want you to forget all this nonsense."

"What nonsense," Mrs Willow said, entering the room.

It was an opportune moment. Penny's mother and Josh must have had a hilarious time at the card table, they could talk about nothing else throughout dinner, and that suited Jordan fine. Penny was subdued, not so much because Jordan had not responded to her overtures as she expected, but more in what he said. He had given her something to think about, and she chewed on it all evening.

CHAPTER 25

A lot changed over the following weeks. Jordan and his assistants faced a long interrogation regarding the procedures adopted to investigate the corpse found in Sherwood Forest; the statements and corroborating evidence was scrutinised far more earnestly than other cases; and the conclusions drawn together on that fateful day the subject for a future Commissioner's enquiry. The outcome cleared CAS of any improprieties, and the enquiry exonerated the team.

Penny was out of her cast and back at work, if she could consider sitting in draughty, formal surroundings as work. By which time her infatuation with Jordan had waned, he thought, but was really only smouldering under the surface; put on hold until the matters at hand had been resolved.

Josh seemed the busiest, and most sort after, since the important ones had discovered his special talent for remembering detail. They assumed it made him the perfect yardstick to measure the facts without any distraction from extraneous personal opinions. Although out of his hands now, Jordan attempted to muddy the waters, by suggesting Josh's talent was open to manipulation.

The Commissioner preferred to believe his own viewpoint of the proceedings, governed by two agendas: one, to discredit

Jordan in the event that he might use his knowledge of the Commissioner's file to disgrace him, and to ingratiate himself if the consensus was that the investigation was a success. The Commissioner was an astute individual, with the well-seasoned ability to find himself continuously on the right side. Jordan could see where this was going.

On the other hand, Chief Superintendent Mulholland ultimately proved to be one of Jordan's staunchest allies. After a lengthy period of inactivity, where he apparently left the enquiry to take its own course, he suddenly appeared at the critical moment and supported the Inspector he had known for thirty years.

In the early stages, Jordan had suspected the Commissioner had used his influence on him, but it soon became apparent that the Commissioner's threats were without teeth; the Judiciary had learnt of Jordan's decision to destroy the dossiers, and they quickly showed their appreciation.

When the dust had settled and the judge presiding over the enquiry made his decision, he declared the case officially closed, while Victor Strand and Cartwright were the only living losers. Benjamin Naseby was beyond punishment; he had paid the ultimate price for his major part in the saga surrounding The Sherwood Forest Man, and by all accounts, the Ayers Foundation was now free to continue.

Christopher Lyle seemed a changed man when he invited Jordan to Naseby's house. An official notification that there would be no charges brought against Naseby's name, or the estate that was to be transferred to the Ayers Foundation, prompted Lyle to leave his plush office in London and visit the house, so that he could hear the news from the man himself: the one responsible for bringing down his mentor.

A cool reception awaited Jordan when he arrived.

The man's character had suddenly changed. Jordan could hardly believe his eyes when Lyle's assistant showed him into the lounge, before continuing his activity of itemising Naseby's belongings on a clipboard he was clasping in his hand.

"Inspector Jordan, Sir," he said.

"Thank you, James," Lyle replied, offering his hand but not standing up, "We meet again, Inspector. Much more different circumstances though."

"Yes they are," Jordan said, walking around a large coffee table and sitting down opposite Lyle.

Lyle looked different. Instead of the drab suit and naïve manner, he now brandished a fashionable blue pinstripe, and his air was confident, even cocky. He was sitting, crossed-legged beside a roaring fire with a large glass of whisky in one hand and an equally large cigar in the other. It was in his mouth when they shook hands, but the whisky remained where it was.

"You don't appear to be upset by Naseby's death. I still expected you to be in mourning, or at least sporting a black arm-band."

"No, Inspector. In fact you've done me a favour."

"I have?" Jordan said, surprised at his remark.

"Yes you have. I expected the old man to linger on for some time yet, but you gave him a nudge for me. Just in the nick of time I might add."

"Well it's all over now."

"I don't think so, Inspector," Lyle snapped back, with a grin on his face.

Jordan stared at Lyle, he was getting sick of people saying; 'I don't think so,' and Christopher Lyle was the last man he expected it from. It looked as if Josh was about to be proved right again. "Now why would you say that, Mr Lyle?"

Lyle placed his drink on the coffee table and reached over the side of his chair. When he brought his hand back there was a small briefcase in it, and he placed it on his lap and drew back the zip. He made a deliberate point of taking his time, looking for something inside, then, with a smirk on his face, he withdrew a file and dropped it on the coffee table in front of Jordan.

Jordan thought he recognised the file. It looked like the same one Naseby told him was behind the cushion of the seat he was sitting in: the file that contained his dossier. The one Naseby said was a copy of the original.

"Go on," Lyle prompted. "Open it...I think you'll be surprised."

"I don't think I have to. It looks like the file Naseby showed me."

When Jordan showed no interest, Lyle snatched it back up again and slipped it back into the briefcase, and returned to his drink.

"It is. You were so clever destroying all the others you forgot your own. My man James found it behind the cushion of a chair in Naseby's room the other day."

"I got the impression you were doing some housekeeping," Jordan remarked. "What are you doing, finding out how much you can get for Naseby's estate? Isn't his fortune enough for you, you have to pick at his things like carrion?"

Lyle laughed, "He was a shrewd man was Uncle Benjamin. He's left all his fortune to the Ayers Foundation in perpetuity. That means it can only be used for that purpose, nothing else."

"He's left you nothing?"

"Only a small allowance and this house."

A broad appreciative smile crossed Jordan's face. "You thought you were going to inherit the files...didn't you? Well that one won't do you any good. I don't care if you print it word for word in one of Naseby's papers. In fact give it to me and I'll let Sarah Bolt have it...she never did finish her story."

"You think you've been very clever, don't you, Inspector?"

"Not really...I've just been doing my job."

"No but...admit it, as you found out Naseby was involved, you decided you were going to nail him to the wall...take down another tall poppy."

"I admit it gave me some pleasure," Jordan responded.

Jordan sensed a turn in Lyle's initial bravado. He was hunting for a way out of his dilemma; sitting opposite the man responsible for his downfall. Yet, despite still having a job with the Ayers Foundation, Lyle was determined to do something that would address the imbalance, and compensate for Naseby's death.

On the other hand, Jordan had to dissuade Lyle, or do something to stop this whole catastrophe from starting over again.

"Naseby was special to you...wasn't he?"

"My second father."

"You called him uncle before, yet he legally adopted you when your father was killed. You were only twelve at the time."

Lyle swung his head back and forth in a matter-of-fact way. "I didn't feel like calling him dad...and he didn't insist. Besides...I knew, even at twelve, that he did it because he wanted an heir; he talked about it enough."

"So he groomed you to take over the Foundation?"

"Not really. You have it backwards. He groomed me to take over his Egyptian business when I was twenty-one...the Foundation was a last resort after the Egyptians closed him down."

"Why did they do that?"

"They found out about what he was really exporting."

"And you were involved in that?"

Lyle laughed. He finished his drink, stubbed his cigar out, and reached over for the bottle on a tray in front of Jordan. He could see Jordan watching him as he poured himself another, and offered him one, "Inspector?"

"I'm on duty."

"Oh...does that mean you're investigating me now? You won't find me a pushover like Naseby. Not by a long chalk."

"I'm on duty all day between eight and five...it doesn't mean I'm investigating you. If you recall, the case is closed... and you invited me here."

"So I did, Inspector," he said, taking another drink.

"If you drink any more of that stuff, you're liable to say or do something you regret," Jordan pointed out. "Don't you think you should ease up?"

"I'm celebrating...or commiserating, I don't know which."

Lyle still looked irate, and Jordan knew he had to neutralise his anger, and the only way to do that was with a shock. It went too far with Naseby, and he hoped he would be subtler this time.

"What do you know about your father's death?"

"Why?" Lyle retorted, looking suspicious.

"Well you were only twelve at the time, and it dawned on me during my last conversation with Naseby that he might not have told you the truth."

Lyle's suspicion turned to disbelief. "What are you talking about? Benjamin told me my father died in a car accident outside Andorra. He showed me the police report and a newspaper at the time."

"He didn't show you all the papers. He didn't show you the one's that disagreed with the findings."

"You're...you're lying. You just want to destroy what's left of his memory."

Jordan reached into his inside pocket and brought out the notebook he used to take down Naseby's last statement, flicked through the pages until he reached the part dealing with Willy Lyle's death. Lyle was curious, but continued sipping his whisky. Then Jordan slapped the notebook down in front of him on the table.

"What's this?" he said.

"Read it," Jordan said, pushing it closer, "It's a record of my interview with Naseby. This page deals with your father's death."

Lyle slowly put his glass back on the table without taking his eyes off the notebook. He picked it up and started reading the open page, looking as though he was reading Naseby's dying confession, but showed little reaction until he reached the important part. His gaze stopped moving forward, remaining fixed on one line, which he seemed to read repeatedly until he stopped, and looked up at Jordan.

"This is all a lie."

"I'm sorry Lyle. I assure you I wrote every detail down as Naseby told me. He said he wanted to clear his conscience, and as there were going to be no further charges, he wanted it on record; and it is. Typed up into a statement, with my signature as a bona fide witness, and put before the Judiciary.

I suspected he killed your father, all the local papers hinted as much, but there was not enough evidence to convict him. And he got away with yet another murder."

"Another Murder? What does that mean?"

"It's all in there," Jordan pointed to the notebook, "Ayers was his first. He killed him in Cairo...another car accident. I would have tied him in with Gallagher's death also, but he was away at the time," Jordan hesitated before continuing. "But on further investigation we discovered your father killed him."

Lyle dropped the notebook on the table and stood up. "This is too much now. You're making all this up. When did my father kill this...?"

"Sergeant Gallagher," Jordan prompted, "He was in the Home Guard, and your father employed him to drive a lorry carrying artefacts belonging to Ayers; stage an accident so that your father and Naseby could rob it and then set fire to the lorry full of fake material. That was the foundation of Naseby's fortune."

"I don't believe any of it...I can't believe it," Lyle shouted.

"Don't you get it?" Jordan continued. "Why do you think Naseby called it the Ayers Foundation? Everything was built on that first shipment."

Lyle was pacing up and down denying everything. Jordan had given him too much to take in all at once. "Come," he said, ushering Lyle back into his chair, at the same time, he picked up the notebook and flicked the pages back to the beginning, and he was thankful he decided to use a new book, "Look...sit quietly and read the whole interview from start to finish. If you know what Naseby and your father did from the beginning, you'll get a better idea why it turned out the way it did."

Jordan watched Lyle. He just sat there staring at the book. He wanted to know what really went on all those years ago, but at the same time, he was fearful that it would prove Jordan was right.

Slowly he plucked up the courage to pick the notebook up and face the first page, and he started reading. As he did so, he reached for his glass and sipped what was left of his whisky, and then settled himself back into the chair. Jordan decided to have another look at the room where it all ended, and quietly left.

When Jordan heard a noise in the hall and turned around, he glanced at his watch. Lyle had taken three quarters of an hour to digest the facts that led up to him inheriting the Ayers Foundation, and surprisingly he looked much calmer. He had lost that bombastic look he had in the beginning, and was his old self again.

"It seems that I owe you an apology, Inspector," he said straight away as he entered the room. He was holding Jordan's notebook, and he passed it to him.

"Accepted," Jordan replied, "although it really wasn't necessary."

"I had no idea. This has opened my eyes."

"I'm glad. I'd hate it for you to go on in life not knowing the truth."

"You said that statement has been written up."

"I did."

"Do you think I could have a copy?"

"I was going to suggest it. Give me a couple of days and I'll send you one."

They walked back down to the lounge where Lyle returned Jordan's file, before seeing him out to his car. He still seemed to be in a daze, but Jordan was sure, now Lyle knew the truth, his life would take a happier course.

It only took another week to disband the Chief Superintendent's brainchild CAS. The Commissioner's idea of possibly turning it into a permanent unit had fallen by the wayside since his suspension, and Jordan really wanted to get back to the college.

Josh had decided to return to Yorkshire, this time as a Senior Sergeant, with a recommendation from the judiciary that he applied for Inspector in the following year. Jordan agreed, even providing him with a two-page testimonial to present at his interview along with one from the Chief Superintendent.

Jordan walked him to his car and leaned into his window to say goodbye, while Penny looked on from the entrance with Sergeant Fawcett; she was too tearful to go any further, she had already said all that was to say.

"Well," Jordan said, a bit choked, "You're off then?"

"Yes, Boss. All packed up and ready to go."

"Are you sure this is what you want to do?"

"I think so, Boss; as sure as anyone can be. I think I need to get out a bit in the next few years. Try a few different things. I think I'll still end up back in a squad like CAS, it suited my talent better, but I need to know more about homicide, and drugs and all that sort of stuff...if you know what I mean."

Jordan laughed, "I do, Josh, and thanks for your help. You were an invaluable asset to the team, I don't know what I would have done without you, except...if you are suspicious about your superiors in the future, don't try and find out about their past...they're not all as reasonable as me."

He laughed, "Point taken, Boss," then he winked, reversed out of his space, and passed through the open gates.

As Josh's car slowly made its way down the narrow Prescott Lane towards the high street, Jordan turned back and saw Penny still standing on the steps waiting for him. He let out a sigh, and contemplated what future lay ahead for them; but somehow he had little doubt it would be a complicated one.

He had longed for the approaching end to The Sherwood Forest Man case so that he could get back to his nondescript life as a tutor, with little more than the mundane dramas in the wardroom to disturb his idyllic life. However, Penny had chosen to stay in Nottingham, working for Inspector Dent no less, in the same capacity as she did for Jordan.

Dent had decided his squad needed a new dimension; and looking at the evidence with a similar eye as Jordan, it suited his new thinking. Of course, he had to find someone to sit behind DS Ward's desk.

"I'm going to miss, Josh," she said.

"We both are. But we must move on, and that means you as well."

"I know, Inspector Dent asked me to drop in on him this afternoon. He said he wanted to discuss my future duties. Did you know he's putting me up for Sergeant?"

"I didn't...you deserve it. You don't have to join him you know," Jordan said, "You've already had three other stations interested in your credentials, and the Chief Superintendent said he would hold onto your transfer papers until Friday."

"I know...I saw him this morning."

"So?"

"I would have to leave Nottingham, and that would mean I wouldn't see you again. I don't think I could stand that."

She stared into his eyes for a response.

Jordan rushed her through the lobby, up the stairs and down the corridor into their old office. He closed the door and pushed her down into Josh's chair.

"Oh dear, Penny," he started, "what am I going to do with you?"

"You could give our relationship a chance."

"We don't have a relationship, Penny."

She looked at him searchingly, "Why not? I know you like me...It's a start. And given time you might even learn to love me."

Jordan bent down and took hold of her shoulders, "Of course I like you...I like you very much, but that wouldn't be fair to you. You're young and vital; there are plenty of young men out there who would be a far better proposition."

"I don't just want anyone."

Jordan let go of her and paced the floor in front of his desk, "No...you want an old warn out derelict of a man who's obsessed with his past."

"You said yourself; you were getting over the nightmares... that the memories were beginning to fade. I'm prepared to wait."

While each collected their things together and placed them into a cardboard box, they continued the debate: Jordan presenting the case for his preferred reclusive existence, and Penny expounding the virtues of love at any age, single or not, until they reached an impasse and agreed to keep in touch. Then with his cardboard box tucked under his arm, Jordan walked Penny back along the corridor to Dent's squad room, and saying adieu, he left her there.

It must have been a week later, after a long staff meeting with the Governor that Jordan finally arrived back at his house in Clifton Beck. It was dark, and the rain that had engulfed the area most of the day, had eased slightly, and had now become a thick unrelenting drizzle.

Struggling out of his car with a box of groceries, Jordan was not aware of the dark shape of a small car farther along the drive. He was almost on top of it before he realised it was Penny. He placed the groceries on his front step, in the shelter of the small roof, walked around to the driver's side, and knocked on the window. A pale, drawn face looked up at Jordan through the rain-spattered glass and a smile appeared across it.

Penny rolled down the window, "Jethro," she said weakly. "At last."

"What on earth are you doing here?" he replied.

"Oh don't be like that. It's Friday…we've got all weekend, and I thought it would be a nice surprise if I cooked you a real meal for once."

Jordan was getting wet, and irritated. "You'd better come inside, but only until I decide what to do with you."

As Jordan picked up his groceries and opened the front door, he noticed the waif-like figure pass by him into the house. A pathetic vision: her body slightly bent, with her arms wrapped tightly around her chest, shivering.

"How long have you been out there?"

She glanced at her watch, "About an hour. I didn't expect you to be so late."

Jordan felt guilty, "No…well, we had a last minute staff meeting. If you'd given me a ring first, I would have told you."

"What would you have told me, Jethro? 'Sorry Penny but I'm busy tonight.'"

Jordan felt doubly guilty, and sorry for the condition she was in: still shivering and looking miserable: all on his account.

Even if she was exaggerating a little, he found it difficult to be annoyed with her, especially since she had come all this way to cook him a meal. Then he recalled what she had said earlier, and wondered if that meant staying all night as well.

"All right," he said, less harshly. "But you're going to have to get warmed up."

Penny's face broke into a broad smile, and she flung her arms around his neck and kissed him, "Oh I knew you wouldn't send me away, Jethro."

He unwound her embrace from his neck, "No, Penny...I mean get yourself into a hot bath, before you catch your death of cold."

She broke away and pouted like a schoolgirl, "Oh all right," she said. "You're wet. Why don't you come in with me?"

"No!" Jordan let out sharply. "I've got a fire to light, and a dinner to start. So off with you, the bathroom is first left at the top of the stairs."

As she left, Jordan shook his head, took his box of groceries into the kitchen, and dumped them on the table, hoping he had enough for two. It was cold, the whole house was cold and damp, and Jordan decided to start the fire first. It was already made, all he had to do was put a match to it, but it would take time to warm the house, which, under normal circumstances, would be all right, but not for a young woman straight out of the bath.

He switched on the gas heating, and although he disliked it, he thought it would warm the place up quickly. It was a legacy from the previous owners, who were too lazy to chop up logs for the open fire. He laughed as he emptied the box, recalling the weeks it took to restore the fireplace, and the continuous soot-falls he had to cope with until he finally rang the chimney sweep.

By the time Penny had finished her bath and walked into the kitchen in Jordan's bathrobe and slippers, the dinner of sliced cold meat, spaghetti and chips was almost ready. Downstairs was becoming nice and cosy and the fire in the lounge was roaring; casting romantic shimmering patterns through the adjoining doorway into the darkened hall, and Penny shrugged her shoulders as she wrinkled her nose.

She was standing in the archway between the kitchen and the hall with the dancing lights behind her, looking as provocative as she could, while Jordan opened the wine. He offered her a glass as he served up the meal, and her coyness appealed to him. She was distracting him as she slipped into her seat at the table, all the time pulling at the long baggy sleeves, as if she was having difficulty covering herself, while attempting to drink from her glass at the same time.

Jordan knew what she was doing, as she clutched at the oversized garment, emphasising the fact that she was naked underneath. Jordan had been there before. It was many years ago, but nonetheless the memory was still as vivid and exciting as if it was only yesterday.

When their meal was finished and Jordan had poured out the last of the wine, the house was warm and cosy, and it was time to move into the comfort of the lounge. As Penny tiptoed across the hall towards the glowing room, Jordan noticed she was unsteady on her feet and needed support until she dropped onto the couch.

Then she kicked off the slippers, leant against one of the arms and tucked her bare feet under herself, and straightaway, he realised there was no way she was going to make that journey back along the motorway tonight.

Jordan opened another bottle, he had no idea why, Penny's face was already showing a healthy glow that stretched all the way from her temples to the line of her jaw, and there was a mischievous sparkle in her eyes. Like her, Jordan's tension had already left him, and despite feeling manoeuvred into a compromising situation; at that moment, he was beyond caring.

"Did you say your nightmares had stopped?" she said, with her eyes closed, and her head tilted towards the ceiling.

"I did…but that doesn't mean they won't return."

"They're not violent…are they?"

Jordan nudged her hand gently with the edge of the glass he had, so that she would open her eyes. She smiled in a dreamy way and took the glass.

He then sat down beside her and replied, "No…it's a horrific nightmare, but as I'm usually the only occupant of my bed, I can't say what I get up to."

"So you could be violent? I'd hate to wake up to you thrashing about."

Jordan decided to skip that hint and started recalling his nightmare: "Usually I'm fighting my way through searing flames, fending off falling timbers and kicking at the flyscreen door to get at my family. They're screaming you see…I have to save them from the flames," Jordan sucked in a deep breath, and a tear started running down his cheek. "But I was too late. That is my nightmare...but in all reality; I was not there: I was too far away to help them."

Penny brushed the tear from Jordan's face, "I'm sorry...I didn't understand."

Jordan looked across at her, sipped his wine as a strange smile crossed his face. "That was all it was...a nightmare. I was out chasing Mau-Mau for burning down a homestead, when all the time it was my homestead, and it was all over by the time I got back; there was nothing left."

"Then why the recurring nightmare?"

"I suppose it's all a matter of viewpoint: Those who don't know think I'm mad; those who do know call me delusional; and my psychiatrist still hasn't made his mind up what to call me?"

Penny hesitated before answering. She was reticent about always being confused for Jordan's wife, but at the same time, she was fearful of the prospect of not seeing him again. "I don't know about you being mad, but I know I shall, if we don't get to bed before I pass out."

Jordan stared into the flames again. He was feeling nervous about breaking thirty years of not committing himself, and now he had to make a decision that might change his life, he was wavering, and Penny's silence was not helping.

He turned to face her. He took her closed eyes as a sign she was waiting for him to kiss her, and he was about to, until he noticed the glass in her hand was on the verge of tipping over. He laughed to himself, and gently eased it out of her fingers.

Then finishing his own drink, he laid both glasses on the floor, and returned his gaze to the flames. There are no demons there now, he thought, just a curling, spiralling kaleidoscope of colours: nothing threatening. Glancing back at Penny, Jordan wondered what the future would have in store for them.

He was sure of one thing though; if he ever had one of his nightmares again, he had the oddest feeling there would be someone there to console him.

As a child in the London blitz, Charles Beagley distracted himself from the horror of his family's situation by making up stories or drawing. His eventual training was at Art School, which equipped him for the many years he spent working in advertising and design. He lived in London initially, did two years National Service in the RAF, worked in Ireland and Belgium and then set up a Design Consultancy back in England for twenty years.

He married and had two sons whose futures concerned him as things were grim economically in 1982 England. He jumped at the opportunity to move his family to Australia when he was offered a managerial position in design. During his years in England, his writing developed as he wrote promotional text and an occasional short story.

Since coming to Australia he has honed his skills, writing many fictional stories, mainly mysteries. *Sherwood Forest Man* is one such novel.